The Graveyard Game

Kage Baker

TOR®

A Tom Doherty Associates Book
New York

This is a work of fiction. All the characters and events portrayed
in this novel are either fictitious or are used fictitiously.

THE GRAVEYARD GAME

Originally published in 2001 by Harcourt, Inc., in the United
States.

Edited by David G. Hartwell

A Tor Book
Published by Tom Doherty Associates, LLC
175 Fifth Avenue
New York, NY 10010

www.tor.com

Tor® is a registered trademark of Tom Doherty Associates, LLC.

ISBN 0-765-31184-4

EAN 978-0765-31184-9

First Tor Trade Paperback Edition: February 2005

Printed in the United States of America

0 9 8 7 6 5 4 3 2 1

This one's for absent friends.
Miss you, Dave.

What Has Gone Before

THIS IS THE FOURTH BOOK *in the unofficial history of Dr. Zeus Incorporated.*

In the twenty-fourth century, a research and development firm invented a means of time travel. It also discovered the secret of immortality. There were, however, certain limitations that prevented the Company from bestowing these gifts left and right. But since the past could now be looted to increase corporate earnings, the stockholders were happy.

In the Garden of Iden *introduced Botanist Mendoza, rescued as a child from the dungeons of the Inquisition in sixteenth-century Spain by a Company operative, Facilitator Joseph. In exchange for being given immortality and a fantastically augmented body and mind, she would work in the past for the future, saving certain plants from extinction.*

On her first mission as an adult, Mendoza was sent with Joseph to England, where she fell in love with a mortal, with bitter consequences.

Sky Coyote *opened over a century later, as Joseph arrived at the research base at New World One to look up his protégée and inform her they had both been drafted for a Company mission in Alta California. Mendoza said good-bye to the one friend she had made at New World One—Lewis—and went with Joseph.*

Near a Chumash Indian village she met a number of the mortal masters from the future, and was appalled to find them bigoted and fearful of their cyborg servants. Joseph learned unsettling facts about the Company that brought to mind a warning he'd been given long ago by Budu, the Enforcer who recruited him.

Why was it that, though the immortal operatives were provided with information and other entertainment from the future, nothing they received was ever dated later than the year 2355?

At the conclusion of the mission, Mendoza remained in the wilderness of the coastal forests, working then alone as a botanist.

Mendoza in Hollywood opened in 1862, as Mendoza journeyed reluctantly to her new posting: a stagecoach inn at a remote spot that one day would be known as Hollywood. There, near the violent little pueblo of Los Angeles (one murder a night, not counting Indians), she was to collect rare plants scheduled to go extinct in the coming drought.

Mendoza found herself now haunted by visions of her mortal lover, and she was giving off Crome's radiation again, the spectral blue fire of paranormal abilities that no cyborg was supposed to possess.

In a local spot known for strangeness, she encountered an anomaly that threw her temporarily into the future. There she glimpsed her friend Lewis, who tried frantically to tell her of an impending disaster.

Into her life came another mortal—Edward Alton Bell-Fairfax, an English spy involved in a plot to grab California for the British Empire. Edward looked enough like Mendoza's first love to have been cloned from him. Mendoza abandoned her post and ran away with Edward.

As they raced for sanctuary on Catalina Island, pursued by American agents and bounty hunters, Edward began to suspect that Mendoza was far more than a coaching-inn servant. Mendoza discovered that Edward too was more than he seemed, in fact was connected to the Company in some way.

But before the lovers could solve their mutual riddle, their luck ran out. Edward was shot to death, and Mendoza went berserk with grief. The Company sent her to a penal station hundreds of millennia in the past—the preferred method of disposing of troublesome immortals . . .

Joseph in the Darkness

You know something, father? Sin exists. It really does.

I'm not talking about guilt, I'm talking about cause and effect. Every single thing we do wrong comes back to get us, sooner or later. You knew that, didn't you? And you told me, and I...well, I was so much more flexible than you, wasn't I? I could see all sides of every question. You saw black and white, and I saw all those gray tones.

For the longest time, I thought I was the one who had it right. I mean, you wound up here at last, didn't you? And I'm still free, as free goes. But whatever you're feeling, in there, I'll bet your conscience isn't bothering you.

You'd have let the little girl die, I know. Sized Mendoza up with that calm ruthless look, seen what she was and given your judgment: unsuitable for augmentation. Sent her back to die of starvation in the dungeon. She'd only have lasted another couple of days, she was so weak. Maybe I'd have let her die too, if I hadn't thought there was a chance they might interrogate her again before she died, and use the hot coals on her this time.

That was why I lied, father. It seemed doable at the time. Rescue the kid, make her one of us, give her a wonderful new life working for the Company. Nobody would ever find out about that freaky little something extra she had. Hell, every living thing generates the

Crome's stuff from time to time. Only one person in a million ever manages to produce enough to do things like walk through walls or be in two places at once. How was I to know...?

You're right, it was still wrong. And did anybody ever thank me for my random act of kindness? Not little Mendoza, that's for damned sure. Not on that day in England in 1555 when I stood beside her watching her mortal lover burn. How could she thank me? Her heart was in shreds and she could never die, no matter how much she wanted to, and it was my fault.

And I wouldn't be here now, either, would I, father? Going from vault to vault, looking up at the blind silent faces, to see if one of them is hers. Hoping to find her here in one of these houses of the near dead, even if I can't set her free this time, praying she's here: because there are worse places she might be.

I guess I was a lousy father to her. I hope I've been a better son to you. Yes, father, there's sin, and there's eternal punishment for sin. It's like a rat gnawing at your guts.

Sorry about the metaphor. Don't take it personally.

Look, we've got all night: and you're not going anywhere. I'll tell you about it.

Hollywood, 1996

SOMETHING ODD had happened.

Unless you possessed the temporally keen senses of an immortal cyborg, though, you wouldn't have noticed, over all the racket floating up from the roaring, grinding city. Lewis, being an immortal cyborg, frowned slightly as he accelerated up Mount Olympus Drive and scanned the thick air. He was a dapper man, with the appearance of someone who has wandered out of a Noel Coward play and got lost in a less gracious place.

Earthquake? No, or there would have been car alarms shrieking and people standing out on the sidewalk, a place the inhabitants of Los Angeles County seldom ventured nowadays without body armor.

Still, there was a sense of insult on the fabric of space and time, a residual shuddering Lewis couldn't identify at all.

He turned left into Zeus Drive and nosed his jade-green BMW into the driveway of the house. Nothing out of the ordinary here that he could see. He shut off the engine, removed his polarized sunglasses and put them in their case, removed his studio parking tag, and carefully put glasses and tag in the glove compartment. Only then did he emerge from the car and look about, sniffing the air.

Other than a higher than normal amount of ozone and an inexplicable whiff of horse, the air wasn't any worse than usual. Lewis shrugged, took up his briefcase, locked the car, and entered Company HQ.

What was that high-pitched whine? Lewis set down his briefcase, tossed his keys on the hall table, and looked into what would have been an ordinary suburban living room if it hadn't had a time transcendence chamber in one wall. Maire, the station's Facilitator, was activating it. She turned to him.

"You should have been here, Lewis. We've had quite an afternoon," she said.

He barely heard her, his gaze drawn to the window of the chamber. He gaped, astonished to see a pair of very uneasy horses and two oddly dressed people in there, just beginning to be obscured by the rising stasis gas.

One of the people raised her hand and waved. She was a sharp-featured woman, with cold black eyes and hair bound back in a long braid. She smiled at him. He knew the smile. It made her eyes less cold. The woman was the Botanist Mendoza.

Lewis had loved her, quietly, for several centuries, and she had never once noticed. They were stationed at the same research base for many years before she was transferred. He thought of writing to her after that, but then lost his chance, because she made a terrible mistake.

So terrible, in fact, that it was impossible that she could be standing there now smiling at him.

Then he connected the horses with the nineteenth-century clothing she was wearing. Was he seeing her, somehow, before the commission of her mistake? Was there any chance he might warn her, prevent the catastrophe?

No, because you couldn't violate the laws of temporal physics. You couldn't change history. He knew that perfectly well and yet found himself running to the chamber as the gas boiled up around her, beating on the window with his fists.

"Mendoza!" he shouted. "Mendoza, for God's sake! Don't go with him!"

She stared, taken aback, and then turned her wondering face to her companion. Lewis realized she thought he meant the other immortal, and cried, "No!"

She looked back at him and shook her head, shrugging.

"No, no!" Lewis shouted, and he could feel tears welling in his eyes as he pressed his hands against the glass, to push across time by main force. Futile. She was vanishing from his sight even now, as the yellow gas obscured everything.

Out of the clouds, her hand emerged for a moment. She set it against the window, palm to palm with his flattened hand, a gesture he would have died for once, rendered less personal by the thickness of the glass.

Then she was gone, he had lost her again, and he staggered back from the chamber and became aware that Maire was standing beside him. He turned and looked into her amazed eyes, struggled to compose himself.

"Er—what's going on?" he inquired, in the coolest voice he could summon.

"You tell me!" was Maire's reply.

In the end, though, she had to explain first. What he had seen was a temporal anomaly—nothing the Company couldn't handle. In fact Maire had received advance warning this morning from Future HQ. It was all listed in the Temporal Concordance. Everyone knew that weird things happened at the Mount Olympus HQ anyway, overlooking as it did Laurel Canyon's notorious Lookout Mountain Drive. It had been built to monitor that very location, actually.

This didn't do a lot to clear up Lewis's confusion. Temporal Concordance or not, it was still supposed to be impossible for anybody in the past to jump *forward* through time. When he mentioned this, Maire glanced at the techs and drew him aside.

"She was your friend, wasn't she?"

"Yes," said Lewis. "A—a coworker. We were close."

Maire said in a low voice:

"Then you knew she was a Crome generator."

Lewis hadn't known. He was unable to hide his shock. Watching his face go pale, Maire lowered her voice even more.

"Lewis, I'm sorry. I'm afraid it's true. Something latent that wasn't caught when she was recruited, apparently. You know what those people are; she might have warped the field any one of a dozen ways. What can I tell you? The impossible happens, sometimes."

He nodded, silent. Maire looked him up and down and pursed her lips.

"Under the circumstances, you see why there wasn't anything you could have done to help her," she said, in a tone that was gentle but suggested he'd better get a grip on himself now.

Lewis gulped and nodded.

Nothing more was said that night, and he thought the matter would slip by without further discussion. But next morning at breakfast, Maire said, "You're still upset. I can tell."

"I guess I made a fool of myself," Lewis replied, sipping his coffee. "She was a good friend."

"I wouldn't worry about it, Lewis," she told him, stirring sugar into her cup. The tech who was on his hands and knees scrubbing a large stain off the carpet looked up to glare at her. She glared back and slowly lifted her coffee, drinking it in elaborate enjoyment. "I might have done the same thing in your shoes. Besides, you're a valued Company operative."

"That's nice to know," said Lewis mildly, but he felt the hair stand on the back of his neck. He modified the slight tremor into a sad shake of his head. "Poor Mendoza. But, after all, a Crome generator! At least the rumors make sense now."

"Yes," Maire agreed. "Cream?"

"Thank you." Lewis held out his cup. The tech made a disgusted noise. He was a relatively young immortal, having traveled to 1996 from the year 2332 and not liking the past at all. He didn't care for decadent old immortals who indulged in disgusting controlled-substance abuse either. Coffee, cream, and chocolate were all illegal in his era. More: they were immoral.

"Unfortunate, but the sooner we put it behind us the better," Maire continued. She rose and wandered over to the picture window, which looked out across Laurel Canyon. It was a hazy morning in midsummer, with the sky a delicate yellow shading to blue at the zenith. The yellow was from internal combustion engines. The air burned, acrid on one's palate, and was full of the wailing of sirens and the thudding beat of helicopter blades. Maire was fifteen thousand years old, but the late twentieth century didn't bother her much; she'd seen worse. Besides, this was Hollywood.

Behind her, Lewis drained his coffee and set down his saucer and cup. "Sound advice," he said. "Well, I'd better hit the road. I'm going up to San Francisco today. That fellow with the Marion Davies correspondence has settled on a price at last."

"No, really?" Maire grinned. "I suppose you'll pay a little visit to..." She dropped her eyes to the tech, who was still scrubbing away, and looked back up at Lewis. *Ghirardelli's?* she transmitted on a private channel.

Lewis stood and took her hand. *Shall I bring you back a box of little Theobromos cable cars?* he transmitted back.

Her smile widened, showing a lot of beautiful and very white teeth. She squeezed his hand. She was a strong woman. *You're a dear.*

"To Fisherman's Wharf? Certainly. Shall I bring you back a loaf of sourdough bread?" Lewis asked.

"You're a dear! Boudin's, please." She glanced down at the tech mischievously. "I wonder if they'll still pack up those boiled crabs in ice chests for you."

The tech looked horrified.

"I'll find out." Lewis slipped his hand free and took his briefcase and keys. "Ciao, then. If I have to stay over, I'll give you a call."

"Oh, stay over," Maire ordered, waving him to the door. "Too long a drive to make twice in one day. Besides, you could use a little vacation. Get this unfortunate incident out of your mind."

"Oh, that," said Lewis, as though he'd forgotten already. "Yes, well, I imagine a ride on a cable car will lighten my spirits."

He wasn't referring to the popular tourist transit. *Theobroma cacao* has a unique effect on the nervous systems of immortals. Maire chuckled at his joke. The tech looked over his shoulder in a surly kind of way as Lewis stepped out into the heat and light of a Southern California morning.

He walked once around his car to inspect it for vandalism. When this Company HQ had been built, thirty years earlier, the gated community in which it was situated was regularly patrolled, to say nothing of being perched so far up on such a steep hill as to deter most criminals. Times had changed.

Sooner or later, they always did.

Satisfied that his leased transport was safe for operation, Lewis got in. Carefully he fastened his seatbelt and put on his sunglasses; carefully he backed out onto Zeus Drive and headed over the top of the hill to the less crowded exit from Mount Olympus. As he descended, he had a brief view of the city that stretched to the sea. Beyond, it had once been possible to see Catalina Island. The island was still there, but the smog hid it. Only once in a great while, when atmospheric conditions were just right, could it be glimpsed.

He proceeded down to Hollywood Boulevard and headed north through Cahuenga Pass, where he got on the Hollywood Freeway. He bore east to Interstate 5. After Mission San Fernando he followed the old stagecoach road, now a multilane highway into the mountains. It took him north, under arches restored since the last earthquake.

Long high miles brought him to Tejon Ranch, where the road dropped like a narrow sawmill flume between towering mountains preposterously out of scale. At the top, the San Joaquin Valley hung before his eyes like a curtain, and far down and away the tiny road raced across it, straight as an arrow.

He shivered, remembering how bad the grim old Ridge Route had been, especially in the season of flash floods, or forest fires, or blizzards, or summer heat so extreme, it made automobile tires explode. The modern road had only the drawback of the San Andreas Fault, which lay directly beneath it.

But there was no earthquake scheduled today, so as he shot down onto the plain through a miasma of burning brakes he muttered a little prayer of thanks to Apollo, in whom he did not particularly believe, but one really ought to thank *somebody* for getting safely down that pass.

For the next four hours the view was the same: the lion-yellow Diablo Range on his left, flat fields on his right, stretching across the floor of the valley to the Sierra Nevadas, the eastern wall of the world. Straight ahead lay the highway, shimmering in the heat. Memory rose like a ghost from the bright, silent monotony.

He did not want to remember himself striding along the front walk of Botany Residential with a bouquet of red roses, and he was even whistling, for God's sake, he was that happy. Could anything have been more of a cliché? Right in through the lobby, past all the mortal servants and the Botany staff leaving for early dinners, and he didn't care who saw him. He waited at the elevator, still whistling. He might as well have had a neon sign on his forehead: I AM A HAPPY MAN.

The elevator doors opened, and there stood Botanist Mendoza, ice bucket in hand. She smiled at him, briefly. She didn't smile at many people, but once at a party he'd been casually kind to her. It hadn't amounted to much; he'd seen her alone at a table, miserably unhappy, and brought her a handful of cocktail napkins to dry her eyes. Could he help? No, she explained with brittle dignity: it was only that she'd once loved a mortal man, and he'd been dead now for forty years, and she hadn't realized it had been that long until something at the party reminded her. She didn't really want company, but Lewis stayed long enough to be sure she was all right.

He smiled and nodded at her now, and she nodded back. They stepped past each other, she to the ice machine and he to ascend into realms of delight. He thought.

As it turned out, he got ice too.

Ten minutes later he was standing outside the elevator on the fifth floor of Botany Residential, in the act of tossing the roses into the trash chute, when the door opened and Mendoza was standing there again, witness to his bitter gesture. Her eyes widened. He drew himself up, summoning what shreds of self-respect he had left, and adjusted his cuffs.

"Hello, Mendoza," he said.

"Oh, Lewis. I'm sorry," she said.

She took him down the hall to her apartment, and he didn't mean to pour out his woes, but he did, and she listened.

They stayed there for hours, until he talked it all out, and then it seemed like a good idea for them to sneak down to the bar in the lobby and go on talking over drinks. For some reason she decided to let him past the wall of sarcasm with which she kept the rest of the world at bay. It couldn't have been his little moment of chivalry with the cocktail napkins. Lewis had been kind to a lot of women. But, laughing with her in that cramped little bar, he spent the best evening he'd had in a long time. And they were seen.

"You went out with the Ice Witch?" hooted Eliakim from Archives. "*Mendoza?* Botanist Mendoza? You took a flamethrower instead of a bottle or something?"

"None of your business," Lewis said. "But it might interest you to know that she's a perfectly delightful woman."

"This is the redhead we're talking about, right?" Junius from Catering leaned over the back of his chair, eyes wide with disbelief. "The workaholic? The one who isn't interested in *anybody?* I tried to kiss her once at a Solstice party, and I thought I'd have to get a skin graft for the frostbite!" He looked at Lewis with a certain awe that Lewis found flattering.

He merely shrugged. "It doesn't bear discussion."

Of course they promptly went out and told most of New World One, and for about two weeks rumors flew. He went to Mendoza to apologize.

"To hell with them," she said philosophically. "Us a couple? Are they nuts? What a bunch of nasty little academic gossips, and what overblown imaginations."

"I just wanted you to understand that none of it came from me," he said, not that pleased.

"I know," she replied, looking at him with a fondness that made his heart skip a beat. "You're a good man, Lewis. You're the nicest immortal I've ever known."

She kissed him, then, on the cheek, and tousled his hair.

They never became lovers, but she was affectionate with him in a way she never was with anyone else. He accepted that. They became great friends. When he was transferred to England, he found he missed her terribly. When he learned what had happened to her, years later in Los Angeles, he was sick at heart.

San Francisco

HE GAVE A SIGH OF RELIEF when at last he turned west through the Altamont Pass, fighting the wind until he got through to the East Bay cities, leaving the golden desolation well behind him.

Chrome and glass, sea air, the Oakland Bay Bridge with its section that had fallen out during the last big earthquake—all nicely replaced now, millions of busy commuters never gave it so much as a thought anymore, but Lewis's knuckles were white on the steering wheel until he had crossed into the city.

He made his way along the diagonal of Columbus, where he turned up a steep and narrow street and called upon a man in a dark rear apartment. A price was named and met; several bundles of cash were removed from Lewis's leather briefcase, to be replaced by a certain packet of letters. Lewis got back into his car and checked his internal chronometer.

Three hours ahead of schedule.

He started the car and took it up the long spiral to Coit Tower, apologizing to the transmission. There he parked and walked to the edge of the terrace, to all appearances a young executive taking an afternoon off to admire the spectacular view.

He removed his sunglasses and folded them away in his breast pocket. He looked out across the bay at Marin County. Somewhere over there...? He transmitted a tentative inquiry. It was returned immediately, from the depths of the city at his feet:

Receiving your signal. Who's that?

Literature Specialist Lewis. Joseph?

Lewis! What are you doing up here?

We have something to discuss in private. Coordinates, please?

Directions were transmitted. Lewis got back into his car and drove down from Coit Tower, apologizing this time to the brakes and promising to go nowhere near Lombard Street's notorious block.

He drove to another tourist attraction instead: the great outdoor shopping mall on Pier 39. Parking, he wandered through the mortal throng, the Europeans with cameras, performance artists, recovering addicts hawking cheap jewelry from card tables. Near the entrance Lewis spotted the location he sought. It was an amusement arcade of the modern variety, promising the thrills, so popular in this late twentieth century, of vicarious mass destruction and simulated murder. Cautiously he went in, politely declining a handbill that would have got him twenty cents off a frozen yogurt cone.

He stood peering down a long dark corridor filled with electronic games, tuning his hearing to sort through the wall of noise. Beeps, crashes, screams, roaring, and a familiar voice:

"...so your place would be the first, Jeff. We're willing to throw in the service plan for free, too. But, you know, I really think this model sells itself. I mean, I couldn't believe it when I saw the resolution, personally."

"Yeah, I like the graphics," somebody said, almost won over but wanting a bit more assurance. Lewis walked around a console where an adolescent boy was piloting a flying motorcycle through flames and winged demons. He beheld two bearded men, spotlighted in reflection from the sunlit world outside.

One was a young mortal, in nondescript casual clothes. The other was an immortal, a short and rather stockily built male in an Armani suit. His ancestry might have been Spanish, or Jewish, or Italian, or Greek; in fact he had been born centuries before any of those nations existed, though he appeared to be in his early thirties. He wore a neatly trimmed black mustache and beard, which gave him a cheerfully villainous look.

Open on the floor at his feet was a bulky white case bearing the logo of a well-known special effects house based in Marin County. He was holding a curious visored helmet in his hands, extending it to the mortal.

Both men turned to look at Lewis as he approached.

"Do you have a soda machine in here?" Lewis inquired.

"Sorry, no," the mortal told him, but the man in the Armani suit reached out a beckoning hand.

"Hey, friend, have you got a minute? Would you mind being part of an impromptu demonstration here?"

"Not at all," Lewis said. The immortal reached out to shake his hand.

What are you doing?

Bear with me.

"Name is Joseph X. Capra, how're you doing today? Great. Listen, I'm just offering my friend here some of the latest virtual reality technology for his business, and I'd like to get an unbiased opinion of this new helmet. Would you mind trying it on?"

"Not at all," said Lewis graciously, setting his briefcase between his feet. "Of course, I don't play VR games much—"

"That's okay, friend. That's even better, you know? You won't know what to expect." Joseph stepped around the case and set the helmet on Lewis's head. He fastened down the visor, and Lewis found himself in total darkness, listening to the voices outside.

"Now, just hang in there a minute, friend. You'll experience maybe a second of disorientation, but I promise you, the room won't be moving. Let's see, would you like to try the walk through Stonehenge? That's a neat one, let's get you set up for that."

"Sure," Lewis said.

Jeff said doubtfully: "I understand the Japanese have stuff now that's five years ahead of anything we have, so this is probably already obsolete—"

"This they don't have," said Joseph firmly. "Trust me on this one, pal. Here we go, the walk through Stonehenge!"

Lewis heard a click, and ethereal New Age music began to play in his headphones as Salisbury Plain opened out before him. He seemed to be drifting across it like a cloud, advancing on the Neolithic monument as it might have looked shortly after its completion. White-robed druids were moving in procession around it, chanting.

Really, Joseph, there weren't any druids yet when Stonehenge was finished. I was one, I should know. "Gosh, this is—quite amazing," said Lewis.

"You like those visuals, huh? Aren't they killer?" *Yeah, I know. What do you want? The artist is a neopagan reincarnated shaman in his spare time.* "But the best part's coming up in just a couple of seconds. Hang in there—"

Lewis felt a hand grip his shoulder, and it was just as well, because there was a sudden flash within the helmet that left him with a pattern of stars dancing before his eyes. The virtual world around him skewed and broke up. He could tell he was supposed to be watching the arrival of the sun god Belenos, but the image was fragmented. He felt sick and dizzy.

"Oh—ah—wow! What an experience!" he chirped desperately. *What in God's name did you just do to me?*

"You like that?" The grip did not leave his shoulder. "Think you'd come back to my friend's operation, here, to play this one?" *I'll explain when we're out of here.*

"Yes, certainly. Can't wait!" *I'd sooner have my liver torn out by harpies!*

"Unfortunately, this is only a sampler program, so you only get an excerpt," Joseph said, as the music stopped and the picture went to black. There was another click, and the Great Pyramid began to loom into view as Joseph lifted the helmet away. Lewis stood blinking, running a self-diagnostic.

Something's wrong! There's an error in my data transmission.

Yeah, it's fried for the next twenty-four hours. Mine too.

He was referring to the constant flow of data that went back to a Company terminal somewhere, the visual and auditory impressions from every immortal operative. It guaranteed that an operative in the field was always being watched over, could be rescued in time of trouble; but it also made private conversation impossible, except through subvocal transmission, which required a lot of concentration.

Are you out of your mind? Lewis transmitted.

No, but the Company's out of yours. Joseph was grinning, shaking his hand again. "I'd like to thank you for your valuable time and opinion. Great meeting you." *Go outside and wait. I'll be finished here in just a minute.* He turned to Jeff and said, "So okay, that's a guy who doesn't regularly use your product, and see the effect it had on him? Now. Because this is practically the prototype, Mr. Lucas feels..."

Lewis tottered outside and groped hurriedly for his sunglasses. He bought a Calistoga water at a snack stand and sat down on a bench with it. His hands shook as he poured the drink into a paper cup and sipped carefully.

He watched Joseph emerge from the arcade with Jeff, deep in conversation. They went across the street to what was obviously Joseph's car—a black Lexus sports coupe, gold package—and loaded the case into the trunk. Finally, Joseph shook Jeff's hand and walked back with him as far as the arcade entrance, talking earnestly and persuasively the whole while. They shook hands again, and the mortal went back inside. Joseph stood there a moment, going through a routine of finding and putting on his Ray-Bans, shooting his cuffs, patting his pockets for his keys, as Lewis got up and strolled toward him.

So, want to take my car?

I'd really rather not drive in this condition, thank you. Lewis frowned slightly as he finished his mineral water and put the cup in a trash receptacle.

Trust me, the dizziness won't last, Joseph told him as they walked across the street, pretending not to notice each other. *But you sounded like you had something private to discuss, and now we can discuss it out loud. Neat trick, huh?*

Remarkable, but couldn't you have invented something a little less painful?

Joseph pulled out his keys, making his car beep twice as it unlocked for him. *I didn't invent it. Total fluke discovery. The particular hardware in that particular helmet plus the glitch in that particular sample program. Nothing the Company could ever have anticipated when they designed us. I'm working on reproducing the effect in something smaller and more portable, though.* He got into the car, and Lewis got in on the other side.

Dear Lord! You'd better be careful, Joseph. Is it safe to talk in here?

"Oh, yeah," said Joseph, looking over his shoulder as he backed out of his parking space. "But I'd wait till we get where we're going."

"Where are we going?"

"Chinatown!" Joseph grinned and peeled away from the curb.

They parked in Portsmouth Square near the Stevenson Monument. Lewis looked around nervously at the towering buildings. "A lot of these are unreinforced brick, you know," he remarked.

"Uh-huh," said Joseph, striding away up the street. "But we both know there's no earthquake today, so what's the problem?"

"It's the principle of the thing," Lewis objected, hurrying after him. "I don't see how you can overcome the basic hazard-avoidance programming."

"You live long enough, you can figure out ways around almost anything," said Joseph, stopping to look up at a rusting pink neon sign. "Come on, this is it. Good old Sam Pan's."

He stepped through a narrow doorway into what was apparently a restaurant, and spoke in fluid Cantonese to an elderly man in a stained apron. Lewis waited in the doorway, peering doubtfully into the tiny dim kitchen. Before him a steep flight of wooden stairs ascended next to the yawning mouth of a dumbwaiter. It opened on a black shaft whose impenetrable darkness stank like a crypt.

The elderly man nodded and sent a slightly less elderly man to lead them up the stairs. On the third floor landing they emerged into a lofty dining room with card tables lined up along the street windows, through which the afternoon sun poured like gold. Flies whirled merrily in the sunbeams. The waiter settled them at a table and shuffled away to the dumbwaiter, where two bottles of beer rose smoothly into sight. He brought them to Joseph and went off to sit at the table by the staircase, where he proceeded to remove his right shoe and sock and examine his corns.

"We're not going to eat here, are we?" murmured Lewis.

"What are you, nuts?" Joseph's eyes widened as he opened their beers. "But isn't this a great place to talk in private? Can you imagine any Company operative coming in here for any reason at all? Get a load of *this.*" He jabbed with a chopstick between two of the bricks in the bare wall; ancient mortar trickled down like fine sand. "Any quake over 6.2 and, boy—"

"Don't." Lewis closed his eyes.

"Hey, it's okay. Next big one isn't scheduled for—" Joseph looked at his chronometer. "Well, a while, anyway. So, what did you want to talk about?" He lifted his bottle and drank.

Lewis drew a deep breath. "You know I was posted to the Laurel Canyon HQ back in '65."

"The Mount Olympus place?" Joseph frowned. "That's the one that monitors the Lookout Mountain Drive anomaly, huh? It's a full-service HQ now?"

"Budget reasons," Lewis said.

Joseph sighed and shook his head. "Jesus. One of these days that whole place will get sucked into some black hole, you know? So, what happened? Was there a disturbance?"

"Yes, apparently, though it was over by the time I got there," said Lewis. He wondered how to tell Joseph what he had to say next. Finally, he just said it. "Joseph, I saw Mendoza."

He wasn't prepared for the reaction. Something flared for a moment in Joseph's eyes, then burned out as fast as it had appeared. He lifted his beer and took another swallow. "Really?" he said casually. "No kidding? How's she doing these days?"

"What do you mean, how's she doing these days?" gasped Lewis, staring at him.

Joseph looked for a long moment into Lewis's white face.

"Oh," he said. He set the beer down carefully. He put his head in his hands.

"You mean you didn't know?" Lewis was horrified. "I'd have thought you of all people would have been notified!"

"Yes and no," said Joseph in a muffled voice.

"All these years I thought you *knew*." Lewis sagged back in his chair. "My God. I was never officially notified myself, I came across the partial transcript in my case officer's files."

"What happened to her?" Joseph lifted his face. His eyes were cold now. "You tell me. I'd rather hear it from you."

"She was arrested," Lewis said. "And... retired from active duty. Joseph, I'm sorry, I never thought—"

"Arrested? What the hell did she do? When was this?"

"1863. She was stationed in Los Angeles, and—"

"L.A.?" Joseph said. "They sent her down there? What did they do that for? She was in the Ventana, she was okay. Nothing grows in Los Angeles! Nothing natural, anyhow."

"Well, things used to, before the 1863 drought. There's that temperate belt, remember? She was stationed in the old Cahuenga Pass HQ."

"Bleeding Jesus!"

"Well, she was doing all right. Apparently. She'd completed her mission and everything, but... From what I can tell, the job ended, and she wasn't reassigned anywhere else." Lewis swallowed hard. "You know how layovers can be."

Joseph nodded. "If trouble's going to happen, it happens on a layover. Every time. Some goddam idiot of a posting officer... Tell me the rest."

Lewis wrung his hands. "I'm not clear on the details. As far as I could make out, somehow everybody was away from the HQ one day except for Mendoza and a junior operative. And... a mortal came to the station while the boy was in the field. She, er, ran off with the mortal. Deserted."

"With a mortal?" Joseph stared. "But she couldn't stand being around mortals! Not since—" He halted. "Who was this guy? Did anybody find out?"

"Oh, yes, the boy testified. It was his testimony transcript I saw, actually. The mortal seems to have been one of those Englishmen their foreign office sent out back then to court the Confederacy." Lewis stopped. Joseph had gone a nasty putty color under his tan.

"You did say Englishman, right?"

"I know. Bad luck, wasn't it? After what happened to her in England all that time before." Lewis shook his head. "Maybe the co-incidence—I don't know. But it ended rather quickly. And unpleas-antly. The Englishman died, I know that much."

"You're sure about that," said Joseph.

"Well—yes."

"What did they do with her? Where did they send her?" Joseph asked.

Lewis made a sad gesture, turning his empty palms up on the table.

"But you said you saw her!"

Lewis nodded. "I told you there was a disturbance. It was in 1862, before the incident happened. She and a fellow operative went into Laurel Canyon hunting for specimens. I don't know what could have possessed them to do it, but they rode up to Lookout Moun-tain Drive. And somehow or other the temporal wave sucked them *forward*, into 1996."

"Forward." Joseph gaped at him. "No, that's nuts, you must have misunderstood. We can't go forward. They must have been pulled from 2062. You heard wrong."

"Joseph, I saw them," said Lewis quietly. "They were wearing nineteenth-century clothes. They'd been riding horses, even the horses had been pulled along with them!"

"But—" Joseph was too stunned to continue.

"I got there just as they were being sent back," Lewis explained. "They were already in the transcendence chamber. And I saw her there, and I just—" He paused. "I tried to warn her about what she was going to do. I had to! And she couldn't understand me through the glass, she just stood there looking bewildered." He had to stop.

Joseph reached out and patted his arm. "It was a good try. There'll be trouble over that, though, you know."

"Oh, it's not that bad," Lewis said. "My case officer and I get along. I think I smoothed it over. It's not as though it did any good." He laughed bitterly. "History cannot be changed."

"Watch out, all the same." Joseph was still puzzled. He looked sharply at Lewis. "When did all this happen?"

"Yesterday afternoon."

"The place must be swarming with techs trying to find out how it happened. How'd you get away?"

"Well, I had business up here anyway and I thought—I thought you knew about her, you see, so you might have an idea where she's being kept. It was one thing to learn about her arrest and feel awful for years, but then to see her! Suddenly I just couldn't stand it anymore. As for how it happened, well, isn't it obvious?"

"No. Would you mind letting me in on the little secret?" said Joseph harshly. "Because in—what, twenty-odd thousand years of going around the block?—this is the first time I've ever heard of anybody defying the laws of temporal physics!"

Lewis looked at him miserably. "It was Mendoza, Joseph. She'd become a Crome generator. *She* set off the temporal wave. You didn't know that either?"

Joseph was silent for about thirty seconds. Then, moving too quickly for mortal sight, he leaped to his feet and hurled his beer bottle across the room. It smashed against the brick wall. The waiter looked at him reproachfully.

"Let's get out of here," croaked Joseph. "I need to do myself some damage." He pulled out his wallet and withdrew a fifty-dollar bill, which he thrust at the waiter as he shouldered past him. He ran clattering down the stairs, Lewis following him closely.

The waiter thrust the money into his pocket and, sighing, got a couple of paper napkins from the cutlery stand. Careful not to step in the broken glass with his bare foot, he crouched to shove it all together in a small pile between the two napkins. He scraped up as much as he could into the napkins. Looking around, he finally dropped them down the dumbwaiter shaft. The rest he pushed up against the baseboard, into a spacious crack there. Wiping his hands on his apron, he put on his sock and shoe again and limped downstairs. His corns hurt.

There are a lot of strange people in San Francisco, and if you work there, you soon grow used to occasional peculiarities in your customers; but the girl behind the cash register at Ghirardelli's decided that this took weirdness to new heights. Two executives in tailored business suits were sitting at one of the little white tables in the soda fountain area, glaring hungrily at the fountain worker who was preparing their eighth round of hot chocolate. They had marched in, put down a hundred-dollar bill, and told her to keep the drinks coming. On the floor between their respective briefcases was a souvenir bag stuffed with boxes of chocolate cable cars, and the table was littered with foil wrappers from the chocolate they had already consumed.

To make matters stranger, they had the appearance of junior delegates from opposing sides of a celestial peace conference: the dark one with his little diabolic beard and the fair-haired one with his fragile good looks. As she watched, the devil jumped up the second his order number was called and went swiftly, if unsteadily, to take his tray. He grabbed the cocoa-powder canister on his return. Sitting down across from the angel, he added a generous helping of cocoa to his hot chocolate. Then, apparently seized by an afterthought, he opened the canister and shook out a couple of spoonfuls onto the marble tabletop. Giggling guiltily, he pulled out an American Express card and began scraping the cocoa powder into neat lines.

"Danny!" She stopped the busboy as he came through the turnstile. "Look at him! Is he really going to—?"

He was. He did. The angel went into gales of high-pitched laughter and fell off his chair. The devil sighed in bliss and leaned down for a pass with the other nostril.

"I don't know what's wrong with them," said the girl in bewilderment. "I swear to God they were both sober when they came in here, and all they've ordered is hot chocolate."

"Maybe they just really like hot chocolate?" said the busboy.

"So, anyway," Joseph said, brushing cocoa powder off his lapels. "Where was I?"

"That thing you were going to tell me about," Lewis replied from the floor, where he was on his hands and knees searching for his chair.

"Yeah. Well, see, I don't think Mendoza's been deactivated. And I'll tell you why."

"I'm glad we're doing Theobromos," said Lewis as his head reappeared above the level of the table. "I don't think I could bear to discuss this if we weren't, you know? I just think I'd cry and cry." He drank most of his hot chocolate in a gulp.

"Me too." Joseph lifted his mug and quaffed mightily as well. "But this is okay. So. You ever go over to Catalina Island?"

Lewis blinked, remembering.

"Once or twice. Second-unit work. Who was I stunt-doubling for? Was it Fredric March or Richard Barthelmess? I know I've been over there. Go on."

"You remember the big white hotel? It's not there anymore, they tore it down in the sixties, but back then it was brand-new." Joseph sighed, remembering. He reached into the souvenir bag and pulled out another bar, unwrapping it absentmindedly.

"Big white hotel. Right." Lewis frowned solemnly. "Oh! The Hotel Saint Catherine. I remember now, because one used to be able to get, uh . . ."

"Yeah, liquor in the bar, because there were bootleggers all over the place." Joseph looked around on the tabletop, trying to see where his chocolate had gone. "Did I eat that already? Christ."

"I hope you're leaving me some of the ones without almonds."

"Uh-huh. So I was over there in 1923. I was trying to corner somebody, Chaplin or Stan Laurel or I forget who, to get him interested in a deal with Paramount."

"Was he?" Lewis drank the rest of his hot chocolate and signaled to the counterman for more.

"Interested? Hell no, complete waste of time. But it was a job. So I'm at the bar, see? And I'm talking up a great line, hoping to make the guy sorry he's not a player, you know, and I glance over into the dining room and—there she is." Joseph gulped. Tears started in his eyes. He reached blindly for his hot chocolate and drank the rest of it.

"Who?"

"Mendoza. I'm telling you, Lewis. Sitting at a table in the restaurant. Sleeveless dress, peach silk with a bead fringe on the skirt, white sun hat, string of pearls. She had a glass of white wine in front of her. So did he."

"Who?"

"The guy," said Joseph, and put his head down on the table and began to weep. It's disconcerting when a baritone weeps. Lewis was at a loss. He looked up as the fountain attendant, who had given up trying to get their attention, approached with their next hot chocolates.

"Um, I think my friend has had enough," he enunciated with care. "You can leave both of those, though, I'll drink them."

"Can you drive?" said Joseph foggily.

"Uh...no."

"Well, I can't."

"That's okay," said Lewis. "We'll just take a cable car."

"I live in Sausalito."

"Oh." Lewis drank half of one of the hot chocolates. "Cable cars don't go across the Golden Gate, do they?"

Joseph shook his head, reached for the cocoa powder again.

"Oh, busboy!" Lewis stood up and nearly fell over. "Would you call us a taxi, please? Thank you. There we go! All settled. So, anyway. The girl in the peach silk dress. She turned out not to be Mendoza, obviously."

"Yeah. No, it was her. I'm telling you, Lewis, I saw her!"

"Who was the fellow she was with?"

"That was what I couldn't dope out." Joseph rose up on one elbow, staring at him. He mopped tears and cocoa powder from his face with a paper napkin. "He shouldn't have been there. Couldn't have been, the big arrogant bastard! But they both looked up and saw me. Recognized me, I'd swear. I pushed away from the bar and went through the crowd to get to them, but that was a hell of a crowded watering hole, and by the time I got into the restaurant, they were gone."

"You're sure they were really there in the first place?"

"No," Joseph admitted. "Except... their wine was still there, on the table. And the terrace door was open."

"Where are you going?" shouted the busboy from the phone, putting his hand over the mouthpiece.

Where indeed? wondered Lewis.

"Sausalito," shouted Joseph.

They sat looking at each other.

"We must find her," Joseph said.

"I was hoping you'd say that." Lewis began to smile.

"It's impossible she managed to escape from wherever they stashed her, but what if she did? She might need help. And I have to know whether or not she was really there."

"We couldn't get into trouble, could we, just making a few discreet inquiries?"

"It might take us years to find out anything."

"So much the better." Lewis held out his hands. "We'll be less obvious that way."

"What was it the man said about the free French garrison, Louie?" Joseph began to giggle again, reaching for Lewis's half-finished drink.

At that moment another immortal entered the room. He was a security tech. He was dressed as a sport cyclist, in the bright tight-fitting cycling ensemble of that era, and carried his helmet and sunglasses under his arm. He swept the room once with a cold gray stare and acquired the two businessmen sitting at the little table under the time clock. He closed on them at once.

"Operatives? You stopped transmitting three hours ago. Are you in need of assistance?" he inquired in a low voice. They stared up at him, momentarily sobered. Someone must have been monitoring their data transmissions.

"Oh, gee, I'm sorry!" Joseph said. "You know what it was? We were in this arcade, and one of the damn electronic games fritzed. We were standing too close to it. Happens every now and then. We're okay, really."

"Honest," Lewis said.

The security tech scanned them and recoiled slightly at the level of Theobromos in their systems. He surveyed the litter of foil wrappers and empty cups, regarded the cocoa powder in Joseph's beard, and sighed. Two old professionals on a sloppy bender. And it was true that there were occasional inexplicable flares and shortings-out in San Francisco, which was as weird in its way as Laurel Canyon, not because of any geologic anomaly but because the place seemed to attract Crome-generating mortals in droves. It made his job more complicated than that of most security personnel.

"All right," he said. "I don't really need to report this, if you two senile delinquents will promise me you won't try to drive in your condition."

"We've already sent for a taxi," Lewis assured him.

"Gonna go home and order a pizza and sleep it off. Trust me, kid." Joseph reached up and patted the security tech's white helmet. He left cocoa-powdered fingerprints.

Lewis sat up abruptly and stared around, wishing he hadn't. He had a terrible headache, and his skin was crawling. He was ravenously hungry, too. At least he remembered where he was: a houseboat in Sausalito. Rank wind off the tidal flats and the cry of sea birds confirmed his memory.

He remained on the couch for a moment, surveying the litter of the dimly recalled previous evening. Five pizza boxes and two empty five-liter bottles of Coca-Cola. Lewis lifted the lid on the nearest box, hoping there was some crust left. There wasn't. How sad. He needed carbohydrates terribly just now.

Resting his head in his hands, he tried to remember his dream, but it was fading so quickly: Mendoza laughing with him at one of the base administrator's parties, over some ridiculous costume Houbert had worn. They hadn't been able to stop giggling. He'd master himself, fix all his features in a look of prim attention, and she'd take one look at him and go into fresh gales of laughter, which would set him off again. They'd had to stagger outside at last, leaning on each other.

Mendoza looked young when she laughed. Apparent age, in immortals, is largely a matter of facial expression. Most of the time she seemed older, austere and withdrawn. Lewis thought he must be the only person who'd ever seen her eyes sparkle, her cheeks flush. That is, outside the mortal men who'd loved her.

Resolutely, he got to his feet and peered into the empty bedroom. The bed was neatly made, though Joseph must have been in bad shape when he woke. Funny how army training never wore off, especially when one had been a centurion. He sent a vague questing signal, and there came a response, faint through hills and traffic: *Getting the car. You can borrow one of my shirts.*

Thanks.

Lewis stepped into the kitchen and opened Joseph's refrigerator. There was more Theobromos, which he couldn't bear to look at. There were several six-packs of Anchor Steam beer. There was a loaf of Roman Meal bread and a package of unidentifiable sliced delicatessen product. Lewis groaned and opened the freezer. Ah! Ten boxes of frozen fettuccine Alfredo. He slid out the whole stack, opened them all, and put them in the microwave. Then he went to take a shower, uttering another silent prayer of thanks to Apollo, lord of civilized amenities.

Only after he'd eaten all the fettuccine did he gather up the pizza boxes and liter bottles and little black plastic dishes and fill a trash bag, which he set carefully beside Joseph's front door. He found an ironing board and was pressing his suit when he heard the Lexus pull into the carport.

A moment later Joseph came across the gangplank and let himself in, rather awkwardly because he was carrying a large cardboard box.

"I got two dozen doughnuts," he said, offering it. "I think there's a couple left. I meant to leave more. Sorry."

"Oh, no, thank you, you needn't have. I ate all your fettuccine Alfredo."

"Okay then," said Joseph, and sat down to eat the remaining doughnuts. No Armani suit today; he was wearing a brilliant Hawaiian shirt over black Levis, and black high-top sneakers. "I phoned in sick," he explained through a mouthful of doughnut, taking in Lewis's stare. "We need to talk to somebody today. Do you have to get back anytime soon?"

"Not immediately, no." Lewis unplugged the iron and pulled on his pants. "With whom do we need to talk?"

"I did some checking," Joseph said, licking glazed sugar from his fingers, "on the operatives who were posted at Cahuenga Pass with Mendoza. One of them is still in California. Right here in Marin County, in fact."

"That's convenient." Lewis tied his tie carefully.

"It gets better. It's the ornithologist. The kid who was there with her when she went AWOL. The one who testified. Who actually saw the Englishman." Joseph's eyes were black and shiny as coal this morning, his gaze hard and direct. "So. We have another six hours before the effect of the helmet wears off and we start transmitting data to the Company again. Here's what we do. We go see this guy right now, somehow or other we get him to put on the helmet and walk through Stonehenge, and then we ask him a few questions. Okay?"

"*Nunc aut nunquam,*" said Lewis grimly, slipping on his coat.

"You said it, kiddo." Joseph picked up his car keys and rose to his feet.

They took Highway 1 north, winding along coastline and cutting over to Tomales Bay. In the late twentieth century this was all pastoral land, dairy pastures on sea-facing hills, with redwoods along the creeks and wild rose and blackberry bramble thick beside the road. Here and there an isolated farmhouse sat back in the shadows under its grove of laurel trees, unchanged in a hundred years except for a satellite dish for television reception.

At last there was a steel-framed gate across a dirt road on their left, with a posted sign. Joseph slowed and stopped as they came abreast of it. It read:

AUDUBON SANCTUARY, TOMALES BAY
RESTRICTED ENTRY

"Good place for an ornithologist," said Lewis.

"Nice and isolated, too." Joseph backed up and made a sharp turn across the highway, pulling up to the gate. There was a little communications box with a push button at one side. He got out and pressed the button. A moment later a voice responded, tinny and distorted by the weathered speaker.

"Are you here to see the smews?"

"Uh—" Joseph and Lewis exchanged a look.

"Or are you here to see the Hitchcock set?" the voice went on, in a slightly annoyed tone.

"Yeah, actually," Joseph said.

"I have to tell you, you're really missing an opportunity if you don't see the smews while they're here."

"Ornithologist Grade Two Juan Bautista?"

"Oh." The voice altered completely. "I'm sorry. Who's that?"

"Facilitator Joseph and Literature Specialist Lewis."

"Okay." There was a loud buzz and click as the gate unlocked. "Please close up again after you come through."

Once through the gate, they followed the road across a meadow and down the hill toward the bay. It led to a promontory where a frame house sat, shaded by three enormous cypress trees, looking out on a little boat dock. The location seemed eerily familiar.

"*Alfred* Hitchcock," said Joseph abruptly, slapping his forehead. "It's the house from *The Birds!*"

"Well, no wonder we drove up here to see it," said Lewis in delight.

"Perfect," Joseph growled, pulling up to the garage from which Rod, Tippi, Jessica, and Veronica made their final desperate escape.

As they approached the house, they heard what appeared to be a violent argument going on between a child and an adult, though it ceased abruptly when Lewis knocked. The door opened, and an immortal stood there staring at them. He wore a khaki uniform with a plastic tag over the pocket that read JOHN GREY EAGLE, SITE DOCENT. His long hair, which had once been silver, was now dyed jet black and braided behind him.

"Hi," he said. There was a violent flapping of wings from the room beyond, and a raven suddenly landed on his shoulder. He reached up swiftly and closed its beak between his thumb and forefinger.

"Whoa." Joseph stepped back, laughing. "Is that one of the cast members still hanging around?"

"No," said the man with a trace of sullenness. "This is just Raven. You guys understand that birds never, ever really behave that way, right? It was just a horror movie. Ravens never hurt mortals, and neither do seagulls, for that matter."

"Well, sure, but it's still a great movie." Joseph thrust out his hand. "Hi. I'm Joseph and this is Lewis. We came to see the set, but—say, what *is* a smew, anyway?"

"I'm Juan Bautista. *Mergellus albellus,* it's a Eurasian merganser, and they're only accidental here, but we have a mated pair! Do you have any idea how rare that is?" said Juan Bautista, shaking hands.

"Amazing," said Joseph. "So. Can we see the house?"

"All right," sighed Juan Bautista, stepping back from the door. Then he stopped, staring at Joseph. "Do I know you from somewhere?"

"Gee, I suppose it's possible. I get around a lot," said Joseph. "Come on, I want to see the fireplace where the sparrows attacked."

There wasn't really much to see, since no attempt had been made to reproduce any of the film's furnishings. Juan showed them through the rooms anyway and recited a few film facts for their edification: that Hitchcock had thrown a lot of innocent helpless birds at Tippi

Hedren, and that the schoolhouse where the ravens massed for their completely out-of-character attack was now a private residence and thought to be haunted, though not by Suzanne Pleshette. The raven clacked its beak derisively.

"Well, isn't that just fascinating," said Lewis.

"Want to go see the smews now?"

"Great," said Joseph.

A smew looked like a fat little black-and-white duck with a crest, though Juan Bautista insisted a merganser wasn't a duck. They admired one paddling about on a reedy backwater for a few minutes, then started back to the house.

"I guess you don't get into the city much," said Joseph as they crossed the lawn.

"Me? No. What do you guys do?"

"Lewis here works for the studios in Hollywood—" Juan Bautista turned to stare at him, impressed. "Dealing in rare research stuff and old scripts."

"I was stationed in Hollywood once," said Juan Bautista. "It wasn't there yet, though, so I never got to see any movie stars."

"Yeah, that's life in the service, isn't it?" Joseph shook his head ruefully. "I don't see many in my line of work, either. I work for— Say, I've just remembered, I have that helmet in the car!"

"That's right, you do," said Lewis. "Let's show him."

Juan Bautista looked from one to the other. "What?"

"You'll love this. It's so cool." Joseph ran to the Lexus and popped the trunk.

"He was showing me only yesterday," Lewis told Juan Bautista. "No end of fun, virtual reality stuff."

Juan Bautista's eyes lit up. "The graphics are still pretty crappy, but I understand they're getting better."

"Wait'll you see this." Joseph chortled, digging the white crate out of the trunk. "Come on, let's take it in the house. It's a prototype. You can try it out."

"You work for *those* guys?" Juan Bautista recognized the logo on the box. "Wow."

"Yeah, but I'm never involved in the movies themselves." Joseph pushed the door open and set the box down. "Right now I'm a salesman for their cybernetic entertainment division. There are certain developments Dr. Zeus wants monitored. You know." He lifted out the helmet. "Just sit down and get comfortable."

"Okay." Juan Bautista handed the raven off to a perch—it gronked and protested—and took a seat on his couch. Joseph stepped close and placed the helmet carefully on Juan Bautista's head. Lewis winced and retreated a few paces. The raven cocked its head to look at him and looked back at Juan Bautista uneasily.

"Here we go!" Joseph took a small control out of his pocket and inserted a minidisc. "This is the sampler. My favorite's the walk through Stonehenge, it's the first one on the program. Check it out." He thumbed the control and stepped well away from the couch. The raven ducked its head and began to flutter its wings, crying.

"Oh, shut up, bird. Hey, this is really something," said Juan Bautista muffledly. "It's a *lot* better than the other stuff I—ow!"

He began to fumble with the helmet. The raven flew off its perch and went straight for Joseph's eyes, screaming, "Get it off him! Get it off him right now!"

Joseph dropped the control to defend himself and got a grip around the raven's wings, trapping them. He held it out at arm's length. Juan Bautista pushed off the helmet, panting. There was a moment of silence.

"Did that bird just talk?" asked Lewis at last.

"Uh—sure. Ravens can be taught to talk, you know," said Juan Bautista, in a frantically reasonable voice. "Just like parrots. All the *Corvidae* are really intelligent."

"Get it off him, get it off him right now," said the raven rather lamely. "Polly wants a cracker, awk, awk, awk."

"Nice try," said Joseph, glaring at it. "Why don't you do the nevermore bit next?"

"I hate that stupid poem," said the raven. Juan Bautista groaned and slid down on the couch. "I'm sorry, Dad," it added contritely.

Joseph grinned unpleasantly. Lewis was reminded that Joseph had worked for the Spanish Inquisition.

"Well, well," he chuckled. "You're not just any birdbrain, are you? Somebody's done an augmentation job on you. Boy, that's really illegal. The Company wouldn't be at all happy if they found out. I wonder who could have done such a thing?"

"Dad didn't do it!" shrieked the raven. "It was somebody else. Not Dad."

"Shut *up*," said Juan Bautista desperately.

"Oh, pal, have we ever got your ass in a sling," Joseph said. "To say nothing of your bird in my hand. But, you know what? This is your lucky day. The Company won't ever find out, because that helmet just shorted out your automatic datalink."

"For a period of twenty-four hours," Lewis added.

Juan Bautista looked from one to the other, then ran his self-diagnostic. "My God, it has," he said after a moment. He scowled at Joseph. "Okay, what's going on? Who are you guys? I'm sure I know you from somewhere."

"Don't worry. We just needed to ask you some questions in private, and the helmet was the only way to do it," Lewis assured him.

"Let Raven go, and maybe I'll talk to you," Juan Bautista said.

"Okay, Raven, are you augmented enough to know what'll happen to you if you go after me again?" Joseph asked her.

"I'll be good," the raven snarled. Juan Bautista put out his hand and she went to him, scurrying up his arm to busy herself with grooming his hair through the whole of the following conversation.

"Look, there's no need for unpleasantness. We just want some information you might have about something that happened to a friend of ours," said Lewis.

"You don't tell anybody about this conversation," said Joseph, pulling up a chair, "and we won't tell anybody about your little friend. A deal? And if there are any inquiries about why you weren't transmitting for twenty-four hours, no problem." Joseph held up his index finger. "We came here to see the Hitchcock set, got to talking, I persuaded you to try on the helmet, and it zapped you. You can tell it exactly as it happened. Then Lewis and I looked at each other and exclaimed, 'My gosh, it must have been the helmet all along. It's defective.' I apologized, and we promised to take it apart tomorrow to see what's wrong with it, which I'm going to anyway, so it's not even a lie. Okay? That's what you tell any security tech who comes to check on you. If they ask us, we'll corroborate, and everybody's happy."

"Do you mind if I ask you a question, though?" Lewis stepped closer. "How did you manage to do the augmentation without being found out?"

Juan Bautista nodded in the direction of Tomales Bay. "The San Andreas Fault runs right along under there. Every time there's any seismic activity at all, the electromagnetic disturbance shuts out transmissions for hours. I have a lot of time to myself, actually. The Company just ignores it, now, since there's nothing they can do."

"Neat," said Joseph in awe. "For Christ's sake don't ever tell anybody else, though."

"I'd heard rumors that storms will do it too," said Lewis.

Juan Bautista nodded. "Bad electrical ones," he said.

"It's true," Joseph admitted. "To let you in on a little Facilitator classified information. But you're not supposed to know. So you don't know, right, guys? And you'll never speak or think about it again, after today." He glanced at his chronometer. "After about fifteen hundred hours today. So let's talk fast."

"Indeed." Lewis came and sat down gingerly on the couch, as far away as he could get from the raven. "Do you remember working with the Botanist Mendoza?"

Juan Bautista's eyes widened. "Yes," he said unhappily.

"You testified against her," stated Joseph.

"Not *against* her," Juan Bautista said. "Just about her! I just— oh, man, can't I ever leave this behind me? I caught hell from my case officer, I had to testify."

"But you have a real nice posting now, and you wouldn't want to lose it, so let's move on," said Joseph flatly. "1863. What happened?"

"I don't know what happened," Juan Bautista said. "I swear to God I don't. All I remember is, Mendoza's job was finished, and her transfer never came through, and she was getting really mean. There was a drought that ruined the rancheros, and all the plants died, and there was smallpox. Were either of you guys there? It was bad. I was only seventeen, my first time out in the field."

Joseph's face twisted oddly. Lewis glanced at him and took the initiative.

"I've heard about it. I was in England at the time, and glad to be there. The man who came to see Mendoza, he was an Englishman, wasn't he?"

Juan Bautista nodded emphatically. "An espionage guy. Like an early-day James Bond. There were American secret service agents, or whatever they had back then, chasing him, and Mendoza was helping him hide."

"You have any idea why she was helping him?" said Joseph.

Juan Bautista looked very uncomfortable. His hand wandered up to stroke the raven's neck feathers, but she clacked her beak at him irritably. "Stop that!" she snapped. "I'm doing the grooming here."

Juan Bautista looked out the window at the bright waters of the bay. "Well—Mendoza and the Englishman, they went to bed together, apparently." He exhaled. "Do you guys really want to know all this?"

"No, no," Lewis said soothingly. "So there was some relationship between them, that's why Mendoza was helping the mortal. How did she explain what she was doing?"

"She said it was research," Juan Bautista said. "There was some kind of British conspiracy going on. Our anthropologist knew all about it. I think this guy was part of the plot. The one that Mendoza ran off with. He came after Imarte left—she was the anthropologist—and suddenly Mendoza was all interested. She told me she was going off to check things for Imarte. I thought it was weird, because she and Imarte couldn't stand each other."

"That's true," said Joseph.

"When I came home that afternoon, Mendoza and the British guy were about to ride away. She told me I had to fix my own dinner." Juan Bautista sighed, remembering. "Didn't come home all night. Next morning two Yankees came looking for the Englishman, said they were his friends. I was pretty dumb back then, but I played dumber. Next thing I know, Mendoza transmitted, said she and the Englishman had to hide out, and could I bring them some food? So I did. I told them about the Yankees. You should have seen her, she was so scared. And mad..."

There was a moment of silence, broken only by the rustling of the raven's feathers.

"What happened then?" said Joseph.

"Nothing. I never saw her again. I was all alone the next two days. The Yankees never came back, either. But the night after that, security techs came and took all Mendoza's stuff, and started searching the place. And in the middle of it Porfirio—he was my case officer—came galloping up, and they started yelling at each other." Juan Bautista closed his eyes at the memory.

"They left with her stuff. Porfirio reamed me out, he really did. Like it was my fault! But then they came back and got both of us. They took us to some place in Los Angeles, and I didn't see Porfirio again after that. They questioned me over and over, but I didn't know anything. Then they transferred me. And that was all that happened."

"What did he look like?" Joseph asked.

"Porfirio?"

"No, the Englishman. Did he look like James Bond?"

"No," Juan Bautista said. "He just looked...like an Englishman. But he was really tall."

Joseph began to pace the room. He took a pencil and paper from Juan Bautista's desk and thrust them at him. "Draw the guy for me," he said. "Give me a photographic likeness."

It was a simple request to make of a Company operative, with total recall and photographic memory at his disposal. Juan Bautista shrugged. He worked for about five minutes, as Joseph and Lewis watched him. Long before he had finished and handed the portrait to Lewis, Joseph was across the room beating his head against the wall.

Lewis studied the portrait: a very tall figure looking down from horseback. He was dressed in the clothing a gentleman wore for travel in 1862, elegantly tailored, which somewhat obscured the fact that he was rather lankily built. He had a long broken nose and high broad cheekbones. Lewis found the picture disturbing, though he couldn't have said why, other than the obvious fact that something about it was making Joseph bang his head against the wall. Juan Bautista watched, horrified.

"You know," said Lewis carefully, pretending not to notice what Joseph was doing, "this fellow reminds me of... the way Mendoza used to describe the mortal she knew in England. The, ah, attitude."

"And how," groaned Joseph. He staggered to a chair and sat down. "Give me the picture."

Lewis handed it to him. Joseph stared at it for a long moment before crumpling it up and squeezing the wad of paper between both hands.

"Did I offend you somehow?" Juan Bautista asked cautiously.

"No. No, you didn't, pal, and I owe you one. We're going to go, now, and with any luck our paths won't ever cross again." Joseph got up. "Come on, Lewis."

"Thank you, Juan," said Lewis. "And rest assured we won't tell anyone about the raven."

Juan Bautista watched as Joseph scooped up the helmet and its case and stalked out, with Lewis following.

"*Did* he know you from somewhere?" Lewis asked quietly, as they paused at the car to put away the helmet.

"He was one of my recruits," Joseph said, slamming the trunk lid down. "Haven't seen him since he was four. Great father, ain't I?"

Juan Bautista went to the window to be certain they left.

"I'm glad they're going," said Raven, fussing with her master's hair. "I didn't like them at all. I wanted to peck out his eyes, that mean man. Just like in the scary movie."

"Hush," Juan Bautista said, watching the two immortals drive away. His hand rose in the habitual gesture to stroke her neck feathers, and this time she let him.

"You're driving rather fast," remarked Lewis. It was the first word either of them had spoken. They were halfway back to San Francisco, following the highway along the cliffs above the sea.

"Sorry," Joseph said. He pulled the car over on the narrow stony verge, stopped the engine, and got out. For a moment Lewis had the strangest conviction that Joseph was going to jump; instead he pulled back his arm and threw something, hurling it with a grunt of fury toward the steel-colored ocean. It seemed to hang in the air a moment before it dropped, a little white ball of wadded paper.

"Would you mind explaining?" asked Lewis, when Joseph got back in and slammed the door.

"We made a decision yesterday when we were both bombed out of our skulls. But the ante, Lewis, just got upped. If you knew just how high it is now," Joseph said, "I don't think you'd want to keep playing."

Lewis turned to stare at him. "I beg your pardon," he said coldly. "That's my decision to make, I believe. Mendoza was my friend. If there's anything I can do to help her, wherever she is now, I'm going to do it."

Joseph sighed. "We may not be able to do anything for her. Even finding out where she is will be dangerous. I may have some chance, on my own. What I do, what we do, depends on what I turn up. But I may not turn up anything for years. You see what I'm saying?"

"Yes, I do." Lewis set his chin. "But you have to understand my position. There she was, about to walk into tragedy, and I knew it but there was nothing on earth I could do."

"Oh, I think I know how you felt," said Joseph bleakly.

"You recognized the man in the picture. Who was he?"

Joseph disengaged the emergency brake and started the Lexus again. Watching carefully for oncoming traffic, he pulled back onto the highway. "Somebody who died and should have stayed dead," he said at last.

They were nearly back in Sausalito before Lewis spoke again. "You'll let me know when you discover where she is?"

"I promise. Now, I think we shouldn't contact each other again for a few years. You may not hear from me until after the war. You probably won't be stationed in L.A. much longer."

Lewis shrugged. "Not the way things are going, no." He looked at his chronometer. "Gosh, how time flies," he said lightly.

Joseph nodded. They were talking about the Oakland Raiders when data transmission resumed a few minutes later.

Lewis reclaimed his car and drove back to Hollywood that afternoon, arriving long after dark. He didn't see Joseph again for thirty years.

Joseph in the Darkness

So, FATHER, YOU'RE the expert on death. Why can't we die?

Right now you'd be giving me that flat patient stare that meant I'd asked a really dumb question. But, seriously, think about this for a minute: what step in the immortality process makes us permanent problems for our masters, instead of just terribly long-lived ones?

The conditioning to avoid danger at all costs can be worked around, if you psych yourself up to it. Takes a lot of practice, but it can be done.

The pineal tribrantine 3 gives us eternal youth, but it doesn't make us indestructible.

The ferroceramic skeletal structure can't be damaged, but the soft tissues around it are as vulnerable as a mortal's to injury—or would be, if we didn't have the speed and agility to avoid bullets, knives, shrapnel, et cetera.

The millions of biomechanicals circulating through us, each one custom-designed to the individual operative's DNA, are tougher to beat. If my heart was cut out of my body (assuming I held still long enough to let somebody do that, which I wouldn't, because I'm afraid of pain), I'd just go into fugue and my biomechanicals would grow a new heart. They repair, replace, revive, detoxify, and probably they could keep us immortal all on their own, if it wasn't for the fact that they're susceptible to damage too.

Each system backs up the other systems, functions overlap, and the whole design works so well that Preservers almost never incur damage bad enough to land them in a repair facility. Smash us to bits—sooner or later we'll rise up in one piece again, like the bucket-carrying brooms in the *Sorcerer's Apprentice,* and go on about our work. Not only that, we make more of ourselves, out of the unwanted orphans of history. And we're smarter than the masters who created us. God knows I'd be scared of me, if I was a mortal.

So I can just imagine our masters sitting around a table in an ivory tower up there in the twenty-fourth century, thumbing frantically through some big book of spells trying to find the one that will turn us off.

But better minds than theirs have tackled the problem, and nobody's ever managed. I'm talking about suicide attempts, of course. All of us immortals have felt like dying, at some time. Some of us have wanted it bad enough to try. There are a lot of stories, hilarious in a black kind of way, about what happened. The best of them is the one about the guy who overcame his hazard avoidance programming enough to position himself at ground zero in Hiroshima. Next thing he knew, he was wandering around in the mountains with big chunks of his memory gone, and the locals were reporting sightings of Charcoal Faceless Ghost-Man.

Why wasn't he vaporized, ferroceramic skeleton and all? I don't know. My guess is, no matter how badly he consciously wanted to die, something in his unconscious got him out of there at hyperspeed at the last possible second.

If we can survive something like that, what can't we survive?

And how would our masters even begin to find out? How could they experiment without tipping us off? What would we do to them if we caught them at it?

But if they did find some silver bullet, how would they manage to hunt down every single one of thousands of ancient, cunning, superintelligent, and extremely survival-oriented cyborgs so they could use it?

To say nothing of the fact that it would have to be one hell of a silver bullet, capable of destroying every single biomechanical in a cyborg's body. If it missed even one, the little thing would reproduce frantically, and soon there would be enough to begin repair. Months or years later, some body would claw its way out of an unmarked grave, and if it wasn't pissed off about the way it had been treated, I'd be real surprised. The masters would be surprised, too. Maybe in their beds, maybe in lonely places.

No wonder they monitor every word we say.

Austin, 2025

THE CEMETERY WAS a modern one, parklike and smooth, with neat flat headstones set flush in the manicured lawn; so it had taken a lot of work and enthusiasm to give it an appropriate holiday look. Garden edging had been used here and there to enclose graves in little pavilions festooned with black and orange crepe paper, or strung with electronic pumpkin and skeleton lights. Every grave had its jack-o'-lantern or bouquet of marigolds and chrysanthemums. The infants' section was particularly bright, with little plastic trick-or-treat buckets, tiny pumpkins, black and orange pinwheels, tissue-paper ghosts.

The living children in their costumes wandered between the graves reading names and dates, or thronged at the edge of the cemetery, where a produce stand had a pumpkin patch and hayride. A row of dilapidated tractors was ranged along the edge of the property line; today there were dummies mounted in the rusting seats, old clothes stuffed with newspaper and surmounted with rubber masks. There was a vampire, a werewolf, Frankenstein's monster.

Señor and Señora Death were busy packing up the leftovers of a tailgate picnic, nesting empty Tupperware containers and wadding up plastic bags. Señor Death turned to look at the horizon, where slate-blue clouds advanced. He frowned. He shouted, "Kids! Are you going trick-or-treating or what? Come on."

They came running from the hayride, the ballerina and Snow White and the baby tiger. Teenage Death strolled after them, being irritating, too cool to hurry.

Señor Death exhaled sharply and shook his head. The ballerina outpaced her little brother and sister and said breathlessly, "Uncle Frio! The man at the pumpkin patch says it's going to rain. Will that short out Daddy's lights?"

"No." Señor Death crouched down by the grave and lifted the wire that connected the four little jack-o'-lanterns carved with the four names: GILBERT, TINA, BRANDY, AGUSTIN. "It's outdoor grade wire, the microchip's insulated. They'll shine all night, no matter what the weather does."

"Mommy, can I have an orange soda?" asked the baby tiger.

"Not in the car, mijo," Señora Death said firmly. "When you get home." The baby tiger started to pout.

"Tricker-treat, tricker-treat, tricker-treat," chanted Snow White, which distracted the baby tiger, and he took up the chant too. They bounced up and down in great excitement.

"You're practically jumping on Daddy's grave!" the ballerina fretted.

"I think he'd kind of like it," Señor Death told her. "They're little, Brandy. It's okay."

Teenage Death made his leisurely arrival and bent to lift the cooler over the tailgate for his mother. He fished inside and drew out a bottle of orange soda. Instantly the baby tiger stopped bouncing and pointed an accusatory finger. "How come *he* gets to have one?" he yelled.

"Because I won't barf all over the inside of the truck, baby," said his brother.

"Agustin, it won't kill you to wait ten minutes until we get home. Put the soda back," Señor Death ordered. Agustin gave him an insolent stare, so Señor Death added, "If you want to go to that party tonight—"

"Nazi," muttered the boy, but he put the soda back.

"Come on, kids." Señora Death was kneeling by the grave, making the sign of the cross. The younger children knelt beside her and crossed themselves too. Señor Death and Agustin stood to pray, reciting the Hail Mary and Our Father with them. When they finished, the children scrambled to their feet and climbed into the truck, crouching under the camper shell. Agustin closed the tailgate on them and stood beside Señor Death, waiting somberly as his mother bent to the gravestone and kissed it. Her white makeup left the print of her lips on the stone that read:

PHILIP BERNARD AGUILAR

LOVING HUSBAND AND FATHER

1990–2021

They got into the truck and drove away, following a road east through low rolling hills and scrub oaks, into a pleasant lakeside housing development shaded by sycamore trees. The storm clouds had advanced with breathtaking speed, bringing early darkness. Already people were putting out lighted pumpkins or turning on strings of Halloween lights. As they pulled into their driveway, a tiny devil and superheroine emerged from the house next door, clutching loot bags.

"Mommy, Robin and Maria are starting!" shrieked Snow White. "Uncle Frio, can't we go now?"

Señor Death shut off the motor and scowled up at the sky. "Yes, go early, that's a good idea. Agustin! Watch them like a hawk. If it starts to rain, go to the Circle K and call me. I'll come drive you home."

"Okay." Agustin slid from the cab seat. "Drive me to Sasha's later?"

Señor Death nodded. Brandy ran into the house and returned with their loot bags and a flashlight for each child. Waving them like light sabers, the children hastened down the street. Señor Death watched them go. He could smell autumn leaves, candle-charring pumpkins, dinners cooking in a dozen kitchens; over all that, the heavy smell of the storm, very strong, worrisome.

He hefted the cooler out of the back and tilted it in the driveway, letting the melted ice drain out. As he bent there, something came through the twilight to him, some signal through the ether he couldn't define. He stood up sharply and stared, turning his bone-white face this way and that, but he couldn't locate it.

Shrugging, he carried the cooler into the house.

Señora Death was just sliding a covered dish into the oven. "You can go first," she told him. "The cotton balls and the Noxema are all laid out." There was a certain courteous reserve in her tone, a formality, respect and affection without intimacy.

"Thanks," he said. He made his way through the darkening house, turning on lights as he went, not out of any need—he could see by infrared—but out of a mounting edginess. Near the door of the bathroom he nearly stepped on a UFO Abductee Barbie. Muttering to himself, he picked it up and went to the door of the girls' room, where he turned on the light before tossing it on Tina's bed. Nothing out of place, everything normal: Brandy's side fussily neat, Tina's a wreckage of toys and crayons. He heard a faint scrape and hiss, smelled something burning. Annette was lighting the jack-o'-lantern and setting it in the front window.

He went back to the bathroom and slipped off his black robe. Leaning forward over the sink, he began carefully removing the white from his face. It was an involved process, because he had to avoid removing the more subtle makeup that disguised him as a forty-five-year-old mortal man.

He was sponging the last of it out of his mustache when Annette was beside him suddenly, her alarm magnified by the black grease-paint around her eyes.

"Porfirio, I thought I saw a man in the backyard."

I knew it, he told himself. "Well, let's see," he said grimly. He stepped into his bedroom and emerged with a shotgun. Cocking it, he stepped out on the back porch and looked into the deepening shadow.

"Luisa said the marshal shot two Freemen in Spicewood," Annette hissed.

"Maybe," he replied. It had been three years since the war, but now and then somebody came lurching out of the back country, desperate for supplies.

But there was no crazed survivalist in this suburban backyard, and nothing out of place either: Gilbert's wading pool full of waterlogged oak leaves, bicycles, the tree house made of pallets, the rope swing over the edge of the lake. For a split second he thought he saw something wrong. An outline, a ghost, in the tree house? As he stared, it melted into nothing. Or nearly nothing. He snarled silently.

Miles away, there was a flicker on the horizon. A long moment later the faint thunder came.

"It's okay," he called to Annette. "Nobody out here stupid enough to trespass."

He went back indoors.

They ate supper in the kitchen, interrupted occasionally by trick-or-treaters. The storm held off. The children came home, and Annette fed the younger ones while Agustin got a change of clothes and his sleeping bag. Porfirio drove him to his party. On the way back the lightning flashes were nearer, the thunder following more closely. As he let himself in, the first drops began to fall, and as he crossed the threshold, a blue-white blaze lit the whole street.

Annette was sitting on the couch clutching his shotgun, her eyes enormous.

He locked the door behind him and shot the bolt. "Did you see somebody again?"

"No. I was getting Gilbert out of the tub, and Brandy came running in screaming she'd seen somebody in the kids' tree house. We looked with the flashlight. I couldn't see anybody, but—"

He came and put an arm around her. "Probably just a coyote.

Too many spooks this Halloween, huh? Don't worry. It's raining pretty hard now, listen. At least they can't get into much trouble at that party. You go on to bed. I'll sit up and watch the yard for a while. Nothing's going to prowl for long if I get a clear shot at it."

Boom! Blue light flared, and the windows rattled with the force of the thunder. She jumped and held him more tightly than she meant to.

"All right," she said, deciding not to argue. In the time since he'd shown up on her doorstep the day after Philip's funeral, she had learned not to ask him too many questions. It was a small price to pay for security, even if she had her suspicions that he was not really Philip's long-lost cousin.

He walked her to her bedroom, turned on the light, checked the closets. Nothing out of place. He kissed her on the forehead and went off to check the locks. Lightning flashed. Thunder split the sky, and rain fell in torrents.

Porfirio went into the dark kitchen and stood looking out into the yard. He could see the man clearly now, huddled in the tree house, flinching at every blast of livid fire. Porfirio grinned. He went into the living room and tapped in a combination on the customized entertainment center. A soothing tone filled the air, inaudible to mortal ears. The children sank deeper into dreams, and Annette, who'd been staring tensely into darkness, suddenly relaxed and was blissfully unconscious.

Porfirio went back into the kitchen and opened the back door. Ozone was filling the air with an acrid electric smell. Between one flash and the next the man stood beside him on the porch, dripping and shivering.

"Goddam storm took forever to break," he gasped. "I've been waiting out there for hours."

"That's a shame," said Porfirio. "Not that you have any business in my yard. You want to tell me who you are and what you're doing here?"

"Joseph, Facilitator Grade One," the other said, jumping when

lightning struck close by. "Can we continue this conversation indoors?"

Porfirio stepped inside, and the other followed him readily. He
went on:

"I know this is sort of unorthodox, but I needed to ask you
something in private, about somebody you worked with once. I'm
trying to find out what happened to her. I thought you might know."

Porfirio looked at him in silence. His visitor was dressed, most
improbably, in complete fly fisherman's gear, including waders, util-
ity vest, flannel plaid shirt, and shapeless hat. "And you had to wait
for an electrical storm, so the data transmission would be knocked
out? Smart guy. I just might report you anyway, pal."

"Aw, don't do that," implored Joseph. He looked around the
kitchen, hungrily inhaling the fragrances of Halloween night. "Nice
place. How'd you get posted with a mortal family?"

"You don't need to know," Porfirio told him, opening the liquor
cabinet and pouring a shot of bourbon. He offered it to Joseph, who
was drifting wide-eyed toward the big bowl of candy on the kitchen
counter.

"My God, those are Almond Joys! May I? Thanks." He tossed
back the bourbon in a gulp. "You're right, I don't need to know.
Look, I'll make this short: back in 1862 you worked with the
Botanist Mendoza, yes?"

Porfirio started. Joseph, watching him, peeled the wrapper off
a candy miniature and popped it in his mouth. "I thought so," he
said, chewing. "I was her case officer once myself. I'm trying to find
out where she went. I'm not asking for your help, just for some
information."

Exhaling, Porfirio got down a couple of highball glasses and
poured out more bourbon. He handed one to Joseph and took the
other. "Let's go sit. And leave the candy alone. The kids will kill me
if it's gone in the morning."

Boom! All over the neighborhood, in other houses people were
sitting huddled up, unable to sleep for the thunder, but Annette and

her children slept on. Porfirio lit the gas logs. Joseph relaxed on the couch, watching the firelight play on the ceiling, watching the jack-o'-lantern's flame.

"I guess this is part of the Gradual Retirement Plan, huh?" he said. "Mendoza didn't get gradually retired, though, did she? She was arrested. Something nasty happened."

"Very nasty," Porfirio agreed, sipping his bourbon.

"I think you tried to help her. I think you went on record as making some kind of formal protest about what they did to her." Joseph gulped his bourbon and set the glass aside. "So tell me, friend: do you have any idea where she is?"

"Out of commission, as far as I know," said Porfirio. "She got a raw deal. Still, she killed six mortals and went AWOL. You don't get off with a slap on the wrist for something like that. I believe she had a lot of drug therapy, and in the end they transferred her to—" He dipped his finger in the bourbon and drew on the table a line of three little arrows pointing left.

Joseph might have gone pale; it was hard to tell in the wavering light. After a moment he asked, "Did you see her after she was arrested?"

"I tried. They wouldn't let me."

"Thank you," Joseph said.

Porfirio looked at him thoughtfully and had another sip of bourbon. "What's it to you, anyway?" he asked.

Joseph avoided his gaze, staring into the fire. "I recruited her," he said.

"And? You must have recruited a lot of kids in your time. You're old. Why follow up on what happened to this one?"

"Most of the time I ship them out, and I never see them after they've been augmented, but I saw Mendoza a lot after she came back. I was with her on her first field mission. She's the closest thing I have to a daughter. I always felt kind of responsible for her."

"Okay, that I can understand," said Porfirio, nodding. His dark stare intensified. "You must have known she was a Crome generator, then."

Joseph winced. "Not really," he lied. "I have this habit of ignoring things that might bother me. So. Was that how she got into trouble? Something to do with the Crome's radiation?"

"No," Porfirio said. "Although now that I come to think of it, maybe it did after all. She'd been throwing Crome's like . . . that storm outside. Every damn night practically, mostly while she was asleep. It was never a problem, though, until one day when she went up into the Laurel Canyon anomaly."

"I heard about that," said Joseph uneasily.

"So you have a good idea why the Company doesn't want anybody to find out what happened there. I'd like to know how *you* found out about it, actually." Porfirio raised one eyebrow.

Joseph just shook his head grimly. Porfirio shrugged and continued:

"She got back okay, but in my opinion it was just a matter of time after that before Dr. Zeus found a reason to put her away. Pretty soon she gave them a reason, too, one in Technicolor." He lifted his glass again and stopped, struck by a thought. "I wonder if that's why they kept delaying her new posting."

"I heard that they left her on layover indefinitely," said Joseph, rubbing his temples. "You're saying the Company *wanted* her to get into trouble so they could take her out?"

Porfirio nodded almost imperceptibly.

"And then the Englishman came," said Joseph in a tight voice.

"I don't know anything about that part. That had all happened by the time I came back."

"Did you see the guy?"

"No. He was already dead by then."

"Do you have any idea who he was?"

"Nope." Porfirio set his glass down.

"You said she killed six mortals. Did she kill him?"

"No. She killed the guys who shot him, and I sure as hell know who *they* were, because it cost the Company a lot to cover up their disappearances. Pinkerton agents employed by the Union government. This was during the Civil War. They were after him for some reason, and for some reason she was helping him. I've always thought she was susceptible to him because of that incident in her file, the thing that happened back in England on her first mission." Porfirio looked sharply across at Joseph. "You were on that posting. You must know all about it."

"Yeah," said Joseph. "She never got over it, really."

"Plus the fact that Crome generators have been known to go nuts," said Porfirio, watching the effect of his words as Joseph flinched again.

"You think she did?"

"Who knows? Something weird happened, that's for sure." Porfirio leaned forward and spoke in a cold voice. "And she's not the only one who suffered for it, my friend. All of us who were there got a black mark in some way or other as a result of that incident. The Company dragged my ass over the coals, let me tell you. They scared the hell out of the only other witness, nice little kid on his first mission. There was an anthropologist who wasn't even there when it happened, and I know for a fact they pulled her in and did a data erasure on her.

"And there was an operative who went with Mendoza on that trip into Laurel Canyon and got pulled into the anomaly too. I sent him along to cover her. Nice guy, had a good attitude, never a moment of trouble for the Company. He wasn't there when she went AWOL either, he was on a job. I was with him, for crying out loud. But you know what? Within twenty-four hours of Mendoza's little mistake, a security team showed up at our camp at Tejon and took him away with them. He just grinned and went. Never seen him since. I can't even find out where he was reassigned, and I've tried."

"Jesus." Joseph put his head in his hands.

"Some body count, huh?" Porfirio's voice was harsh. "And maybe it's all because an operative got careless one time, when he was scanning a potential recruit, and didn't bother to check for Crome's. You think that's maybe the case?"

"Could be," said Joseph in a muffled voice.

"I've carried the same guilt," said Porfirio reflectively. "How did I miss what was coming? Was there any way I could have stopped it? Could I have helped her? And poor old Einar, I was the one who gave him the order to go with Mendoza into Laurel Canyon, and now he's out of the picture. I thought I was responsible. Maybe I'm not, though." He turned to Joseph. "Maybe I'll just dump all this guilt on you now, pal."

"Thanks," said Joseph listlessly.

"You're welcome. Listen: I told you all this because I respect the fact that you're trying to help your daughter. And she was a good operative, before the incident. Mendoza did good work." Porfirio sighed. "But I have family of my own I'm looking out for, so I don't ever want to see you or hear about this again."

"Family?" Joseph sat up, sudden comprehension in his face. "Is that what you're doing here?"

Porfirio nodded. "They're descendants of the brother I had when I was mortal. I've kept track of them all down the years."

"The Company lets you do that?"

"They want to keep me happy. I'm a problem solver."

"Oh," said Joseph in a small voice. "One of those guys who gets rid of—"

"Yeah. Anyway, this is all your responsibility now, right?" Porfirio stretched. "Find out what happened to her, if you can. Help her if you can. If you can find out what happened to a Zoologist and Cinema Preservationist named Einar, that would be nice too. But I never met you, I never talked to you, and you're going to stay the hell away from me and my family for the rest of your eternal life."

"You got it," Joseph agreed. He looked across at the window, where the rain beat steadily but with less and less punctuation of lightning. "I guess I'll be going now. Thanks for the help, all the same."

"You need a ride anywhere?" Porfirio relaxed somewhat.

"No, that's okay." Joseph gave a slightly embarrassed grin. "My canoe's tied up at your neighbor's dock. I'll just row back up the lake to the public campground. I'm supposed to be on a fishing vacation, it's part of my gradual retirement. Smooth, huh?"

Porfirio almost smiled. He stood, and Joseph stood, and they went out through the kitchen, where Joseph cast a longing eye at the Halloween candy.

"One for the road?" he suggested.

"What the hell." Porfirio tossed him an Almond Joy. He caught it neatly and slipped out through the back door into the steadily falling rain, silent as a coyote. Porfirio went to the window and watched. A moment later he saw the dark shape of a canoe moving out on the lake, and a dark oarsman rowing. It backed around and headed north, and a moment later was lost in the rain and the night.

Porfirio locked the door and slid its deadbolt home. He keyed in the security combination that protected the house. Returning to the living room, he turned the lever to extinguish the gas fire, went to the front window, and drew the drapes against the night. He leaned over the pumpkin and blew out its little candle. Darkness, and a plume of white smoke.

Joseph in the Darkness

WELL, THAT WAS THAT. Now I knew where Mendoza was, if only in a general way. I knew I couldn't rescue her myself; and Lewis had no chance at all. There were only two immortals I could turn to.

One of them was Suleyman, the North African Section Head. He's built up a private power base in Morocco, a huge machine, employs mortals and immortals alike as his agents. They do a good job for him, too, because he's a good man. Believes in all that Honor, Integrity, and Service stuff that was so important to you, Father. I'd trust Suleyman with my life...but I didn't think he would trust me. We go back a ways, he and I, so it would be sort of hard for him to believe I was really only trying to find my daughter. See what happens when you get a reputation for being a slimy little guy?

The other one was you, Father, and I hadn't seen you in a thousand years. You'd turned rogue, gone underground, and I hadn't lifted a finger to help you. Never even looked for you, though you gave me a clue. It sat undecrypted in my tertiary consciousness for ten centuries, because I was scared to look at it. It might even be useless by now. I guess you'd tell me it serves me right. But Mendoza, and the operatives she took down in her fall, is paying for my cowardice.

The whole sin thing works just like the Almighty said it does: innocent people get punished for things they didn't do. Unto the fourth and fifth generation. You make your mistake, and not only do you get screwed forever, the screwing spreads out in circles like ripples from a body dropped into quiet water. A body with a millstone about its neck.

That's why slash and burn was your way of dealing with the bad guys, wasn't it? Make examples of them, terrify the others so they'll never dare to break the laws. Free will? Forget it. Obedience was what you demanded and got. Very Pentateuch.

I wonder... did you ever work around Ur of the Chaldees? Ever lay some law on a shepherd named Abram? With Company special effects, maybe?

But theater was never your way. You'd have marched up to the shepherd, grabbed him by the front of his robe, and told him you would be running his life from then on, for his own good. You didn't beat around the bush.

Times changed, though. The Company had to stop being that direct. I think you understood this, maybe you alone of all the old Enforcers; though it didn't help you in the end. You realized what was going on when your kind began disappearing, didn't you? You knew how the Company was solving the problem of operatives it no longer needed.

Did you do what I'm doing now, investigating, searching? But it's a little harder for me, Father, the Company's more devious these days, as 2355 draws closer. The Preservers are being given a nice package deal. It's called gradual retirement.

The argument is that as the future world comes nearer, there's less work for us, who were created to rescue endangered things from humanity's folly. Mortals, finally becoming wise and good, don't need our services as much to preserve their priceless works of art from the ravages of war, to prevent extinctions of rare plants and animals due to overcrowding, overdevelopment. There is very little and soon will be *no* more war, overcrowding, or development.

Personally I have my doubts about this. Maybe they've just run out of stuff for us to save.

But anyway. We've all been told the Company will start rewarding us now for our millennia of faithful service. Giving us little treats, vacations, personal lives. This is the way it'll be all the time after 2355, they say: we can go anywhere we want, do anything we want. Just as though we weren't slaves.

It's taken me so many years to be able to say that word.

Slaves? Us? Not when the Company is starting to let us choose our own postings. Not when the Company is permitting us lasting relationships with the mortals with whom we have to work. Not when the Company is relaxing the old rules about personal property, schedules, and Theobromos consumption. We have choices now, at least some of the time. We can live our own lives, except when the Company needs us to do something.

The reason gradual retirement is so gradual, of course, is that all our programming directly opposes the idea of retirement. We have to be eased into a life of leisure. Our work is all we want, all we need, all that has kept us going through centuries of immortal heartbreak. Time on our hands makes us seriously uncomfortable. Look what it did to a Conservationist like poor Mendoza. Drove her crazy...

I assume she went crazy when she killed those mortals. A Conservationist killing, that's unheard of. Guys like you made pyramids of trophy heads, I know, and problem solvers like Porfirio work their silent way through the sewers of the world taking out two-legged vermin. Even Facilitators have been known to do a little quiet unofficial termination now and then.

But Mendoza? I'd never have thought her anger could push her that far. It was a rotten trick the Company played on her, taking her work away, letting her sit there in the middle of desolation with nothing to keep the old memories at bay. No wonder she went with the damned Englishman...

But which Englishman?

Who the hell was he?

What was he?

London, 2026

Trevor and Anita sat waiting in the front parlor of the shop in Euston Road. They were uncomfortable. It was a very well known antiquarian bookshop, the kind that did almost no business out of the shopfront but relied principally on private clientele and Web orders. Nevertheless there was not a speck of dust anywhere, and the furniture in the parlor was expensive.

Trevor and Anita were not well off. They were hoping to be; artistic, creative, and talented, they were busily working at several concurrent schemes to make a bundle. One of these schemes was buying and restoring old houses, doing the work themselves to cut overhead, and reselling at handsome profits. Although to date there had been no profits, due to the union fines they had to pay. Then they found the old box.

It was so old, its leather panels were peeling away, and now it was wrapped in a green polyethylene garbage sack. Trevor held it on his lap. A white cardboard carton would have been more elegant, or brown paper. Looking uneasily around at the fifteenth-century Italian manuscripts under glass, Trevor and Anita regretted that they had found nothing better to put the old box in.

After a half hour of raised eyebrows from immaculately groomed persons who came and went through the office, Trevor and Anita were ready to sink through the floor. They had just decided to sneak out with their nasty little bag when a young man descended the stairs from the private offices on the first floor. He looked inquiringly at them.

He too was immaculately groomed, and wore a very expensive suit, though it seemed a little too big for him. He was handsome in a well-bred sort of way, with chiseled features and a resolute chin, rather like a romantic lead from the cinema of a century before. His eyes were the color of twilight.

"Excuse me," he said. "You wouldn't happen to be my three o'clock provenance case, would you?"

They stared at him, nonplussed.

"Um—you described it on the phone? Old wood-and-leather box found in an attic?" He gestured helpfully. "About this big? Full of possibly Victorian papers?"

"Yes!" The couple rose as one.

"So sorry I kept you waiting," he said, advancing on them and shaking hands. "Owen Lewis. You must be Trevor and Anita? Is this the box?"

"It is—"

"There was an iron bed frame in the attic room, and I don't think anybody had moved it in just, well, ages—"

"And this was wedged in underneath, we would never have known it was there if we hadn't moved the bed, and it took both of us—"

"The lid just fell apart when we prized it off—"

"Gosh, how exciting," Lewis exclaimed, rubbing his hands together. "Let's take it up to my office and have a look, shall we?"

He led them up the stairs, and they followed happily, completely set at ease. This was a nice, unintimidating man.

"My, this really has come to pieces, hasn't it?" said Lewis, when they were all gathered around his desk and he'd gingerly cut away the green bag. "Good idea to have brought it in in plastic. This is what we in the trade call a basket case."

Trevor and Anita smiled at each other, validated.

"A pity the box fell apart," Trevor said.

"Don't feel too badly," Lewis told him, taking a pair of latex gloves from a drawer and pulling them on with fastidious care. "From the pieces I'd say it's early Victorian, but rather cheap for its time. Mass-produced. You say it was in the attic? Where's the house?"

"Number 10, Albany Crescent," Trevor and Anita chorused.

"Ah." Lewis lifted away the ruin of the lid, piece by piece. "I know the neighborhood. Upstairs-downstairs, once, with a full staff of servants. Parlormaids and footmen and undergardeners and, here we are! A packet of letters. Let's just set these aside for the moment, shall we? This looks like a certificate of discharge from the army; this is a clipping from the London *Times* for—" Lewis tilted his head to look at it. "13 April 1840. And here's an old-fashioned pen."

"I thought people wrote with feathers back then," said Trevor.

"Not by 1840, actually. See this? It's the sort of wooden pen you could buy cheaply in any stationer's shop. I think all this belonged to a servant. The stains here? These are your man's fingerprints, just imagine!" Lewis set it carefully aside. "More newspaper clippings. Something underneath, looks like a book, and...a picture..."

"Oh," said Anita, leaning forward to look. "An old photograph! Do you suppose this is him?"

There was a moment's silence. Trevor and Anita looked up to see Lewis staring fixedly at the old picture. But he lifted his eyes to them, smiled, and in a perfectly normal voice said, "Probably not. This man's in a naval officer's uniform. A daguerreotype, too, I should say from about the year 1850. Somebody the servant knew, perhaps."

"He's rather odd-looking," Anita said, frowning at the image. "So stern."

"Yes, well, naval officers had to be." Lewis gave a slightly breathless laugh. "But let's see the book, shall we?" He lifted it out and opened it gingerly. "This'll be your real treasure, or I miss my guess. Your man must have been the butler at number ten. This is his household accounts book. Not a record of the finances, you understand, sort of a handbook he'd have compiled on how to run that particular household. Everything from recipes for silver polish to how to cure hiccups in a lady's maid. Here we go—here's his name, Robert Richardson, 19 January 1822. Two hundred and four years ago."

"Is it worth money?" Trevor said.

"The book? Almost certainly. I can put you in touch with at least three or four research libraries who have standing offers out for this sort of thing." Lewis set the book down.

"How much money are we looking at?" Anita said.

Lewis spread out his hands as though inviting them to guess. "Four thousand pounds? Five? The material has to be verified first. I can get to work on it at once, but it may be a few days before I can give you a real estimate."

Trevor and Anita looked at each other. Four thousand pounds would enable them to finish installing a modern climate-control system and pay off the union bully for the next month.

"Please go ahead, then," Trevor said.

While they waited, Lewis opened each of the letters in turn and ran a scanner over them to make a quick electronic record of their number and contents. There were two letters of reference from former employers and one from a regimental colonel attesting to the worthiness and reliability of Robert Richardson as a servant and soldier. There were three letters from someone named Edward, of a personal nature. The newspaper clippings were scanned and recorded, the book recorded page by page, the daguerreotype image recorded. The ancient pen and a half stick of sealing wax found at the bottom of the box were also duly noted.

Lewis transferred the scan to a master and opened the keyboard of his desk console. He keyed in a command to copy. A moment later the console ejected a little golden disk.

"And there you are." Taking it carefully by the edges, Lewis slid it into a plastic case and presented it to Anita. "Your record. Sign here on the tablet and leave your contact site, please. I should have some preliminary results for you by tomorrow afternoon."

Trevor and Anita left the office walking on air, and drifted away through the London afternoon into the rest of their lives, which do not figure further in this story.

Lewis sat alone in his office, contemplating the heap of yellowed paper, the blackened fragments of the box, the daguerreotype in its felt-backed case. At last he took up the picture and looked at it directly.

There could be no doubt.

It was an authentic image. The mortal wore the uniform of a naval commander, and from the cut Lewis guessed the image dated from about the year 1845. The young commander's face was extraordinary. Lewis had seen that face only once before, in his long life, and it was distinctive enough to stand out from any other.

As the mortal woman had remarked, the commander looked very stern, stiffly upright with his cockaded hat under his arm, frowning at the camera. He had high cheekbones and a long nose. His eyes were deepset, colorless silver in the image, perhaps pale blue. His wide mouth looked mobile and businesslike, ready to rap out some sort of nautical order or other. Ordinary features, but in their composition there was some quality that defied description, that fascinated or repelled. His hands were big but beautifully shaped.

And if the plaster Roman column against the backdrop was any measure of scale, he had been an extremely tall young man.

Lewis sighed and closed his eyes.

He saw in the darkness, for a moment, the commander's face; then the sketch he had seen thirty years earlier, the arrogant stranger staring down from horseback. The two faces were identical. They faded, to be replaced by a woman's face.

Her face, pale with unhappiness, looking paler in the darkness at the back of the booth. Where had they been? The old El Galleon at New World One, to be sure, in a secluded booth suitable for lovers...

Mendoza had lifted her glass and gazed into it a moment without drinking.

"Nicholas was the tallest mortal I ever saw," she said. "I had no idea they came that tall. He couldn't walk through any doorway without having to duck. And I had to tilt my head back to look into his face, and—and such a remarkable face he had." She closed her eyes, red from crying. "Even looking sullen like that. How he disapproved of me! Little Spanish Papist girl, he thought. Daughter of Eve, source of all sin. I'd say we're Lilith's children, though, wouldn't you...?"

She opened her eyes long enough to take a sip of her drink, and closed them again, the better to focus on her memory. "Big Roman nose, broken once. High cheekbones, wide mouth, quite a sensual mouth too, as I found out..."

Mendoza opened her eyes again and stared at Lewis, with that black intensity that connected like a physical blow. "I'm not giving you any idea of what Nicholas looked like, am I? He must sound absurd to you, homely as a mule. I tell you, though, no god was ever more beautiful."

"I can't see the man," Lewis admitted, "but I can see the man's soul, I think. You're describing what your heart saw when you looked at him."

She nodded in emphatic agreement, her face flushed. "His soul, yes, it was the animating spirit in his eyes that was so...I couldn't stop looking at them. Winter-sky eyes paler for colorless lashes, kind of small, actually, way up there peering out from their caves...But when Nicholas regarded you with those eyes..."

Her breath caught, and she looked so young, with the scarlet color draining away and leaving her pale as ashes again. Lewis caught his breath too, but the moment had gone; the young girl had retreated, and there was the austere old woman, the widow pulling her shawl closer against the cold.

She shook her head and picked up her drink again. "You see? All these years later, and I still go to pieces. Is God a cruel bastard or what, to make love so painful?"

He reached out and took her hand. "And mortal love is the hardest," he said.

She laughed harshly, tilting her glass to peer at the last of her margarita. "Oh, look, we're out," she said. "Shall we order another round? 'Stay me with flagons, comfort me with apples; for I am sick of love...'" And she crumpled into herself in such an agony of grief that Lewis hurried to her side and put an arm around her. She wept in desperate silence as he held her.

Lewis opened his eyes now and looked at the old picture.

It was the Englishman Mendoza had run away with in 1863. What had been the name Lewis glimpsed in the arrest report? Bell-Something? And yet Nicholas Harpole too must have looked very much like this, Mendoza's Nicholas who had been burned for his faith in 1555. Lewis was seeing, suddenly, the extraordinary quality she'd tried so hard to describe. His heart lurched. He wasn't sure what to make of this.

He sat up in his chair and put the daguerreotype and the other contents of the old box in a neat white carton. Drawing off his gloves, he set the carton aside, went to his bookcase, and withdrew a slender volume. It was not what you'd expect to find in an antiquarian's case; it had been printed only a half century before, and big bouncy letters on its cheaply lithographed cover announced that it was the *Chocoholic's Almanac,* containing all sorts of interesting lore and legends to delight lovers of *Theobroma cacao.*

He sat down at his desk with it and drew out a manila shipping envelope, addressing it in neat script. Then he keyed in an order to his printer, which hummed and promptly provided him with a copy of the image on the daguerreotype. He scribbled something across the bottom and slipped it into the *Chocoholic's Almanac;* wrote a brief note and enclosed that too, and sealed up the book in the envelope. That done, he arose, slipped on his coat, took his package across the landing to the office's postal franking machine, which scanned, weighed, and inked it with the necessary bar code.

Lewis ran lightly down the stairs and out through the lobby to the street, leaving his package in the office's outgoing parcels bin. The parcel courier's van was already pulling up as Lewis rounded the corner and walked away down Tottenham Court Road.

Houston, 2026

You GOT A PACKAGE, boss," said Musicologist Donal, peering at it as he returned to the breakfast nook.

"Have you been sending off for more of those bondage fetish disks again?" asked Muriel innocently, looking up from her coffee. She was an Anthropologist.

"Ha ha," said Joseph, scowling at her. He accepted the package and peered at the label. "One of these days I'm going to find out which one of you did that, and then—"

He was interrupted by the Art Preservationist, who came thundering down the stairs, pulling on his coat. "My alarm didn't go off. Why didn't anybody wake me?"

They gaped at him in surprise as he buttoned his coat.

"We didn't know you were on that tight a schedule, Andrei," Muriel said.

"My car's in the shop, and I've got to be in Corpus Christi by noon," he said, grabbing a brioche from the basket on the table. "The hurricane's scheduled to hit on the twenty-seventh, you know. I don't have much time, and there's even less if I have to take goddam public transit on this job."

"Okay, okay," sighed Joseph, getting up and tucking the unopened package into his briefcase. "I'll drive you. It's not as though

I had anything important to do today. Just kiss Governor Gleason's
ass until he agrees to veto that land appropriation bill. But I can do
that any time, right? I'm under no pressure, not old Joseph."

"I appreciate this," Andrei said, dancing in impatience by the
door. "I'll even mail the governor's office for you in the car while you
drive. Tell him you're calling in sick or something."

"Let's go," Joseph said, following him out the door and down
the hall.

"Have a nice day," Donal called after them.

Outside the apartment building it was already uncomfortably
warm, and Andrei had shed his coat by the time they got into
Joseph's black Saturn Avocet. However, the temperature fell rapidly
over the next two hours, and he was bundled up again by the time
Joseph dropped him off on the outskirts of town.

"Will you need a ride back tonight?" Joseph leaned out the
window.

"No. I'm probably staying a few days this time. I'll call HQ later
and let you know, okay?" Andrei shouted, turning up his coat collar.

"Okay," said Joseph.

"Bye." Andrei waved, and sprinted off to get out of the wind.

Joseph circled back to the highway. Before he had gone very far,
however, hail began dropping out of the sky. He cursed and pulled
off to the side of the road to wait out the cloudburst. Other motorists
were doing the same.

He sighed and switched off the engine. His gaze fell on his briefcase; carefully he took out the package and opened it.

There was a note and a book: *The Chocoholic's Almanac.* He
nodded gamely, setting the book aside. He read the note.

> Hello there, old man! Came across this in an estate sale
> and was reminded of the days when we used to paint the City
> cocoa-powder brown. You might find it instructive. Can you
> get Ghirardelli's in the Lone Star State?

I'm in the other City now. Come across for a weekend,
and we can discuss old times over a cup of Cadbury's, ha ha.
Vale, Lewis.

Grinning, Joseph picked up the little book and opened it. He
came upon the printout of the naval officer tucked inside, and his grin
froze on his face. The officer regarded him severely. Under the picture
Lewis had written, in a waggish scrawl: NO THEOBROMOS PERMIT-
TED IN THE DORMITORY.

Joseph drew a long breath through clenched teeth, eyes fixed on
the picture. The hail was coming down harder now, big stones hitting
the Avocet's shell and putting a thousand little spiderweb fractures in
its just-waxed finish, but Joseph barely noticed. When the storm
passed, his was the first car to leave the side of the road, lurching out
and fishtailing slightly as he sped away through the slush. He might
have maintained better control of the car if he'd kept both hands on
the wheel, but he was busily making a flight reservation on the dash
console as he drove.

London

Lewis spotted him from the end of the street, a businessman in a rumpled if costly suit, waiting on the front step like a patient dog. Joseph rose to his feet, grinning as Lewis approached, but there was a certain flinty quality in his eyes.

That was quick, Lewis transmitted to him.

"Hey, Lewis, great to see you." *Where did you find that picture? Who is he?*

"Joseph, you old rake." Lewis bounced up the steps and shook hands vigorously. *His name was Edward Alton Bell-Fairfax. I have a lot to tell you. Did you ever perfect that signal disrupter?*

"Nice place the Company's set you up in." Joseph waved a hand at the building. "Restored Georgian, isn't it?" *Not quite yet. Anyway we shouldn't use it this time out. Somebody would be bound to wonder why we fry our circuits every time we get together.*

"Yes." Lewis keyed in the entry combination. "Lots of style, but the closets are impossible and the heating bills are worse. On the other hand, I needn't commute, and there's a really first-class vindaloo place around the corner."

The door swung open, and he gestured for Joseph to precede him. Joseph put his suitcase down in the hall and looked around brightly, scanning. "Quite the bachelor pad, huh?"

"It's all done in Mid–Twentieth Century Revival," Lewis said, keying in the security, lighting, and temperature control. The rooms had a certain spartan, masculine style, black vinyl and brass, framed abstract prints, a whole wall given over to books. Everything was spotlessly clean and in perfect order. It looked like a movie set for an espionage film.

"Boy, you must sit here in the evenings and pretend you're James Bond," said Joseph, hanging up his coat on the hall stand.

Funny you should say that. "It's quite comfortable, all things considered. How long can you stay?"

"Oh, just for the weekend. I'm taking a suborbital back Sunday night." *What did you find out?*

More than I can tell you subvocally. Are you sure it's dangerous to discuss out loud, even in here? "Well, let's make good use of our time. Come on, I'll give you the grand tour. That's the den, and the kitchen's in there. Lavatory and two bedrooms upstairs. You'll want to unpack, I imagine." Lewis led Joseph up the stairs.

Especially in here. I know what we can do, though. Got any DVDs?

"And maybe you'd like to watch a movie after dinner?" Lewis suggested. "I've got rather an extensive collection of classics."

"Great." Joseph edged into the tiny guest bedroom and looked around. It was all navy blue and brass, with yachting prints on the walls. *We just put on a movie and settle back to watch it. Then we can talk subvocally without having to improvise chatter for some security tech's benefit.*

Seems a bit paranoid, but you're the Facilitator.

After Joseph unpacked, they walked down to the corner for takeaway curry, chatting pleasantly and audibly on unobjectionable topics. The nearest wine shop had closed for the day, in accordance with the tighter new laws, but Lewis had a cabinet nicely stocked with Californian white varietals. He filled a couple of goblets, and they sat on his black couch in companionable silence, eating from the cartons as they watched Humphrey Bogart face down Conrad Veidt in the latest remastered rerelease of *Casablanca*.

So, you were saying? Edward Alton who?

Bell-Fairfax. Nice young couple of mortals renovating an old house found an ancient box of papers in the attic and brought it to me, pound signs dancing before their eyes. Among the papers was that daguerreotype. He's the man the ornithologist sketched, isn't he? That day we went to the Hitchcock house?

Maybe. What he definitely is is the exact double of a first-class son of a bitch named Nicholas Harpole, whom I had the pleasure of watching burn at the stake in 1555.

The man in the daguerreotype looks like Nicholas?

The spit and image.

How remarkable, transmitted Lewis calmly, though his pulse was racing.

Remarkable ain't the word, Lewis. I wonder what we're dealing with here. Coincidence? Genetic hyperstability on this damn little island? You've lived here on and off for centuries, Lewis. Did you ever see another Englishman who even remotely resembled that big scarecrow?

Actually he seemed rather well-dressed to me. But—no, I can't say that I have. I've been trying to find out more about him.

You've tracked down his death certificate, I hope?

I haven't, though there's a registry of baptism in an obscure little country parish, and he's listed as illegitimate.

That figures.

There's more. He appears to have written three of the letters in this collection. The young master writing home to the old family retainer, as it were. I've been using the references in the letters to track him, to follow his career. He was in the royal navy for a while, but then he left under something of a cloud.

I'll bet.

I've only started seriously looking, but I have several leads to follow up. Did you find out where Mendoza was sent?

Yeah.

Where, for God's sake? When were you going to tell me?

Joseph shifted uncomfortably on the couch, as Paul Henreid ordered a champagne cocktail for himself and Ingrid Bergman.

I was getting around to it. Lewis, we can't help her. She ... Did you ever hear rumors about a place called Back Way Back?

Lewis reached out in a leisurely way and picked up his wineglass. His hand shook only very slightly as he took a sip of chilled Chardonnay.

I see, he said at last.

She may be perfectly okay! But she's out of the picture, Lewis. Permanently. Even if there was something I could do for her—and I'm not ruling that out—there's sure as hell nothing you could do.

Lewis set his wine down carefully. For a moment his face was astonishingly transformed by rage. *Damn them. And damn you. Are you writing her off?*

Look, Joseph said, *all this is beside the point. Wherever Mendoza is, she'll be staying put. I'm following another lead right now, something completely unrelated, but it just might give me some leverage. I'll need all the advantages I can get if I'm going to even attempt to help her. See? So you must bear with me.*

What sort of lead?

Somebody gave me a set of coordinates once ... I'll tell you the story sometime, but the bottom line is, I need to look them up. What I'm searching for may be long gone by now, but I have to see. One of the locations is in Yorkshire. You know that area?

Yes, actually. I had a job there a few years back.

Great. Do you have a car?

I can get the Austin from the garage. It might be an overnight trip, though.

It's only a couple of hundred miles. Just pretend you're back in California. And even if we do stay over, I have my own credit line these days, I can pay for a hotel. All we need is a plausible reason for visiting there, so we don't rouse suspicions.

Lewis frowned thoughtfully. *A literary pilgrimage? Lot of writers in that part of the world. The Brontës, Herriot, Knollys ...*

*Sounds unbelievably boring, but what the hell. You're a litera-
ture guy, right? Any Theobromos action up there?*

I don't believe so.

*Oh, well. We can always get some Aero bars at a newsagent's or
somewhere for the trip.*

Lewis sipped more of his wine. *You're on another jag? I'd better
lay in a few dozen tins of spaghetti. So you think this search of yours
might help Mendoza?*

Possibly. Though she's been out of the picture since 1863.

*Aren't you forgetting something? You saw her in 1923. And she
was with* him, *wasn't she? That man in the daguerreotype, who
looks just like her Nicholas?*

*Lewis, that has to have been a hallucination. I couldn't have
seen either one of them. I know that now. Even if she managed to escape Back Way Back somehow, what about him? That picture dates
from, what, 1850? By 1923 he'd have been damn near a hundred.
But he wasn't. He didn't look a day older than the last time I saw
him, just before a powder keg turned him into a human torch.* Joseph
crunched into a pappadum savagely and continued. *In any case, what
does it matter? We know that the gene pool over here produced not
one but two of the rotten stinking lousy guys. We know that somehow, by the worst coincidence in the world, guy number two managed to find my poor little recruit and screw up her life even worse
than guy number one did. End of story, except that if this island
somehow manages to produce another one, I swear I'll kill him myself, because God only knows what's left for him to do to her.*

Lewis looked at him sidelong. *Would you mind not gnashing
your teeth? You're spitting pappadum flakes all over my couch. You
really hated the man, didn't you? It's affecting your judgment, you
know. You've completely overlooked one possibility.*

Which would be?

*Mendoza was a Crome generator, Joseph. There have been no
other immortals with that condition. It's impossible to say what she
can do.*

True. But all the same—

She loved Nicholas desperately. I know. She was never reconciled to his death. What if she somehow reincarnated him?

Lewis, that is nuts. Have you been reading romance novels?

Of course I have, but that's beside the point. In the nearly two thousand years I've been alive, I've seen my share of the inexplicable. And if you tell me you haven't seen more anomalies than I have in your twenty thousand, then all I have to say is you're either blind or a damned liar.

Joseph picked up his wine and drank it down like water. He sagged back in the vinyl upholstery, staring at the old film, watching the exquisite play of black shadow on white, on silvertone, on ash gray, silhouettes of palm fronds, window blinds, pale smoke curling in the midnight air. Bogart took another drag on the cigarette that would kill him and pondered the cruelty of chance meetings.

Yorkshire

This used to be Ermine Street, didn't it?" Joseph asked, squinting into the wind.

Lewis drove an Austin Taranis electric convertible, gunmetal gray, and the sporty windscreen didn't deflect much. "Good old Roman roads," he said, slipping them through the last poky A1 traffic emerging from London and cautiously increasing his speed. "I daresay you've marched along a few of these in your time."

"Yeah," Joseph replied, a little gloomily. "This very road, if you want the truth."

"Really? I wish I'd been stationed here then. Or in Rome. I never really got to know that side of my organic heritage, you know. The Company sent me straight into Ireland as soon as I graduated, and I was stuck there for the next few centuries," Lewis said. "By the time I was finally stationed in England, Roman Britain was long gone. I've always rather regretted that."

"You like army life?" Joseph unwrapped an Aero bar and took a bite.

"Well, no—at least, I don't suppose I would. Literary Preservationists don't see a lot of that sort of assignment," Lewis said. "But, you know, all those legions tramping through the mists, the sort of thing you imagine when you listen to Respighi's music. It has a certain romantic appeal."

"Respighi should have done some time carrying a hundred-pound pack through Cumbria, that's all I've got to say," said Joseph. "And your feet froze all the time in those damn caligae. What brain trust came up with an open-toed combat boot? Goddam slaves got better shoes. And of course the poor auxiliaries died like flies from the cold, because we had guys from Africa and Hispania sent up here, naturally, and ex-Visigoths sent down to patrol villages in Egypt. Military intelligence."

"Eat the other Aero bar, for God's sake." Lewis shifted gears and sped around a lorry trundling Japanese sewing machines to a minor industrial town.

"Okay, okay. Let's see, what can I say that's positive about the Roman army? Good engineers, but everybody knows that. Lots of incentives, and they really took care of their veterans. Had to; most stayed in the service until they were gray and toothless, which wasn't actually all that long, given the life expectancy in those days." Joseph balled up the wrapper and stuffed it in the Austin's map pocket after looking around vainly for an ashtray.

"I suppose I shouldn't ask further." Lewis sighed. "Not if I want to keep any illusions about the blessings of the Pax Romana with all those centrally heated public buildings and orderly little towns."

"A little Rome went a long way, believe me," Joseph said.

Lewis pulled over to let a speeding Jaguar pass him. "Now—it's funny, I've known for years you'd been a centurion, but it's only just occurred to me to wonder—what on earth would one of us be doing in *any* army? How could you possibly have dealt with being on a battlefield?"

"I ducked a lot," Joseph told him. "And as for what I was doing there, you don't need to know."

"Ah," said Lewis, nodding sagely, and appeared to concentrate very closely on the road for the next few miles.

No, seriously, can you tell me what you were doing?

The Company needed an observer to fill in an event shadow. I was with the Ninth Hispania, operating out of Eboracum. York, I mean.

The Ninth? The famous lost legion?

Yeah.

And the Company planted you among them so you could find out what happened to it?

That's right.

But I thought it turned out they were never lost after all. Didn't someone discover they were simply transferred to Cappadocia or somewhere?

Those were the replacement guys. Haven't you been in this business long enough to know that most questions have to be answered with yes and no? There was a good reason the legend of the lost legion got started.

Well?

We got sent on a stupid march through the Pennines, and about a million Brigantes came down on our heads. It wasn't as bad as when Quintilius Varus got massacred, but it was bad enough. They cut us into little pieces. All except me, of course. Joseph unwrapped the other Aero bar and ate it in three bites.

That's all?

It didn't take long, either, the Ninth was already in such bad shape.

But... why were no remains ever found? No rusting armor, no spears, no coins?

Why do you think? Joseph stared out at the green countryside, where a bulldozer was methodically destroying a hedgerow eleven centuries old.

Lewis's jaw dropped. He put the car on autopilot a moment while he went through the motions of opening out the audio case for a leisurely inspection of its contents. He selected one disc at last, a symphonic piece by Ian Anderson, and slipped it into the music system. Only then did he place both hands firmly back on the wheel and ask, *Are you saying the Company had you strip the bodies?*

Joseph gave a barely perceptible shrug. *Something like that. You know how much future collectors will pay for authentic relics of the lost legion? With the old IX Hispania insignia?*

I can imagine, Lewis said. He drove on, pale and shaken, as a flute melody of haunting sweetness wafted out of the Austin's speakers. At last he shook his head. *You know—I've been thinking, lately, that all this paranoia and strong-arm work was something new for the Company, some reaction perhaps to the fact that we're nearing the year of the Silence. I assumed that Dr. Zeus used to operate in a more civilized and humane manner.*

Nope.

North and north the car sped on, along the well-metaled road.

They went west on the A635 and meandered westward for a while to the A629, past Denby Dale, past Kirkburton, through Huddersfield and Halifax, and at last Lewis announced brightly, "Well, we're almost there. Stop one of our Yorkshire literary tour. We'll see the famous parsonage at Haworth, where the ill-fated but creative Brontë family lived, loved, and died to the last member. You've read the novels, of course?"

"I've seen the movies," Joseph said. "I worked at MGM when they were making the *Wuthering Heights* with Larry Olivier."

"So you've never read the novels?" Lewis's lips thinned slightly.

"I might have scanned them in school." Joseph shrugged, refusing to admit to anything. "Real men don't read *Jane Eyre*. Unless you're a Literature Specialist, I guess," he added soothingly.

"Thank you." Lewis downshifted with a bit more force than was required. "Well, you're going to enjoy this anyway, damn it. Look at these heathery moors! Look at the wild and lonely prospects! Imagine those fantastically talented and sickly children in their claustrophobic little parsonage, growing up into doomed, brilliant youth. Not a one of them made it into their forties, did you know that? They burnt out like flares. Is it any wonder they were able to produce masterworks of savage passion and searing romance?"

"*Jane Eyre*, that was the one with the governess, right?" Joseph yawned.

"You know perfectly well it was. Look, there's the parsonage museum." Lewis turned off and steered for the car park.

"Do they have a souvenir stand?" asked Joseph.

They stopped and got out. There for their edification was the little church with its parsonage, islands in a sea of tombstones, and the moors rolling down on the back of the parsonage like a never-breaking wave. There were a few other cars in the park, but no tourists visible. The two immortals strolled toward the parsonage.

Is this going to help you at all in your investigation?

Not really. We need to go farther north. Still, it's a good blind. We'll see the sights, buy a couple of souvenirs, and move on, okay?

How very cloak-and-dagger.

As they came around the corner, they saw an impressive conveyance, a long wagon with a team of six coal-black draft horses in its traces. It was an omnibus of some kind, fitted with rows of seats and roofed over by an awning. A man in nineteenth-century coachman's dress waited, immobile as a waxwork figure by the horses. Joseph and Lewis halted, staring at the moment out of time.

Before either of them could comment, the door of the parsonage opened, and out filed a line of persons, also in nineteenth-century costume in varying funereal shades, all looking rather self-conscious except for the formidable lady at their head. She spotted Joseph and Lewis gaping at them. Directing her companions to the wagon, she turned and made straight for the immortals.

"If you are interested in the tour, gentlemen, you must purchase tickets in the gift shop," she said. She was a small stout lady of the iron-sinewed maiden-aunt variety. "However, I must advise you that appropriate dress is required, which fortunately you may rent for a reasonable sum from the wardrobe mistress."

"Okay," said Joseph.

"Oh! Oh! This is one of those total immersion reenactor events, isn't it?" said Lewis in excitement. "How utterly magical! And I imagine you're Charlotte Brontë?"

"I am, sir," said the actress.

"Delighted to make your acquaintance, Miss Brontë." Lewis swept her hand to his lips. "I have so enjoyed your novels. May I introduce myself? Mr. Owen Lewis, and this American gentleman is my friend, Mr. Capra."

"Hi," said Joseph.

Charlotte Brontë inclined graciously and peered down at the watch pinned to her bosom. "Thank you. Today's tour includes the authentic locations that inspired my late sister Emily in her depiction of the principal scenes from *Wuthering Heights*. We depart presently; shall we wait for you to join us?"

"How much are the tickets?" Joseph asked.

"Thirty pounds," said Miss Brontë coolly. "Per person."

"Jesus H. Christ," Joseph said.

"You may, of course, elect to wait in the parsonage until the costumed tour returns in three hours, when the bargain-rate tour will be given." Miss Brontë stared him down. "Though I must warn you that the parsonage has, of course, no central heating, a fact that led, indirectly or otherwise, to the early deaths of several of my dear sisters."

"Joseph, you'll regret it if we pass up an opportunity like this," Lewis cajoled. "I know I will."

"I said I had a credit line, not a money tree."

"We won't be a moment," promised Lewis, and grabbing Joseph by the elbow, he hurried away to the parsonage. Miss Brontë sauntered back to the omnibus, swinging her reticule with an air of triumph.

"That cost a goddam fortune," growled Joseph five minutes later, as they emerged from the parsonage decked in Inverness cloaks and rather poorly made felt top hats. "And this is *really* not a guy thing, Lewis."

"For heaven's sake, can't you at least enjoy the irony of it all?" said Lewis. *Besides, if you don't want the Company to think you're planning something, this is certainly a good cover. What possible reason could you have for doing something like this other than impulsive, spur-of-the-moment fun?*

Joseph just growled again. They hurried to the omnibus, presented their tickets to Miss Brontë, and took their seats.

Three hours later they returned to the car, pausing to open the boot of the Austin.

"I can't believe you didn't enjoy that," said Lewis, as Joseph carefully loaded in the six jugs of Brontë liqueur he had purchased at the gift shop.

"I guess I'm just not literary," Joseph said, changing his mind and removing one of the jugs. He carried it around to the front of the car and got in.

"You've no appreciation of high romance, that's your trouble," Lewis said, climbing in and starting the motor.

Joseph nodded somberly. "Boy meets girl, girl loses boy, everybody dies. I just don't get it. What those kids needed was some tuberculosis inoculations and a whole lot of Prozac." He broke the seal on the jug and sampled the liqueur. "Wow. Or this. Want some?"

"Not while I'm driving. Do you want to get us arrested?" Lewis headed back in the direction of the A629.

"At least that would be a guy thing," Joseph retorted.

They zigzagged back and forth across the Yorkshire Dales, gradually working their way north. They stopped at a Herriot museum and had their photographs taken with a Clydesdale horse; bought *All Creatures Great and Small* tea towels and a Yorkshire Dale cake in a tin enameled with scenes from Herriot's books; passed through villages with names like Blubberhouses, Winksley, Snape, and Patrick Brompton.

"Where are we going now?" Joseph said, taking another gulp from the liqueur jug.

"Quite a historically significant spot, actually," Lewis said, brushing crumbs of Dale cake from his tie as he accelerated. "Swaledale Anti-Farm, home of the late Audrey Knollys and setting of her celebrated heroic epic trilogy, *Commonwealth of Innocents*. Don't tell me: you haven't read it."

"What, the Beast Liberation lady?" Joseph shrugged. "Wrote kind of a cross between *Animal Farm* and *Watership Down*? I've heard of it. Those are the books that will get the Mandated Vegan Laws passed over here, right?"

"And over there, too, in what will be left of the United States," Lewis said. "There's already a Beast Liberation Party flexing its muscles in London. Ironically enough, none of the locals want it here; the economy's still based in farming. Eventually, though, the BLP will get the Herriot places closed down as mere glorifications of beast exploitation. Hang on to those tea towels; they'll be worth a fortune someday."

"I guess so," said Joseph in awe.

He was silent as they continued west, and silent when they turned north at Hardraw. A short distance on, he sat upright and peered around suspiciously.

What's wrong? Lewis transmitted, keeping his eyes on the road.

Nothing. Nothing now, anyway. But it was right around here that the Ninth got creamed.

Gosh, really? Lewis slowed the car, looking about as if he expected to see hapless auxiliaries being chased by howling blue savages.

I guess I sort of erased the memory. It wasn't fun. But, you know something else? This is also pretty damn close to the coordinates I was tracing.

Lewis gnawed his lower lip. *That's an awfully big coincidence. It's also rather close to the location of that job I had up here.*

No kidding? Weird.

They drove on in silence. A moment later they came upon a wayside inn and gift shop styled THE INNOCENTS, beyond which loomed the flank of a steep hill.

Suggest that this looks like a good place to stop, transmitted Joseph urgently. *Out loud, now!*

"I wonder if this shop sells Bournville bars?" mused Lewis obediently, pulling into the row of graveled parking spaces. "Would you mind if we looked? I must confess I'm finding the scenery a bit depressing."

"Sure," said Joseph in his most casual voice. "Say, look at those clouds. Might be a good idea to remember there's a hotel here, if we get caught in a storm. Should we put the top up?"

Lewis keyed in a command on the dash, and the convertible's top creaked out over them like an opening wing. "May as well do it now, in case it starts while we're inside." *What is it? Have we reached your coordinates?*

This is the spot.

They got out and crunched across the gravel to the shop, looking up doubtfully at the dark sky. A bitter cold wind was sweeping under it, piercing through their coats. They opened the door and stepped into the relative warmth of the shop and an atmosphere of tinkling chimes, fragrant incense, and a vast distant mooing that Lewis, after a millisecond's startled analysis, identified as recorded whale songs.

"It's California again," muttered Joseph.

As if on cue, an American voice spoke from behind a display of crystal pendants. "Can I help you find something?"

"Hello?" Lewis peered around the display and beheld a thin intense lady wearing purple and a lot of Neolithic-styled jewelry. "Do you have any Bournville bars?"

By way of answer the lady pointed to a display stand gratifyingly loaded with sweets. "Right over there, next to the books."

"So they are." Lewis smiled his thanks. Joseph followed him around to inspect them.

"Get me some mints too, will you? Hey, look," he said loudly. "Here are those great books you were recommending. The, uh, *Commonwealth of Innocents.*"

Must you be devious about everything? Lewis said in exasperation.

"Oh, you have to read those!" the lady informed him, heat and light coming into her voice. She emerged from behind the counter possessively. "You know where you are, don't you? You're right smack in the middle of where all her stories are set."

"I thought Swaledale must be nearby," Lewis said. "I've read them, of course."

"Aren't they just—?" The lady put one hand on her bosom, expressing that words failed her. "We named this place for the trilogy, you know, Jeffrey and I. We just couldn't believe it when we got up here and found out that there's no museum or plaque or *anything* about Knollys up at the Anti-Farm. It's just sitting there vacant! We're starting a fund to establish a museum. Donations are always welcome."

"What a wonderful idea," said Lewis, gallantly pulling out his wallet.

The lady nodded in vigorous affirmation, ringing up his purchases.

"Right up the road a couple of miles is the meadow with the copse where Silverbell the Gentle is martyred," she went on, referring to the eponymous bovine saint of the trilogy's first volume. "And, you won't believe this, but right in back of us is the very hill where Jeremiah the Valiant leads the Innocents against the Vulpos!"

She was referring to the trilogy's controversial third volume, wherein the peace-loving barnyard folk band together to exterminate all foxes in one great crusade to rid their world of vicious predators. Lewis explained this in a brief transmission to Joseph, adding:

There have always been rumors of a new trilogy Audrey Knollys was working on at the time of her death, in which the Innocents go after cats and dogs too. No notes ever surfaced, but the mere idea has already caused a schism among her followers.

Joseph gave Lewis a bright inquisitive look. *I bet there really were notes, in fact I'd bet there was a completed first draft. Gee, I wonder what could have happened to it?* He opened the mints and popped one in his mouth.

I had nothing to do with her accident, if that's what you're implying, Lewis said sharply. *I simply got there before her executors did.* He pressed a ten-pound note into the lady's hand. "No, keep the change for the museum fund. Please. Is there any kind of tour one can take? Any guidebook to the real-life locations?"

The lady shook her head. "It's shameful, but there really isn't. Someday, I just know there will be, but right now—" She lowered her voice. "It's this country. Don't get me wrong, I love England and all, but there's just no initiative here. You know what I mean? I mean, haven't you noticed that?"

"Absolutely. Is there anybody local we could pay to show us around?" said Joseph.

At this moment a youngish man shouldered open the door, puffing with effort because he was quite stout. He set down the cardboard boxes he'd been carrying and straightened up to glower at the two immortals. He wore black and more Neolithic-styled jewelry, and had cultivated a little sinister beard and mustache to rival Joseph's.

"Jeffrey, these men are interested in a tour of the trilogy sites," said his wife hopefully.

"And we'll pay," added Joseph.

"Well then," Jeffrey said, drawing himself up. "Five pounds apiece, just to cover the gas, okay? I'll take you in the Land Rover."

"Deal," Joseph said. Lewis fished out another ten-pound note.

Ten minutes later they were rumbling along a cow path in an old Land Rover, listening to Jeffrey talk. Jeffrey spoke sonorously, pontifically, and at great length, and if either Joseph or Lewis had been actually interested in the trilogy, Jeffrey would have been a great guide, because he clearly knew the books by heart. As it was, they were able to hold a fairly uninterrupted subvocal conversation during his narration, only pausing now and then to murmur appreciatively when he emphasized something with a dramatic silence or sweeping gesture.

They wobbled past the semiruined Swaledale Anti-Farm, acres of weedy earth and a few stone buildings, "the site of Audrey Knollys's magnificently daring Nonhuman experiment"; they visited various chattering becks or heathery hillsides that had inspired scenes where unforgettably heroic beasts had loved, suffered, and/or died; and at last they charged bumping up a great hill, following its ridge as along the spine of a beached whale. At the highest point Jeffrey turned off the motor, set the emergency brake firmly, and announced:

"We're getting out here, gentlemen." He swung open the driver's door and stepped into a roaring blast of wind.

"Er... I don't like to seem overcautious, but isn't this spot rather exposed to lightning?" Lewis said, clambering from the Land Rover after him. Joseph followed even more reluctantly. They stood there with their coats whipping behind them as Jeffrey struck an attitude.

"Now, *this* is my favorite spot. From this point you can see just about every important place mentioned in the entire trilogy, except for the parts set in Leeds, of course. But, see? Back there is the Anti-Farm, and Silverbell's Copse is clearly visible just over there, and..."

Lewis was smiling and nodding, pretending to follow the lecture attentively even as his teeth chattered. Joseph wasn't watching. He was staring fixedly into a place just below where they were standing, a smooth depression in the flank of the hill, more than a ledge, less than a valley. It was the sort of place where exhausted hikers might sprawl before going on to the top, or perhaps where a handful of desperate men might make a last stand, unable to go any higher.

This is what he was remembering:

Brigantia, A.D. 120

WELL, *THIS ISN'T GOING* to work," said Ron, staring down at the last of the Brigantes, who had noticed their retreat. He was very, very big—all six of the "Cimmerians" were very, very big men with dun-colored hair and light blue eyes. They also shared other distinct and unusual physical characteristics, which was why the Company had felt it advisable to slip them into the legion as auxiliaries from a non-existent northern race. Joseph came to peer over the edge and backed away, pale.

"Do you think they'll try to come up here after us?" he asked, groping for his short sword.

"Oh, yeah," said Bayard, coming to stand beside Ron. "As soon as they're done mopping up down there. Poor old Ninth. Ouch! They just took out Gaius Favonius. That's it. The last of the Syrians are running like hell."

"Are they getting away?" Gozo and Albert came to watch. The four giants stood there a moment in silence, staring, before Ron said briefly:

"Nope."

Bogdan and Pancha, who had been scanning the hilltop above the ledge, gave up and joined them, and after a moment's hesitation Joseph edged close again. He looked out on the carnage below and shuddered. "I'm sorry," he said desperately.

To a man, the Enforcers shrugged.

"It was their fate," said Ron. "Soldiers kill, soldiers get killed. Don't feel bad. You can take some revenge on the Brigantes, if you want. They're going to be up here any minute."

Joseph's blade trembled in his hand, and Gozo burst out laughing.

"Don't sweat it." Leaning down, he knocked playfully on Joseph's helmet. "We'll do our job, centurion baby. We got what the Company wanted, didn't we? You were able to observe the whole thing. Now this event shadow's filled in, Dr. Zeus knows what happened to the original Ninth, and all we've got to do is clean up."

"There's still the goddam Brigantes," said Joseph through his teeth, pushing his helmet back on his head.

"You can say that again." Ron's voice sharpened as he stepped back. "Here they come. Joseph, stay down, and we'll keep them off. You're the observer; just keep those cameras rolling. Axes, guys!"

Joseph sheathed his sword and crouched down, fighting every programmed instinct to wink out in hyperfunction and not touch ground until he was a good five miles away. He obeyed his orders, which had not come from Rome; he held his tiny patch of ground and kept his eyes open, recording what he saw.

The Enforcers cast away the little round oval shields and drew from their cases the particular native weapons of their own unit. These were not blades, nor were they slings or curved bows. They were flint axes of enormous size, bound to oak hafts in leather thongs, beautifully worked, heavily weighted to crush with the blunt ends, slice like razors on the edge. Each Enforcer had two axes.

"Hhhhaaai-ai-ai!" Bogdan said reverently. "Death!"

"Ready them," said Ron. "Hand-to-hand in thirty seconds. Shit, look at that. Down axes, prepare for javelin cast! Take out that front line!"

Joseph dragged himself to the edge and looked down. The Brigantes were coming, not swiftly. Winded from the fight below, they advanced almost lazily, chatting among themselves as they came up the face of the hill. They were followed by the fresh reinforcements that had just arrived, walking easily through the mutilated bodies and the ruined baggage train. He estimated their number at a hundred and six.

The foremost looked up at the ledge, and Joseph saw their eyes widen slightly. Then he heard the noise behind him, the creak of leather armor on six bodies bending all together like the great machines they were, just before they fired in perfect unison and with inhuman force.

No mortal eye could have seen the flight of spears, so swift it was; but Joseph watched them hurtling down the hill and through the Brigantes. Literally through, men two and three deep were falling, shrieking, with gaping wounds front and back as the spears shot on downward, clattering to rest at last on the stones of the little stream below.

The advance halted. The barbari looked at one another big-eyed, drew into groups, muttered together, stared up at the ledge uncertainly now. Joseph turned to look too. The Enforcers had taken up their axes and come to the edge and were just standing there, six very big men, motionless as mountains.

Joseph could see the Brigantes looking, turning to each other and mouthing, *Is that all?* and shrugging at last and beginning the cautious advance again, flatfooted up the hill, keeping their eyes on the very big men.

Ron drew a deep breath.

"Father of battles," he moaned. "Lord of justice, drink the blood of the unjust!"

The whole line of the Enforcers began to sway together, in that eerie unison with which they had launched their javelin cast. Their pupils had dilated enormously. To a man, they were smiling now as they rocked in place and contemplated the advancing mortals. First one and then another began to chant, softly at first, apparently disconnected phrases in a language forty thousand years old, a chaos of harmonies that unified into descant on a single melody, beautiful and terrifying, sweet tenor voices from those monstrous chests, those thick necks.

Joseph remembered the language. It was a very simple song: its meaning was only that the wicked must be punished so the innocent might live in peace.

Albert and Bogdan stepped forward and began to walk down the hill, still singing, swinging their flint axes in either massive hand.

The Brigantes halted, gaping; then someone screamed, and they charged, swarming up the hill.

Almost at once Albert and Bogdan vanished in the press of mortal bodies. You could see the axes rising and falling, though, and occasionally catch a glimpse of a great red hand or arm. Pancha and Bayard were walking down now, reaching out almost casually to knock in the skulls of the first Brigantes to reach them, disappearing in their turn under the screaming mob. Ron and Gozo waded in after them.

It didn't last long. The fighting moved back down the hill, for the simple reason that none of them could keep their footing, everyone was sliding in the blood and mud. Not only mortal blood, now; Joseph saw a lucky blow take off Albert's head, the trunk fountaining scarlet as it fought on a full ten seconds before dropping in fugue. Bayard was down, he'd been damaged. Brigantii were all over him like flies on a corpse, desperately trying to knife him where he lay, but his arms still rose and fell, rose and fell like machines, beating and breaking any mortal thing in range. The terrified mortals were stabbing frantically at the other Enforcers, delivering wound after wound with dagger or sword or spear, and the big men slowed as their blood ran down, but they did not stop killing.

Then it was over, all at once. Ron was the last one standing. He staggered back and sat down heavily. Joseph heard him sigh. There was a silence, except for the wind coming up the valley. There wasn't a Brigante left alive.

Joseph was on his hands and knees then, scrambling and crawling down the hill to Ron's side.

Ron blinked sleepily, not even looking at the mess that had spilled into his lap, though he was making an effort to hold it in with one hand. He was bleeding from wounds on every exposed surface of his body, from little thin scratches to the worst one in his neck, which had a short sword rather comically still protruding from it. It looked like a party novelty.

"That was close," he told Joseph, and spat out blood. "Got 'em all, though."

"The other guys are all down," Joseph meant to say firmly, but it came out in a whimper. "Don't worry. The retrieval team will be along any minute. I'm so sorry."

"Aw, don't be," Ron said. He looked down at the hideous carnage with a fond expression. "Damn, that was fun. That was like old times. How long has it been since a bunch of the Old Guard have been able to get together for a party like this?" He coughed and spat out a piece of something; Joseph avoided looking to see what exactly. "And I'll bet that's about the last time we get to mix it up. We look too different now from the mortals. I ain't looking forward to being demobilized, I can tell you."

Joseph shook his head. "They won't stick you behind a desk. They'll have to find something better for you. Maybe you can fly transports or something fun like that."

Ron smiled at him. "Company'll manage. They made us like killing. Maybe they can make us like something else. Just reprogram us, I guess." He shrugged and winced; putting his hand up in bewilderment, he encountered the sword sticking out of his neck. His incredulous giggle turned into a roar of laughter.

"Look at this stupid thing! How long were you going to wait before telling me some mortal left his sword in my neck? I wonder when that happened?" He took a firm grip and pulled it out. A gout of bright blood followed.

"Uh-oh." Ron's face grew still suddenly. "Not good. Blood loss unacceptable. Going into fugue, I guess. Bye-bye, Joseph. See you sometime..."

He closed his eyes and sank backward, like a tree going down in a storm.

Joseph got unsteadily to his feet. Panting, he looked around at the desolation. After a long moment he sighed and went down the hill, slipping and falling a few times in unspeakable muck, to retrieve Albert's head where it had rolled into a gorse bush. He had even nastier work over the next few minutes, locating the other Enforcers under piles of chopped Brigantii and hauling five enormous bodies up the hill to lay them out beside Ron.

He was standing there, gasping, watching Albert hopefully to see if the head might reattach where he'd set it on the neck stump—he didn't think so, the process of fugue was too far advanced, already the wounds had exuded the antiseptic ichor and sealed themselves over—when he heard little bells ringing. He turned.

Winding its way along the crest of the hill above him was a pack train of mules, bells on their harnesses announcing their approach. They were led by an immortal he vaguely recognized, accompanied by two maintenance techs.

"Facilitator Grade One Joseph, I presume?" called the leader cheerily. "Nennius, Facilitator General for the Northern Sector. Another successful mission, eh?"

"I guess you could call it that," Joseph said. He watched as they negotiated their way down the steep slope. "I thought they'd send an air transport."

"Are you mad? It's broad daylight. Anyway the mules will do perfectly well, the repair facility is nearby." Nennius tsk-tsked as he saw the Enforcers. "Poor old fellows! Blood lust got the better of them again, did it?"

Joseph shook his head. "Actually it was a last-minute bunch of enemy reinforcements. You should have been here! The bastards just kept coming. Our guys followed orders, sir, you'd have been proud of them."

"I'm sure I would have." Nennius nodded, gesturing. The two maintenance techs lifted Albert's body between them and threw it over the back of a mule, where they bound it in place. A moment later they came back with a bucket for his head. Nennius watched briefly and then turned back to Joseph.

"So. The lamentable end of the original Ninth Hispania! All the details were recorded for data transmission?"

"Yes, sir." Suddenly the horror of the last three days caught up with Joseph, the long trailing march, the snipers and skirmishes, the inexorably rising body count, the last full assault on an exhausted and demoralized remnant legion. His knees wanted to buckle. He settled for sitting down in the presence of a superior and leaning his head on his arms. "These are the last. No survivors. You'll find the previous casualties in cairns along the route. I left a signaling device at each one."

"They've already been collected," Nennius assured him. "And if you'll just be kind enough to do the same for the bodies down there, a transport will be along to get them after dark."

"Okay," said Joseph wearily. "Do you want the Brigantes too?"

"Heavens no. Leave them where they fell. We only want the legionaries, and of course all the gear and material from the baggage train. Mustn't leave any evidence to conflict with recorded history, after all." Nennius smiled graciously. "Though of course you know that, experienced field operator that you are. Really, you handled this very well, Joseph. Full marks."

"Thank you," Joseph replied, looking up to watch as Ron's body was hauled away to the pack train. Nennius turned and pulled out a good-sized leather satchel and dropped it beside Joseph.

"Now, when you've finished sorting and stacking the corpses, you'll need to remove everything you're wearing and leave it with the rest. There's a change of clothing for you in here, as well as money and trade goods to get you to the west coast. There'll be a ship waiting in Morecambe Bay. We're sending you back to Spain for a while, but you need to stop at a particular village on the way..."

Joseph just recorded and nodded, letting his awareness slip away.

He was back down on the field, poking through the bodies of his mortal command, when he glanced up to see the pack train winding away along the skyline, making for an even bigger and more steep-sided hill in the near distance. The next time he looked up, laboring antlike under his burden of carrion, the pack train had vanished.

Yorkshire, 2026

...WHERE THE WAVES of Vulpos plunged screaming from their foul dens, racing in their sharp-toothed hatred toward the firm hooves of the Innocents!" shouted Jeffrey at the top of his lungs, flinging his arms wide as his black coat billowed theatrically behind him. As if on cue, there was a blue-white flash, and thunder boomed. For a second the mortal looked panicked, and then very pleased with himself indeed.

"Oh, dear, I think we'd better head back, don't you?" said Lewis from inside the Land Rover, where he had more or less materialized a split second after the lightning struck. Joseph, however, remained where he stood, staring slack-jawed at the high steep hill, the setting of Jeffrey's narrative.

"If you like," Jeffrey said grandly, sauntering back to the car. "Sorry if I alarmed you. As you can see, this is a place of Powers."

Joseph came to himself and scurried for the car.

You seemed spellbound, said Lewis worriedly. *I didn't think he was all that good a storyteller, frankly.*

It had nothing to do with him, Joseph replied. *I just made a connection, that's all.*

You'll have to tell me about it later.

Sure. Later.

Jeffrey drove rather recklessly down through the rain that had begun to fall. By the time they reached the Innocents, it was a solid torrent, sheets of water drenching them as they ran into the shop.

Jeffrey was in an expansive mood, suddenly more talkative than Lotus (the lady in purple) and very much in charge. They must stay for dinner, he informed them: savory tofu lasagna with its perfect accompaniment, Australian merlot. And they really ought to stay the night. This storm was not about to let up before morning, if *he* knew anything. The charge for a night was normally ninety pounds, but if they were short of cash—

"No, no, that's all right." Lewis waved his fork dismissively. "We'd planned on staying somewhere in the vicinity, and why not here? What remarkable luck we stopped in, eh, Joseph?"

"Mm," said Joseph in a ghost of a voice.

"Your friend seems shaken by our little experience up there," Jeffrey told Lewis, filling their glasses. He settled back in his chair, basking. "Understandable. It's a powerful place…"

"Yes," Lewis agreed, tasting the wine, "it simply reeks of power."

"Normally I prefer not to let—well—outsiders in on our secrets, but you seem to be fairly discreet gentlemen," Jeffrey began.

"There are all kinds of local legends!" said Lotus, coming back from the kitchen with the Choc-Tofu-Treats that were their dessert. "The name of the hill behind us is Arthur's Seat, you know."

"Oh?" Joseph turned to look at her.

"Is it really?" Lewis said. "How fascinating. Any connection with King Arthur?"

"Well, they say that—"

"It's the sleeping knights legend," Jeffrey said, firmly retrieving the lead. "You can find it in a few other places in England, but this is our local version. Supposedly there's a cave somewhere under that hill where Arthur's knights lie sleeping in their armor, waiting until Arthur comes again. When England's in its greatest hour of need, they'll wake and join in the battle of good versus evil."

"Personally I think it's Guinevere who's coming back, not Arthur," asserted Lotus.

"No, really?" Lewis looked fascinated, managing at the same time to conceal most of a chunk of lasagna in his paper serviette. "What an original idea."

"I have reason to believe that the whole legend predates Arthur and Christianity and all the rest of them." Jeffrey raised his voice a little. "And I'll tell you something: Audrey Knollys knew that when she set the scene of the final battle out there. She knew it was a place of power. There are certain people who hold the opinion," he leaned forward and dropped his voice like a garment, "that her death was *no accident.*"

"She knew too much?" said Lewis, unobtrusively conveying the serviette into his coat pocket.

"No, that she didn't really die at all! That, in fact, she was able to arrange her own advancement to a higher plane of existence to continue her work more effectively," Jeffrey told him, perfectly serious.

"You don't say," said Lewis in a shocked tone.

Joseph had been looking steadily grayer as the conversation progressed, but here he asked, *Did this lady really die?*

She was attempting to get a muffin out of a toaster with her fork and got electrocuted, Lewis replied, sipping his merlot and listening to Jeffrey with a rapt expression. Gratified, Jeffrey expanded on his revelations of mystic power and theories of ancient gods.

Outside, the dining room window made a tiny square of light in the miles of darkness. The rain fell, the thunder rolled, and the high steep hill loomed behind the house as though it were watching.

After a while the yellow light winked out, to reappear shortly in another window higher up, and then there were three lights briefly; then darkness entire.

Joseph sat on his bed, eating Polo mints one after another and waiting until the mortals slept. He was still wearing the suit and overcoat in which he'd traveled all day.

Shortly after midnight he rose in silence and left his tiny cold room, going down through the house to the private entrance. As he slid the bolt, he heard light quick steps descending the stairs behind him, and turned to look into Lewis's narrowed eyes.

I knew you were going to do something like this, Lewis said angrily.

This is so classified, you can't even imagine. Please go back and forget you saw anything.

I haven't seen anything. What is it, for God's sake? Something to do with your mysterious coordinates? What did you discover while we were up there?

Yes, it has to do with the coordinates. I wasn't going to investigate further this time, because I have you with me and it's just too dangerous. But then the electrical storm started and our datafeed to the Company went down again.

Yes, I noticed that.

I just can't pass up the chance. Do you know how long I had to wait to get the timing right before I could get a private interview with Mendoza's last case officer during a storm and still make it look like it happened totally by accident? Twenty-five years. And we come here, and another storm is just thrown in my lap! I have to go out there to see.

Well, whatever it is you're looking for, I'm going too.

Joseph shook his head sadly. He opened the door, and they went out into the rain.

The back garden rose in terraces up the hill a short way, ending in a line of leaning snow fence that was easily stepped over. They found a little track through the heather up there, someone's favorite ramble perhaps, and they followed it around the lower slopes and up the northern face a few hundred meters. The storm hadn't stopped. They tramped on through mud and bursts of painful illumination backlighting the falling rain, bringing out garish and alien colors in the purple heather.

Suddenly Joseph stopped in his tracks and pointed. Lewis looked up uncertainly, wiping the rain from his eyes.

There, that rock face. Look close. What do you see?

A nasty place for climbing, a treacherous rotten stretch of over-hung rock that any hiker would avoid. It looked crumbly and diffi-cult to get to. Even the little animal trails went above or below it, but nowhere near. This is what a mortal would have seen, would have been intended to see. Joseph and Lewis, staring intently and using a visual filter mortals didn't possess, saw more.

They beheld a smooth path leading up to a sealed door.

"God," said Lewis faintly.

Joseph strode up the path. He crouched in the overhang, exam-ining the door. There was a via pad there, tuned to Facilitator-grade clearance. He flattened his palm against it. After a moment the door opened smoothly, revealing utter darkness that breathed out a cur-rent of warm air, a promise of dryness, cleanliness. Half frozen in his soaked clothing, he found it pleasant.

He became aware that Lewis was standing beside him, staring with horror into the dark.

"This is what you were after," Lewis said.

"I guess so," Joseph said.

Lewis swallowed hard. "Is Mendoza down there?"

"I have no idea." Joseph tilted his head and considered the black depth. "Probably not, though. How could she be? We both know where they sent her. No, I'm looking for somebody else."

"But—even if Mendoza was sent back a million years, she'd get to the present eventually, just by living through the past a day at a time," stammered Lewis. "Wouldn't she? I mean, I never believed those rumors of Back Way Back for just that reason. If the Company wanted to get rid of its immortals, sending them into the past wouldn't be a permanent solution."

"You have a point there," said Joseph, advancing cautiously through the doorway, scanning as he went.

"So—she might be here after all. Is that what you think is down there? Some kind of holding facility for immortals?" Lewis's teeth were chattering in his head. He attempted to follow Joseph across the threshold but drew back, gasping as though he'd been struck a physical blow.

Joseph turned swiftly. "You ought to be able to cross that threshold," he said, puzzled. "I deactivated the repulsion system. What's wrong with you?"

"Well, let's see: violent electrical storm making my hair stand on end, crumbling cliffs in danger of dropping on us at any minute, and the only safety a yawning mouth of darkness. I suppose I'm terrified."

"You ought to be able to come in even so, there's no physical barrier. But stay here. I'll try not to be long. Just stop talking."

Lewis fell silent, and Joseph paced away into the darkness.

As tunnels into the absolute black unknown went, it wasn't bad: smooth and gradual of descent, full of a faint fragrance that was unidentifiable but familiar. Joseph could, of course, see perfectly well in the dark, and every programmed instinct he had was telling him he was much safer here than out in the middle of an electrical storm.

He had descended perhaps a hundred meters, and the tunnel had begun to level out ahead of him and reveal a glow of blue light, when he heard a clatter of shoes behind him. Lewis was racing down the tunnel, eyes wide.

What? Is something after you?

No, I just—had a hallucination or something. I can't be alone up there!

Joseph bared his teeth in exasperation and stalked on ahead. *I warned you.*

I know. Gasping, unsteady, Lewis followed him.

A few meters farther on, though, he staggered and fell. Joseph swung about to find him huddled against the wall, pale and sweating.

What the hell is wrong now?

Lewis turned a sick face up to him. *I seem to be having some sort of suppressed memory retrieval.*

Of what?

I, uh, appear to be remembering my death.

Joseph crouched beside him. *We're immortal. We don't die.*

I'm perfectly aware of that, thank you.

You know we're not supposed to be here, right? So you're probably feeling whatever trauma you went through before the Company recruited you as a kid. Dr. Zeus uses them to keep us in line, like the conditioning nightmares. Break the rules, and you start reliving whatever jam you were in before some nice Company operative appeared out of nowhere and rescued you. Me, I remember the guys who exterminated my tribe.

But I never went through any trauma like that, Lewis said. *I was taken by the Company as a newborn. I have no memories of mortal life, you see?* He drew his knees up and stared at the blue light with haunted eyes. *That's not it. But something happened to me in Ireland once, and I think it gave me amnesia...*

We don't get that either, Lewis. Joseph rose to his feet impatiently. *But you stay put and remember whatever you're remembering. I have something to check out.*

He walked away down the tunnel and vanished into the blue light.

Lewis hugged his knees. There had been a child chained in a cell. Not a child. Something all malevolence, hideously wise. There had been a mortal man, a Christian monk. The images were crowding on Lewis thick and fast, incoherent, inexplicable, impossible, and he realized that he could not sit there alone with them. The blue unknown was less horrible. He clawed his way upright again and went tottering off down the passage after Joseph, fighting panic every step of the way.

When he finally emerged from the tunnel's mouth, though, he stopped in blank surprise. It wasn't what he had expected at all.

He stood in a great vaulted bunker opening out before him into gentle gloom. The blue light was coming from regeneration vats, which were arranged in neat rows under the vaults. There were hundreds of them, and every one he could see was occupied by a pale floating figure. Joseph was sitting on the floor with his back against the nearest one. He lifted a tear-streaked face as Lewis came forward into the bunker.

"Oh, man," he said hoarsely. "I wish you hadn't come in here."

"But—it's just some kind of infirmary. These are only regeneration vats," said Lewis wonderingly. He came closer, peering up at the floating body. After a moment his mouth fell open in astonishment.

"Good God," he cried. "What are they?"

The vault's occupant was an immortal male, but there any resemblance to Lewis or Joseph ended. He was enormously tall, even allowing for the magnifying qualities of the transparent tank, probably eight feet if he were standing; enormously broad and deep in the chest and shoulders, with a peculiar articulation of the powerful neck and arms.

His head was even more peculiar, not human at all, with a wide-domed helmet shape. The face was comparably strange: great protruding brows made caves of the blind eyes. An enormous nose, flat cheekbones, the suggestion of unusual dentition in the heavy jaws. The skin was fair. The hair and beard, long and drifting in the tank's slight current, were the dun color of an autumn field after rain.

He wore nothing but a circlet of copper-colored metal on his brow.

The vault next to him contained another such, not identical but clearly of the same strange race. So did the one beyond that vault, and the one beyond that, and so on as far as Lewis could see. They were all males.

"They're...Neanderthals?" Lewis guessed. "No, they can't be, they're so big. That's not quite the skull shape, either. All the same... what kind of monsters are these?"

"They're not monsters," Joseph said, wiping his eyes on his sleeve. "They're heroes."

Lewis stared at him in incomprehension.

Joseph got to his feet, slowly, moving like an old mortal. "There's more than one kind of operative," he said.

"I know," Lewis said. "Facilitators, Conservationists, Techs."

Joseph shook his head. "Those are all Preservers. You, me, Mendoza. All you've ever seen is Preservers. The Company doesn't make these big guys anymore. We used to call them Enforcers."

"What did they enforce?" Lewis looked up at the sleeping giant nervously.

"Peace," replied Joseph. "You've heard of the Great Goat Cult?"

"Certainly. They were a fanatic religious movement back in prehistory. Insisted on tattoos. Wiped out any tribe that rose above a certain technological level. They delayed the birth of civilization by ten thousand years, and the Company was powerless to stop them."

"It wasn't." Joseph shook his head sadly. "Dr. Zeus got tired of waiting. Wouldn't you have got tired of waiting? Watching *Homo sapiens* work its way up from the monkeys, and just as it starts to produce art and culture worth preserving, somebody starts a religion that demands mass slaughter of sinners. The Goats were pretty good at it, too, they killed half the population of Europe and Asia before the Company made the decision to interfere.

"But the Company couldn't send in Preservers to stop the cult. We were designed to run, not to fight. We're sneak thieves, smooth talkers, nice guys. We don't get involved in mortal quarrels. We let mortals go their own way to hell while we rescue what we can, and we never, ever risk our own skins. Pain scares us. We don't do danger."

"Rather unflatteringly put, but essentially true." Lewis couldn't take his eyes off the man in the vault.

"Yeah, well, the Company needed somebody who *could* do danger. They played around with the available gene pool and came up with these guys."

"You mean they made recombinants?" Lewis asked, horrified.

"No, just some controlled breeding experiments, which is nastier, if you ask me. Where they got the results they wanted, they made the kids into immortals, but not Preservers: killers. Warriors, though, not assassins. Braver than you or I could ever possibly be, guys who'd think nothing of charging into oncoming spears, guys who could be shot so full of arrows they would look like porcupines and still keep fighting." Joseph glanced up at the vault, remembering.

"I can't imagine that," Lewis murmured. He jumped as the big man moved galvanically, flexed, and then relaxed.

"You're programmed not to," Joseph told him. "So am I. Not these guys. Anyway, the Company turned them loose on the Great Goat Cult. Kill all killers. Simple instruction. And they weren't stupid, either; these guys were as smart as you or I, just motivated differently. They went after any mortals who practiced violence. You know why mortal civilization was finally able to get started? Because these guys did their job."

"Perhaps they shouldn't have stopped, given the way civilization progressed."

"They thought so, too," said Joseph quietly.

"Oh," Lewis said. After a poignant silence, he went on: "And so the Company locked them up here? No wonder you didn't want me to find out about this."

"I didn't know about it," said Joseph in a wretched voice. "I just guessed. The problems were supposed to have been worked out. The Enforcers were supposed to have been retrained, reprogrammed, reassigned. Mostly to Company bases, because as time went on, the mortal races started looking different, and these guys couldn't pass anymore. I used to see a few of them now and then, back in the early days. Less and less as time went on. I didn't think anything of it. I didn't want to."

"What changed your mind?" Lewis drew back as the giant clenched his enormous and well-made hands, then relaxed them.

"Looking for Mendoza," said Joseph. "I hadn't wanted to think about *her*, either. I just shoved my official notification of her arrest into a file in my tertiary consciousness and never accessed it until that day in Sam Pan's when you told me you saw her."

"I remember. But—"

"I had other data in that file," Joseph went on steadily. "And when I accessed the notification about Mendoza, it popped up. It was information somebody passed me a long time ago, something I didn't want to know anything about because it was really dangerous."

"Those coordinates?"

Joseph nodded.

"And they led you here?"

"The first set did."

"You mean there are other places like this? Full of these...?"

"Probably. This is the first one I've checked." Joseph sighed. "I didn't want you to know about them at all. You're now one of probably ten people in the world who have seen this place, and we are in sooo much trouble if the Company finds out, Lewis. Remember back in San Francisco, when I said the stakes had got way too high for you? You should see them now."

"I heard a rumor, once." Lewis began to pace along the rows of vaults, looking at their occupants. "Supposedly passed back from some operative in the future. It's that, when we finally do reach the twenty-fourth century, our mortal masters will make us all wear an emblem. A clock with its hands missing. They'll tell us it's a badge of honor for all our work in time, but really it'll be a way to mark us out for the day when they... dispose of us somehow."

"I heard that rumor too."

"But I never believed it. And I've seen..." Lewis was walking faster now. "What were you hoping to find?"

"Somebody I owe." Joseph followed him. "Somebody who might be able to help me free Mendoza, if she can be freed. If he's here. If I can get him out of here."

They moved along the aisles between the vaults, looking up fearfully at the occupants.

"At least it seems humane enough," Lewis whispered. "They're safe. They're alive. They're not in any pain. I spent ten years in one of these tanks, once."

"Jesus, what happened to you?"

"I'm not sure. It was after Ireland."

"Maybe you did nearly die, then. Ten years! They must have had to replace most of your organic parts." Joseph shuddered. "You never mentioned this before."

"Would *you* want to talk about it?"

"But what kind of danger could a Literature Preservation Specialist get himself into—" Joseph stopped at one vault, and Lewis came instantly to his side.

"No," said Joseph, both relieved and disappointed. This vault's occupant was a Preserver, a woman, but not one he knew. She looked tiny, elfin compared with the Enforcers; her black hair waved around her like long silk. After a moment Joseph and Lewis moved on.

There were five hundred vaults in the bunker, four hundred and eighty of which contained sleeping Enforcers. Of the remaining twenty, nine contained Preservers, six males and three females, none of whom was Mendoza. Eleven vaults were empty.

There were rooms opening off one side. One room contained drums of regenerant concentrate and cleaning supplies. Another seemed to be a repair area, with an operating table and cabinets that might have contained tools. The third room had a bank of terminals, blinking quietly, and a cot. On the wall was a chalkboard, on which someone had printed, in straggling Latin:

ABDIEL HAS DONE HIS APPOINTED WORK HERE
9 NOVEMBER 2025–30 NOVEMBER 2025

There was nothing else.

"How many other bunkers like this are there?" said Lewis, aghast.

"You don't want to know," Joseph said.

"And your friend might be in any one of them. We'll have to search them all, won't we?"

"No way." Joseph stopped and glared at him. "Not you. Lewis, what have I been telling you over and over again? I'm a Facilitator, there's less danger for me. Is this how you wound up in a tank for ten years, taking stupid risks?"

Lewis scowled back. "I took a vow to help Mendoza, and I'd keep it even if the Company locked me away for a thousand years." He considered the nearest one. "How long do you suppose these poor devils have been here?"

"About two thousand years," said Joseph in a lifeless voice. "That one, anyway. He was brought here in 120 A.D. So were those five over there. We were in the Ninth Legion together."

Lotus and Jeffrey were terribly disappointed next morning to discover their guests had departed early, though they were somewhat comforted by the considerable tip the gentlemen had left.

Shortly afterward, the clerk in the York Rowntree Factory shop was startled by the abrupt appearance of two men at her counter. Their eyes were red-rimmed with exhaustion, their expensive suits needed pressing, and they had in their combined shopping baskets at least a hundred pounds' worth of assorted chocolate bars. They seemed a bit on edge.

Lewis dropped Joseph off at London City Airport and watched him board his suborbital flight. Weaving a little as he climbed the boarding ramp, Joseph turned at the door and threw Lewis a shaky Roman salute.

"*Ave*," murmured Lewis, waving back. "*Magna est veritas, et pravalebit.*"

A full century was to pass before they saw each other again.

Joseph in the Darkness

So now I had opened the great big Pandora's box from hell in my hunt for you, father. I was finding out a lot more about the Company's secrets than I'd ever wanted to know, and Lewis—what kind of box had he opened for himself? All kinds of things were swarming out of the darkness of his memory to say hello to him. Poor bastard.

At least he was too busy to think about them much. We were all overworked in the second half of the twenty-first century, gearing up for when things were going to get crazy. Way too much to do for a lot of follow-up on the other bunker locations. I did find a couple, one in New Mexico and one in Siberia, but I wasn't able to do more than locate the concealed doorways. The Company kept me running.

Here's what would have interested you about that century, father: Information was king, and technological advances went at breakneck speed, if unevenly. Electric cars everywhere except the United States. Bullet trains, boom and bust, new religions, new leases on life for old religions. Fossil fuels began to run out. Islam sheathed its sword and went sort of Amish, concentrating on farming, at least in the former OPEC nations. They hadn't much choice.

The neopagan religious movement, with all its Wiccan and quasi-Wiccan subsets, finally realized that what it lacked was a certain coherence of doctrine. In 2082 they all got together in Malta to hold the First Maternal Synod. They debated questions like divine polarity

(Was the Great God equal with the Great Goddess? They decided he wasn't) and whether males had souls. They agreed on common goals: the ancient city of Ephesus and its temple to the Goddess, for example, had to be reclaimed and restored for the faithful.

There were a couple of schisms—both the Diannic Feminist extremists and the Sons of Cernunnos walked out of the synod, and terrorists from both factions bombed each other's shrines. At the end of a year, though, they'd managed to put together a book of holy scripture and forge a new maternalistic religion every bit as violent and repressive as the old paternalistic ones had been. With the shoe now firmly on the other foot, the nonsecular world limped on.

I don't think it was a judgment of Jehovah—or Diana either, for that matter—but about this time the Sattes virus swept through the prisons of the world, killing off most of the inmates as well as the guards and their families. In every nation on Earth. How much did you know about that one, father? Was it planned? Would you have forbidden it, if you'd been able? Well, the mortals lived up to your expectations, I'm afraid. The stupefying improbability of it all was mostly ignored, the official investigations perfunctory at best, because everyone was so secretly grateful.

Then the virus broke out in the world's armies, and they weren't so happy anymore.

When it ended, abruptly and mysteriously as it had begun, there were a lot fewer people; but the infrastructure for the new world was intact, so a boom period of prosperity followed. Wages were up, labor was satisfied. No wars for a while, except in places where it never stopped, with or without armies.

Like Northern Ireland. Somebody nuked Belfast, with a dirty little stolen bomb, probably one of the old ones misplaced by the former superpowers. Nobody's quite sure who was responsible. But, surprise: when the mushroom cloud dissipated, the place was neither green nor orange. It was dead. Did that teach them anything? You'd bet it wouldn't, father, and you'd be so right.

America had its troubles too, race wars and a growing antifederalist movement, until the epidemic hit. Things went steadily on to hell in California, with two big earthquakes and an urban war in the south before the epidemic. Most of the population fled to the northern end of the state. Fusion power finally made the scene, and New York sued New Jersey to get its garbage back, now that the stuff could be used to power generators. Taxes went up. The pieces began to fall into place for the Second Civil War. I saw it, working in Texas, which was a big economic giant flexing its muscles. None of the mortals saw it coming, though.

Things went on in China and Africa about like they always had, insane repressions and bloodbaths in some places that made the news, peace and relative prosperity in other places that didn't. Same with India. Quebec split from Canada and tried, without success, to join the European Union. The Inuits got a full-fledged nation to themselves up in the Arctic Circle. Parts of Japan sank following three major earthquakes in a row, and Mexico suddenly found its lap full of yen. Europe manufactured things and grew a lot of genetically improved vegetables.

The first Luna colonies were founded, and boomed, because the colonists got rich in short order. Even the janitors became millionaires up there. High wages, nothing to spend them on, good benefits. People fought to go.

And the Recombinant was born. And died.

In the Netherlands, as it happened. Some laboratory had been working away, unfettered by any laws against genetic engineering, and one day announced proudly to the world that they'd produced the first designer human being. Not only that: they'd done it six years ago, and the perfectly normal, healthy boy was now of an age to make statements to the press.

Though he didn't, much. I remember seeing the footage of a terrified little kid at a press conference, holding tight to the hands of the two scientists who'd raised him. He was slender and dark, and all he said for the cameras was that he was very happy to meet people and really looked forward to going to school. That didn't disarm the people who screamed that his very existence was blasphemy. Maybe in time they would have been disarmed; but then the new plague began, all around the boy. Children he played with got it. People he shook hands with got it.

A mob broke into the house where the kid lived and shot him and the scientists who'd raised him.

They burned the house, with the bodies and the laboratory and all the records of the experiment. I personally doubt that the work was lost. Dr. Zeus must have had somebody on the scene to retrieve all that data. But every nation in the world signed an agreement: Never again would anyone attempt to create another Recombinant.

And if there were any of us immortals who still believed that the day would come when Dr. Zeus proudly introduced us to an astonished world—Look, these are the wonderful cyborgs we created to save the planet for you, and now that they're retiring, they'd like to move into your neighborhood—if there were any of us who still believed that, well, we must have been a little shaken.

The twenty-second century arrived, and the year 2355 was another century closer.

London, 2142

LEWIS WALKED QUICKLY along Euston Road, past the bomb crater where the antiquarian bookshop once stood. He'd cleared out its treasures in one exhausting night just before the bomb went off, and managed to invite all his mortal coworkers out to breakfast an hour before the explosion, so that when the blast came, they were all sitting in a cafe arguing the merits of Thai iced coffee over Thai iced tea.

That was the last time he was able to afford inviting anyone out to breakfast.

England was poor now, like Lewis. Cutting loose Northern Ireland had seemed a good idea, but nobody had foreseen Belfast, and now there were roving Ulster Revenge League bombers carrying out reprisals for the Great Betrayal, as they termed England's disengagement. A number of historic buildings were no more, including Lewis's former place of employment. So far King Richard IV (dubbed Lucky Dicky because of his uncanny ability to dodge snipers' bullets) and Parliament (who were less skilled in that regard than their sovereign, and died frequently) had been unable to come to terms with any of the several faction leaders demanding restitution.

It hadn't helped when Scotland broke away. Terrorism was too tame for the Scots: they used lawyers. Richard's predecessor, George VII (even less lucky than Parliament), signed away the Union of Crowns and was promptly assassinated by an enraged imperialist.

Now Wales was threatening to exit what was left of the United Kingdom, though its separationists were presently quarreling too violently among themselves to be able to draft a resolution to that effect.

London was once again a chilly place where people stood in queues for food, where children played in bombed-out ruins, where amputees hauled themselves along begging for change, where shopwindows were boarded up. Things would improve, eventually. They generally did.

Lewis pulled his coat tight about himself and sprinted up the dark narrow stair to his garret bed-sitter. Safely locked in, he took off his coat long enough to unpack the groceries he'd been carrying strapped to his body, chlorilar pouches worn like a diver's weight belt: beans, consommé, mixed pickle, tomatoes, pilchards, raspberry jam, green peas. Not his favorites, but what he'd been able to get, and a nicely balanced haul. He lined them up on his shelf, rejoicing in a sense of abundance.

No evidence of mice this afternoon. Perhaps his latest strategy had worked. He made himself a jam sandwich, whistling, and wandered over to his communication terminal.

He had no fear the power wouldn't come on. In these days of cold fusion, even England had dependable electricity. Not only that, the streets were kept tidy as people scavenged for trash to sell to the reactor stations. Taking a bite from his bread and jam, Lewis sat down and logged on.

On the little table at his elbow, Edward Alton Bell-Fairfax stared out at the world. Lewis had himself purchased the daguerreotype, and now it was one of several framed images Lewis owned and represented to his occasional mortal guests as long-departed family members. Usually, after identifying various nonexistent grandfathers and great-aunts, he'd tap Edward's daguerreotype fondly and tell some story about a great-great-great-uncle who'd been a disgrace to the British Navy. His guests were invariably amused, and this kind of faked incidental detail never hurt when one was passing oneself off as a mortal.

Lewis had been working sporadically on what he had come to think of, ever since that long-ago weekend in Yorkshire, as the Edward Mystery. He hadn't heard from Joseph in decades. For all he knew, Joseph had been arrested, and in any case Lewis didn't want to think about underground bunkers and what was inside them. He had refused to admit that he was powerless to help Mendoza. He had stubbornly clung to the notion that following the long-cold trail of this mortal man might turn up some helpful detail, some useful clue.

Besides, Lewis found he had become unaccountably fascinated by Edward Alton Bell-Fairfax himself, who in some way was also the reincarnation of Nicholas Harpole. Lewis was beginning to understand how Mendoza could have loved these mortals to such a degree that she never stopped mourning one and threw away her career for the other.

Taking another bite from his bread and jam, Lewis clicked in. A particular combination of keystrokes encrypted all he saw and everything he was to upload that afternoon. Anyone monitoring his automatic transmission to the Company would read it as a long series of entries on the literature of the Socialist movement in Britain, guaranteed to send them channel-surfing on to monitor some other operative's more interesting datafeed.

He opened the file headed EASILY AND BEST FORGOTTEN. There before him were the three letters in facsimile. The originals had long since passed into the possession of a museum in Southhampton, where they no doubt lay forgotten in some cabinet. It didn't matter. Lewis knew them by heart now.

16th May 1843

My dear Richardson,

Here he is in all the full glory of his dress uniform—you'd scarcely know him, would you? Pray accept this remembrance from The Damned Boy as a token of his sincerest regard.

I fear all your assertions in respect to Navy life and morals prove more true than I can conveniently relate, and I would not grieve you in any case with a recitation of my adventures. Suffice it to say that I cannot thank you enough for that advice on the removal of certain stains from one's dress tunic, to say nothing of where to find the best purveyors of French letters.

You may hear something of the *Osiris* and her crew soon. I fervently hope so. Ten weeks of whist parties with the best small gentry of Southhampton—elderly daughters and solicitous mammas—I leave it to your imagination! I would welcome a howling Buonapartist, pistol in either paw. Especially at one of these whist parties.
I remain
Edward

10th February 1847
My dear Richardson,

You will undoubtedly have been informed by now. I maintain, and will maintain, that I did no wrong. I was derelict in no duty, disobeyed no order, indulged in no cowardice, conspired in no mutiny. I did strike a superior, if a vicious and stupid monkey in a uniform may be dignified with that title.

I am fully aware that my case is lost before it has even begun. Neither my conduct in the late engagements with the blackbirders nor the testimony of the common sailors whose capricious murder I prevented will weigh in my defence, given the birth and breeding of Captain Southbey.

Indeed, my only regret is that I did not kill the man outright, since his continued career ensures a drain on Her Majesty's purse and certain danger to any men so unfortunate as to come under his command. There are certain offences to which I intend to testify, knowing full well they will not serve to acquit me but which must be shouted aloud. 'Tell truth and shame the devil,' says the poet, and so I must. He, at least, will suffer the indignity of hearing his particular monstrousness named before his peers. I WILL NOT BE SILENCED.

You cannot receive this news with any light heart, I know.
Moreover, it has been forcibly given to me to understand that
He of Whom We Must Not Speak has been seriously displeased
by the news of my impending trial. How little I esteem his
opinion you may well imagine, but the prospect of grieving
your good heart is intolerable to me. You MUST understand
that I have done nothing of which you would be ashamed, nor
ever shall.
I remain
Edward

23rd September 1852
My dear old Richardson,

It grieves me more than I can express that I am unable to
visit you at this time. None but you taught me the meaning of
Duty, and mine requires my continued efforts here for the
present, as I am certain you will understand, old soldier that
you are. There will not pass one hour of the day when you are
not continually in my thoughts.

You must get well, old man, you must obey Dr. Malcolm
in every particular and avoid all care! I cannot imagine how
No. 10 could continue without your 'mailed and terrible fist'
to keep them all in line, and moreover, to whom shall I write if
you leave me quite alone in this world?

For though One had the natural title and refused it, and
Another assumed the title but bore it *in absentia,* God knows
only you have ever done the office of a true Father to
your Damned Boy
Edward

Lewis sighed, as he usually did on reading the last paragraph.
There wasn't a lot of material to run with, but over the years,
through patient hours of cross-referencing and through the meticu-
lous search of ancient archives, he had been able to piece together the
following story.

On approximately August 1, 1825, a boy—almost certainly illegitimate—was born in a small country house near Shipbourne, owned by one Mrs. Moreston, who kept the establishment to accommodate well-born young ladies who needed a nine-month country retreat. One week later he was baptized Edward Alton Fairfax in St. Nicholas's Church in Sevenoaks.

At this point in time, the property at No. 10 Albany Crescent in London was owned by one Septimus Bell, who resided there, childless, with his wife, Dorothea, and servants, chief of whom was the butler, Robert Richardson, a former sergeant in the 32nd Regiment of Foot. Mr. Bell's occupation was listed as Gentleman.

Lewis had never been able to determine just how the infant wound up in the Bell household, but in 1836 young Edward Alton Bell-Fairfax was enrolled in Overton School, and his guardian's address was given as No. 10, et cetera. On discovering this, Lewis searched out Mr. Septimus Bell's bank records, and found evidence of quarterly deposits of large sums of money beginning in 1825, though so far he had been unable to trace the source. The deposits continued even after Mr. and Mrs. Bell were lost in a shipwreck off the coast of Italy during a grand tour, late in young Edward's first term at Overton.

Edward's progress in school was exceptional, particularly in maths, at which he excelled, though there were disciplinary actions on two occasions for fighting. Scholastic brilliance notwithstanding, at the age of fourteen he was pulled from school and entered the Royal Navy as a midshipman. Admiralty records revealed that young Edward progressed with remarkable speed to the rank of lieutenant, and within five years was given command of a schooner and sent to the coast of Africa to patrol against the slave trade.

This was not the reward it might appear. It was dirty work and dangerous, given to young officers in no position to protest being sent in humble little boats to chase after slave ships. It appeared, however, that Edward turned the slight to his advantage. Mangrove swamps, poisoned spears, fever, alcohol, shipwreck: none of them managed to take him out. He distinguished himself by conducting a ferocious campaign against the slave traders, proving so effective a fighter that he was promptly pulled from the job, made a commander, and reassigned to a man-of-war doing nothing in particular off the coast of France.

And this appeared to be his downfall; he "violently quarreled" with a Captain Southbey over the matter of a flogging ordered for an ordinary seaman "in excess of a hundred strokes." However violent the quarrel may have been, Edward must have received some help from the unknown benefactor he so disdained; for the threatened court-martial never materialized. He was instead allowed to retire, retaining his rank of commander and on half pay. Captain Southbey, on the other hand, was murdered by his own crew the following year.

That was all the Admiralty records had to say on the subject of Edward Alton Bell-Fairfax, and for many years Lewis was unable to trace him any further.

But Lewis was patient as only an immortal can be, and had decades of gray London evenings to spend combing through every records cache that had survived the intervening centuries.

No record of marriage for Edward, no record of children, no record of what duties kept him from going to see Robert Richardson in his last illness—the old soldier died on October 10, 1852, and was buried in a churchyard in London, one of the tiny crowded places Dickens described. Lewis went to the grave site, found the ancient stone with its nearly effaced inscription; but there was no corresponding stone for Edward in any cemetery that kept records.

Lewis checked the ones without records, too, spent interminable sunless weekends pacing between leaning headstones, broken angels, toppled urns, wildernesses of moss and ivy. Passersby sometimes glanced through rusted railings and were startled by the slight man in the long coat, like a ghost himself.

Year after year Lewis searched, not knowing what he wanted to find or what he sought to prove. He cautiously admitted to himself that the hunt for Edward Alton Bell-Fairfax had become more than a hobby for him. The mystery possessed all the elements of a novel: the highborn foundling infant, the brilliant boy cut off from human affection except for an old servant, the heroic career at sea and in the coastal swamps of Africa, the furious protest against injustice and evil—and then nothing but the hint of some secret duty that prevented him from coming home. How did the story end?

Or, rather, how did it end with Edward's dying in Mendoza's arms in far-off California? How had this man, who'd risked his life repeatedly to prevent slaves from being taken, wind up shot to death by agents of a nation fighting to end slavery?

Lewis invented half a hundred scenarios, none of them satisfactory. To be a Literature Specialist is not necessarily to be able to write, though Lewis longed to. The fantasy was like a fire that kept the chill out of his immortal bones: he'd gaze off between the crumbling tombs and the willows and see the couple embracing there for a moment, the bright wraiths of the stern young man and the black-eyed girl. Edward smart in the uniform he'd worn for his portrait and Mendoza happy as Lewis had never seen her, wearing a summer dress of peach silk...

The image sustained him somehow. And it kept away the quiet horrors of his own life.

The nightmares came on Lewis gradually, after the return from the Yorkshire trip, and had nothing to do with the downscaled standard of living or the bombs in the streets, or even with living alone in a garret. They had everything to do with what he had forgotten about Ireland.

Sometimes he would be fine for years on end, and then something would set the nightmares off. Once he was in the Tube when the lights failed, and that did it. Once he tuned into a BBC program on the pathetic survivors of the human cloning experiment (it had worked, but the resulting children all suffered from progeria). Once it was no more than a customer bringing in a book to sell, a late-twentieth-century facsimile of the *Book of Kells*.

The symptoms were always the same, just what mortals suffered:

shortness of breath, pounding heart, cold sweats. He'd sit up reading until he was exhausted, fearful of turning out the light. The nightmares would come eventually anyway, sometimes when he thought he was still awake.

They tended to begin with sleep paralysis. He knew he was awake, sitting up in a well-lighted room, safe and in full possession of his immortal faculties. He was completely paralyzed, however, and as soon as he acknowledged this to himself, the real horror began, a sensation of slipping downward into shadows.

After that followed chaos, darkness, and a sense of imminent and personal danger. There was a voice that spoke in Latin. A cell with a trick door. Children crowding into a tunnel. A suffocating smell. Red lightning. Sometimes the specific sequence of these events was confused, but they built, always, to the same conclusion: he would begin to go gradually blind. He'd be lying somewhere, helpless, unable to see, and he could hear his own voice saying, *My God, is this what it's like?*

Lewis never woke screaming. He'd get his sensation and his sight back a little at a time, finding himself at last perched on a chair or sprawled on the daybed in his clothes. He would be cold as ice, shivering, nauseated. Running a self-diagnostic never revealed anything wrong with him.

And then six months ago, something different happened.

The nightmare began again—this time simply an oddly familiar face glimpsed in the street had done it. He fell into dreams and was shuddering in the dark, fighting back the panic, knowing he was too damaged to stop them, knowing he might die, really die, the way mortals died—

Someone took hold of his hand.

Complete sensory confusion, sight flowing up his arm from his hand, caught hard in the grip of the other hand. It was pulling him out of the darkness. The sight reached his eyes, and he found himself staring into Edward Alton Bell-Fairfax's stern young face.

Edward kept pulling, and the darkness snarled and flowed away from Lewis like a fast tide receding. He found himself standing on a London street in his modern clothes, as the shuttle traffic roared past, as cripples pulled themselves along and shopkeepers unlocked their iron gates for the morning's commerce. But Edward was still standing there before him, in his nineteenth-century naval officer's uniform, frowning down at Lewis from his great height.

Pale blue eyes, just as Lewis had always thought, and high color in his face, yes, just as Mendoza had described it. Mendoza! If he could only tell Edward, if he could warn him, as he hadn't been able to warn Mendoza—

"I will not be silenced," Edward said grimly, looking him in the eye. Having said that, he straightened, kept going up and up, lengthening, and he seemed to have stepped back into the facade of a building too. No, he had *become* part of the facade behind him. For a second Lewis could still make out his face, rigid in stone; then the features faded, and Lewis was staring up at a great Ionic column, one of three holding up the pediment of an enormous neoclassical public building.

He knew the building, it dated from the early twenty-first century and was a copy of the Temple of Zeus at Lemnos. Lewis looked around in confusion, uncertain whether he had just awakened after a spectacular episode of sleepwalking. Cripples, pigeons, shopkeepers, traffic, all very real, and here was the morning sunlight just creeping over to illuminate the inscription in sedate Roman capitals on the front of the building:

NEW SYON HOUSE
2355 BOND STREET

"Surely, that's wrong, though," he found himself saying to his reading lamp. He sat up. He was in his room in the gray morning light.

And in fact the address proved to be wrong, when he showered, shaved, and went running out into the real morning of London to see; though only in respect to being at No. 205 Bond Street. Every other detail was just as he had seen it in his nightmare. Was that even a suggestion of an aloof face, in the design of the capital on the middle column?

Lewis murmured a prayer of thanks to Carl Jung. He even did a little skipping dance in his honor as he hurried home, for this was the intuitive leap he had needed to make.

New Syon House was some sort of government office. You could go in and fill out forms on the ground floor, and the clerk would forward them somewhere for you. Lewis knew, as any other operative of Dr. Zeus knew, that the place was actually a dump for outworn state secrets. It was an archive of documents that had never been declassified but that were now so old, there was nobody left alive who even knew why they had been secrets in the first place or (in the case of some encoded material to which the keys had been lost) what they even were about.

When the time came to transform moldy sheepskin into magnetic ink, somebody dutifully encrypted everything and shredded the originals. There the secrets hid, to this day, in databanks never accessed from one year's end to the next, masses of arcane gibberish.

For an immortal with empty nights to fill after eight hours a day in a grubby little bookshop, and no transfer to a better posting in sight, New Syon House was like one of those old Christmas calendars with twenty-five little windows: a new one to be opened every day, with no idea of what treat might be behind it, while one grew closer and closer to the window with the ultimate treat.

It took Lewis three months to scan the inventory. It took another month to sort out encryptions dating from the nineteenth century. Two weeks sufficed to break the old-fashioned code; all he had to do then was search for any occurrences of the name Edward Alton Bell-Fairfax.

The first reference was a list of members of a Redking's Club for the years 1849 to 1869. The list was profoundly interesting. For a smallish club, Redking's appeared to have had a disproportionate number of members whose names had made it into history books. There were politicians, there were men of science, there was a writer or two—and a virtual nobody, a retired naval officer on half pay. Lewis marveled. What was Edward doing in company like this? And why was this information classified?

Lewis found another peculiarity on the members list: the name of one William Fitzwalter Nennys. Lewis remembered this man perfectly, for the simple reason that he was in reality Nennius, an immortal with whom Lewis had worked briefly in the 1830s. Nennius was a Facilitator, and nothing was more likely than that he'd be strategically positioned in an exclusive club whose fellow members were in politics.

The next reference to Edward turned up when Lewis found a list of members of a Gentlemen's Speculative Society. Edward Alton Bell-Fairfax was one of their number. So were most of the other members of Redking's Club, including William Fitzwalter Nennys.

Lewis frowned as he read. Wasn't there something disreputable about the Gentlemen's Speculative Society? A moment's hasty access of *Smith's History of Esoteric Cults*, volumes 1 through 10, brought it back to him:

In the year 1885 a mortal named David Addison Ramsay held several public lectures, claiming to be a representative of a hitherto secret brotherhood that presently went by the name of the Gentlemen's Speculative Society. He was unwise enough to mention several prominent statesmen and academics who he claimed were fellow members.

He said further that their purpose was to advance humanity to a state of perfection through scientific means. This, he claimed, was where similarly well-intentioned secret societies had missed the mark: by clinging to outworn magical and religious rituals.

Ramsay then displayed what he claimed were inventions that had been suppressed out of religious superstition and ignorance. He apparently got quite a reaction out of his audience with his "thermo-luminous globe," "speaking automaton," "true philosopher's stone," and several other remarkable objects. These inventions, he claimed, were not new; the Gentlemen's Speculative Society had rescued and collected them from laboratories of persecuted martyrs to the cause of Science. Da Vinci had contributed several, as had Dr. John Dee, who had also been a member of the Society, though in a former time when it bore another name.

Ramsay concluded by saying that the purpose of this demonstration was not merely to enlighten or entertain, but to enlist uninitiated Britons in the great cause for which he and his fellow Gentlemen labored. He admitted that his brother members did not entirely agree with him that the need for secrecy was past, but he believed that in this age of steam propulsion and industrial capitalism, mankind was ready to understand what science might achieve, if unfettered. He intimated that all the fantastic possibilities of legend were not beyond man's grasp, even, indeed most particularly, immortality itself.

All that was wanting was *capital*. He stood ready to accept the donations that must flow in from the noble Britons in his audience, who surely understood that every rational man must labor in the cause of the perfection and advancement of humanity.

Ramsay wasn't quite hooted off the stage, but the papers very nearly murdered him. His inventions were denounced as nothing more than brilliant stage effects. Worse, the powerful individuals he named all stated flatly that they never heard of him, or of the Gentlemen's Speculative Society to which they supposedly belonged. He was a common charlatan, they said, a humbug, an utter sham.

Ramsay hotly denied these charges and promised to provide proof. He didn't; he simply disappeared, along with his inventions.

This was the sort of thing that professed skeptics liked to giggle over. Even Lewis, himself an immortal being created by the efforts of a cabal of scientists and investors, smiled as he read the account. His smile faded as he considered the fact that he'd just found evidence— in classified documents, no less—that there *had* been a Gentlemen's Speculative Society, at least as early as 1849, and that the august persons who denied knowing David Addison Ramsay *had* been members. And so had Edward Alton Bell-Fairfax.

And so had William Fitzwalter Nennys, who, like Lewis, was an immortal being created by the efforts of a cabal of scientists and investors...

What on earth had Nennius been doing? What had *Edward* been doing?

Lewis followed up his next hunch: searching for other references to the Gentlemen's Speculative Society in the classified records. He was mildly astonished at what he found.

It was the Gentlemen's Speculative Society since 1755; prior to that its members called themselves the Fellowship of the Green Lion, during which time Sir Isaac Newton was one of their number.

The Fellowship of the Green Lion was reliably recorded as having existed as far back as 1660. It seemed to have sprung from a group calling itself the House of Solomon, almost certainly led by Sir Francis Bacon.

That particular fraternity of scholars previously met under the name of the Servants of the Temple of Albion, an organization that could be traced back through the era of Elizabeth I—persons as disparate as Dr. Dee and Sir Francis Drake were members—to the year 1250, when Roger Bacon was apparently its guiding light. There were intimations that Bacon inherited a tradition that began at an even earlier date.

All of this in a file the British government had chosen to keep secret, had chosen to keep *so* secret, it went to the trouble of encrypting it and burying it far from the light of day in New Syon House.

It was at about this time that Lewis began to feel a creeping sensation of knowing too much for comfort.

So he turned his attention to the biographical data on William Fitzwalter Nennys.

Born 1803—ha ha. Lewis knew for a fact that Nennius had come over in a galley at the order of the emperor Claudius; this he learned in the course of a pleasant evening in a coffeehouse back in

1836, during a chat with Nennius about old times. Lewis's current identification disc gave his own date of birth as the year 2116, when 103 A.D. was nearer the mark. Well, and what had Nennius done with that lifetime?

Here were the names of parents he never had, followed by a list of schools he never attended; and here the statement that in 1832 he became headmaster of Overton School...

Edward's school. He'd been Edward's headmaster.

Lewis's gasp in his chilly room puffed out like smoke. Distractedly he got up and turned on the climate-control unit, standing in front of its heating vent while he collected his memories and spread them out to try to make sense of them.

Nennius *had* been a headmaster, yes, that was what the meeting at the coffeehouse was all about—Nennius brought a sheaf of inky student papers to deliver to Lewis for the Company archives. Lewis didn't ask why, Lewis didn't even read them, just passed them on to the Company courier who came for them the following week. Dr. Zeus was always making off with ephemera like that. Lewis was more interested in the prospect of pumping Nennius for details about the old empire. They sat up late, getting mildly buzzed on drinking chocolate and laughing about how it was impossible to find a decently heated room in Britain since the legions pulled out...

Closing his eyes, Lewis dived back through his visual record. There! There were the papers, he was laughing with Nennius as he opened the leather case, and Nennius was saying:

"—lad may be somebody someday, but you know how it is with the archivists, they ask for the damnedest trivia—"

Freeze frame. Part of the top page was visible. What did it say? Enlarge and enhance. There were the slightly uneven letters of a boy not yet perfect in his copperplate hand: *Dulce et decorus pro patria mori, which is very true I think if you have got no other way of helping anybody or, for example, stopping the Hindoos from doing things such as burning up their widows. I would like to—*

Reeling slightly, Lewis put a hand to the wall. Compare frame with EASILY AND BEST FORGOTTEN file documents A, B, and C. Points of similarity? Singularity? Statistical likelihood of the same hand?

Ninety-five percent.

And though the feeling of impending danger was very, very strong just then, Lewis leaped out into the middle of his room and executed a few shuffling tap steps, finishing on one knee with both arms flung out in triumph.

Nennius was young Edward's headmaster. Nennius belonged to the Gentlemen's Speculative Society and Redking's Club at the same time his former pupil was a member of them. Coincidence? Or had he sponsored Edward's admission into those august bodies? Given Edward's obscure birth and blighted naval career, it seemed likely he had. Why? Unless of course Edward was admitted at the urging of the unknown benefactor who prevented his court-martial and paid for his upbringing. But, then, what did Nennius have to do—?

Lewis was barely able to sleep that night, but he had no nightmares. Not that night, not any night since the plot began to thicken. And this was why he whistled, today, tapping away at the keyboard in his room.

He couldn't remember when he'd been happier, even as his awareness of risk grew. He very nearly got in touch with Nennius (a scan of Company records showed him that Nennius was currently stationed in the Breton Republic), but common sense prevailed. He was contenting himself now with following up Nennius's subsequent career.

It appeared that his fellow immortal had worked a very long shift indeed as William Fitzwalter Nennys, finally pretending to die in 1886. All the appliance aging makeup must have been hideously uncomfortable.

Ah, but not so uncomfortable he hadn't been able to—what was this? To attend a last meeting of the Gentlemen's Speculative Society. Yes, and vote with the other members, old and new—and, my, what interesting new members had joined since 1849, George Bernard Shaw and young Herbert George Wells, for example—to *change the name of the Gentlemen due to the recent scandal.* What did they decide to call themselves this time?

Lewis read on eagerly and then stopped.

He got up, made himself a cup of tea, went to the window, and stared down into the street for a while. When he finished the tea, he went to his tiny sink and rinsed out the cup, setting it carefully in the drainer. At last he walked back to his workstation, pulled out his chair, sat down, and looked again at the screen.

Yes, it really did say that the new name they chose was the Kronos Diversified Stock Company.

The reason Lewis was having trouble believing what he saw, of course, was that Kronos Diversified was one of the names under which Dr. Zeus, Incorporated, did business throughout the centuries.

He got up once more and went to his cupboard. Taking out a bottle of gin, he poured himself a small silver cocktail and went to the window again. He half-expected to see Edward Alton Bell-Fairfax looking up at him from the pavement, as the late traffic went by.

You won't be silenced. You meant it, didn't you? thought Lewis. *Have you refused to let go, are you haunting me somehow? What does all this mean about the Company, and why have you shown me? Are you trying to tell Mendoza? Can't you find her, either?*

Fez

"IF THERE'S AN ETERNITY, boy, I wouldn't mind spending it like this," said Joseph, drifting gently into the coping at the edge of the pool.

"Contemplating the eternal stars?" Suleyman leaned back to look up at them where they glittered in the wide square of night sky, framed by the high white walls of the old garden.

"Floating in your pool with a piña colada, actually."

"Ass's milk, you infidel moron," jeered Latif. "Do you want to scandalize the servants?"

"All right, so it's coconut pineapple asses' milk with extract of Jamaican sugar cane," Joseph said. "God forbid I should upset the help, you lousy little squirt."

Latif, who had known Joseph since childhood, just sneered at him. He had long since attained his considerable adult height and had the lean and dangerous profile of a North African corsair. Suleyman laughed quietly and thumbed the control that lowered his deck chair into a reclining position so he could view the stars in greater comfort. Suleyman was very dark, with the classical features of Mali, so he didn't look like a corsair—though he had been one in his time.

"Isn't that something, about poor old Polaris?" he mused. "All these tens of centuries it's been the one thing you could depend on, in this hemisphere, anyway. Byword for constancy, and what does it go and do but slip out of place at last? What will mortals use to navigate, with the North Star gone astray?"

"Things change," said Joseph.

"So they do, little man. So they do."

A silence fell, with a shade of meaning in it that the two younger immortals missed. Donal sighed in contentment and switched off his headset, flipping up the televisor.

"That was that," he informed the others. "The Pirates took the match, six to nothing. Not one goal for the Assassins."

"The office pool is mine," said Latif.

"Yaah," Joseph said.

"Yaah yourself, you loser," Latif told him, grinning white in the darkness. He sprawled backward like a man at his ease, but there was an alertness in the lines of his body. He went on: "So, this vacation thing you're doing. You actually want to go see a *necropolis* tomorrow?"

"That's what I said, kid."

"Well, that's certainly my idea of a good time. Ride out into the foothills, where it gets hot enough to boil rice on the rocks at noon, and crawl around a bunch of mortal graves all stuccoed over to look like the biggest seagull splash in the world. What's that phrase, *whited sepulchers*? What a party guy you turned out to be."

"It's psychological," Joseph said, pushing away from the coping and rotating slowly in his pool float. "People are designed by nature to need a last resting place. The idea of one, anyway. We immortal guys never get graves. The programming we're given in school keeps the urge off for the first few millennia, but after a while you find yourself wondering what it would be like to just—lie down in a tomb and stop moving forever. So it helps, see, to go and look at the reality. Bones and dust. Makes you glad to be alive."

"Really?" Donal sounded appalled.

"No, he's giving us a lot of bullshit as usual," Latif said.

"Sounds creepy to me," Donal went on, shuddering. "I was recruited out of some kind of tunnel or catacomb place. I'd never want to visit one."

"I'll show him the necropolis," Suleyman said. "I know what he's talking about, after all. You kids go hang out at the bazaar. Milo Rousseau's added a third show at Palais Aziz, did I tell you? If you hang around the window and whine, I'll bet you can get tickets."

"What's his backup band?" Latif sat bolt upright.

"The Dead Weights."

"We're there," Latif said. He regarded Donal with curiosity. "Now, what was that about catacombs? I thought you were recruited out of San Francisco."

"Plenty of catacombs in San Francisco," Joseph said, draining his glass and setting it on the coping. "Place has everything. Of course, the catacombs are mostly in Chinatown," he added, tilting to peer at Donal. "You were an Irish immigrant kid, right?"

"As far as I know," said Donal. "I was only about three when the Company rescued me."

"So what were you doing in a catacomb?" Latif persisted.

"He may not feel like talking about it, you know," Suleyman said.

"No, it's okay. It's just—it seems so *silly*." Donal shook his head. "I was supposed to have been rescued from the 1906 earthquake, but I don't remember that at all. I remember something else entirely..."

"Which was?" Latif prompted.

"This sounds so stupid. As God is my witness, what I remember is that the Bad Toymaker carried me off, down to this place with all these dead Chinese guys. And then Uncle Jimmy—I mean Victor, that's the operative who recruited me—came and rescued me."

"Dead Chinese guys," said Joseph thoughtfully. "That would fit with your being in a catacomb. It wouldn't explain who took you there, though, or why."

"Bad *Toymaker*?" Latif looked incredulous.

"See, it's all mixed up in my mind." Donal closed his eyes in an attempt to think. "There was this show my mortal parents took me to, on that last night. I found out since it was *Babes in Toyland*, by Victor Herbert. So what I remember is mixed up with the Bad Toymaker and some bears. I thought it was a big bear at first, but it was a man. I thought he was going to break my neck. He'd hurt Uncle Jimmy already, there was blood on Uncle Jimmy's shirt." Donal's voice slowed unconsciously, took on traces of an early accent. "I was scared, but then Uncle Jimmy spit on him, and it, like, broke the spell or something. The Toymaker had to let me go. We climbed a ladder. Then I got to ride in a motor car, the little Chinese doll gave me chocolate, and we went on the ship."

"That's very interesting," said Suleyman at last.

"It sounds like some of it was just a nightmare," said Latif.

"Yeah, that's what I've always thought, too." Donal sighed. "I still see that big bear sometimes in my sleep, and the bunks down there, and the dead men. Uncle Jimmy, Victor I mean, arguing with him."

"Victor," said Suleyman. "The Facilitator Victor? Little white man with a red beard, usually plays an Englishman? Did you ever ask him about it?"

"I only met him once, since then," Donal said. "I couldn't ask, somehow. He was, I don't know, sort of stiff and formal, not at all like when he was being Uncle Jimmy. Do you know him?"

"He stops in to see Nan, when he's in this part of the world," Suleyman said. "And he is a little unapproachable, I must admit."

"The big-bear guy," asked Latif, "what did he look like?"

"*Big.* Twice as big as Uncle Jimmy. A giant, an ogre. And he smelled awful. It'd knock you down, that smell, not like dirt but like musk. He had huge teeth, a big nose."

Joseph splashed a little. "What color were his eyes?" he asked, perhaps a shade too casually.

"His eyes? I don't remember. Yes, I do. Really pale blue. Like, uh, Coke bottle glass used to be?"

"Weird," Joseph remarked.

"And you say he was arguing with Victor," said Suleyman. "Can you remember what they were arguing about?"

"It must have been a hell of a fight," said Latif. "What kind of mortal could draw blood on one of us, no matter how big he was? It's impossible."

Joseph said nothing.

Donal groped for his drink. "This is creeping me out. I don't want to think any more about this. Not to be rude—"

"No, it's all right," Suleyman assured him. "We all have our own nightmares. Let's change the subject."

"Thanks. I'm sorry, I just—"

"It's okay, kid, perfectly okay," said Joseph.

Latif looked narrow-eyed from Suleyman to Joseph. However, one of the qualities that made him an able second-in-command was his ability to sense, without being told, when to leave something alone. So he yawned, stretched, and said, "How about those Pirates? What were you thinking, Joseph? You *knew* Wilker's averages."

Joseph, about to reply colorfully, caught his breath as a woman emerged from the lamplit terrace and came down the steps into the garden.

She was tiny, like an ebony figurine, with exquisite aristocratic features. Over her nightdress she wore a blue silk robe, the same shade as the evening sky. Her bearing was upright, she walked unconcernedly with her hands in the robe pockets; but there was a certain darkness in her gaze that brought to mind storm clouds.

Instantly the mood in the garden changed. Suleyman rose to his feet.

"My apologies, Nan," he said gently. "Were we keeping you awake?"

She shook her head. "I hadn't retired, to tell you the truth. I thought I'd sit out here and watch the stars for a while." Latif was already up and opening a lawn chair for her, arranging the woven cover and pillows with the deference one shows a princess or a widow. She

stood watching in silence, unnervingly motionless. When he stepped
back with a gesture of presentation, she gave him a smile.

"Thank you, dear," she said, and sat down.

"How's the work going?" Donal asked.

"Quite nicely, thank you," Nan replied. She wasn't referring to
the mosaic she was restoring, and neither was he; but no one there
wanted to speak of what she had been doing, alone in her room at
her workstation, making endless inquiry for information she could
never seem to get, searching for a man who had disappeared.

Joseph watched with compassion as she stretched out and sighed,
turning her face to the sky, making an effort to relax the stiffness
of rage. He couldn't think of anything to say that wouldn't seem
clumsy, but he remembered that she loved the music of the twenty-
first-century composer Jacques Soulier. He began to sing, very softly,
Soulier's wordless *Sea Lullabye*. His baritone resonated off the water,
off the high walls that enclosed them. He hadn't a bad voice.

After a moment Suleyman took up the bass part, and the two
voices wove together, becoming the slow currents in the night sea.
Donal listened for the first tenor part, describing the reflection of the
evening star, and joined in on cue. Latif took the second tenor part
when its turn came, the music of the breakers on the reef, that was always played by trumpets when the piece was done symphonically.

It was late, they'd been drinking a little, felt no need to cramp
themselves to sound like mortal men. Within the house an old servant awoke and lay silent, listening in joy and terror. He had lived
long enough to know that Allah did things like this, sometimes,
beautiful and inexplicable things like sending angels to sing in a garden at night. It wouldn't do to blaspheme, though, by running to the
window to see if they were really there. The music was gift enough.

Nan looked up at the stars and wondered, for the thousandth
time, what had happened to Kalugin.

I have a question for you, little man.
Joseph looked off blandly across the floor of the desert, where

the tombs shone like impossible snow. *I'll bet it's the same question I was going to ask you.*

Suleyman shifted gears on the little electric Moke, and it charged the next hill with a whine before he replied, as they went bumping on, leaving the elegant city farther and farther behind them, *Quite probably. But I outrank you, and I brought the subject up first.*

Okay.

You listened pretty attentively when the boys were discussing Donal's memories. Why?

What, about the Toymaker? You were paying close attention yourself, I noticed. The guy just sounded like someone I used to know. Joseph looked out at the tombs again and wiped sweat from his brow. "It's hot," he said out loud. "I bet this used to take forever on a camel, huh?"

"Just about," Suleyman said. *Is Budu the name I'm groping after, by any chance?*

Joseph's eyes widened. "Say, is there any tea left in the thermos, or did you finish it off?" he said in a bright voice. *Budu, Budu. Old Hungarian name, isn't it?*

"Plenty of tea. Help yourself." *Stop this. I need to know.*

Why do you need to know? Joseph groped about and found the thermos. He gulped thirstily.

Because I've been on his trail for the last three centuries. Suleyman shifted gears again, and the Moke obeyed him, complaining.

So have I, give or take a century. I can't imagine what he'd be doing in an opium den in San Francisco right before the 1906 earthquake, but it sure sounds like him.

I see. Why are you looking for him, Joseph?

Isn't everybody?

Answer me, please.

I owe the guy. And I need help, and he's the only one I can think of to ask.

Tell me why you owe anything to a mass-murdering Neanderthal freak.

He's not a Neanderthal, you know, they were really short. All the Enforcers were hybrids.

Hybrids? What are you talking about?

There was a protracted silence, as the Moke bumped along in the ruts of the road.

Let's start over, said Suleyman. *I have been looking for an Immortal named Budu. Very large, resembling a Neanderthal in certain respects, evil incarnate and able to travel nearly anywhere in the world without the Company being able to find him. Officially AWOL since 1099 A.D.*

I see.

Now you talk.

I've been looking for a big ugly guy named Budu who has coincidentally been on the lam from the Company since 1099. The one I knew wasn't evil incarnate, though. Or a freak. He was just an Enforcer, the best and smartest of them. He never hurt anyone who was innocent. He saved my life when I was a kid. Recruited me.

Suleyman nodded, narrow-eyed with anger but controlling it well.

All right, now I understand your point of view. You should know, though, that he kills without discrimination these days, and so do his people.

His people? But—all the old Enforcers have been retired.

I'm not talking about the old Enforcers, Joseph. I'm talking about a cabal hidden within the Company, operatives he's managed to talk around to his point of view. He wants the Earth's population forcibly reduced. Kill them all, and God will know his own, wasn't that the old motto for soldiers?

Joseph did not reply, staring forward through the dust of the windscreen, clutching the thermos bottle.

Suleyman exhaled and continued. *You remember when the epidemics started up again, in the late twentieth century, even before Sattes? AIDS, all those hemorrhagic fevers like Ebola and Marburg? Do you remember how badly Africa was hit? All we were supposed to do, my people and I, was watch. Salvage certain cultural treasures the Company wanted and perhaps the occasional child for recruitment, but nothing else. Let the mortals die, it's their fate after all, history can't be changed. Do you think I could do nothing more than watch? Do you know how many millions on this continent died, while the rest of the world looked the other way? Well, I didn't look the other way, Joseph. I worked with the epidemiologists. We tracked the outbreaks to their sources. Do you know what we found?*

Joseph shifted in his seat. *I always heard it was stuff that had been around for centuries, only it'd lain dormant in the rain forests until people started cutting them down.*

No, Joseph. We traced most of them to one point of origin, a cave in Mount Elgon. One cave, Joseph. And there the epidemiologists hit a dead end, literally, couldn't figure out how the diseases had all originated in one simple little hole in the earth. They left, defeated.

But it wasn't a simple little hole in the earth, Joseph. It was the entrance to a Company supply tunnel. That was when I knew.

Joseph squeezed his eyes shut. *Jesus.*

Someone within the Company was doing it. Using Africa as a testing ground, I think.

Not Budu. He'd never have done a thing like that, never in a million years. You didn't know him. Anyway he wasn't with the Company by that time. He's been on the run since 1099, you said so yourself. Where did you get the idea it was him? How did you even find out about the old Enforcers? They were way before your time.

I was old before the first stone was set in Zimbabwe's wall, you know that. I knew there were warriors once among the immortals, used for a specific purpose and then reprogrammed. Set to constructive tasks. I'm told you'd never know, now, what they used to do, they're indistinguishable from the rest of us. Suleyman steered expertly around a dead dog.

Well, there you're wrong. Joseph ground his teeth. *They were a different model from us, Suleyman. They were braver than lions, and they loved justice. War was their element, like air for the birds. Dr.*

Zeus designed them that way. You think Budu was a freak because you never saw the others.

They sound like monsters.

Maybe they were. But they did their job, and you know how the Company thanked them once they'd done their job? Tricked them into underground bunkers one by one and took their brains offline. Budu was the last. He went rogue so it wouldn't happen to him. I can see him going after Dr. Zeus, maybe, but not doing the kind of filthy work you're talking about.

Suleyman looked at him sidelong as he drove. *I'm sorry. But I went hunting, Joseph, I set Latif and the best of my people on this. I can show you the evidence they've gathered. There is a group operating within the Company, betraying its ideals. Such as they are. The Sattes virus was their work. The Church of God-A took the blame in the history books, but Budu's cabal was guilty. It took him centuries to build it up, but he got a circle of disciples among the Preservers. I've seen their master plan. By the year 2355 there'll be so few mortals left, they can be rounded up and kept in patrolled villages. Peace at last. And any of the immortals who dispute their agenda will be taken out. How, I haven't discovered yet.*

"Boy, it's hot," said Joseph, pulling out a tissue. "I'm sweating bullets." He mopped tears from his face. *I can see him targeting the armies and the criminal population,* he admitted. *But why would he go after Third World civilians? Or homosexuals?*

Who would stand up for them? Suleyman responded grimly. *They're the easiest target. And look how well the economies of the world are doing, now that there are fewer people. Just like it was after the Black Death. Little towns abandoned and going back to nature. The grass grows greener, the trees grow taller with nobody to cut them down. The air is cleaner. But millions have been sacrificed for this.*

You have proof. Joseph sighed. It wasn't a question. Suleyman just nodded.

They drove along in silence for a while. At last Joseph blew his nose and asked, *Is it at the highest levels?*

Not really. But it goes deep.

You know—all I started out to do was find a friend of mine. A kid I recruited, once, who got into trouble.

The Botanist Mendoza?

Yeah. Christ, you wouldn't know where she is?

No. Just that she was a friend of Nan's. I take it she's become one of the disappeared, like poor old Kalugin?

Yeah.

This is why you want to see the necropolis, isn't it? You think there's a bunker underneath. You think your child might be in there.

She might be.

You think Kalugin might be in there?

Who knows? But we can't check today. You can only get into these places under cover of an electrical storm, so your datafeed to the Company gets knocked out.

Is that what you've been doing? Suleyman glanced at him, grinning. *Waiting for storms? Aie! How long has it taken you to get even this far? Pay attention, now, little man, and learn something.*

He sent the Moke charging recklessly up the nearest slope, swerving over the most rutted part of the road deliberately, at a decidedly unsafe speed. Joseph yelped and held on; but all that happened was that at the crest of the hill the Moke suddenly froze in its tracks.

"Shit." Suleyman thumped the steering wheel. "The power cell's knocked loose again. Give me a hand, here." He swung open the driver's side door and hopped out, pulling a tool kit from under the seat. Joseph got out and came around the fender uncertainly, meeting him in front of the car.

"Here," Suleyman said, thrusting the tool kit at him. "Open that and get me out a C-rod spanner."

Joseph obeyed and looked on as Suleyman lifted the hood of the car and peered in, making a disgusted sound. "Look at that. I tell that kid and I tell him, bungee cord's no good. Replace the hold-down clamp, I tell him. Does he listen? Kids!"

The power cell had indeed jumped half out of its little shaped space, and one connection had jostled loose. Suleyman tugged at his gold earring in annoyance. Then he reached out and grasped the connection with one hand, while reaching for the spanner with the other. In the second that his hand touched the spanner that Joseph still held out to him, there was a brief flash and click.

"And no more datafeed for the next six hours," Suleyman announced.

"Wow," Joseph said. "That's brilliant. I never thought a simple car power cell would have enough charge to blow out the link!"

"They don't." Suleyman tugged his earring again. "But this does."

Joseph stared openmouthed. "My God. Where did you get that?"

"Latif designed it. Clever child, wouldn't you say? We used to have a few virtual reality games, back when they first came out. Some of them had some interesting glitches."

Joseph said something profane in a long-dead language. "Do you know how many years it's taken me to make one of those? And it's twice that size!"

Suleyman just smiled and reconnected the power cell. They got back in the car and drove on.

"Now, you understand," Suleyman resumed, "that I can't trust you."

Joseph sighed.

"We've known each other a long time, and I mean it as a compliment when I say you're the most Company man I've ever seen. You're also a lying little bastard when you need to be. That's a good thing, given your line of work. Unfortunately, I think you lie to yourself, too.

"If you're working for the Company and reporting on what I'm doing—well, it isn't as though I haven't tried to tell them. I think the Company knows about Budu's group, and they're tolerating him because the Company can benefit from his work without getting its own hands dirty." Suleyman pulled up before the necropolis and switched off the engine. "However, the devil will call for payment one of these days."

They got out and trudged toward the gleaming white terraces. The heat was astonishing, making the horizon dance and waver in currents of boiling air.

"The other possibility is that you're here from Budu himself," Suleyman went on composedly. "You've made it clear you still think of him as a hero. You wouldn't feel that way if you walked with me through a children's hospital in Uganda, though, unless you've changed a lot from the days when you and I worked together. And we immortals don't change. It's one of the things that makes us immortals."

"My point exactly," said Joseph. "Budu wouldn't change either, not to the point where he'd orchestrate something like this."

"Maybe. Anyway—if you *are* here from your old Enforcer, if you're leading me into a trap, disabling me won't help you. Quite apart from the fact that little Latif would be very, very annoyed with you, and he knows where you live, by the way, I've taken a lot of pains to see that my work will go on without me."

"I work alone, myself," Joseph said. "I wish I had the kind of resources you have."

"I made some good investments when Dr. Zeus started permitting us private incomes," Suleyman conceded. "Latif, too. And it helps, of course, to have advance knowledge of the market."

"How did you manage that?" Joseph asked, as they made their way up a long mud-brick stair between walls so white, their shadows were iridescent blue, under a sky blue as blue tile. "You'd have to get a look at the Temporal Concordance to get information like that, and everybody knows we're not allowed to see that stuff."

"Nor do we," Suleyman said imperturbably. "If we could get a look at the Temporal Concordance past the present calendar date, we'd be all omnipotent as gods. Latif just analyzes the Company investments, and we go with his projections. I said he's a clever child. Strong, too. I recruited him out of a slave ship, you know. Watched him, down there in the hold, beside his dying mother. Frightened little baby, but he was angry. His anger made him strong. We're all of us angry when we come into this immortal life; keeps us motivated to fight for humanity against evil.

"The question is, how long can we fight without coming to see humanity itself as the source of evil?" Suleyman stopped on the stair, turning to Joseph. "Of course, we've been given immortal wisdom, with immortal strength, to avoid such a pitfall."

"Well, there's that old saw of Nietzsche's about becoming a dragon yourself if you fight dragons too long," Joseph said, drinking from the thermos again. "I still don't think Budu's guilty. And I haven't led you into an ambush. In fact, I'm going to show you something really useful, to somebody with the ability to use it." He climbed again, scanning as he went, until he abruptly stepped off to the left into one of the white terraces.

He paced along a short distance, Suleyman following closely, and stopped at one particular tomb midway along the line.

"Ah." Suleyman looked close. "This door is in good repair. Very unusual."

"Isn't it?" Joseph ran his hand down the frame. He found what he was searching for, what any operative with Facilitator clearance could have found, if he knew it was there. The door clicked and swung inward.

There were several dead persons in the tomb, in varying degrees of becoming dust. The front and side walls of the tomb were of mud brick; the back wall was the hillside itself, an irregular rock outcropping. Joseph pointed at it silently, and Suleyman nodded.

"Clever," he remarked. Had any one of the mortal occupants of the tomb come to life again for a moment, he would have been astounded to watch as Joseph and Suleyman walked toward the rock wall and through it, vanishing into a gloom deeper than even a corpse would be comfortable with.

But Joseph and Suleyman, able to see by infrared, clearly saw the smooth and sloping walls of the tunnel they traveled.

It was just like the tunnel in Yorkshire had been, to look at; had the same faint pleasant scent, too. Presently they emerged into another vast and vaulted room, blue-lit from the rows of regeneration tanks, each with its floating occupant.

"This is some kind of repair facility," said Suleyman, frowning.

"You'd think so, but look at these guys." Joseph went close. "See! Here's your proof. *These* were the old Enforcers."

Suleyman followed him reluctantly, staring up at the vaults. His eyes widened.

"Name of the Merciful," he said quietly.

"What else do you do with an immortal you don't want anymore? You can't kill them," said Joseph. "I guess you could blast them into space, but they might find a way back, and then—"

Suleyman looked up at a chalkboard on the wall. There, in Latin, were the words:

ABDIEL HAS DONE HIS APPOINTED WORK HERE
6 MARCH 2143–23 MARCH 2143

He looked back at Joseph's anguished face. "All right," he said. "I bear witness."

Joseph began to hurry back and forth among the vaults, looking up at the occupant of each one, and Suleyman followed him.

"You're not looking for your child," Suleyman realized. "You're looking for Budu."

Joseph nodded. "I think they must have caught him at last. I'm betting he's in one of these vaults. If I can find him, and wake him up—I pity whoever spread all those viruses from that supply tunnel." He skidded to a stop in front of a vault where a male Preserver floated. "Kalugin might be here, too. Would you recognize him if we found him?"

"I would," Suleyman replied grimly, standing beside Joseph. "I performed his marriage ceremony."

"They got *married*? He and Nan? Two immortals?"

"It happens," said Suleyman.

"Amazing." Joseph turned a corner and started working his way along a new row of vaults. "So I guess we're wondering just exactly what Donal saw in 1906? How did the Company catch up with Budu? Why did Budu grab Donal? It was right before the big earthquake. Was Budu maybe doing some recruiting?"

"Unlikely," Suleyman said. "Unless his people have a way of performing the immortality process themselves, and if they'd managed to infiltrate the Company far enough to get *that* secret, they wouldn't have needed to send their own leader into a salvage zone to steal one mortal child."

"I guess so," Joseph said. "Donal said Budu and Victor were fighting, didn't he? Victor had blood on his shirt. Can you imagine what it would be like fighting with an Enforcer? Why wasn't Victor smashed like a bug?"

Suleyman nodded in agreement, stopping in front of one vault to peer at someone he thought he recognized. After a moment he moved on. "Donal said that Victor spat on Budu. That suggests the use of some kind of toxin."

"Poison? But *no* poison works on us. And if the Company finally found one, why wouldn't they use it to kill off all these Enforcers instead of keeping them here?"

"I don't know." Suleyman looked up at an olive-skinned girl with a sweet-sad face. "Unless it only disabled the old monster."

"Here's another scenario. What if Budu did start some group to try to change Company policy? And what if his people double-crossed him, and somebody else has been running the cabal since 1906? Have your people found any trace of Budu in the last two hundred years?"

After a long moment Suleyman said, "As a matter of fact, no. Not since the end of the nineteenth century. Plenty of evidence of his group, though."

"There," Joseph said. "There's your answer."

"It's not an answer, little man. It's many, many more questions."

"You know who we have to talk to now, of course."

"Victor." Suleyman came to the last row of vaults and turned, starting back.

"And Victor's either on the side of the Company or he's one of the bad guys." Joseph strode to keep up. "If he's still Company, he may be the problem solver who finally caught up with Budu."

"A dangerous man to talk to, in either case."

"I liked Victor," said Joseph plaintively. "The guy did me a favor once, when he was stationed at New World One."

"He's always been the most pleasant and courteous of guests, when he stops in to visit Nan," Suleyman said.

"They're old friends?"

"So it seems."

"Would she talk to him? Can she find anything out for us?"

Suleyman looked down at him as they walked. "What are the chances that any of this will help her learn what happened to Kalugin?"

"I can promise to look for him," said Joseph. "I already have a shopping list of missing operatives."

"Then she'll talk to Victor."

They emerged from the tomb unseen. A plume of dust rose up behind them as they headed back for the city. Joseph sagged in his seat, watching the distant minarets against the sky.

"This is really depressing. At least I'm starting to get an idea of what will happen in 2355. There's the Company, and then there's this antihumanity cabal within the Company, and then there are people like you and me who are just trying to do their jobs. I can think of a lot of ways the Silence might fall."

"I guess we'll find out," Suleyman said.

"And the Company has it coming. Will we all wind up in those bunkers, or wearing those clock emblems? It's just the kind of thing I can see the twenty-fourth-century investors ordering. We make them nervous."

"I don't blame them for being nervous. It's sad...Now and then, to obtain something the Company wanted, I've had to impersonate supernatural creatures."

"Me too."

"I've played a djinn, once or twice. There's some interesting folklore about djinns. The story goes that Allah made men from clay, but the djinns he made from subtle fire. In his wisdom Allah gave them tremendous power, but gave mankind chains to bind that power, lest the djinns prey on them. So djinns were slaves to wise men and served their purposes. King Solomon commanded whole armies of them."

"I've heard that too."

"The story goes on to say that the djinns must continue as faithful slaves until Judgment Day. Then, when the first blast of the trumpet sounds, they all die, since they have no souls with which to enter Paradise."

"Talk about raw deals." Joseph grinned bitterly.

"Who argues with the Almighty?" Suleyman made a gesture with his hand as though flicking away a speck of dust. "No point. Maybe the djinns don't mind. Maybe they're glad to rest at last. Don't forget that Allah is all-merciful and utterly just. Unlike the mortal masters who created us."

"Now I'm *really* depressed," muttered Joseph.

The city grew nearer. After a while Joseph asked, "So. If I wanted to get a message to you without going through Company channels, how would I do that?"

Suleyman chuckled. "You do count on trust. I'll tell you, though. Look up a religious order calling themselves the Compassionates of Allah. If you're in the right city, and you leave a message, it will filter back to me."

Fez

THEY STROLLED TOGETHER through the city, the immortal gentleman and lady.

He was a dapper white man with small precise features. His eyes were green as a cat's, his hair and pointed beard red as fire. He wore a white suit of perfectly pressed, tropical-weight linen, rather retro in its cut, and a wide-brimmed hat against the sun. Formal as his appearance was, there was a sense of deliberate parody, a hint of the bizarre. Something too much like an insect's pincers in the way his oiled mustache swept up; something suggestive of a mime's exaggeration in his walk. Despite the heat, he wore white gloves.

Nan wore a peacock-blue afternoon ensemble from the premier designer house in Senegal, with matching hat and veil, like a beautifully dressed doll. Her parasol threw a shadow of deeper blue.

Slowly they made their way along the old streets, in and out of the islands of shadow from the great palm trees, through arcaded quarters plastered and painted in all shades of white and blue. They spoke quietly together. That either of them could hear what the other said was remarkable, given the small mortal child who danced along behind them, following closely as though drawn on a string. He carried on his shoulder a SoundBox 3000 that screamed out the latest album by Little Fairuza: ten songs of love and longing in the teen world of Islam.

Every now and then a passerby frowned severely at the child. It wasn't so much that the music's content was objectionable—when has any culture approved of love and longing for the under-sixteen set?—but for such a big SoundBox the speakers were execrable, buzzing and roaring with distortion. The child danced along, oblivious.

The white man cast a dubious look over one shoulder as they walked slowly down Rue Meridien. "You're quite sure this is necessary?"

"Yes. The generator renders our conversation unintelligible."

Victor nodded, stroking his beard. "Well. Lunch alfresco? I seem to remember a place in the next street over that does a splendid b'stila."

"I'd like that." Nan took his arm, and they bore right through a winding maze of connected courtyards, emerging at last in a dim garden where a central fountain played. There a waiter served them from a cart, presenting them with two neat chlorilar plates of b'stila and uttering brief harsh words to the child, who hopped over the garden wall, turned up the volume, and busied himself with an exhibition of ape dancing for the edification of onlookers.

Nan and Victor set their plates on the wall and nibbled away tidily at their crispy pastries. Victor made sounds of dignified pleasure, lifting a forkful of savory filling to admire it.

"Of all the things one never thought one would miss," he said, "I must say *chicken* is the most unlikely. Do you know it's impossible to get over there at all, now?"

"Really?"

"Yes. Thanks to the Beast Liberation Party, chickens are no longer being bred. They're very nearly extinct in England."

"Extinct?" Nan looked astonished.

"Poor creatures were apparently too stupid to make use of the gift of civil liberty," Victor said, carefully brushing confectioner's sugar from his beard. "Wandering onto motorways or into the path of packs of feral dogs, who have made much better use of their civil liberty."

Nan shook her head. "Why do all these attempts to stop cruelty result in greater cruelty?" she said.

"Cruelty is a natural element in the world, like sand," Victor said, smiling thinly. "Mortals may shovel it out of one place, but it merely accumulates in a pile somewhere else. Clear your house and bury your neighbor's. Yet the futile efforts persist."

"As we do," she said.

His smile faded, and he looked down at his plate again. "Have you had any success?"

"I haven't found him, no. Though I wouldn't say my efforts have met with complete failure."

"May I hear what you've learned?" Victor asked, taking her empty plate on his and dropping them, with the forks, down the nearest fusion hopper. He then pulled off his soiled gloves and tucked them away in one pocket. From another pocket he produced a fresh pair and pulled them on. Nan waited patiently, setting her parasol on her shoulder again.

He offered her his arm, and they strolled from the garden. The mortal child took up his SoundBox and moved after them.

As they paced across the courtyard outside the university, Nan said, "I was able to break into his personnel file, but there isn't much after 2083. Kalugin was at Kamchatka, he finished whatever he was doing there, he returned to Polar Base Two. He requested recreational leave, and then he was transferred to a location designated only by a number. After that his record simply stops."

"Perhaps he's still on duty at that site?" Victor suggested. "Involved in something classified."

"He'd have sent me word, in all these years," said Nan quietly. "You know that."

Victor reflected that she was right, that violating a mandatory communications lockdown to talk to his wife was exactly the sort of thing Kalugin would have done. He didn't say this, however. He simply watched Nan from under the brim of his hat and wondered, for the thousandth time, what his life might have been like if Nan had not loved Vasilii Vasilievitch Kalugin.

"So he would have," he said. "You've found nothing further, then?"

"I didn't say that." Nan glanced over her shoulder, and the mortal child walked nearer. She spoke in a measured, dispassionate way, as though she were discussing a subject of only mildly mutual interest. "It occurred to me to study the phenomenon of disappearance itself. Does it happen often? To whom, and why?"

"Sensible way to approach the problem," Victor said.

"I accessed Company personnel files, traced them, cross-referenced them. Never mind how I obtained the codes. I learned that disappearance is not recent, not the result of our masters' paranoia as we approach their time period.

"It has always happened. There are any number of files that simply stop, Victor. After a certain date they contain no entries. Sometimes it happens following injury."

Victor nodded. "Pretty damned infrequently, I'd think."

"More often than you'd think. An operative will be sent to a base for repair—and never released. Sometimes, it follows an arrest. An operative is sent to the nearest base for disciplinary action and counseling. After that, the operative is reassigned, but to a numbered location that cannot be traced in the Company files, regardless of what search parameters are used."

"I see." Victor smoothed his mustache uneasily.

Nan's voice sharpened as she went on: "Then there are operatives who disappear simply because they were associated with operatives who also disappeared." She let go of his arm and turned to face him abruptly. "They go to numbered sites too, Victor. Why? What did they witness? Do you know?"

Victor caught his breath at her fury, at her perfect lips drawn back from her white teeth. He raised his hands in a palms-up shrug, aware that the gloves made the gesture outrageously theatrical.

"I'm only a Facilitator, Nan. But we're both old enough to know the Company has its ugly little secrets. Dr. Zeus may have found it convenient to lose some of us."

"How can it just *lose* us?" Nan demanded. "I remember being told that I might sink under the polar ice, or be buried in an ocean of sand, and the Company would still be able to rescue me."

Victor took her arm again. She let him. "If you never incur the wrath of all-seeing Zeus, you'll be rescued. But certain persons... certain persons, madame, may have been careless."

She looked at him without speaking, and for a moment he thought she was going to strike him. His pulse quickened, but she turned away. The little mortal behind them looked from one to the other and frowned.

"Forgive me," said Victor.

Nan shook her head. "You were only telling the truth."

"Not always a prudent thing to do."

"And we mustn't be imprudent, must we?" Her voice shook slightly. "It's a mortal weakness."

At the word *weakness* Victor thought of Kalugin. Nan, gazing out across Rue Atlas, was thinking of something else...

"No, that would be weak. I wouldn't ever fall in love with any-body," eight-year-old Mendoza had announced, chinning herself on the bar. She pulled herself along and dropped into the swing next to Nan's. "Look at the stupid things mortals do when they're in love." She rolled her eyes to heaven and clasped her hands. "Ooh, darling, I can't live without you! I burn for your kiss! I die!" She threw herself backward recklessly, almost falling out of the swing. Catching herself at the last moment, she added, "Would you ever want your life to de-pend on somebody else's?"

"If I was really in love with somebody, it would be worth it," Nan had insisted. "People need other people. I bet you start singing a different tune when we hit puberty."

"Yuck! I bet I won't," Mendoza said, swinging faster now, punctuating each rise with "Never, never, *never*. Love! Who needs that kind of grief? Why take the risk?"

So saying, she had launched herself from the swing at the top of the next arc, hurtling into open air with outstretched arms.

Why take the risk? thought Nan bitterly. She turned now to regard Victor, standing beside her with eyes downcast, lost in equally bitter memories.

"Will you do something for me, Victor dear?"

He looked up, startled, and his gloved hands flew to his heart. "Anything, madame! What may I do?"

"Do you know the Facilitator Joseph?"

She watched as his face changed, became cautious and closed. The mortal child watched too, and decided it was time to set down the SoundBox. He stepped between them, shaking a tiny fist, and angrily told the white man he'd better not insult the *reine noir*.

The SoundBox wailed on:

How can I tell my mother of our love?
How can we hide from my father and my brothers?
The world has a thousand eyes to spy on us!
Oh, why did the Almighty make me a teenager in love?

Mexico

On his lunch hour, Joseph strolled between the street vendors' carts of Little Kobe, looking up between the carved and gilded beams where the fish banners flew. It was a tourist trap, but a great place to get a fast bowl of rice. There was the beef bowl home-style, gray ribbons of beef on brown rice with julienned carrots, or the beef bowl Mazatlán-style, brown shreds of beef on orange rice with cubed carrots. The taste depended on what sauce you poured over it.

His present posting was unobjectionable. He was a departmental supervisor in a civic office that granted permits to archaeologists, and all the Company needed him to do was ensure that certain permit requests were granted and others refused. He was allowed to keep the weekly salary he earned (another benefit of gradual retirement), which enabled him to live in a very nice little box in a high-rise not two blocks from his office. Sticking up twenty stories, the building looked like a soda straw by comparison with the surrounding adobes. The Japanese developers couldn't seem to break themselves of the habit of conserving space, even in a country of sprawling deserts. The view from his one tiny window was fabulous, though.

Joseph finished his rice and dropped the paper bowl into a conveniently placed fusion hopper, where it vanished with a whoosh. Consulting an internal chronometer, he decided he had time to check his mail before going back for the afternoon shift. He wandered up to the nearest public terminal and stood in line, waiting patiently for his turn. Then he stepped up to the keyboard and tapped in his communication code.

Yes, he had mail. Water bill, a public service announcement about Park Beautification Week, and a letter from Morocco. Well, well.

It was encrypted, like most personal correspondence. He shunted it into his tertiary consciousness undecrypted, paid his water bill, and stepped away, relinquishing the terminal to a harried-looking little abuela with a string bag full of groceries. Hands in his coat pockets, he wandered back to his office.

At his desk he was able to decrypt the message as he busied himself with inputting a monthly report. The letter was brief:

Victor would prefer to speak with you privately. He feels that Regent's Park in London is a suitable location. His communication code is VdV@24Q83/09.
Very best wishes,
Nan D'Araignée

Joseph finished his report and leaned back from his keyboard, rubbing his neck. He closed his eyes and concentrated on draining the blood from his face, giving himself an unsightly pallor. A little careful work turned the skin under his eyes dark. He checked his reflection in a pocket mirror and hastily revised a little; he wanted to look sick, not dead. Then he got up and tottered into the manager's department to explain that he'd apparently eaten a bad tuna roll and needed to go home early.

His color returned to normal as he hurried down the street to his building. In his room he paused only long enough to pack an overnight bag. Back out on Calle Nakamura, he found an unoccupied public terminal. There he purchased a ticket to London for a tenth of what he'd spent the last time he went there, and sent a message to a certain bookstore in Gower Street.

Stepping away from the terminal to let two small members of a soccer team log on, Joseph spotted an electric tram trundling toward its stop. He sprinted to catch the tram, and rode standing as it took him out to the airport. He made his suborbital with ten minutes to spare, settling back in his seat as the flight attendant offered him a chlorilar pouch of green tea.

London

FORTY-FIVE MINUTES later Joseph stepped through the exit at London City Airport, having satisfied the customs officials that he was not a URL terrorist with a concealed explosive device. He boarded the Tube and exited at Gower Street, after shaking off the attentions of three desperates who wanted his overnight bag.

"What the hell have things come to in this country when a man has to fight for three pair of cotton socks and a shaving kit?" he growled as he strode into the small dark shop, redolent of moldy paper, where Lewis sat behind a counter.

"Oh, I'll bet there are pajamas in there, too," Lewis said. "You have no idea what flannel pajamas go for over here."

"So, hi." Joseph set down his bag. "Long time no see. I'm in town on business, and I thought I'd bunk at your place, okay?" *And I can bring you up to speed on what I've found out lately.*

"I'd love the company, though I'm afraid this isn't nearly as nice as where I was last time," Lewis said brightly. *I have rather a lot to tell you, too.*

"Hey, how bad can it be?" Joseph said, waving his hand dismissively.

"A rathole," he remarked fifteen minutes later, in Lewis's garret. "But *spacious.*"

"Artistic and airy, too," suggested Lewis. "All I need are a few half-finished canvases and a bong."

"This is the kind of place the Company puts you up in nowadays?" Joseph set down his bag, looking worried.

"I've lived in worse," Lewis said, wrestling a bulky object out of a cupboard. He set it on the floor, yanked a lever, and staggered back as an air mattress self-inflated with a roar. "There, you see? I can even accommodate a guest. And we've plenty of gin. Let the good times roll."

No security techs snooping around? No fallout from that trip to Yorkshire? Joseph asked, poking doubtfully at the air mattress with his foot. It gulped in air in a last hissing spasm, like a dragon with gas, and lay quiet.

Techs? No, nothing like that. A few bad dreams now and then. Lewis reached deeper into the cupboard and pulled out a sleeping bag, which he unrolled on the mattress with a flourish. It lay there sullenly exuding a smell of British army surplus shop.

This was how it began sometimes, Joseph thought uneasily, postings that got worse and worse, jobs that got more and more pointless. Never any official acknowledgment of Dr. Zeus's displeasure, but over the great span of years the Company had to play with you, an ever-increasing number of opportunities to hang yourself, and lots of rope.

"The worst time was during the Blitz," Lewis mused. He folded back the slatted screen that closed off his bathroom, displaying the dingy porcelain delights beyond. "Those poor mortals. At least the bombs don't generally fall from the sky anymore. And look, all the hot water your heart desires, and no shillings needed. It's a vast improvement on the old days, let me tell you."

"Gin, huh?" Joseph rubbed his hands together. "Are the bootleggers any good?"

"Oh, the best," Lewis assured him. "It's all brought across the border from Scotland. Though if you'd like a cider or beer, they're still legal. There's a sandwich shop on the corner with a nice selection. I can't afford to eat there myself, but—"

"My treat," said Joseph, suppressing an urge to wring his hands. "Come on, let's go down there."

The place was small, dark, and overheated, but Lewis seemed to revel in the atmosphere.

"Gosh, this is like the old days," he said happily. In the dim light his face looked gaunt. Joseph staved off feelings of guilt by remembering that Lewis looked like a tragic poet at the best of times. He ordered most of the menu.

"You gentlemen aren't driving or operating machinery after this, I hope," said the barmaid sternly, bringing their beers.

"No fear!" Lewis toasted her, grinning. She seemed about to respond with a reluctant pleasantry when she gasped and dived for the floor, just as the sound of some heavy vehicle roaring by outside filled the room.

"Down!" Lewis yelled, and Joseph needed no urging. He found himself crouching in the darkness under the table as shots chattered in the street. There were a few screams and a lot of curses. He heard the distinctive ping and rattle of a bullet coming through a windowpane.

"Don't worry," Lewis said, sipping his beer, which he had brought under the table with him. "It's all safety glass in these places."

"Great," Joseph muttered. Three more shots followed in quick succession and broke another window, the lamp over the bar, and the holo-pinball machine in the corner. The machine didn't die quietly; it began to short out in great gouts of sparks and flame, to say nothing of low-level microwaves. The barmaid shrieked and scrambled on her hands and knees for a fire extinguisher. Joseph, who knew an opportunity when he saw one, reached into his coat pocket and switched on a tidy little device Suleyman had given him. He felt a click and a slight chill. So did Lewis, who lowered his beer and looked questioningly at Joseph.

The vehicle roared on, and now one could hear sirens screaming in pursuit. The barmaid got up and doused the fire. Grumbling, she went behind the bar for a potholder, with which she unplugged the defunct machine.

"I *knew* this bloody thing wasn't safe," she said. "Edwin! Get the tape, please."

A slender youth emerged from the kitchen and proceeded to tape brown paper over the broken windows. This seemed to be the signal for the other diners to emerge from under their tables. Within five minutes the glass had been swept up, candles had been lit at the bar, and conversation resumed as though nothing out of the ordinary had happened. Actually, nothing out of the ordinary *had* happened, except to the two immortals at the table near the door.

"I gather you've finally perfected that little device you were working on?" Lewis said, taking another sip of beer.

"Sort of," Joseph replied. "We can talk for about six hours."

"Good," Lewis said. He set down his beer. "Any new clues in our mystery?"

"I'm still following up leads." Joseph lifted his beer and drank, after scanning it cautiously for broken glass.

"I've continued sleuthing too," said Lewis. "You remember our friend Edward Alton Bell-Fairfax?"

Joseph grimaced and set down his beer. "That guy. Lewis, he's even deader now than he was when you found his picture. What's the point of investigating *him*?"

"I've learned several positively fascinating things," said Lewis. At this point the barmaid brought their orders: chips and beans, vegemite sandwiches, and spaghetti carbonara made with SoyHam bits.

"I'm not really interested in him, Lewis," Joseph said, looking around vainly for salt for his chips. He settled for vinegar.

"He's part of a bigger picture. Tell me, wouldn't you be interested in finding out how Edward—after being as good as court-martialed—gained entrance to one of the more exclusive clubs in London? And to an even more exclusive secret society whose origins are lost in the mists of time?"

"You're going to tell me he was a Freemason, right?" Joseph said, splashing vinegar all over his plate.

"Ever hear of the Gentlemen's Speculative Society?"

Joseph shoveled in a mouthful of chips. "Sounds like something that meets at a grange hall."

Lewis pointed with his fork. "Nowadays they call themselves the Kronos Diversified Stock Company."

Joseph choked slightly. "That's a Company DBA," he said when he had his breath back.

"Precisely," Lewis said. "And it means that the Company doesn't begin in 2318, as we've always been told, but much earlier. When that bunch of twenty-fourth-century technocrats get together and incorporate under the Dr. Zeus logo, they'll just be taking a new name. I'm beginning to suspect they're not even responsible for the technology that created us."

"They will invent pineal tribrantine three, though," Joseph said. "I've talked to the guy who came up with that. An idiot savant mortal by the name of Bugleg."

"Really? Well, I'm positive they didn't invent the time transcendence field on their own. Almost the first thing the Company did was guarantee its own existence by setting up a temporal paradox and stationing operatives throughout time in this one secret society. It's been based in Britain, almost from the beginning; though there's some indication that it was relocated before recorded history began from what is now Egypt. Tell me, did you ever go by the name Imhotep?"

Joseph jumped as though he'd been shot.

"Ha! Well, somebody using that name passed a few Company secrets to a progressive-minded group of priests, and carefully guided what use they made of the material. You might have been part of it without even being aware. And Edward Alton Bell-Fairfax was closely connected with the Victorian group, the Gentlemen's Speculative Society." Lewis pushed aside the empty plate that had contained the spaghetti and started on the beans and chips.

Joseph gulped down half his beer. "I guess you have proof."

"This time a month ago I had nothing more than inferences and conjectures—a few suspicious coincidences, one or two blatant clues. Evidence that the Company had closely monitored the progress through life of our friend the young naval officer, but no reason why." Lewis speared three chips on his fork and nibbled them delicately. "Ah, but then!"

"What?"

"I was able to break into the files of a long-defunct department of the British Foreign Office." Lewis grinned at him. "Doing semi-public business as the Imperial Export Company of London."

"Oh, for Christ's sake. Like in the James Bond books? Lewis—"

"No, no, that was Universal Export. You really ought to read something besides Raymond Chandler, you know. Anyway, need I tell you that the gentlemen involved in Imperial Export were all members of the same London club *and* the same secret fraternity? And that one of them was a retired naval officer by the name of Edward Alton Bell-Fairfax?" Lewis leaned across the table and spoke in a lower voice. "I found his dossier, Joseph. You wouldn't believe the things he did for Queen and country."

"I'll bet I would."

"A lot of them weren't very nice," Lewis admitted. "But he was awfully good at his job. Something of a problem solver, you see? Until he disappeared on his last job, in California, in 1863."

Joseph put down his sandwich. "Does this place sell hot chocolate?"

"Yes, but you're going to want to hear this first."

"I don't want to hear what he did to Mendoza."

"Listen, Joseph. There was a full-scale expedition to California, supposedly under the auspices of the Foreign Office but spearheaded by the Gentlemen's Speculative Society. The object was to secure Santa Catalina Island for Great Britain."

Joseph stared. "The place the chewing-gum guy owned? With the Avalon Ballroom? And the hotel where—"

"Where you thought you saw Mendoza, yes." Lewis leaned back and steepled his fingers like Sherlock Holmes. "And oh, Joseph, the things I've found out about Santa Catalina Island! Were you aware the Company maintains a steady presence there, in fact has quite a few research facilities and other involvements? And do you know why the Company remains interested in the place?"

"Because it's a safe zone, like Switzerland and Canada, where nothing ever happens," Joseph said.

Lewis shook his head. "It's a safe zone because the Company has made it so, Joseph. The Gentlemen desperately wanted something that was thought to be located on that island!"

"What?"

"I haven't found that out yet," said Lewis. "The records keep referring to something called Document D. It was discovered in the Royal Archives by a highly placed member of the Gentlemen's Speculative Society who had security clearance—and who was nudged in the direction of his 'discovery' by one of our operatives. And promptly thereafter they sent their covert invasion force."

"But the Brits never invaded Catalina," Joseph objected. "Hell, they never even tried."

"As a matter of fact, they did try." Lewis took up his fork again and began to finish off his chips and beans. "It's quite a story, once you track down all the details. They set up a base camp on the island in 1862. Though the expedition found what they'd been searching for, apparently the Yanks twigged to something and prevented them from taking it away.

"But the Gentlemen persisted. After the war they came back, they bought mining rights, and they kept trying to purchase the island itself. They were never able to buy it; but they do seem to have finally made off with the mysterious object."

"This is Indiana Jones stuff, Lewis," said Joseph wearily.

"And just how much do you know about the Ark of the Covenant, may I ask?" Lewis retorted.

"I forget. Barmaid?" Joseph waved. "Could we get a couple of hot chocolates over here, please? Thanks, sweetheart."

"What got the Yanks suspicious by 1863 was a breach of security, some inexperienced political who was caught, and talked. He'd left a valise containing incriminating evidence in a stagecoach inn in Los Angeles," Lewis continued.

Joseph groaned. "The one where Mendoza was stuck between postings."

"And Edward was sent to retrieve the valise, and this is where he disappears from history," Lewis said. "I could probably find out more if I were able to get into the Yanks' classified archives, and perhaps after the war I shall. The British Foreign Office never knew what happened to Edward, although the Yanks evidently never got hold of the valise. There's a confused report of a mystery ship that moored off the island near the British base there, where some sort of massacre evidently took place. Then the ship disappeared before they could investigate further.

"They kept Edward's file open for years before they declared him missing, presumed deceased. He had a reputation for surviving sticky situations. Of course, they didn't know what we know."

"That he dragged Mendoza into whatever trouble he was in," said Joseph hoarsely. "That the Pinkerton agents blew him away right in front of her eyes, and she went nuts and killed them. And the Company stepped in and mopped up so the mortals would never find out about her."

"Or about *him!*" Lewis said. "Hasn't the import of all this sunk in on you? The Company wanted Edward mopped up after too. He was on Company business when he died. Mendoza was helping him. In fact—" He halted before he could blurt out what had just occurred to him.

The barmaid, coming to their table, looked in concern at the American gentleman who'd ordered the hot chocolate. "Here, is he all right? Shall I call a medic?" she asked his friend.

The American lifted his head and gave his friend a look that quite unnerved the barmaid, who (as should be evident by now) did not unnerve easily. Without waiting for a reply, she set down the chocolate, murmured something polite, and scuttled away to the safety of the kitchen.

"They set her up," said Joseph through his teeth.

"I—I suppose."

"They left her there deliberately so she'd meet him. They knew it would happen! She helped him get rid of the evidence. If she hadn't, the Yanks would have found out about what the British were looking for and grabbed it for themselves, and maybe then there would never have been any Dr. Zeus Incorporated."

"And then the Company arrested her and put her away," said Lewis in a ghost of a voice, "but not because she'd gone AWOL. Not even because she killed those mortals. A Crome generator who has the ability to go forward through time could find out what happens when the Silence falls in 2355 and—"

"Lewis, don't go there. Okay? Not another word about that, if you value my life, let alone your own," said Joseph quickly. He noticed the chocolate and grabbed for it. "But that wraps up a whole bunch of problems for them, like what do they do with an operative who's a Crome generator when the Company says there aren't any. Thanks, Mendoza, for helping us get started, and here's your one-way ticket to two million years ago."

Lewis sat silent, horrified. He looked down at the last piece of his sandwich and set it carefully on his plate, as though it might explode.

"Great Caesar's Ghost. And Edward—"

"Edward was their goddam bait to snare her!"

"But, don't you see? He was set up too," Lewis said. "I've traced his whole life—the Company groomed him for the work they wanted him to do. From the time he was at school. Our people were there monitoring him, Joseph, I've seen the proof. The Company wanted a man who'd be willing to die for a cause, a man with no family, a man who could disappear. He was a member of the Gentlemen, he knew their secrets and must have believed in their work. He was their operative!"

"You don't have to tell me any more about the guy." Joseph drank down his hot chocolate and made a face. "What is this made with, soy milk?"

"How can you just sit there?" Lewis demanded, his voice shaking. "Knowing what the Company did to Mendoza!"

"Yeah, soy milk, all right," said Joseph woodenly. "Who am I going to jump up and kill, Lewis? I never got a shot at Edward Alton Bell-Fairfax."

Regent's Park

THE TREES WERE still there, and so was Queen Mary's Garden; but its lawns hadn't been mown in years, so most of the park was hip-high weedy wilderness and young woodland. There were stories that tigers had been released into it when the London Zoo was closed down, and lurked in the tall grass even now, leaping out to eat the occasional homeless person. It wasn't true, of course. The tigers had been dutifully flown to Asia and released into a preserve there, where they were promptly shot by poachers.

There had been a movement to box up the swans and ship them off to wherever it was swans hailed from originally, but no one was really sure that swans didn't belong in that part of the world, and anyway they were free to go if they wanted to. It was pointed out, moreover, that the act of catching them even for the purpose of repatriation would be a violation of their civil rights. There the matter rested.

So one could still stand in the middle of the footbridge and watch the swans gliding to and fro where there was open water, and this is what Joseph and Lewis were doing as they waited for Victor. That, and arguing.

No, I've known Victor for years, Lewis insisted. *He was at New World One for nearly a century when I was there, don't you remember? He did the most wickedly funny imitation of Director General*

Houbert. Before that I think he was based in Europe, at least I recall seeing him once at Eurobase One—

He broke off with an odd expression on his face.

I did see him there, he went on. *But that was right after I—*

Lewis, this is not a social visit, said Joseph. *You may be old pals, but he won't be expecting to see both of us. He may not feel like talking to me at all, if he sees you here. Not to be rude or anything, but—*

All right, I'll go poke around in the ruins of the mosque. I know when I'm not wanted. Lewis pulled his coat about himself and stalked away into the jungle that grew along the Outer Circle.

Joseph watched him go and sighed. Almost at once he was aware of another immortal approaching from the opposite direction, and turned on his heel to see Victor staring after Lewis with an expression of dismay.

"It's Victor, isn't it?" Joseph bustled up to him and extended a hand.

After a moment's hesitation Victor shook his hand, without removing the gloves he wore. "Wasn't that Lewis? The literature fellow?" he asked.

"Uh—yeah." Joseph cursed silently. "That's right, you would have seen each other at New World One, wouldn't you? Small world. He'll be sorry he missed you."

Victor shrugged. "We were slightly acquainted." *I agreed to talk to you alone.*

We're alone now. Joseph surveyed Victor. He looked thin and pale, as everyone did in London; but he was considerably better dressed than most, in smartly tailored clothes that had come from somewhere expensive on the Continent. "Some coincidence, huh?" Joseph said.

"Quite," replied Victor coldly. *I understand you have questions about something that happened in San Francisco. Why do you need to know?*

I'm looking for somebody who disappeared. You recruited a Musicologist named Donal there, yes? From the 1906 earthquake?

Victor's eyes narrowed and became, if such a thing were possible, colder. He glanced elaborately at his chronometer. "Heavens, look at the time. I'd love to stay and chat, but—"

Wait. I need to know—because your kid barely remembers it. Who did you rescue him from? Was it Budu? "Can I ask you a favor, first? Do you know of any snack stands around here? I'd kill for a Mars Bar right about now."

Victor stood for a moment, apparently lost in thought. "You know, I believe there is one here. Or was. I think it's over this way. I wouldn't mind a Mars Bar myself, now that you mention it."

He turned and started off along the trail, and Joseph hurried after him, thinking that Victor had changed. He'd noticed a similar alteration in some operatives and had assumed it had something to do with being out in the field too long. Certain lines of strain around the eyes, a certain indefinable sense of shadow.

You were one of Budu's recruits, weren't you? Victor asked warily.

Yeah. Though I understand he went crazy or something. Look, let me set your mind at rest. All I want to know is if the old guy is all right. Did they finally bring him in? Did the Company repair him? This is kind of a filial duty thing for me. It just breaks my heart to think of him roaming around damaged on his own somewhere, lost—

Spare me, please.

Where is he?

I was his recruit, too, as it happens.

Joseph halted at that, and pretended to have trouble with a shoelace. "Hang on a second, something's caught my shoe. Say, there aren't any tigers roaming around here, are there? That's just one of those urban legends, right?" *Really?*

"Of course. There are no tigers." *Yes. And, since we both know the sort of creature he was, why don't you drop the pretense of filial love?*

But I did love him, protested Joseph. *He was a hero. I'll admit*

I've heard stories, and maybe they're true—but he must have gone nuts. Was that him in San Francisco, in 1906? He straightened up. "Okay, lead on."

Victor turned and walked. *He was there, the night before the earthquake.*

You saw him? He talked to you? Donal seemed to think there was a fight of some kind. That's absurd, though, because nobody fights with Budu and wins. He was damaged, right?

He was damaged.

And so obviously you got Donal away from him, and Dr. Zeus was able to get Budu back, and he's okay now.

No, Joseph.

No, Dr. Zeus didn't get him back, or no, he's not okay?

Both. "Oh, dear," said Victor. "This doesn't look promising." The refreshment pavilion loomed ahead of them; boarded up and in an advanced state of disuse.

"Damn! Can we go up close and see? Maybe they're just closed for lunch," said Joseph. *Please tell me. Was he arrested?*

No, Joseph, he wasn't.

He got away?

No, he didn't.

For Christ's sake, what then?

They made a slow circle around the refreshment pavilion, trying all the doors, before Victor replied. *I can tell you where to look for him. You understand this is classified?*

Please.

"No, I'm afraid we're out of luck, old boy," said Victor. *He's in Chinatown. On Sacramento Street, about a block up from Waverly Place.* "You might try the newsagent's in Marylebone Road." *And if you should find him at home—pray tell him that Victor sends his sincerest regrets.*

Regrets? Is that sarcasm?

No. I never loved him, and he knows it, but I'm ashamed of what I did there. Tell him that. I had no idea what would happen.

I've since taken steps to make sure that it won't happen again. Victor wrung his gloved hands briefly. "And now, if you'll excuse me? I really must run."

He strode off in the direction of Chester Road.

Joseph stood staring after him, openmouthed. Finally he shivered and looked around him at the abandoned pavilion and the high weeds, uncertain whether he heard a low staccato growl, caught a glimpse of striped flank. He set off for the Outer Circle, making his way along the overgrown path in some haste.

So, what did he have to say? transmitted Latif, emerging from the trees behind him and pacing after in silence. Joseph started violently but managed to avoid looking around.

Give a guy some warning! How long have you been there?

Before either of you.

What do you have, some kind of masking field?

Right, like you need to know. Want to tell me what Victor said so I can get the hell out of here and back to a civilized country? One that's not so cold, anyway.

Joseph turned along a loop of trail and wandered aimlessly, kicking at fragments of bombed wreckage. *It was pretty cryptic. He doesn't think much of Budu either. But it sounded like Budu's out of the picture, some way or other.*

Did Victor know where he is? Did he tell you?

Sort of.

Joseph heard the exhalation of impatience. *Are you going to tell me?*

I'd kind of like to see for myself first. Can you cut me that much slack? I'll let you know everything once I've got the truth. If it's something really bad—I'd rather it was me found him. He recruited me. How would you feel if it was Suleyman?

Suleyman wouldn't go that way.

I never thought Budu would, kid.

Okay. As soon as you know anything, though, you send us word. Suleyman says he told you how to get in touch with him.

He did, and I will. Trust me.

He also said you were right about something.

What?

We reviewed all the information we've collected on Budu. There isn't anything after 1906. No sightings, no intercepted messages, no evidence he was running the Plague Club after that time. All the evidence indicates Facilitator General Labienus stepped into his place immediately after Budu dropped out of sight.

That guy. Joseph shivered.

You know him?

Cold-hearted SOB. I've had to work with Labienus a couple of times. Never liked him.

He taught me. I can't say I'm surprised he'd be part of this cabal. The man's ruthless.

He is. So, why don't you set your machine on him?

We already have.

Well, that's nice to know. Joseph picked his way to the Outer Circle and stood looking across at the ruins of the London Mosque. Lewis, wandering in the rubble, had picked up a piece of old inscribed tile and was studying it, head cocked to one side.

That's Lewis, isn't it? The guy who used to run Guest Services at New World One? transmitted Latif.

That's him. Do you remember that New Year's ball, when you were tiny? You came and sat at the table with us, and he was there too.

Of course I remember. You and Lewis and that lady, the Botanist, Mendoza.

The Botanist Mendoza. Yeah.

Do you remember what she said that night? Something about how the four of us would probably never find ourselves together in the same place again? But here we are, you and Lewis and I. Almost all of us.

Almost.

Joseph in the Darkness

IT WAS LIKE—like I set out to find just the pieces of the puzzle with blue sky, but somehow I kept reaching into the box and coming up with bits with fishing boats, rooftops, and elephants. Details I didn't want or need, and the growing feeling that the picture I was going to see when they were all assembled wouldn't be the nice simple scene I'd expected.

What had I learned so far?

A lot, actually. I knew that my old heroes the Enforcers had been double-crossed, were stashed away indefinitely, along with some of the Preservers.

I knew that Mendoza's fall from grace had been engineered, that the Company had used her for its purposes and thrown her away.

I knew that the goddam tall Englishman was connected with the Company somehow, that he'd been used and thrown away too, and I didn't really want to think about the implications of that. I should have, though.

I knew that the Company was a lot older than it said it was, and it didn't want that fact known. I knew it had lied about other stuff, like our being unable to travel forward through time—though maybe that wasn't exactly a lie. Maybe only Mendoza had ever managed that.

I knew that the Company had found something it wanted really badly on Catalina Island, something for which it was willing to sacrifice people.

I found out that there are at least three groups competing for power within the Company: the people officially in charge, who are probably Old Ones, like Nennius, who pull the strings of our mortal masters; the Plague Club, who favor biological warfare against humanity, and who may have been started by you, father; and Suleyman's people, who are working against the Plague Club. Hell, you could probably count a fourth faction if you throw in the mortal masters themselves. If they have any brains at all, they must have some plot in the works to take their immortals out.

So who gave the orders to put Mendoza in harm's way? Who put away the Enforcers? Who the hell thought it would be funny to resurrect Nicholas Harpole Edward Alton Whatever-His-Name-Was and use him as a mortal Company operative? And how did they do that?

Why should the Company hide the fact of its origins from its own operatives?

And who was Victor working for, and where the hell were *you*, father? Were you masterminding a really evil bunch of people from a subterranean lair in Chinatown? Or were you living there in quiet gradual retirement, a victim of slander? How did you manage to disable your datalink?

Every time I thought I'd found an answer to something, it turned out to be a fistful of questions instead, and they were multiplying geometrically. Lewis was no help, plunging ahead with more enthusiasm than good sense, like a man digging for treasure and tossing sand into the hole somebody else was digging, completely unaware that a tidal wave was coming in...

So I left his chilly little garret and flew back to my cozy little box in Mazatlán, and tried to push everything to the back of my mind in the hopes it would straighten itself out.

My plan was, I'd go looking for you next. Eventually. I wanted to hear the story from your mouth. I knew if push came to shove, I'd have to side with Suleyman's people. But maybe he was mistaken about you. I hoped like hell he was.

Though Suleyman is almost never mistaken, about anything.

But I had to wait and let a good amount of time go by before I took any spur-of-the-moment vacation weekends to San Francisco. The Second American Civil War was just about to start, and Company personnel were quietly getting the hell out of the States. Even without benefit of the Temporal Concordance, we all knew the Yanks were headed for trouble.

I guess the main difficulty was that their founding fathers never did really solve the problem of E Pluribus Unum back when they put their constitution together, in that locked room with the press kept firmly away so the American people wouldn't know what they were doing. Small wonder the succeeding generations of government felt they weren't accountable to the public; things had been done that way from the beginning, hadn't they?

Eventually, though, the public had enough. Everybody knew the government lied to the people. It lied about assassination conspiracies, unidentified flying objects, unpopular wars. So the powder and fuse of resentment were ready and waiting for the spark.

It went off in 2150. The West had fallen on hard times. Industries shut down or moved east. There were plagues. There were earthquakes and floods. The government made things worse by closing down the military bases. Dumb move, as it turned out.

You know your history, you know what happens when people think they have nothing to lose but their chains. A handful of cranks with a lot of guns took the California state capitol building and read an antifederalist manifesto. They were in the right place at the right time and hit the right nerve. Suddenly California was seceding from the Union. Nobody was surprised when Montana and Utah seceded, too, but then Nevada went, and Colorado. What really tore it was when Texas joined the secessionists, because Texas had money and an intact infrastructure.

Within hours, most of the other western states had declared, and the South woke up in astonishment and jumped on the wagon, too. Everything was happening so fast, and everyone was so confused, there might have been a real shooting war, with bombers and disrupter rifles this time, if the earthquake hadn't hit.

It was estimated at a ten on the Richter scale, and it hit the Eastern seaboard. The last time that happened, in the middle of the nineteenth century, the Mississippi river ran backward for three days.

It did it this time, too. New York was destroyed, Washington D.C., was destroyed, any place with high-rise buildings and a dense urban population was destroyed. Millions of people died. The remaining United States found themselves with no way to refuse the secessionists.

Funny thing happened, though. The Americans were aghast at what had happened, abruptly aware of how vulnerable they were. Hurried meetings were held among the survivors. A loose federation was patched together, all parties agreeing to disagree.

The result was a bloc composed of most of the northeastern states, a bloc of southern and central states, an independent Republic of Texas, and a handful of Native American nations. The Mormon Church got Utah. Canada debated whether to accept the few bordering strays who petitioned for admittance. California fragmented into about five little independent republics. Hawaii set up a constitutional monarchy, since it had thoughtfully kept its royals. All parties retired to lick their wounds and burn their dead.

And that was it. You couldn't really call it a war, because Mother Nature was the only one who did the fighting; but Second Civil War sounds good in the history books. A lot of wealthy Asian and European countries looked thoughtfully at the mess and wondered what might be grabbed. Things might have gone badly for the Yanks if some guy in the American Community hadn't discovered—or, rather, rediscovered—antigravity.

What a joke! Antigravity proved to operate on a principle so moronically simple, most scientists refused to acknowledge it at first out of sheer embarrassment, except for a few rogue Egyptologists who laughed and laughed. The American Community had the sense to see it had been dealt a trump card, though. Cash flowed into the renascent union, and the old experiment of government of the people, by the people, for the people was back up and running. With all their politicians buried under tons of rubble, they just maybe had a chance this time.

It's easy to rebuild after an earthquake when you have antigravity to help you, and Megalith Nouveau became the next hot architectural style. The Yanks became the world's first manufacturer of the antigravity car, after having been the only holdouts in the world who were still stubbornly making internal combustion engines.

You can zip all over the known landscape in an agcar, you can even take them across water on a still day, they use almost no power and are a whole lot cheaper to make than electric cars. Everyone in the world wanted antigravity technology. The Yanks made a fortune selling the secret, until other nations figured out how simple it was.

Just as people were congratulating themselves on things returning to normal, the plagues broke out again—in China and India this time. Millions more died. Labienus's work, I guess. And then a good-sized earthquake hit England, of all places, and took out a lot of high-rise London. That was in 2198.

The Brits rebuilt with antigravity technology. By the year 2205 London was back in business, though there were a lot fewer people. At least the last of the terrorists seemed to have been killed in the earthquake. England had enough of chaos: it reinvented its peerage and gave ruling power to a house of lords, hereditary bureaucrats who promptly formed social committees and tidied up everything. Europe went pretty much the same way: the Hapsburgs (talk about comebacks) emerged from the woodwork and made the antigravity trams run on time, and people were only too glad to let them.

In a way it was the post-holocaust world people had been expecting since the atomic age: old familiar institutions gone, humanity scarce on the ground and returning to feudalism. Instead of grinning leather-clad bandit punks, though, corporate functionaries were the rulers. People clustered together in smaller communities, linked online, and held tight to their comforts. Technological innovation stopped dead after antigravity. We had the global village at last and, surprise, a village was exactly what it was. With a shared culture, mortals became more provincial, not less.

The world looked inward, not ahead, and history-reenactment clubs became more popular than they had ever been. Even the people going out to Luna carried historical clichés with them, proud to be pioneers seeking Lebensraum. The future was looking more and more like the past, especially to anybody who watched Rome's long slow slide into night.

Oh, and Japan kept sinking. They had one earthquake after another, though none of them did much damage anymore, because most of the Japanese had relocated to Mexico. By 2205 about all that was left above sea level was Mount Fuji, and downtown Mazatlán was really crowded at lunch hour. By that time I was glad to be working again in Spain, which had changed beyond recognition in some ways and not at all in others.

Just like everything else.

London, 2225

Lᴇᴡɪs ᴄʜᴇᴄᴋᴇᴅ ʜɪs internal chronometer and wondered whether he ought to finish up lunch. It didn't really matter whether he took one hour or three, because almost nobody ever came into the Historic Books Annex of the London Metropolitan Library. Some days he never saw a single patron. It wasn't surprising; *historic* books were the only kind that existed anymore, as nobody had printed on paper in decades.

The fact that the entrance to the annex was on a dark little side street made traffic less likely still. Lewis reflected that he might have indulged in a seven-course meal with brandy and cigars, if he'd wanted to (and if such things still existed); the chances of seeing a mortal before closing time were one in a hundred.

On the Buke screen at his desk a little animated figure of Edward Alton Bell-Fairfax stalked up and down on the quarterdeck of a nineteenth-century warship. The sea pitched and rolled most realistically, and about every seventh wave a seagull would swoop across the upper right-hand corner of the scene. It had taken Lewis months to program, getting all the details right, and he was rather proud of it. He no longer kept the daguerreotype on display—it was fabulously antique now—but he liked being able to see Edward.

Lewis leaned back in his chair and picked again at the mixed green salad, wondering sadly how a country so thoroughly vegan as Britain had gone could somehow fail to produce decent lettuce. He peered at what might have been a wholemeal crouton or a piece of romaine and gave up in disgust, tossing the catering box into the dustbin. No matter. He'd skip over to Paris this weekend and treat himself. He could afford to do such things nowadays. The gold letters on the inner door read LEWIS MARCH, CHIEF CURATOR.

Yes, the wheel of Fortune had turned; now he had a nice modern house in one of the New Parks that had been created on the site of the former high-rise district. Plenty of central heating and plumbing, all the sunlight London ever offered, and something else that hadn't used to be available at all in an urban area: fresh air. His present assignment—buying old books for the library and smoothly making off with the rare ones Dr. Zeus wanted—was unbelievably dull, but it left him a lot of time for his private research. Lewis didn't mind gradual retirement much.

He had been quietly monitoring the present-day activities of the Kronos Diversified Stock Company, and had noted that two of his fellow immortals sat on its board of directors. He had also hacked into the American classified archives—as he had suspected, this became a great deal easier after the war—and was able to confirm a great many details of the 1863 incident, including the unsolved disappearance of six Pinkerton agents. There was no record of any capture of a British agent, however, or even of one being shot while trying to escape, and nothing about any woman that might have been Mendoza.

The nightmares marched on relentlessly. He dreamed, often, about a sixth-century monk with the sort of sideways tonsure the Irish had defiantly worn. A big man, bearded, with ink on his hands. Lewis almost knew the mortal's name. He didn't want to.

It wasn't that he was afraid of the mortal—the man seemed quite nice, in fact he was trying to remind Lewis of something—but Lewis invariably woke in a cold sweat just as the man was about to tell him what it was.

He brushed away the crumbs of his lunch, standing up to be certain he hadn't got salad oil on his beautifully pressed trousers. Satisfied, he settled down and cleared the screen for the personal project he was working on, his secret indulgence. He opened it and reviewed what he'd written that morning, frowning thoughtfully.

Lieutenant Dumfries saluted and said nervously, "But, Commander, how are we to penetrate the mangrove swamps against the tide? There's not a breath of wind to fill the longboat's sails!"

By way of answer Edward drew his cutlass and vaulted ashore, where a few brief efficient chops at a stand of bamboo produced three serviceable poles, each some eight feet in length when trimmed.

"Were you never at Cambridge, man?" he snapped. "Pretend the damned thing's a punt. Now, gentlemen, step lively! We've got a good deal of this damned swamp to cross if we're to rendezvous with Jenkins's men before Señor Delarosa and King Dalba—

Before they what? Lewis ran a hand through his limp hair, sighing in frustration. What exactly was the point of the rendezvous? And did bamboo grow in Africa? And wouldn't it be faster for them to sail across the lagoon rather than work their way through the swamp? And how had King Dalba met up with Señor Delarosa again so quickly?

Lewis wrote a few more lines and then stopped, realizing he hadn't mentioned Edward's vaulting back *into* the boat before it pushed off. He was busy deleting when the outer door opened, and Edward had just leaped athletically onto the gunwale (a move that would almost certainly have landed the heroic young commander in four feet of swamp) when the inner door opened. Someone came to the counter and stood there.

Lewis turned in his chair. "May I help you—?" was as far as he got before he choked and levitated out of the chair so quickly, he knocked it over. He stood behind it, shaking. The nightmares were coming again, he could hear them baying for his blood in the distance. His visitor did not seem to have noticed the accident.

"I have to use a terminal," said the visitor.

Lewis scanned, controlling himself. Nothing to be afraid of after all. His visitor was only a mortal, rather a small one with some kind of developmental disability. Male, about thirty-five, badly dressed, with big weak-looking dark eyes that reminded Lewis of a rabbit's. Pasty complexion. Big-domed oddly shaped head with an extremely receding hairline. He was carrying a string bag containing a sipper bottle of water and an orange.

"Er, sorry about that," Lewis giggled in embarrassment. "I'm a little jumpy today. What are you looking for, Mr.—?"

"I have to use a terminal," repeated his visitor in a drippy little voice.

Lewis walked out into the main reading room and pointed to the closest bank of terminals. "Here you are. Please let me know if you need any—" But the visitor had already marched past him, sat down, and begun to type away with blinding speed. Lewis retreated behind the counter gladly enough.

"I'll just continue my research, then, shall I?" he said, for no reason he could think of. The visitor ignored him. The rattling of keys in the echoing room sounded like a hailstorm.

Lewis sat down again, attempting to return his attention to the adventures of Commander Bell-Fairfax. What part of a boat was a gunwale anyway? And should it be cane instead of bamboo Edward cut for the poles? Mendoza could have told him . . .

He was accessing internal datafiles for his answers when the pattering of keys stopped. Lewis felt the hair rise on the back of his neck and turned in his chair to see the visitor advancing on him. What was so familiar about the creature?

"That terminal doesn't work," said the man.

"Oh, dear," Lewis said. "What are you trying to locate? Perhaps I can—"

"I need to call home," said the man, staring at him.

"Oh, I see, you need a public terminal," Lewis said. "I'm so sorry for the misunderstanding. None of these are linked to a public line, I'm afraid. They're for accessing information in the archives."

"Oh," said the visitor.

"Yes," said Lewis.

"Got any Nasowipes?"

Lewis pulled out a handful of tissues and thrust them at the visitor, who accepted them without a word, turned, and went back into the reading room. Lewis leaned over the counter, staring after him.

"But don't you want to—?" The visitor gave no sign of hearing him. Lewis shrugged and went back to his Buke. After a moment of staring at the last line, wherein Commander Bell-Fairfax had just rescued a frantic British tar who'd fallen into leech-infested water, Lewis adjusted his chair and console pullout so he was no longer sitting with his back to the reading room.

"Please, Commander, get 'em off me!" begged Johnson desperately.

"Courage, man." Coolly, Edward lit up a long cheroot. "This is likely to be a bit unpleasant. Close your eyes." The other sailors looked on in horror as Edward, having produced a red and glowing ember on the end of his cigar, reached down with his fine hand and applied it carefully to the horrible

"Got any paper clips?" the visitor asked, appearing at Lewis's elbow like a ghost. Lewis restrained himself from levitating again and groped in a pigeonhole of the desk. He found a handful of paper clips and offered them to the man.

The man took them, turned, and headed back to the reading room. Lewis looked after him, wiping his hand on his coat lapel unconsciously. The man's hand had been long, thin, and clammy.

Lewis revised:

applied it carefully to the disgusting

"Any magnedots?" asked the visitor. Lewis yanked open the drawer where he kept file labels and fished out a strip of magnedots for him. The visitor took them without a word and trudged away. Lewis sat jittering a moment before he resumed:

applied it carefully to the loathsome, blood-engorged

The street door was opening. Two mortals came hurriedly toward him, a man and a woman, passing through the inner door. They wore uniforms and were radiating alarm.

"Excuse me, please," said the young woman. "We're looking for a little man."

"Ah," said Lewis.

"We're from the Neasden Adult Residential Facility," said her companion. "We were taking our guests on an outing to the library, and Mr. Fancod seems to have wandered off. He's about five feet tall—"

"Mr. Fancod!" exclaimed the young woman, catching sight of the visitor through the reading room arch. "How clever of you to find your way in here. Come along now, dear, your friends are very worried about you." She rushed into the reading room, closely followed by her associate.

"I have to call home," said Mr. Fancod.

"Oh, but we're going home, Mr. Fancod," the man assured him.

"I'm not finished yet."

"Well, I'm afraid we really must ask you to come along anyhow..."

"Ask the cyborg if he has any raisins."

Cyborg? Lewis sat perfectly still, heart pounding. He heard the male attendant stifling a chuckle. "Now then, Mr. Fancod, I think it's time you stopped having fun with us. If you'll come along now, we'll stop at Prashant's, and you can buy more raisins."

"Okay," said Mr. Fancod, and Lewis heard them coming out of the reading room. He glanced up cautiously. The two mortals were making apologetic faces at him. Mr. Fancod, following them obediently, had taken out his orange and was peeling it as they went along, staring at it in utter absorption. He dropped pieces of peel on the floor as he walked.

Gnawing on his lower lip, Lewis watched them go. He looked down at his Buke and typed in:

applied it carefully to one of the loathsome, blood-engorged??????

He saved the document and closed the Buke. Rising, he got a tissue and carefully collected all the discarded orange peel. He tossed it in the dustbin. Wiping his hands, he ventured into the reading room to see if all was well.

It wasn't.

All the consoles, except the nearest one, bore a cheery greeting above the logo and menu for the London Metropolitan Library. That was normal. What wasn't normal was the black screen on the nearest console, crossed from top to bottom in something that resembled binary code but wasn't quite. Lewis approached it reluctantly and stood looking down at the screen. He reached out at arm's length and gave the command key a tentative tap.

The inexplicable code went away and was replaced by a menu. It said:

DR. ZEUS COMMUNICATION REQUEST
INITIALIZE
INITIAL REPLY
MEMO
DEPARTMENT METHODICAL
LEFT MODE
ENTER PERSONAL NOW:

Lewis looked over his shoulder and looked back at the screen. He leaned forward and examined the console. It was a moment before he found the small panel that had been broken out at one side, and the little alteration sticking out of it, made of paper clips and magnedots.

He looked around the room once more before crawling quickly underneath the seat recess to unplug the console. He found an OUT OF ORDER sign and spread it across the screen before scurrying back to his desk.

Opening his Buke again, he linked up with the Greater London Communication Listings and entered a search request for the name FANCOD.

There was only one. Thurwood Fancod, care of Neasden Adult Residential Facility. Registered challenged adult. Employed: Self-Reliance In-Home Data Entry Program. Sponsor: Jovian Integrated Systems.

Jovian Integrated Systems was one of the holding companies for Dr. Zeus Incorporated.

Lewis leaned back. "Oh dear," he murmured. He exited the listings and swiveled in his chair, this way and that like a compass needle seeking true north. He closed his eyes to concentrate more deeply and at last found the frequency he sought.

Xenophon? Literature Specialist Lewis requesting reception.

Xenophon receiving, came the reply.

There seems to have been a security breach of some kind. My cover's been compromised.

Specify.

A mortal named Thurwood Fancod has access to material quite a bit beyond my need to know.

Xenophon swore electronically. *Details?*

He identified me as a cyborg in front of two other mortals. They didn't take him seriously, but he knew. And...he modified one of the library terminals to hack into a Dr. Zeus database. Seems to have been going after something classified.

Damn!

Should I run?

Yes, you'd better. We'll send a team over right away to confiscate the modified unit and replace it. I suppose somebody had better deal with Fancod, too. Where can we reach you?

Lewis gave him a set of coordinates.

Very good. Your new assignment and paperwork will be forwarded to you at that address on 7 March. Vale, Lewis.

Vale.

Sighing, Lewis got up and slipped his Buke into its case. He made a quick search through his desk drawers for any personal items he might want. There were none. He pulled on his coat, stowed the Buke case in an inner pocket, and took one last wistful look at his name in its gold lettering before walking out.

In the morning someone with unquestionable credentials as his next of kin would tearfully notify the library of an accident, or sudden death, or some terrible emergency. Shortly thereafter a person with splendid references would be perfectly positioned for promotion to the position of chief curator, and the space Lewis March had left in the world would vanish like a footprint in sand. It was standard operating procedure for a security breach, and he'd been warned that this sort of thing might begin to occur more frequently as he got closer to the Company's end of time.

He caught an antigravity transport at the corner and rode the short distance to his house, where he packed a suitcase with his shaving bag and a change of clothes. Just before closing it, he went to a cabinet and took out a little bubblewrap package containing the old daguerreotype of Edward, nesting it between two shirts.

Lewis carried his suitcase down to the front hall and paused again, looking around at the comfortable rooms, the entertainment center, the furniture, the paintings. Within the next six hours there would be Company techs in here loading everything into a van. This time tomorrow the place would be spotless, silent, and empty, awaiting a rental agent's powers of description. It had been nice while it lasted.

He put that out of his mind as he stepped outside, locked the door behind him, and walked away. Immortals say a lot of good-byes.

It wasn't until Lewis was on the LPA transport bucketing along to Newhaven that he groaned and smacked his forehead. "The cheroot!"

he said out loud. "How would he light the damned thing?" A mortal woman looked across at him in affronted silence. She wasn't affronted enough to go inform a Public Safety Monitor that there was a man talking to himself on the transport, however, so Lewis made it to the Dieppe ferry without incident.

Once on board, he went quickly up to the deserted upper deck and found himself a cozy seat near the tea station, a corner booth with a table. There he wedged his suitcase in securely, took out his Buke, and within minutes was lost in the problem of how to light a cigar in a longboat in a swamp on the Guinea Coast in 1845.

He had concluded that it really wouldn't be all that improbable for Edward to be carrying sulfur friction matches (might even have had one of the new boxes with a safety striking surface), when two men clambered unsteadily onto the upper deck and sat down opposite the tea station.

Lewis frowned down at his last paragraph. Leeches. *Loathsome* and *blood-engorged* were a little overripe. So was *slimy*. What about...*vile gray creatures*?

But leeches were black, not gray, weren't they? Lewis sat back to think. Slugs were gray, and so were—he raised his eyes to scan the mortals who sat across from him. His mouth fell open in surprise.

They got up abruptly and came and sat on either side of him.

"Don't shout," said one of them.

"No," said the other one.

Lewis stared from one to the other. "I beg your pardon?" he said at last.

"No use to beg," the first speaker told him.

They were very odd looking mortals. White suits in England? In March? And very large black sunglasses, and fairly stupid hats: one wore a knitted ski hat, the other a shapeless canvas porkpie. They were small and spindly enough to make Lewis seem like a gorilla by comparison. Both had drippy little voices, just like Mr. Fancod's.

They were quite the most feeble and ridiculous things Lewis had seen in a long while, even including Mr. Fancod. Nevertheless, he felt a sudden urge to leap over the side and swim back to Newhaven.

Getting a grip on his nerves, Lewis affected a certain composure as he saved and closed his novel once again.

"Would you mind telling me who you fellows are?" he said.

"Yes," said the man in the ski hat.

Lewis returned his Buke to its case, scanning them more closely.

"You're carrying weapons, aren't you?" he said. They started.

"Yes," agreed the one in the ski hat.

"No," said the one in the porkpie.

"No," the one in the ski hat corrected himself.

Lewis pursed his lips. "I see. But you were threatening me, weren't you? And if you're not carrying weapons, how do you propose to make your threats good?"

The two men looked at each other in silence for a moment. Then they nodded and each drew from within his coat a pistol and pointed it at Lewis.

"We have weapons," admitted the one in the porkpie.

Lewis looked at the pistols. They appeared to be modern disrupters but were not of any design he'd ever seen. All he could determine, on scanning them, was that they contained circuitry whose purpose seemed to be generating a wave field of some kind.

He folded his hands on the table and thought very carefully about the situation in which he found himself.

No danger at all, on the face of it. He might simply wink out from between the two little men, run down into the main lounge, and alert the Public Safety Monitor that there were lunatics with weapons on board. Of course, then there would be a scene, which was not something a running operative particularly wanted. No way to avoid being asked to make a statement to the authorities, and perhaps to the press, either of which would be in direct violation of Company policy as regarded quiet exits.

He could wrest the weapons away and throw them overboard,

which seemed like a good idea actually, though Lewis disliked hurting mortals. These particular mortals looked as though they might snap like toothpicks if he tried anything the least bit forceful, and that would cause a scene as well.

If he were Edward Alton Bell-Fairfax, he'd have casually killed the two with a backhand chop five minutes ago and tossed them, guns and all, discreetly over the side into the Channel. He wasn't Edward Alton Bell-Fairfax.

"Well, then," Lewis said, as politely as he could. "What do you want?"

"To take you home," said the one in the porkpie.

Lewis suppressed a smile. "Um—and what happens if I don't want to go home with you?"

"We shoot you," the other one informed him. "Then we take you anyhow."

"Yes," the one in the porkpie agreed.

"I'd rather you didn't shoot me," Lewis said, drumming his fingertips on the table.

"Yes. We know," said the one in the ski hat.

Realizing in panic that he was looking at three and a half more hours of conversation like this, Lewis attempted to transmit to Xenophon. There was no response. He felt the proverbial sensation of ice water along his spine.

"Are you jamming my signal?" he asked.

"Yes."

"So you know what I am?"

"Yes." Both of them nodded their heads. "You're a cyborg."

"How do you know?"

"We have been looking for you," said the one in the porkpie.

Lewis closed his eyes. Ireland. In that moment, years of denial ended abruptly. The nightmares had him. Grinning, they pulled off their masks, and he remembered the cave under Dun Govaun, the creatures who hadn't been children after all but small men, weak and stupid, yet masters of a weapon that could disable the cleverest cyborg, if he walked into their hiding place. And Lewis had. The erasure field had crippled him, but it hadn't quite killed him. His captors didn't mind, because they had him now, so they could take him apart and see how he was made and make the weapon stronger, better, more deadly...

"Well then," he said in a light voice, opening his eyes again. "If you've been hunting me this long, you must know I don't want to be caught."

"Yes," said the one in the ski hat, nodding again.

"I think it's only fair to warn you, I'll probably run as soon as we get off this boat," Lewis said.

"That would be dumb," said the one in the porkpie, disapproval in his voice. "Because we'd shoot you, and then you'd be broken."

"Well, probably; but that's all the more reason for me to do something desperate, you see?" Lewis spread out his hands as though presenting them with an irrefutable argument. "So, there it is. If you're smart, you'll keep those guns trained on me."

"Oh, we're smart," the one in the ski hat said.

"We're the smartest ones," said the one in the porkpie.

"Yes, I can see that," Lewis agreed. "Well. I can't run anywhere until we land at Dieppe, so I think I'll just go on with my writing."

"It won't help," said the one in the ski hat.

"Then there's no reason for you to stop me, is there?" said Lewis smoothly, drawing his Buke from its case again. His captors appeared to be thinking that over.

"No," they said at last.

Lewis called up a Company line, and found to his frustration that although he was able to access the channel, he was unable to send any messages. Apparently whatever was jamming his personal transmission was able to block the Buke's as well. After several efforts he entered in the last communication code he had on file for Joseph.

Joseph wasn't home. His automatic response picked up the call, and Lewis beheld a brilliant yellow screen with bouncy red letters, giving the following cheery message in Castilian Spanish:

Hola! If you're calling about the sofa and loveseat, they're still for sale. I'm on vacation this week, but please leave your comm code and I'll return your call as soon as I get back. If this is really important, you can reach me care of the Hotel Elissamburu, Irún, Eskual Herriraino, at HtEli546/C/882. I'll be there until the 30th. Bye.

Lewis exhaled in annoyance. He attempted to leave a message, but was blocked once again. After staring at the screen in frustration, he logged off and reopened his story file again and typed:

applied it carefully to one of the filthy little creatures, and had the satisfaction of watching it shrivel and drop away.

Over the next three hours Edward Alton Bell-Fairfax and company got rid of the leeches, found their way through the mangrove swamp by a secret shortcut that was actually faster than sailing across the lagoon, descended on one of Delarosa's notorious barracoons, and burned it to the ground after setting free all the slaves, one of whom was the captive daughter of King Bahou, and very grateful she was too. But just as she was about to express her thanks, who should emerge from the steaming, fever-ridden jungle but the treacherous Diego Luna, determined to make good his threat to kill the English commander...

Lewis, on the other hand, sat in an increasingly chilly upper deck lounge praying that somebody would come open the tea station and perhaps notice his unwelcome companions. Nobody did.

Dieppe, en Route to Paris

IT WAS DARK BY THE TIME the ferry landed at Dieppe. Lewis put away his Buke and groped for his suitcase. "Well, gentlemen, it's time to disembark," he told his captors.

"Not yet," they said together, threatening with their pistols. "We're supposed to wait until everybody goes."

So they waited, as the passengers from the lower decks trailed up the gangway, departing in ones and twos for the customs building. When the last one had trundled his baggage ashore, the little men rose to their feet.

"We're supposed to go now," said the one in the porkpie. "You're supposed to walk in front of us."

"Okay," Lewis said, hauling out his suitcase. "But I'm warning you, I'll almost certainly try to run away."

"Stupid cyborg," said the one in the ski hat. Lewis shrugged and walked ahead of them, down to the main deck and up the gangway to the quay. They followed closely, keeping their pistols trained on him the whole time. As he approached the customs building, Lewis glanced over his shoulder at them.

"I'll probably make my attempt in here," he said, and walked quickly up the ramp into the lighted hall with the turnstile and customs officers at its far end. They followed him, keeping their guns well up and pointed at his head. It was a long, long walk across the floor.

"Bonsoir, Monsieur," yawned the guard at the nearest turnstile.

"Regardez-vous les disrupters, s'il vous plait," Lewis said through his teeth, smiling. The guard's gaze skimmed past Lewis at the two little men and their guns.

"Merde!" he cried. The two little men stopped in their tracks, startled.

"Merci. Bonsoir," Lewis said pleasantly, largely unheard in the commotion of five large customs officers tackling his would-be captors. He walked over to Luggage Analysis, set his suitcase on the conveyor belt, and followed it through on the designated footpath without incident.

Before boarding the express to Paris he stopped at the snack bar and bought three Toblerones, and had finished one by the time he was seated in the deserted passenger car. The train left the station and picked up speed. Lewis was unwrapping the second Toblerone with trembling hands when two more strangers in white suits emerged from the car behind him and sat down, one to his left and one immediately in front of him.

They were quite similar to the first pair, though not so perfectly matched in·size; one wore a beret, and the other a baseball cap. The one with the beret also had a tiny chin-tuft of beard.

"Don't try that again," he told Lewis menacingly. "We have weapons too."

"How many of you people are there?" Lewis asked.

"All of us," the one with the cap said.

"I'd really rather not go with you," said Lewis. "Why do you think you can frighten me with your guns? I'm a cyborg, you know."

"Because these can hurt you," the one in the beret said, gesturing with the hand he was careful to keep firmly in his pocket. "We hurt you once before. We have these now. We can do it again."

"Please don't." Lewis swallowed hard and leaned back into his seat.

Eogan, that had been the mortal's name. Lewis was in Ireland se-
curing illuminated manuscripts for the Company. He'd been working
at the remote monastery with Eogan. A monk had been carried off in
the night by persons unknown, presumably the fair folk. The abbess,
aware that Lewis had some unusual abilities, sent him out with Eogan
to search and rescue if possible. They ventured into a hollow hill
where the fair folk were thought to live. Lewis didn't believe in fairies,
of course, the whole thing seemed like a lark; but when he found the
concealed entrance under Dun Govaun, he was so intrigued...

So he and Eogan went down the passage under the hill, Lewis
confidently assuring his companion there was nothing to fear, until
they stepped across the metal plate set in the floor, and Lewis knew
rending agony for the first time in his immortal life, and then red
darkness.

A confusion of impressions after that, blurred perhaps by the intensity of his fear and pain: a quiet, venomous little voice telling a
story about three brothers. Two were strong and clever, but the third
was weak and small, stupid except insofar as he was able to devise
wonders to hide him from his brothers. The strong brothers tried to
steal the devised wonders, but the weak one fled and hid himself in a
cave. So did his children who came after him, and the hunt continued
over the ages as the weaklings were driven to invent greater and
greater wonders to keep themselves hidden, a branch of humanity
lost in shadows, forgotten except in legend.

The storyteller went on to say that always the weaklings managed to keep ahead of their pursuers, until from the other end of time
the strong ones came up with a device of their own: immortal servants, full of machinery, who were cleverer and stronger even than
their masters. These cyborgs succeeded in finding the weaklings'
caves and robbing them.

So then they had to work harder, poor little weaklings, they had
to find a way to break the cyborgs. With all the moronic intensity of
their peculiar genius, they devised a disrupter field to disable biomechanicals. And Lewis, their first experimental subject, lay paralyzed

in their warren, seriously damaged by the field, self-repair offline and organic components dying inside him.

But he didn't die, not inside the hill. Eogan escaped with him, carried him out. He tried to make Eogan understand about the distress signal to Dr. Zeus, that the Company would come for him. The monk wept, tried to save Lewis by baptizing him so he'd have an immortal soul. A nice thought, but it didn't help. His organic heart stopped. His organic parts began to die.

He looked now at the two little men. "Tell me something," he said wearily. "Why me? It's been two thousand years. You're not immortals. You weren't even born when your people caught me before. How did you know to look for me?"

"We all remember," said the man in the cap.

"Everything," said the man in the beret.

Lewis nodded slowly. "Hive memory? I see. And what are you going to do with me, now that you have me?"

"Take you back," the man in the beret said. "You got away before we could learn about you."

"Ah." Lewis sighed. "That's right. You were going to take me apart, weren't you?" He felt something beading on his brow and realized it was the sweat of mortal fear. Then something occurred to him. "Wait a minute. You mean you've been hunting for me all these years simply because I happened to be the one you caught before?"

"Yes," said the one in the cap.

"But you could have learned what you wanted to know from any Company operative. You mean you never tried to capture any of the *others*?" Lewis's voice rose with incredulity, and he began to grin in spite of himself.

"Yes," said the one in the cap, looking confused.

"Don't laugh at us!" The one in the beret scowled. "You won't laugh when we get you home, slave."

Lewis sobered. Sweat was running down his face. He calmed himself and concentrated, trying to bring a greenish cast to his features. It wasn't particularly difficult.

"Oh, dear, no, I'm frightened," he assured his captors. "I'm so frightened, I think I'm going to be sick. It was Mr. Fancod, wasn't it? You found me through him."

"Yes," the one in the cap said.

"But he's stupid," said the one in the beret with just a trace of pride. "He's not like us."

"No, he couldn't be, could he? He lives with humans. Though I suppose you're some form of humanity too—" Lewis made a choking sound and hastily pulled out a tissue. "I really am going to be sick."

His captors backed away in alarm, but not far enough.

"Please let me go to the lavatory," Lewis gasped, rising in his seat. "You don't want vomit on your shoes, do you?"

"No," said the one in the cap. They let him get up but pushed closely behind him as he stumbled in the direction of the door marked HOMMES. He went in, and they crowded into the tiny space after him, so tightly packed that they were unable to raise their arms from their sides.

That was when he winked out and slammed the door from the outside, twisting the handle until the metal bent, effectively jamming the lock. He heard a splash and a faint cry from within; perhaps one of the guns had fallen into the toilet. He tore apart the nearest seat and pulled out a tubular piece of steel, which he punched through the lavatory's door jamb as an impromptu bolt.

Even as he was doing this, however, he felt a tingling sensation and numbness in the hand that had touched the door. He backed away, terrified. Turning and grabbing his suitcase with his left hand, he ran down the aisle between the seats to the opposite end of the car. There he crouched, staring back in dread as the train rattled on through the night, and the distant lights winked out across the black fields.

Lewis flexed his hand and felt sensation returning. A hasty self-diagnostic told him that there was some tissue damage, ruptured cells, biomechanicals compromised but resetting themselves. Drawing himself up, he shoved through the exit and stood for a moment on the tiny swaying platform between the cars, expecting to see Rod Serling standing there on the point of going into a speech.

Gasping for breath, he disabled the alarm and forced the boarding door. He focused on the passing terrain and, timing it to the split second, hurled first his suitcase and then himself out into the darkness.

Being an immortal, he landed lightly on his feet and pitched forward to lie flat on the embankment until the train had roared past. Then he got up, dusted himself off, found his suitcase, and walked back along the tracks to Neufchatel.

There, on a quiet residential street, he stole an agcar. He felt rather badly about it. He hadn't stolen anything from a mortal since that briefcase of Ernest Hemingway's, three centuries past. He drove all night, through Normandy, through Maine, through Anjou and Poitou, where once he had been a troubadour.

At daybreak he abandoned the car in a field and walked into Bordeaux, where he caught a train that took him across the border into Biarritz, and there he checked into a very nice hotel. Having showered, shaved, and put on a fresh suit, he went down to the hotel's restaurant and ordered lunch. His hands were still shaking.

While waiting for the regional specialty to arrive, Lewis fortified himself with a glass of real wine (France and its neighbors to the south had refused to have anything to do with the ban on alcoholic drinks, thank God) and set up his Buke. He keyed in the communication code to the Hotel Elissamburu and confirmed that a Joseph Denham was registered there. He left a message indicating he would be interested in purchasing the sofa and love seat and would call at the hotel to discuss it that afternoon. He sent the message, holding his breath; to his relief it went through, and the hotel confirmed reception.

Leaning back in his seat, he took another swallow of wine and peered cautiously at his right hand. Full sensation now; in fact, it hurt. It looked badly bruised, purpling under the surface of the skin.

He set down the wine and leaned forward again over his keyboard, spinning the story like a cloak, wrapping the words around to comfort himself.

"I will regret having defeated you, Commander Bell-Fairfax," sneered Diego Luna. "For I assure you, only in you have I ever found an opponent worthy of my steel!"

Edward looked along his cutlass at the wily Portuguese.

"You may find," he drawled, "that I'm a rather difficult man to kill."

Irún del Mar, Basque Republic

JOSEPH SAT IN THE hotel garden, all suited up as a tourist on vacation. He wore a brilliantly colored sweater emblazoned with the logo of the local pelote team, black beret, and terrorist pants. He wasn't wearing espadrilles only because it was March. He was in a strange mood.

There were several reasons why. He hadn't been back to what was now Irún del Mar in twenty thousand years, give or take a few centuries, and the degree to which things had changed (and hadn't changed) was profoundly unsettling to him.

He'd also been speaking Euskaran for the last week, which was enough to bend reality on its own.

Then too, he'd just received a cryptic mailing from Lewis, which probably meant that Lewis had news of some kind. It might be good news, or it might be some further tidbit about the life and exploits of Edward Alton Bell-Fairfax, of whom Joseph was sick of hearing. Mostly, though, he was bemused by a local phenomenon he had observed, and didn't quite know how he felt about it.

He waved cheerily enough, though, as Lewis, looking even more gaunt than usual, came to the garden gate. "Hi," said Joseph.

"What have you been doing, blowing up Spanish peers?" Lewis asked, regarding Joseph's ensemble in horror. He sat down at the table.

"I've been trying to summon a sense of ethnic identity," Joseph said.

"Is it working?" Lewis signaled to a waiter.

"No," Joseph admitted. "But check this out." He pointed at the transport trundling slowly down the street. It was a double-decker, and the upper deck was filled with some kind of sporting team, cheering rowdily and waving little pennants.

Lewis looked at them, and his mouth fell open. "Great Caesar's ghost," he said. "You've been cloned!"

"Weird, isn't it?" said Joseph. And in fact, every person on the bus could have been Joseph or a near relation. Short and stocky to a man and woman, same black button eyes, same ironic mouth. Lewis stared at them until the waiter came, and as he looked at the mortal to order a gin martini, he nearly jumped out of his skin. Joseph appeared to be in two places at once, a very badly dressed Joseph seated at his left and a Joseph in a white apron standing deferentially to his right, waiting with a little order plaquette.

Lewis changed his mind. "Hot chocolate, please," he said. Joseph repeated the order in Euskaran, the waiter keyed in his order and went away, and Lewis sagged backward in his chair.

"You know what's *really* weird?" said Joseph. "Nobody notices."

"Just when I thought things couldn't get any stranger, I was proven wrong." Lewis began to giggle helplessly.

"You don't look good," Joseph observed, frowning at him.

"I don't suppose I do. I've had a difficult couple of days, and I'm a little short on sleep."

"What's wrong? Are you in trouble?"

Lewis went into gales of high-pitched laughter. Passersby on the sidewalk turned toward him and frowned just like Joseph, which didn't help. Joseph looked around uncertainly and finally reached for his water glass, preparing to dash the contents into Lewis's face, but Lewis sobered abruptly. "Don't. This suit is Bond Street linen," he snapped. "And it's my best silk tie. I'm sorry. I'm running, if you must know."

"Christ! Somebody blow your cover?" Joseph set down the water glass.

"Yes. It was very strange. A vile-looking little idiot savant named Fancod walked into my office, modified an archives terminal with paper clips, and proceeded to break into the Company's database," Lewis said. "When his keepers came to take him away, he publicly identified me as a cyborg. They didn't believe him, of course, but he'd done it all the same. Then he threw orange peel all over the floor on his way out."

"Fancod?" Joseph stared.

"I cleaned up what I could, including the orange peel, you know procedure, and I ran." The waiter brought Lewis's hot chocolate, and Lewis reached for it desperately. "Oh, my, look at this, real whipped cream."

"Bad break, but it doesn't sound like it's your fault." Joseph waved his credit disk, indicating to the waiter that he was paying. "I don't see how that could get you in trouble."

"Mm." Lewis gulped hot chocolate. *Then on the boat two more vile-looking little idiot savants attempted to abduct me. They had some kind of disrupter pistols. I shook them off at customs and got on the train, and two more popped out of the woodwork. We had quite a little chat. I got away from them too, but not before they managed to do this.* He held up his right hand for Joseph to see the bruise there. *This happened seventeen hours ago.*

Joseph's eyes widened. He leaned forward and examined the bruise, which ought to have vanished within an hour of Lewis's injury.

There's worse, I'm afraid. I've found out more than I ever ought to have known—and I remembered exactly what happened to me in Ireland—and I'm sorry to go to pieces like this, but I think the Company is out to make me disappear. Lewis drained the last of the chocolate and slumped in exhaustion.

Joseph looked around. *Okay. I was confused before. Now I'm scared and confused. We need to talk somewhere.* "I wouldn't worry," he said out loud. "You've always done your job. Look, you need to relax. I was just about to go catch some People's Shakespeare. Why don't you come along? Ever seen Shakespeare in Euskaran?"

"I can't say that I have." Lewis opened his eyes, remembering in amazement that he had thought everything would return to normal if he could just contact Joseph.

"Neither have I, so this ought to be interesting." Joseph pushed back his chair and got up. "Come on."

They walked down a few streets to a park, where a big flatbed freight hauler had been parked to make an impromptu stage. Several dozen Joseph clones stood or sat around watching the performance, which was being given by a group of young people, also Joseph clones, in worker's clothes. The front of the truck was draped in red banners and Marxist slogans.

"They're Communists?" Lewis asked.

"It takes a while for ideas to reach this country," Joseph explained, embarrassed.

Lewis nodded in mute acceptance as a stalwart maiden in work boots strode to the front of the stage and held up the tree branch, decorated with a star and crescent moon cut of sheet metal, that signified this was the Wood near Athens.

Readers will have to use their imaginations to picture what Euskaran (a language that renders "I take the glass from the waitress" as "Glass the waitress the from in the act of taking I have it from her") would do to *A Midsummer Night's Dream*. The performance took eight hours without counting intermissions. Plenty of time for Lewis to explain what a long strange trip he'd had and why, as he and Joseph relaxed on a park bench and fairies fought over a mortal boy.

It was almost dark by the time Lewis finished. Peaseblossom, Cobweb, Moth, and Mustardseed were leading Bottom away in chains of flowers.

Joseph was silent a long moment, nodding thoughtfully. *These little morons, do you think they're human? Some branch of the mortal race who became troglodytes? And with inbreeding or whatever, autistic genius became a dominant genetic trait?*

And lack of fashion sense, added Lewis, shuddering.

But, you know something? I don't think this is the Company's doing. If the Company wanted to get you, they'd have done it by now.

You think so? But the alternative is even more frightening, Joseph. It means that the Company has an enemy out there with comparative technology, and they know about us. Me, anyway. What's more, they have a way to disable us.

Joseph moved to one side as a stage manager climbed on the bench to hang a probe light from a tree branch. *I'll bet the Company knows a lot more about what happened to you in Ireland than they've let you know. I'll bet that's why it took ten years to get you back online. They must have been studying what the little creeps did to you so they could work up a defense. Wouldn't you think? I'd be really surprised if every operative recruited after that time hasn't got some kind of protection built in. Hell, I remember being called in for an upgrade around 600 A.D.! I bet we've all got it now, you included.*

What about this? Lewis flexed his right hand.

It's healing, isn't it? Whereas when they got you the first time, they fried your biomechanicals, from the sound of it. You weren't in as much danger this time as you thought.

I'd certainly prefer to believe that.

You know what you've got to do now, of course: make a full report to the Company. Joseph looked hard at him. *Tell them everything that happened, or it will look funny. Worse! If these people have come up with some new improved way of getting to us, or you at least, the Company needs to know so they can take countermeasures. They'll cream the little bastards. Hell, if a Literature Specialist could outguess them, think what a team of security techs could do.*

I resent that, Lewis said, glaring at the stage.

No offense, pal. But you weren't designed for cloak-and-dagger stuff, were you? You were made to traffic in manuscripts and first editions, not dirty tricks. It's time to step back and let the profes-

sionals take over. Joseph leaned across and patted him on the shoulder. "I don't know about you, but this is getting real old. What do you say we go get some dinner?"

As they walked back to the hotel, Joseph transmitted: *The only thing that doesn't fit is this Fancod guy. Who the hell is he? You said he's working for the Company? He's got access codes? And yet he's one of these little creepy people?*

Yes! As much like the others as—as you're like all these Basques. That was why I thought it was a Company double cross at first. What is the Company doing employing one of them?

Maybe he was a spy, Joseph speculated. *Posing in an adult care facility as an autistic genius so he could hack into Company files.*

You think so?

Maybe. I don't know. But it makes a good story, and if I were you, I'd tell the Company that's what you think *he was. And I'll bet they give you a pat on the back for being so smart, and that's the last you'll hear of the business, except for maybe an update later on, telling you they've caught the guy and everything's been taken care of.* They turned in at the garden entrance and crossed the courtyard to the indoor dining room. Joseph stopped in the lighted doorway to look seriously at Lewis.

Sounds peachy, Lewis replied bitterly. A waiter appeared—not quite so much of a clone this time, more like an elderly uncle of Joseph's—and led them to a cozy dark booth. *I don't suppose you've had any leads on your friend since last we met?*

Only negative ones. One of the bunkers is up here. I got inside it two days ago. Lots of missing people, lots of Enforcers, but not him. So we can rule this one out.

I'm glad you've been doing something, at least—

"Hi, guys, sorry I'm late," said an immortal, sliding into the booth beside Lewis. "Security Tech Chilon. Literature Specialist Lewis? You okay? What the hell's been going on?"

"About time one of you people showed up," said Joseph. "My friend here's had quite a run. Waiter?" He flagged down the elderly mortal, and they had a brief but infinitely convoluted conversation in Euskaran.

"A lot has happened," Lewis said.

"Your transmission's been broken or intermittent since you got on the boat at Newhaven," Chilon informed him.

"That's nothing." Lewis stuck out his right hand. "Look at this."

"What?" Chilon peered at it in the dim light.

"There's a bruise."

"Oh." Chilon looked more closely. "So there is. How—"

"It's a really bloodcurdling story," Joseph said, settling back. "I've just ordered us wine and a couple of roast ducks. My friend here needs to make a full report. Get your ears on; this'll take a while."

It lasted, in fact, through dinner, dessert, and after-dinner drinks. Chilon, who was rather pleasanter and a bit more intelligent than most security techs Joseph had met, listened with an increasingly grim expression, though he was unfailingly polite and sympathetic in his reactions to Lewis's story.

"It sounds as though we have a lot of work to do here," he said when Lewis finished. He was pushing his glass of Pernod around on the table without drinking.

"Indeed." Lewis leaned forward and tried to look confidential. "Now, I realize I've inadvertently turned up some information the Company didn't want generally known, and I can't tell you how embarrassed I am. I'm only a Literature Specialist, after all. I'd really rather not get involved with any of this. But, you know, it seems to me that the mortal Fancod must be some kind of spy for these creatures. How else could he have known about me? And he's been getting into Company files! I realize my opinion doesn't count for much, but something ought to be done about him, don't you think?"

Joseph applauded silently.

Chilon said, "You're absolutely right about that. We've already handled Fancod, so don't worry. As for the other stuff—well, you aren't likely to go blurting the information out to anybody, are you? Other than to Joseph here."

Joseph held his breath, but Lewis nodded and caught the ball. "I reported to the first Facilitator I could find. Technically it should have been Xenophon, I know, but I wasn't sure I could reach him, and for all I know that channel's not secured."

Right answer. Both Chilon and Joseph relaxed.

Chilon had a sip of Pernod. "Good point," he said.

"So, what happens now?" Lewis looked from one to the other.

"We're going to monitor you pretty closely for a while, to be sure these people leave you alone," Chilon said. "We'll see if we can grab the ones being held by the French authorities. I imagine the guys you trapped in the toilet had some explaining to do." He grinned. "But we must do some event effacement too, so the mortals don't get a lot of messy information they don't need. Don't worry about any of that. In fact, we can do a memory wipe, if you want."

Lewis's knuckles whitened on his glass, but he just shook his head with a slight frown. "I'd rather not go that far, thank you. If I meet up with them again, I want to be able to defend myself."

"You're right there." Joseph nodded.

"Okay." Chilon finished his drink. "Then here's what I propose: you could use a vacation anyway, after all this, and I know you were going to Paris, but why don't you hang out down here for a couple of weeks? Joseph and I can keep an eye on you while the Company clears up the fallout. Paris is a little crowded right now."

"Sounds like a plan," said Lewis cautiously.

"They'll probably want you to report to Eurobase One for a debriefing and a diagnostic," Chilon went on smoothly. "To see why that bruise is still there."

"Absolutely, yes."

Joseph's eyes flickered from Chilon to Lewis and back. "So what do you want to do now, Lewis?" he said. "You want to get a room here? We can take in one of those Minoan-style bullfights they're reintroducing. Or, I was planning on going to the Painted Cave Museum tomorrow. You want to tag along?"

"Oh, my gosh, I forgot." Lewis's face lit up. "They're your mortal father's paintings, aren't they? What an experience for you. I'd love to come. I left my suitcase at the hotel in Biarritz, though."

"No problem," said Chilon. "I have a car. I'll take you there tonight and bring you back up tomorrow. I ought to stick close anyway, until the operation's in place. There may be more of the little morons running around."

Lewis shivered.

It was growing late, so Chilon and Lewis left to walk back to Chilon's car. Joseph stood in the doorway of the hotel, watching them go down the street in the lamplight as they chatted about the fabled luxury of Eurobase One. The larger man put his hand on Lewis's shoulder, in a friendly way.

Joseph sighed, wondering if he'd ever see Lewis again.

But next morning there came no call officially informing him that Lewis had been transferred to a distant location, and as Joseph was sitting over his breakfast, he heard the two coming through the hotel lobby, discussing the relative merits of Toblerone over Perugina.

"In here." He leaned out and waved from the restaurant. They saw him and smiled. He thought that Lewis looked more tired than the day before, if that was possible, with new lines of strain in his face. Lewis seemed cheerful enough as he sat down and ordered coffee, however.

"No weird visitors lying in wait at your hotel, I guess?" Joseph inquired.

"Nope." Lewis shook out his napkin. "Though I can't say I had the most pleasant dreams."

"How's the investigation going?" Joseph asked Chilon.

"Up and running," Chilon said, reaching into the roll basket and selecting a brioche. He broke it open and daubed it with fruit paste.

Joseph knew better than to ask for details. He turned to Lewis and said casually, "So, are you all ready to give me emotional support? This should be some experience. I haven't seen those paintings since I was twenty, when I sealed them up."

"Wow," said Chilon through a mouthful.

"Will we have to do any spelunking or anything like that to get to them?" Lewis asked, worried. "Because I'm not really dressed—"

"No, no, we won't be going into the real cave. That's been re-sealed. This is the exhibit they built outside. It's all holosimulation. They say you can't tell the difference, except that you can walk through without getting mud on your shoes, and there's a gift shop."

"So you won't really get to see your father's paintings, then," said Lewis.

Joseph shrugged. "What's real? I'm a simulation too, when you come down to it. Besides, a lot of people died in that cave. I've put off coming back here my whole life, to be honest. Now that there's this nice sanitary replica, I thought I'd see if I could take it."

"This was where your mortal parents were killed?" Chilon asked.

"That's right," said Joseph.

The site was in a pleasant wooded valley, only a kilometer inland from the sea. Along one side were cliffs bordering a river, with a rock overhang that had long been known as a Neolithic shelter. The cave itself opened out of an escarpment some thirty meters east, and the modern exhibit and carpark were located in a meadow just below.

They drove up in Chilon's car and paid their admission. They walked through the museum with its display of flint tools and skulls, through the hall of dioramas with its creepy models of fur-clad ancients poised around cook fires, and at last to the painted cave itself. Chilon paused at the gift shop to rent an audio unit before they went in.

"You want one?" He gestured at the display rack as he put on his earshells.

"Nah. What can they tell me I don't already know?" said Joseph. They walked into darkness and memory.

The first area, skillfully lit as if by rush lamp for maximum dramatic effect, was the Gallery of the Dancers. It reminded Lewis of the opening night of Stravinsky's *Rite of Spring*, with the bear-robed shuffling figures that dominated the last act. Not that the pictures showed anything that easily identifiable: hundreds of wavy black lines only gradually resolved themselves for the eye and became capering thighs, a pair of arms outflung, a profile bowing over a flute. No single form was complete and coherent.

Lewis and Chilon looked up respectfully. After a moment Chilon's audio docent directed him into the next chamber, and he moved along obediently.

Lewis sidled over to Joseph, who was stone-faced. "Why are the lines all drawn on top of each other?" he whispered.

"Because nobody'd invented erasers yet," Joseph replied. "And the man was a doodler. He couldn't finish anything."

"Oh."

"It drove my mother crazy." Joseph surveyed the illusion and found a particular fall of rock, reproduced in perfect holographic detail. "She died right over there," he added, pointing. "Great Goat cultist with an axe."

"I'm sorry," said Lewis, appalled.

"I don't feel anything. Funny, isn't it?"

There followed a silence, in which they listened to Chilon's footsteps getting fainter as he moved farther in.

I'm going to transmit a code to you. Lewis reached out and touched Joseph's forehead. Before Joseph could reply, the code came, a jumble of something that might have been binary but wasn't quite. Joseph blinked, received it, and shunted it into his tertiary consciousness.

What the hell was that?

It's what Fancod used to pull up a Company menu. I tried it last night, when I couldn't sleep. I got into the personnel files, not the general biographies but the classified material. I thought I'd see if I could find out what Mendoza was doing on Catalina with Edward in

1923. Joseph, the Company sent her Back Way Back, but they didn't keep her there. She was sent to Agricultural Station One on March 24, 1863, linear time. But later that day she was transferred from there to a place called Site 317. That's the last entry in her file.

Jesus, Lewis!

Listen to me. It's more involved than it sounds. Agricultural Station One existed from 200,000 B.C. to 50,000 B.C., and it was on Catalina Island too. They kept her there from 153,000 to 150,000. She was in Back Way Back three thousand years, Joseph, before they let her out! I couldn't find any information on the other place, Site 317. But if you saw her on Catalina in 1923, and Site 317 is her last known location, maybe they're one and the same.

Lewis, are you crazy? Didn't I warn you about this? "Come on," Joseph said, striding after Chilon. "I'm getting depressed here."

They walked unseeing through the Grotto of the Lions, the Red Room, and the Room of Noah, and caught up with Chilon in front of a whole wall of silhouettes of human hands of every possible size.

When they emerged blinking into the morning light, Chilon said, not unkindly, "Did you make peace with your ghosts?"

"There weren't any," Joseph said. "Can you beat that?"

"Perhaps because it's only a replica," suggested Lewis.

"Could be. But none of the rest of the landscape does anything for me either. I thought I'd feel a connection or something, you know? A sense of belonging, coming up here? I don't. No kinship at all, even when every guy in the street looks like my twin brother."

They contemplated that while getting into the car. Chilon switched on the agdrive, and the car rose to its accustomed two feet above the surface of the ground. The propellant motor bore them away.

"I had the same experience," Chilon remarked. "When I went back to Sparta thinking it would feel like home. I don't know if it was that so much time had passed and everything about my memories was totally irrelevant, or what. But I wasn't one of those people. They weren't part of me."

"We're Company men," said Joseph gloomily.

"I guess so."

Lewis settled back and gave thanks yet again that he had been acquired by the Company before he could form any memory whatever of mortal life. He had enough problems as it was. "Have you ever thought," he said carefully, "of where you'll live after 2355? Assuming, you know—"

"Yeah," said Chilon.

"Beyond gradual retirement, we can live anywhere we like, right? Settle down?"

"I'd always kind of thought I'd come back here," said Joseph. "I don't guess I will, though."

"I'm not sure where I'd go," said Lewis. "Just what it would have to have. Fine libraries and shops. A certain degree of gracious civilization. Good restaurants. Decent weather."

"Santa Barbara," Joseph suggested.

"No wine or gin there anymore," Lewis reminded him. "Paris, maybe. Or Monte Carlo. And yet, you know, I've never felt culturally identified with the French? What a pity we can't go backward. I'd love to live in Old Rome at the height of her glory."

Joseph had, and very nearly said something pungent and to the point about Old Rome. He looked at Lewis's weary face and confined himself to remarking, "No gin."

"I suppose not." Lewis sighed.

"And no Theobromos either," Chilon said. "The future's all there is, guys. Pie in the sky as time goes by."

"Good one," Joseph chuckled, and Lewis smiled politely.

Chilon left them off in front of Joseph's hotel while he looked for a place to park, because the technological advances of the twenty-third century had not yet solved that problem. They went back to the lobby to see about getting two more rooms.

Will you check into that code? Lewis asked.

When it's safe. When I'm alone. Lewis, do you have a death wish or something?

Absolutely not. Lewis looked grim. *I found that out on the train from Dieppe, believe me. But this information was dropped in our laps, and we'd be insane not to make use of it. A mere Literature Specialist can't find out where Site 317 is, but a Facilitator might. Don't you want to solve the mystery once and for all?*

Joseph did not reply immediately. They stepped up to the front desk, and he had a long conversation with the clerk in Euskaran that amounted to, "My friends are staying on. Do you have two more rooms?" and "Yes. Please sign here." As Lewis was signing in, Joseph transmitted, *Something to think about, Lewis. Suppose we find Mendoza, switched off in one of those vaults. What will we be able to do for her? Get her out? Revive her? Hide her? Where the hell can we hide from the Company? What would she do with herself? The next chapter in that story is that all three of us wind up in vaults in the same bunker, per omnia secula seculorum.*

Lewis blanched, but answered doggedly, *I don't believe she's in one of those vaults, Joseph. What if they let her go after she served her time Back Way Back? We have no idea what Site 317 is. If it's the Hotel St. Catherine on Catalina Island, if for example that's her gradual retirement, and she's still there with Edward—*

Will you let go of that? You know damn well the Edward guy died, and the odds against Nature's spitting out not two but three *guys who look just like him—it's absurd.*

Lewis gestured impatiently at the lobby full of Josephs playing backgammon. *Somehow it doesn't seem as unlikely as it used to.*

Joseph looked around and went pale. *Oh, no. You don't suppose there's some weird little genetic pocket in England like there is here, do you? I never thought about that.*

Well, think about it now.

All right. I'll see what I can find out. But you have to drop this, Lewis! Mendoza was my recruit, after all. If I'm not obsessed with this past the point of good sense, you shouldn't be. What was she to you?

My dearest friend, Lewis told him. *You should understand, after where we've been today. We don't have families, we don't have homes, we don't even have nationalities. Nothing remains except us, and all we have is each other.*

Joseph was silent a moment. *Sometimes,* he replied. *Mostly, all we really have is ourselves, Lewis. Do you want to lose yourself? You spent ten years switched off once. Do you want that permanently?*

There are worse things. Joseph, I'm tired of worrying about me! We live such miserable lives when we live for ourselves. When our work is over, what will I have? A nice little villa for one somewhere and an endless supply of reading matter?

Hey, you might meet somebody. It's been known to happen.

Never to me. And very seldom to any of the rest of us, as far as I can tell. Except Mendoza. She loved, and gave up everything she had for it. And then three thousand years in prison, Joseph!

I know.

Don't you see? When all this is over, I don't really care if I'm relegated to a vault or rewarded with a villa in St. Tropez. What I want, with my whole heart, is to know that Mendoza's story had a happy ending. That love triumphed, and bravery, against impossible odds. That you really saw them together there on Catalina Island.

And if you get yourself arrested or worse, trying to make the story come out right? What does that leave for you, Lewis?

My honor.

You are the most dangerous incurable romantic I have ever known. Joseph spotted Chilon and waved. "We got you a room. Come in and sign for it," he called.

"You would not believe how far I had to go before I found a parking space," groused Chilon.

Joseph in the Darkness

I WENT WITH LEWIS to Eurobase One. Father, you wouldn't recognize it now! When I was little, when you led the troops out to battle and we kids watched you in breathless admiration, it was such a raw place: partly a twenty-fourth-century field camp with a limited budget, partly a Neolithic stockade, but one hundred percent military base, up in those rough cold Cévennes.

You should see it today. It's a neoclassical Art Deco kind of fantasy, like a resort hotel might be if the Olympian gods built one. I always thought New World One was classy, but it had nothing on this place. Statues by Praxiteles and a lot of other classical masters, gorgeous landscaped gardens, Roman-style banquets with French culinary style, and a bathhouse like something dreamed up by William Randolph Hearst. Aegeus, the guy who'd been running it the last two millennia, had picked and chosen the best elements of the ages that rolled by the place.

There was a big staff of mortal servants to keep it all immaculate too, fairly surly French peasants. I heard rumors while I was there that this hadn't always been the case, that Aegeus had got away with some exploitative stuff that would have made our mortal masters' hair stand on end, if they'd known about it. But that, if it happened, was long in the past. I didn't see a single togaed girl or boy slave while I was there.

Lewis was too nervous to enjoy it much. This was the place he'd been brought after the little stupid guys fried his circuits the first time, after all, the place where he spent ten years in a regeneration vat. More unpleasant memories seemed to be bubbling up to the surface of his consciousness, but he didn't talk about them much. And though he tested out physically okay, with the damage to his hand all self-repaired, and though he got through his debriefing without arousing any suspicion (as far as I could tell), something was wrong.

He seemed to expect to see little freaks in white suits everywhere we went. In the sensational neoclassical gymnasium he thought he saw them lurking behind the homoerotic Greek bronzes. In the vast billiard parlor hung with lost Renoirs, jolly studies of boozing sports parties, he thought he spotted them under the tables. In the restaurant (Le Grenouille en Vin, a five-star place if ever there was one, the wine cellar alone went down five stories into the bedrock of the Cévennes), he jittered when a white-coated waiter stepped out a little too suddenly from behind a potted palm. Even the Robert Louis Stevenson shrine, with its holo statue of the writer, gave him pause. Maybe it was those huge starry eyes Stevenson had and the pipe-cleaner skinniness of his limbs. I knew the guy; even in the flesh, Louis looked too weird to be human.

But no phantoms seized the other Lewis. After about a week, his new posting orders and identification disk arrived, and the Company sent him on to a nice safe job in New Zealand, pilfering old documents from a university library. I saw him to his transport and then got the hell out of Euro One myself. I was tired of all the grandeur.

I sound pretty philistine, don't I? But this was my first home, other than that rock shelter. I had some good memories of the old base, when I was young and as idealistic as I was ever going to be. The world was a swell place, and we were all safe, father, because of you and the rest of the big guys. Nobody thought you were monsters then.

But what did the old stockade have to do with this pink carpeting, indirect lighting, gilt and crystal? And where in this world would you fit, now? I'm not so sure I fit myself anymore.

I went back to my job in Spain, assistant to an archaeology team sponsored by the local rabbinical school, making sure they uncovered the miraculously preserved relics of a twelfth-century synagogue, digging up what Nahum and I buried so carefully all those years ago. I made plans to go back to California the next time I could get a few weeks off, but somehow the time just sped by. Was I scared to come look for you, father? Probably. I sure as hell didn't feel like going to Catalina to see if Mendoza was shacked up there with another Englishman, no matter what I'd promised Lewis.

Things are safe enough in the American Community, at least, no worries about that. Everything is prim and proper and politically correct there now. They've outlawed alcohol again in most of the former states. Also meat, dairy products, tobacco, coffee, tea, chocolate, refined sugar, recreational drugs of any kind, competitive sports, and most great literature. So has England, and so have most of the rest of what used to be called First World countries.

This means boom economies for those little nations, like the Celtic Federation, who thumb their noses at the others and continue to produce whiskey and lamb chops. Still, most of the world's farmed acreage is given over to soybeans. Religion isn't illegal but is increasingly being regarded with genteel horror by most people, except the Ephesians. Faith is so... psychologically incorrect.

Sex isn't illegal, but there isn't a lot of it going on these days. There's talk about how it's a distasteful animal urge, how it victimizes women and robs men of their primal power. It creates codependency. It presents a terrible risk of catching a communicable disease. Relationships of any kind, in fact, are probably a bad idea.

I don't know exactly when this problem became widespread among the mortals, but I know that a lot of operatives of my acquaintance are climbing the walls or beginning to date other immortals, which is sort of unusual. We're not really comfortable in bed with each other as a rule, you know?

There is something beginning to be wrong with the mortals, a certain lack of interest and ability. The birth rate has plummeted all over the world. There are millions of inner children and fewer and fewer real ones. I remember seeing a holo feature on a certain famous amusement park: roller coasters and merry-go-rounds packed with forty-year-olds clutching the wonder of childhood to themselves like harpies, and not one little face in the crowd. Neverland has been invaded by the grownups, no children allowed. It's better than having lots of real kids starving in gutters, at least.

Mind you, it isn't like this everywhere. There are still plenty of places a retrograde old guy or gal can be an adult. You can get a beer, a steak, or a roll in the hay, and merry-go-rounds be damned; but you'll be branded a sociopath if anybody finds out.

Not surprisingly, a lot of people have taken to alternative lifestyles, like living outside national boundaries so they can indulge what appetites they still have without interference. How do they manage this?

It's being called the Second Golden Age of Sail.

Steam ended the days of the old sailing ships so long ago that most mortals can't imagine why such lovely, graceful craft were pushed out of existence by squat metal tubs. Being mortals, of course, they weren't around in the days when foot-long cockroaches swarmed in wooden forecastles or sailors clung to frozen ropes, attempting to take in sails with numb hands. Probably for that reason, a tall ship has come to symbolize the romance of the high seas in a way no chunky cruise boat can ever match, no matter how many Las Vegas revues it books.

Forget about space cruises. Think of an economy air transport, only more cramped, with worse food, and no chance in hell of surviving an accident. People don't go to Luna to have fun; they go there to work. And Mars will be even more work once mortals are able to go there.

No, consumers wanted something pretty, something comfortingly retro. Tall ships were the answer, updated with modern technology.

You don't need to climb to dizzying heights or learn a bunch of arcane phrases: the ship's computer will do it all for you now, with smoothly efficient servomotors and composite cables. It judges the wind and keeps to a course as ably as the crustiest old salt, with the added advantage of weather satellite links. Add a little fusion drive to get you places in a dead calm, and the system is nearly perfect. Employ a couple of able-bodied sailors in case of fouls or repairs, and you even keep the unions happy. Any dope can sail a three-masted clipper now, and lots do, and that means Freedom.

On a good-sized vessel you can store enough booze and contraband food to last a couple of years, and you can enjoy them without a Public Health Monitor breathing down your neck, as long as you stay outside the jurisdiction of the local coast guard. You can play music as loud as you want. You can be overweight, light up a pipe of tobacco, and indulge in other behavior that would get you shut away in a mental hospital if you tried it anyplace else nowadays.

Mortals have taken to the sea in droves, becoming semipermanent residents. Little piddly thirty-foot yachts have become the trailers of the new age. People with real money have custom sailing ships built, mansions under acres of sail.

For a while there was a lot of enthusiastic talk about how eco-friendly sail was, since it utilized wind power, and a lot of commercial freight vessels got built before people figured out it was cheaper just to send stuff by big fusion-driven cargo barges. But for the private sector sail is in, it's stylish, it's a political antistatement, and so waterfronts are once again forested with masts.

I have to admit they're easy on the eyes, those big graceful square-riggers flying along under clouds of canvas; and, unlike the old days, there are no rats, roaches, rotting timbers, or rotting food.

Freedom and adventure on the high seas. Cruise lines make a fortune on consumers who can't afford their own ships by offering six-month package tours during which they can partake of forbidden pleasures like pizza or hot fudge sundaes.

I guess that was why Lewis utilized some gradual retirement time and booked himself a cruise on the Olympian Clipper Line's *Unrepentant Monarch*.

The Company must have decided it was the perfect place to bait the trap.

Three Days out of Auckland, 2275

Take that for you?" asked the deck steward, gesturing at Lewis's empty martini glass.

"Thanks." Lewis looked up from his text of *The Moon and Sixpence*.

"Another?"

"Not now."

Lewis turned his attention to the bookscreen again, but at that moment a little party boat came into sight to starboard, tacking about to give its passengers a better view of the *Unrepentant Monarch*. They hooted and screamed and waved at the great ship, clinging to the rail of their schooner, and there seemed to be a costume party in progress, because most of them were dressed as pirates. As Lewis smiled and waved back, somebody on board fired their signal cannon. Ping, a broadside, if they had been using shot instead of a sound chip. But even if they used shot, the cruise vessel would have no more noticed a one-pound ball than an elephant would notice a mosquito.

The mortals on board the schooner nevertheless danced and whooped, and the mortals on the *Unrepentant* catcalled back to them as though there were a real assault going on.

Lewis, who remembered vividly what it was like to be on a ship under attack by French privateers, offered up a prayer of gratitude to Neptune. All things taken into consideration, he preferred reclining in a deck chair with a novel to running around on a blood-smeared deck dodging real cannon fire.

Though the experience had made for one of his better chapters, he felt. The scene where Edward and his command take on the slaver *Whydah Queen* was his favorite, full of authentic little touches, the one he'd rewritten least over the years. *The Tall Englishman* was unbelievably long now, seventeen volumes at last count.

Lewis had hit a dry spell lately, as he drew inevitably closer to the point where Edward (now a political, supposedly in the pay of Her Majesty's Foreign Office but in reality an agent of the Gentlemen's Speculative Society) was to be given his assignment to go to California. Quite apart from the fact that he wasn't looking forward to killing off his hero, Lewis had certain qualms about depicting Edward's relationship with Mendoza. It seemed an invasion of privacy, unforgivably frivolous to dramatize something that had resulted in heartbreak for her, not to mention ruin.

He had made some attempts to block out a different scenario, one with a happy ending, but it had given off no more warmth than a painted fire. Nothing to do but set the whole project aside for a few decades and see if something suggested itself...

Lewis sighed and leaned back, looking up at the sky with its Mercator lines of cable crossing. Vast canvas walls straining in the brisk breeze, the *Unrepentant Monarch* skimmed along like a seabird. Perhaps Edward had come to America on a clipper. Ought Lewis take notes for a future scene?

He couldn't let the story alone, could he? He closed his eyes, sorted through his mental list of gods, and invoked Apollo and the Muses to grant him inspiration.

"I say, aren't you Literature Specialist Lewis?"

Lewis opened his eyes. There before him, leaning on the rail, was Facilitator Nennius, nattily dressed in white cruise attire. In some other dimension, Apollo smirked and threw Lewis a salute.

"Nennius, isn't it?" he said, after a moment's stupefaction. "Heavens, how long has it been? 1836, wasn't it?"

"To be sure. That evening at Johnson's." Nennius stepped forward, surefooted though the *Unrepentant* was rising on a particularly mountainous swell just then, and settled himself into the deck chair next to Lewis. He was a tall immortal, dark and aristocratic-looking. "Well, well, what are the odds of this? Are you taking the whole cruise?"

"As far as Panama. I'm on my way to my next posting," Lewis replied, fighting down panic. Was it so remarkable they should run into one another again, after four hundred years? He looked on as Nennius ordered a bottle of Chateau Rothschild from the deck steward and wondered how on earth he could refrain from leading the conversation around to Edward, whom this man had actually known, spoken with, perhaps even set on his course in life.

"I'm on holiday, personally," Nennius said, lounging back. "And a damned well-earned one, I might add. I've just come off forty years as a politician in Australia. I envy you Conservationist chaps, I really do. When you're done with a job, you've at least got something to show for it. How I'd love to have an old book or a painting or *anything* I could point to and say, 'There, that was my work, I rescued that for the ages.' But nothing we Facilitators do shows, you know, in the long run."

"Well, but surely that's the point," Lewis said. "If your work's done well, it doesn't show. It's a much more difficult job being a Facilitator. You're the men behind the scenes, the stage managers for history, the men in black."

"A very flattering assessment."

"True, all the same."

"Well, thank you."

They fell silent as the steward brought the wine—service was superb on these cruises—and Nennius accepted his glass, inhaled, sipped, and approved. The steward, waiting until Nennius's nod, vanished unobtrusively. Nennius watched him go and shook his head.

"What that chap could teach his fellow mortals. Does it seem to you they've gotten ruder as the ages roll by? To think the day would come when you'd have to go on a cruise like this to experience courtesy!"

"It's one of the things promised in the brochure," Lewis said. "Every one of the staff has to take social interaction classes."

"Not like the old days, eh?" Nennius drank with relish. "The little monkeys might have been ignorant and bloodthirsty, but by God they knew how to be polite when they had to. Remember that night we sat up talking till all hours at Johnson's? That waiter *waited*, there in the corner, and not a word of complaint or a cough or an impatient look from him."

"Johnson's," Lewis said, remembering.

"Abominable coffee, but a lovely place for privacy. Gone long since, I suppose."

"Utterly. That whole block went during the Blitz."

"That's right, you were stationed over there then, weren't you? You've had some lively postings over the years. I was there until the twentieth century. Then I was off to Greece, thank God." Nennius waved indulgently at the mortal pirate party, which was making another pass along the starboard bow. "Look at the silly little beggars. They do everything they can to make their world as dull and inhibited as it can possibly be, and run off at weekend to pretend they're having adventures. They do love their adventures."

"So few of them ever get to have real ones," Lewis said.

"True. Good thing too, on the whole. Though I remember one who did, by God!" Nennius reached for his glass. "Do you recall those papers I gave you for the archives, that night in 1836? Nasty inky schoolboy mess the Company wanted, for some unimaginable reason?"

Lewis felt the shiver of warning, sensed the pit thinly screened with branches. He stared out at the wide horizon, pretending to think. "Vaguely. I was more interested in your anecdotes about Londinium."

"So you were. The leather-knickers-down-the-well story." Nennius sniggered. "And to think they ended up in a museum exhibit! Anyway. I was a headmaster at a public school at the time, and the papers were nothing more than exercises I'd set one of my pupils. Remarkable boy, really, though I thought he'd no future at all. Illegitimate, you see, even if he was the bastard of somebody awfully important. They'd paid to send him to Overton, at least. But you know how it was back then: you simply had no place in the world with that kind of mark against you, unless you cut one out for yourself.

"I never thought the boy would manage it. Too fond of using his fists to answer an argument, though he was certainly a clever little fellow. He was shaping up into a scholar of some promise, actually, but then he was nearly sent down for fighting, so his people—whoever they were—took him out of school and sent him off to the Navy for a midshipman, and I thought, well, that's the last I'll hear of *him*. Our padre was desolated. He had some idea the little brute could have gone out for divinity!"

"Was he a religious boy?" Lewis asked.

"Oh, he was full of idealistic nonsense at first, but he woke up to the reality of the world pretty damn quickly. No fool he."

"Really," said Lewis, trying to sound bored but polite.

"Edward Bell-Fairfax, that was his name," Nennius said, and Lewis's heart contracted painfully. He raised a hand in a casual gesture, and the deck steward stepped within earshot, inquiringly.

"Another martini, please," Lewis said. The steward ducked his head and hastened away.

Nennius went on: "So anyway, a dozen years went by, and then a few more, and I'd long since forgotten about Bell-Fairfax. In those days I used to belong to Redking's Club. There was a cabinet minister I was dogging on the Company's behalf—you don't need to know whom, of course, but it was more of what you so kindly call stage-managing history. Well, we had our annual function welcoming new members, and to my utter astonishment I found myself seated opposite Bell-Fairfax."

"What a surprise," agreed Lewis. "I suppose that sort of man didn't get into that sort of club?"

"I should say not! But there was no mistaking Bell-Fairfax: remarkably ugly fellow, big horse-faced gawk with a broken nose, so tall he couldn't walk through a doorway with his hat on. Beautiful speaking voice, though," Nennius said, "and tremendously charming when he wanted to be. At any rate he'd charmed his way into the club. A retired naval commander on half pay, mind you! I thought it must be his people who'd arranged it, of course. Funnily enough, I was dead wrong." Nennius poured himself another glass of wine.

"Was he some sort of hero?" Lewis said carefully.

"Oh, I gather he'd served with some distinction off the Ivory Coast. Been sent out there to fight the slave trade, you know, probably some of that youthful idealism coming to the fore. But he got himself into trouble again. Nobody spoke of it to his face, but the rumor was he'd very nearly been court-martialed. Fighting again, just as he'd done in school. This time he'd laid his hands on a superior officer, and from what I heard, the only reason he was allowed to retire honorably was that he threatened to make the damnedest scandal." Nennius looked arch. "The captain in question was notorious for certain things, even by the standards of the British Navy."

"Rum, sodomy, and the lash," quoted Lewis.

"Oh, rather worse than that, I think. However it happened, Bell-Fairfax came out of it all right." Nennius watched as the deck steward set down Lewis's martini and slipped away. "After all, there he was, across the table from me. Properly respectful, of course, to his old headmaster, and I was obliged to converse with him. I was gratified to discover that he hadn't rotted away his brain on grog, or turned into one of those blustering seafaring gentlemen. Actually rather learned, for a Navy man. Superb command of rhetoric, though his Latin was abysmal."

"Not much call for it in the Navy, I suppose." Lewis took a bracing sip of his cocktail.

"No. No. But still a fine raconteur, quite dryly clever, and I found myself liking him. We became friends, as much as a former pupil and master can, saw one another at the club when he wasn't traveling abroad. He did a lot of traveling abroad," Nennius added in a meaningful tone.

Lewis merely raised his eyebrows in inquiry, not trusting himself to speak.

"You'll recollect I said I was wrong to assume his people had bribed the admittance council," Nennius continued. "Well. He had been sponsored by one of the Old Members!"

"You don't say," said Lewis faintly, marveling at the permanence of certain things Victorian.

"It seems he got in with a rather remarkable set." Nennius lifted his glass and studied it. "A clique of Foreign Office people with certain esoteric interests."

"Freemasons?" Lewis wondered to what god he ought to pray just now. Mercury, god of liars? Minerva, goddess of wisdom?

"No. You remember how it was back then, most of the ruling classes were Freemasons. That was old hat compared with what Bell-Fairfax and these other people—most distinguished some of them were, too—were doing." Nennius looked sternly across at Lewis. "Did you ever hear of the Gentlemen's Speculative Society?"

Mercury, Lewis decided, and as he wrinkled his brow in apparent perplexity, he uttered a silent but profound prayer of supplication. "Debating team at Oxford?" he said at last.

Nennius laughed. "Not likely," he said scornfully. "Imagine a secret fraternity that might admit Victor Frankenstein, Jules Verne, and Indiana Jones on equal terms. Sounds like a hoax, doesn't it? However, I happen to know it was very real indeed, and Bell-Fairfax was a member."

Nennius himself had been a member. Did he know Lewis knew? Was this a trap? Or was he simply leaving out his own involvement in order to be able to tell the tale? "Your mortal must have had no end of adventures," said Lewis.

"Perfectly astonishing ones, if rumor prove true," said Nennius.

"Of course, at this late date very little evidence remains. I can assure you, though, that there were any number of quasi-scientific expeditions authorized by my cabinet member, who was also one of the Gentlemen's number, as were some of the best scientific brains in England at the time. Their goal seems to have been world domination, in a mild sort of way.

"That was where Bell-Fairfax fit in, you see. He was no scientific genius, but he was frightfully clever and a damned good man of his hands, if you take my meaning: he'd grown accustomed to dirty work in a just cause and could be relied on utterly. He was one of their best agents, I believe."

Lewis giggled shakily. "What a novel this would make."

"If mortals read such things anymore," said Nennius, looking out at the pirate ship in contempt.

"Well, but go on. This is fascinating," Lewis said, remembering his martini and gulping half of it down. "I worked in Hollywood once, you know. I can't help thinking what John Ford might have done with such a story."

"Unfortunately, I don't know many details." Nennius shook his head. "They sent him to Egypt, and Jerusalem, and once—I believe—to a Jewish ghetto in Prague, of all places. Bell-Fairfax was a closed-mouthed chap, though. Wouldn't have been much of a political if he hadn't been. No, I got most of what I learned of his adventures from my cabinet member, who was rather a fool."

"A ghetto," said Lewis. New chapters were dancing before his eyes, in spite of his fear.

"The only mission I have any detailed knowledge of is his last one: poor old Bell-Fairfax disappeared, presumed killed." Nennius sighed. "We kept his room at the club for seven years. Still, the adventure must have been choice. Ever hear of Santa Catalina Island? But you must have, you worked in Hollywood. I understand it became a fashionable resort in the early twentieth century."

Lewis nodded, light-headed. "Twenty-six miles from the mainland. One used to be able to see it, on clear days, when there still were any in Los Angeles. I suppose one can again, now."

Nennius leaned forward and lowered his voice. "As near as I could piece it together, the Gentlemen had got hold of a mysterious document that dated back to God only knew when and lay forgotten in the royal archives. An early explorer was out there, it seems, and discovered something damned queer on Santa Catalina. There were supposed to have been artifacts with the document, but I was never able to confirm that. The rumors, though! Hints about Atlantis, the Fountain of Youth, fabulous treasure. Whatever was actually there, the Gentlemen felt strongly enough about it to send an expedition, and so of course they prodded the Foreign Office into mounting one."

"Now we're getting into George Lucas's territory," said Lewis, surprised at his own sangfroid.

"Yes, aren't we? The only difficulty with the plan was that the Yanks found out about it, and weren't about to let a foreign power grab a bit of their coastline, especially when they had a civil war going on. This was in 1862, you see.

"Something went wrong, just as the expedition was beginning to make real progress. Bell-Fairfax was sent in to salvage what he could from some fool's mistake. They never saw him again."

"And did they ever find the treasure?" asked Lewis.

Nennius shrugged. "My cabinet minister died not long after, so I lost my primary source of information. I have a general impression they kept sneaking back to search for it, and for Bell-Fairfax too. Do you know, you're the only person I've told about this, in the four centuries since it happened? It seems like the wildest cheap literature, I know. I wouldn't believe it myself if I hadn't known the parties involved."

"You say they kept searching for Edward?" Lewis asked distractedly.

Nennius was silent a moment, noting his familiar use of the name. He smiled at Lewis, thinking that it certainly wasn't difficult to snare a Preserver. All one needed for a literature drone was a good story.

He yawned and said, "Perhaps they hoped he wasn't really dead, after all the tight corners he'd got himself out of without a scratch. I'd like to believe that. I was rather fond of him, at least as fond as one can be of the monkeys."

"But he must have died," Lewis said.

"Well, of course. And yet, you know, rumors persisted that he'd been seen, much later than was possible for a mortal."

Lewis caught his breath. "Really?"

"Yes. Who knows? Perhaps all that nonsense about a Fountain of Youth was true. Certainly they did find something remarkable, in a cave on the windward side of the island." Nennius observed Lewis's reaction. "Or so I heard. I must admit I've felt the urge to go out there and see for myself if Bell-Fairfax is still strutting about. Wouldn't you? What if he somehow dragged himself into that cave and cheated death?"

Lewis smiled but was silent, thinking very hard. Not hard enough, however, as it turned out.

That night he dreamed of a cave in the hills behind Avalon. He was in the long passage that led into the cave, terrified, though it was a pleasant passage, full of sweet melancholy perfume. It glowed with a white light that deepened to blue as he went farther in and farther down. Joseph was with him.

They emerged into a great vaulted room that stretched away into unfathomable darkness, lit only by white screens where films were playing, old films from Hollywood's golden age, when he'd lived there. He saw Sean Connery and Michael Caine being British adventurers: *The Man Who Would Be King*. And there was Harrison Ford in Egypt in *Raiders of the Lost Ark*, and there was Ford too on another screen seeking the Holy Grail with Sean Connery. A silent film flickered in all shades of ash-silver and gray, biblical-era people dancing on the steps of an impossibly big temple set. On another screen,

Jackie Cooper waded ashore from the beached *Hispaniola* onto the sands of Treasure Island, singing Yo Ho Ho and a Bottle of Rum. On yet another screen, Rudolph Valentino rode down the side of a dune.

"That's Pismo Beach, really," Joseph said knowingly.

Lewis turned away from the screens. "Father of Lies," he told Joseph, indignant, though he knew Joseph was right.

"No, I'm the son of lies, and you are too," Joseph replied.

And there was Mendoza, so sad but so beautiful: she was sleeping in a vault, in a light like blue cellophane, dreaming peacefully, shrouded round in her fiery hair that drifted, drifted. Lewis ran toward the vault.

"What a cheap horror matinee," Joseph said, because a skeleton came flying into Lewis's path, but anyone could have told it was mounted from a boom and jointed together like a puppet. It was a very big skeleton, though, and a strange one. The skull's top had been sawed off and reattached with wire. That was only done during autopsies, though, wasn't it?

Lewis knew whose skeleton it was, hanging there so silly beside Mendoza's vault with its bones still rattling: Edward's. Edward hadn't cheated death, he'd been shot and died in Mendoza's arms. No happy ending. Lewis began to cry. Joseph leaped on the skeleton in a fury, and it fell to the floor, scattering like ivory dice.

"Bastard!" Joseph was screaming. "You got her into this condition, now you'll have to marry her!"

"Aye, but he's dead," Lewis objected.

"But he won't *stay* dead!" Joseph kicked the strange skull across the room, and Lewis realized that his friend had become a werewolf—no, the jackal-headed god Anubis, or was it Imhotep? No, he was only a coyote, after all. He pointed his muzzle at something over Lewis's shoulder, and Lewis turned and caught his breath.

There they were together on the biggest screen of all, Edward and Mendoza, alive. He wore his commander's uniform, she wore a sleeveless gown of beaded peach silk. He had brought her down an aisle of great palm trees to a caravanserai. Sinuous sensual music was playing, a piece Lewis remembered from the late twentieth century called "Mummer's Dance."

He was unable to take his eyes from the romance. Edward led her to a high white room, shutters open to the blue sky. They undressed, smiling, clothes falling effortlessly like dropped scarves, and on a great wide bed of tapestry silk, all dark colors, gold, wine, burnt orange, green, he lay her down. Her arms went around his neck, and they kissed.

Lewis watched everything he'd ever guiltily imagined.

Joseph, behind him, was barking and howling, because they had come for Lewis at last, the little stupid men with his death. It didn't matter. He reached up his arms to the lovers, and the realization came to him: *This is my salvation.* Dissolving in tears, he melted into the moving images and was lost, and it was so peaceful.

But he woke shaking and cold in his cabin. He sat up and turned on the gimbal light: no pale men, only a white dress shirt over the back of a chair and his own pale face reflected in the mirror over the dresser, its round brass frame like a halo. Shivering, he got up and fumbled with the thermostat. He sat huddled in his bed until morning, staring at the wall, and he never got warm.

New Hampshire, 2276

AFTER UNPACKING his suitcase and testing the bed, Lewis glanced at his chronometer. Two hours yet until his job, and the cemetery was within walking distance. He adjusted the room's climate control—nothing seemed to warm him these days—and sat down at the courtesy terminal. He tapped in Joseph's code and waited for the screen to clear.

Joseph, mouth ringed in white foam, was brushing his teeth. "Make this quick, okay?" he said. "I'm turning in."

"Are you going on vacation any time soon?"

"Yes, as a matter of fact," Joseph said. "I just came off a job. I was thinking of San Francisco."

"What a coincidence," Lewis said. "I was going out to the West Coast myself, for a couple of weeks. Why don't we relive our madness in Ghirardelli Square."

"You all right, Lewis?" The green face—this was a cheap hotel and the terminal's color values were abysmal—loomed grotesquely close to the screen in a gigantic parody of concern. "You don't look so good."

"Do I ever?" Lewis said.

"Any more of that trouble?" Joseph held up his hand in a pistol-shooting gesture.

"None whatsoever."

"You realize we can't get any Theobromos at Ghirardelli Square. All those laws the Yanks passed."

Lewis gave a theatrical sigh. "Well then, what about Santa Catalina Island?"

Even with the awful picture resolution, he could see the lightbulb going on above Joseph's head. "Hm," Joseph said. "Independent republic, lots of little loopholes to let people party. We might be able to score a couple of bars at that. I haven't been over there since—when was it?—1923, I think."

"It's settled, then? Where shall we meet?"

"Where are you now?"

"New Hampshire. Little town called Arkham."

"Ah," Joseph said. "I know what you're doing there. You should be done by noon tomorrow. When you finish, book the next flight to Santa Barbara. I'll meet you in the Street of Spain, and we'll drive to the ferry from there. Bring a lot of cash. I hear it's expensive."

"I have cash to burn these days," Lewis said.

"How nice for you. So, you got that?"

"Street of Spain," Lewis said, accessing a map and locating the ancient shopping quarter of the tiny republic. "I expect to be there at twenty hundred hours tomorrow."

"See you. And, Lewis?"

"Yes?"

"Take care of yourself, okay?"

"Always, old boy."

"Good. Mañana."

Lewis signed out, got up and showered, and took some pains combing his hair afterward. He wanted to look his best. A few minutes past twenty-one hundred hours, a yet unknown young Eccentric would limp into the local cemetery with an old pillowcase full of his writing, intent on offering it and himself in a fiery holocaust to shame the philistine world. There the youth would meet a kindly stranger who would talk him out of it, or so his autobiography would later state: a small fair-haired man in an expensive suit who would give him cash for the contents of his pillowcase, enough cash to pay off the writer's debts and buy him that all-important ticket to New York...

Avalon

"AT LAST," LEWIS SAID, spotting the old Casino looming white at the entrance to Avalon Bay. "I don't see why we couldn't have taken a ferry from San Pedro."

"Did you really want to drive through Los Angeles?" Joseph asked, and Lewis shuddered.

A little Island Guard cutter sped close and abreast of them for a few miles, scanning the *Catalina Thunderer*. It was doing this primarily for show; on Catalina it was illegal to sell liquor, meat, refined sugar, dairy products, or other proscribed substances, but it was not illegal to *own* them. This careful loophole brought the island a great deal of happy tourist trade. Avalon Harbor was packed with luxury craft at every mooring, and bigger vessels anchored discreetly farther out to sea, sending launches ashore.

"So here we are," Lewis said, looking at the little white town, the steep green mountains rising behind it forested with ironwoods. *This is where Mendoza was, Joseph, all those years, and we never knew. A beautiful place, isn't it?*

A lot better than it was in the twentieth century, Joseph admitted. *I don't remember all these trees.*

The reforestation project has been under way for three centuries now, Lewis said. *I read it in the guidebook. And, look, there's the Hotel Saint Catherine. Remember? Of course, it's been rebuilt, but*

*the book says it's an exact restoration. We can go to the bar where
you thought you saw her.*

I don't know if I want to do that, Lewis.

Well, I do.

Joseph leaned on the rail and considered Lewis obliquely. He was
more than a little concerned about his friend. He had run a surrepti-
tious scan on him and found no malfunction, though Lewis was
manufacturing compounds associated with severe stress. Lewis still
hadn't explained why they were making this trip.

You really think we'll find her, Lewis?

I don't know. She might be here.

Then I guess it's worth a look.

*That's what I thought. See that little tower, up on the cliff? It's a
bell carillon. It used to strike the hours; the islanders disabled it
when they adopted the slogan Where Time Has Stood Still. You
won't find a public clock anywhere. All the agcars are required by
city ordinance to look like early automobiles, and there are never
more than fifty allowed on the island at any one time. New buildings
have to be as nearly as possible copies of former ones, and there are
only two styles permitted: Mission Revival and Victorian.*

So . . . it's perpetually 1923 here?

*You could say that. To quote the commercial, "Our island
throngs with pleasant ghosts: Laurel and Hardy, Charlie Chaplin,
John Wayne, and other immortals from Hollywood's Golden Age.
When you encounter the costumed actors portraying these celebrities
of olden days, feel free to interact with them and ask questions about
their lives and films. Each one is a certified historical reenactor capable of providing you with hours of informative conversation."*

Jesus. There's retro and then there's retro.

It's a mecca for reenactors, I understand.

I bet. What is this, Disneyland West?

*DisneyCorp doesn't own any of it. It's all run by a preservancy,
which is run in turn by the Company. They have extensive offices
over at the west end.*

*I'm not surprised the Company's invested in it. You know how
Dr. Zeus is about places that don't change.*

And this certainly doesn't change, Lewis said as their ferry pulled
up to the mole. He turned to contemplate the little front street, and it
did indeed look almost exactly as it had during his visits in the 1920s,
with the exception of the slightly awkward Model A Fords floating
two feet above the quaint old pavement. Yes, and there were a pair of
actors portraying Stan Laurel and Oliver Hardy parading along, tipping their hats grandly to the tourists and posing for holocards.

Joseph and Lewis went ashore, and spent an interminable thirty
minutes in customs. When at last they passed through the turnstile
and onto the old promenade that led into town, the hotel jitneys had
long since departed, so they had to walk all the way around Crescent
Avenue to the opposite side of the bay, dragging their suitcases. It
was a picturesque walk, at least. Bright fish flitted in the clear water,
and up every steep street that rose from the bay they caught glimpses
of old gardens where clouds of bougainvillea in all its colors grew
below steep gabled roofs. Beyond them loomed the jade-green mountains of the interior.

There were inviting streetside bars, where of course you couldn't
buy drinks, but you might buy glasses full of ice, and if you poured
something you'd brought ashore with you into one such glass, it was
nobody's business but your own. Ice came very dear in Avalon. There
were amusement arcades, as there always will be in any seaside town.
There were adorable little shops full of wildly overpriced clothes.
There were elegant old hotel lobbies and the front porches of little
flea-bitten hotels. There were terraced restaurants shaded by olive
trees, promising (but only promising) an abundance of dishes they
could not legally sell, but could, for a nominal charge, prepare and
serve to the determined diner who brought his own ingredients.
There were stuccoed arches in the Old Spanish Days style and walls
faced with Art Deco–patterned tiles in soft primary colors. There
were tidy beds of bright flowers.

It was impossible to believe that twenty-six miles away, across a cold stretch of deep water, lay the walled gray port of San Pedro, full of machines, and beyond its walls the war-blasted urban desolation of Los Angeles. If you looked closely at the horizon, you could see the alert gunships of the Island Guard making sure that Los Angeles stayed where it was, too.

Neither Joseph nor Lewis looked. They were too intent on the long, long walk to the Hotel Saint Catherine, in neighboring Descanso Bay. At the neck of the rocky peninsula that divided the two bays, Joseph stopped and stared up in awe at the Casino, which sat square on the middle of the peninsula, towering above them like a twelve-story cake.

"*That* wasn't here in 1923," he gasped. "I'd remember something that size."

"No, indeed," Lewis told him. "The guidebook says it was completed in 1929. No one has any idea why it's called the Casino; all it contains is an early-twentieth-century cinema downstairs and the world-famous Avalon Ballroom upstairs. And there are the murals in the lobby arcade by our old friend Beckman. Remember him?"

"I was posted on the Humashup mission with Beckman," said Joseph, staring fixedly at the murals, which featured an undersea garden motif. A narrow-faced mermaid looked askance at him, hair curling behind her like wet fire. "You know what this looks like? Right before we went to Humashup, Mendoza and I! The New Year's ball. Remember the big tent that Houbert put up? It looked like this."

"You're right," said Lewis. "Dear God. That was the last evening I ever spent with Mendoza. Is this an omen, do you suppose?"

Watch your mouth.

You know, I think I'm beginning to fail to give a damn what the Company hears or doesn't hear anymore.

Lewis, for Christ's sake, the Company owns this place. What's wrong with you?

I don't know, Joseph. I want to find her, that's all. Lewis didn't add, *And him,* though he might have. For months the images from his dream had been with him waking and sleeping. He had secretly begun to entertain the possibility that perhaps Edward hadn't really died, and that even now in one of these old gardens the lovers might be embracing... All that beauty and strength, warm if unattainable.

He sighed and took the pull handle of his baggage again, and so did Joseph, and they set off along the graceful promenade into Descanso Bay like two old children trundling wagons after themselves.

The Hotel Saint Catherine rose at the end of the promenade in all her restored glory, early-twentieth-century Moderne at its stately best. She consisted of a white central building flanked by two white wings, embracing a green lawn that went down to the sea. The grounds were shaded by tropical trees; the little strip of shingle beach was clean and inviting. Even more inviting was the hotel bar on the beach, roofed with palm fronds in best South Seas tradition, where a white-jacketed attendant stood on duty shaking a silver canister vigorously. Joseph and Lewis groaned like sea lions and trundled straight for him.

It turned out he was only mixing soy-milk smoothies, but that was enough of an excuse to stop. They collapsed into chairs, gulping their drinks gratefully. You have to be pretty damned hot and thirsty to enjoy a soy-milk smoothie, but they were, so it was okay.

This might be a good time to tell me what we're doing here, said Joseph, looking out at the square-rigged cruise ships that moved gracefully into Avalon Bay.

I made a discovery, Lewis said. *In my research. I have a hunch— actually more than a hunch—that we might find something important on this island.*

Such as?

Information about what really happened to Edward.

Joseph controlled his temper carefully. *We came all this way to find out something about Mendoza's dead British secret agent boyfriend. Okay.*

It's more than that, Joseph. I can't go into a lot of detail, but... you remember when I told you the British were hunting for some-

thing mysterious here? I've turned up a clue as to its whereabouts.
Lewis's knuckles were white as he held his glass.

Joseph reached out and took it away from him before it shattered.
*Aren't you forgetting something? If there's anything valuable hidden
on this island, the Company will have taken possession of it long ago.*

*Not if it's never been found. And I have reason to believe it hasn't
been.*

*Okay, Lewis, we'll look for it, whatever it is. Do you have any
idea where it is?*

*We need to go over to the windward side of the island. There are
hiking trails, aren't there? We could go hiking.*

We could go hiking. Joseph swirled the starchy mess in the bottom of his glass and decided not to order another round. *Lewis, how
have you been since Eurobase One?*

*How have I been? Well, not exactly at my best, but the damage
to my hand self-repaired perfectly. I've been a little jittery, I'll admit.*

Still having nightmares?

*Yes, but now at least I know what's causing them. No more
buried memories.*

No other signs of the little freaks?

None at all, thank God, though I still expect them at every turn.

*They have to be long gone. Anybody with a technology that
might put the Company's operation at risk isn't going to get to keep
it. You know the way Dr. Zeus defends its interests.* Nothing Joseph
was saying seemed to be registering with Lewis, so he leaned forward
and looked into Lewis's eyes.

Lewis looked back at him. *I don't think the little men are out of
the picture, Joseph.*

*All right. Look ... if they ever come after you again, and you
can't get in touch with me? Try to contact the North African Section
Head, Suleyman. Look up any chapter house of the Compassionates
of Allah and leave him a message. It might not do you any good, but
who knows? It's always a good idea to jump out of the way of the
rooks and the bishops when the game gets hot.*

Are we nothing more than pawns, then?

That's all we are, Lewis. Doesn't mean we can't have a nice vacation, though. Come on, let's go check in. Joseph took up the handle of his carryall.

If you say so. Lewis followed Joseph up the long sloping lawn of the hotel. The wind rolled in over the sea, rustled in the palm fronds that shaded the little bar, went on up across the green lawn, and in through the terrace windows of the restaurant.

The interior of the hotel was all early-twentieth-century charm, spiced up by murals of a certain naughtiness celebrating the first golden era of bootlegging, among other things. The staff were all in twentieth-century costume, too, like a revival cast of *The Cocoanuts*: desk clerks in stiff wing collars and black tailcoats, bellboys in scarlet tunics and pillbox hats. They probably delighted the largely reenactor clientele. Joseph and Lewis, who really had been there during the 1920s, felt disoriented.

After Joseph hung up his shirts and secured his room, he came out to look for Lewis. Sending a faint inquiring signal, he was answered from the hotel's first floor. He hurried down the grand staircase and saw Lewis at the edge of the lobby, peering into the hotel restaurant. He had a sudden mental image of Lewis being wafted out through the terrace door like a blown cobweb. The image quickened his pace as he crossed the lobby and caught Lewis by the arm.

"You want to eat? Let's go into town. There's supposed to be a great dinner buffet at the Metropole. Come on, I'll call us a cab."

Was it here? Were Edward and Mendoza in here? Lewis asked.

Hell, how should I remember? Anyway it's all wrong. The colors are wrong. And it was early afternoon. That bar's in the wrong place, too. The restorers must have been working from a picture off a reversed negative, it's all mirror image—

You must have been right over there. And they must have been sitting at that table over there, by the terrace doors, to slip away so quickly. Lewis's eyes were haunted, intense with what he was seeing. Joseph scowled, trying not to look into the room.

Will you come on? I'm starving, and I don't want to eat here.

Why? Lewis turned to him. *You're afraid you'll see them again, aren't you?*

No. But it gives me the creeps, Lewis. Let's go, please.

Lewis sighed and allowed Joseph to drag him away.

They floated back to town in one of the Model A agcars, piloted by a costumed driver who was doing his best to speak the American of the period, faithfully reproduced from old films.

"Say! Are you guys having a swell time?"

"Yes, thank you," Lewis said.

"Gee, that's swell." The driver peered at them in the mirror. "Come over here for relaxation, huh? I know a lot of places that deliver the goods, but plenty, if you know what I mean."

"Actually, we were thinking of hiking," Lewis said. "Are there many hiking trails over here?"

"I'll say. Why, people hike up to the old Wrigley place all the time, and what a view, folks, what a view! And how!"

Do I sound like that? Joseph asked, gritting his teeth in silent mortification.

Of course not, Lewis assured him. *Not all the time, at least.* "Yes, I bet that's a great view. What about the interior, though? Are there any trails that go over to the windward side of the island?"

"Say, what would you want to go *there* for? That ain't no fun, chum, there's nothing over there but what belongs to the preservancy. No booze, no dames, and no trespassing." The cabbie shook his head emphatically as he pulled up to the taxi island in front of the Metropole Hotel. "You want a hot tip? Try the old Pilgrim Club up the street. Plenty of action for a couple of guys like you, believe me. But if you run out of steam, just give me a call." He half turned and presented them with a printed card, grinning. "Ask for Johnny."

"Swell," muttered Joseph, tipping him.

The dinner buffet at the Metropole was swell indeed. It seemed that under Catalina's unique interpretation of vegan laws, seafood qualified as a vegetable. Of course, nothing actually looked like what it was—no staring fish eyes or other recognizable parts, that would have been too much for twenty-third-century sensibilities; everything had been chopped/flaked/formed into nice anonymous shapes and baked or steamed healthily—but there was no mistaking it for soy protein.

Having dined well, Joseph and Lewis opted to forgo the delights of the Pilgrim Club and strolled instead along Crescent Avenue, looking at the shops. This year there were a lot of bright silk garments on display, as there was currently a movement to ban silk on behalf of the silkworms and nobody knew how long supplies would last. In one window was a peach-colored silk dress. Lewis paused before it a long moment, long enough for Joseph to start clearing his throat and shuffling his feet.

It was growing dusk, the blue hour when solid things take on a certain transparency and phantoms become palpable. The olive trees on the promenade began to sparkle with little shifting lights. The shop interior was only half lit, and the reflection of the figures passing in the street created the illusion of busy throngs *inside* the window, a whole world silent on the other side of the glass. Suddenly there was a face above the classic neckline of the peach silk dress, an enigmatic smile, and Lewis muttered an exclamation and turned swiftly.

You thought you saw her? Joseph asked. *Lewis, she isn't here.*
You can't know that.

Why would the Company assign anybody to this place? There's nothing to save here. It's all reconstructions of other things, other times.

Only the town. The interior is all forests. Look, look up here. Lewis hurried to the next building, the brightly lit visitors' center. The walls were faced with interactive exhibits displaying the island's natural history, its unique endemic flora and fauna. In the middle of the room, however, was a dais, and rising from it was a perfect model of the island in holo, just as it would look seen from the air on a bright summer day at noon.

Lewis paused on his way to the reforestation exhibit, struck by the perfection of the model. He walked around it slowly.

"Wow," Joseph said. "Godzilla's-eye view, huh?" He looked down at the little square grid of toy houses, the toy canister of the Casino on its platform of rock.

Lewis did not reply. He had stopped at the southern windward face of the island. Here it dropped away abruptly in high steep cliffs above the sea, a palisaded wall of rock, unassailable from below. There were caves visible. It was directly behind Avalon, perhaps eleven kilometers away in a straight line.

Joseph, I think I've found what I'm looking for.

That'd be nice. Joseph walked around to his vantage point. He frowned. *Nasty cliffs. We don't have to climb those, do we?*

I don't think so. But see the caves above them? We need to investigate there.

I see. And I forgot to pack hiking boots.

Joseph, we have to look!

Okay, we'll look. Joseph peered down at a tiny incongruity in the green wilderness, a stone tower and sweeping battlements embracing a garden. It was about midway between the town and the palisades. "Hey, check this out. This is supposed to be the Wrigley Monument, Library, and Botanical Garden. You want to go see this library tomorrow? It's supposed to be *the* big collection. Most of what they salvaged from the Library of Congress wound up here."

"Great idea," Lewis said, coming around the holo to see. "Oh, yes, we must visit that. I wonder if there's an admission fee?" *It's right on the way. We can scout out the road tomorrow.*

Joseph and Lewis walked out again into the evening and strolled back to the Hotel Saint Catherine. It was warm, with a sky full of stars now that the last glow of sunset had faded, and from every terrace and balcony came music, and the determined laughter of mortals enjoying lost pleasures. As they passed the old Encanto, a man came reeling drunkenly out into the street toward them, the very image of a South Seas derelict in stained tropical whites and a battered hat.

They braced themselves as he accosted them; but he turned out to be merely an actor re-creating Charles Laughton's performance in *The Beachcomber*. They tipped him, and he went away.

Back at the hotel, there was a crowd getting very rowdy on Singapore Slings that may or may not have contained authentic gin. A man at a piano was pounding out "The Sheik of Araby." In the old-fashioned cage elevator, the elevator boy in bandbox uniform insinuated he could get Joseph and Lewis the real thing, and how, if they wanted some fun. All they had to do was ring the desk and ask for Johnny.

"Do you suppose he meant liquor or prostitutes?" wondered Lewis as they trudged down the hall to their rooms.

"Liquor, probably," Joseph said wearily. "If you ordered up a whore here, you'd probably get a theater major doing Joan Crawford as Sadie Thompson. I wonder what would happen if I ordered a Hershey bar?" His eyes lit up for a moment. "I wonder what would happen if I ordered a whore *and* a Hershey bar?"

"You'll never know unless you ask," Lewis said.

"How true." Joseph peered back down the hall toward the elevator. "Well. Nighty night, sleep tight, don't let the bedbugs bite, okay, Lewis?"

"Good night," said Lewis, and unlocked his door and stepped inside.

The hotel room was lovingly re-created to look like any one of the dozen hotel rooms he'd lived in during the twentieth century. Of course there was a modern entertainment center in the period-styled armoire, and of course the plumbing and heating were state of the art; but the narrow bed would be authentically empty when he lay him down to sleep.

He went to the window and looked out at the night. Dark branches, rustling in the night wind, and the sigh and crash of breakers on sand. Faint music, laughter, Joseph's door opening and closing, voices. The clink-clink of rigging and blocks on the little pleasure boats rocking at their moorings.

But not *their* voices anywhere, Mendoza's voice shy and young as it must have sounded once, Edward's voice strong and confident.

No, Lewis could fantasize all he liked, but the stony likelihood was that Edward was dead, long dead, and Mendoza was alone, wherever she was. There would never be the ending Lewis hoped for, with the gallant commander somehow claiming his Spanish lady.

I will not be silenced.

Lewis turned, electrified by an idea. It was the same empty room it had been a moment before, but now the air was full of voices. The yellow pool of light around the table lamp was like an island in the night sea, welcoming, full of promise. With trembling hands he pulled his Buke out of its case and set it up in the lamplight. He turned it on and opened a new file.

It asked him for a name. After a moment's hesitation he typed in HAPPY ENDING. Then he paused over the keyboard, biting his lower lip. He'd never read much science fiction; he'd never written any. True, he had seen the classic Hollywood epics... But the future hadn't turned out the way they'd imaged it.

"Don't leave me, Captain!" begged Zorn, reaching out a bloody hand.

"He's done for, Hawke," Moxx grunted. "And if we don't get back to the ship soon, O'Grady will take off without us!"

Captain Marshawke Daxon paused to fire another laser blast at the pursuing Company troops before he snapped, "I don't care! I'm not leaving anyone to be interrogated. If they find out about the contraband, we're *all* done for!"

"I'll put him out of his misery, then—" began Moxx, but scarcely were the words out of his mouth when he found himself staring into Captain Daxon's icy blue eyes, lit with the glare of deadly rage usually reserved for the smuggler chief's worst enemies. He had taken hold of the front of Moxx's spacesuit and hoisted him bodily into the air, and Moxx's jackboots dangled a full twelve uncomfortable inches from the ground.

"You shoot any member of this band, and you'll have me to reckon with, do you understand?" roared Captain Daxon.

"Aye, Captain!" gasped Moxx.

"We haven't got time for this," Berenice reminded them, ducking as a laser beam shattered the top of the rocky outcropping behind which they had taken cover. "They're advancing again, Hawke!"

"Right." Captain Daxon dropped Moxx and turned decisively. He bent swiftly to Zorn and hauled the wounded man over his shoulder. "We'll run for it. Go! Go! I'll keep you covered!"

The smugglers took to their heels, scrambling frantically over the rugged island slopes as laser fire shrieked out on all sides. Over the next ridge they could just glimpse the silver nose of the *Starfire,* with clouds of smoke coiling up around her: O'Grady must have already started up the star drive.

Captain Daxon brought up the rear, a towering figure in black smuggler's leathers, turning frequently to rake the advancing Company troops with withering laser fire as his band ran for their lives. He was slowed only a little by Zorn's considerable weight, but it proved to be, fatally, enough: for as he turned and fled again, leaping skillfully from rock to rock, a blast screamed terribly near and he felt a sudden sickening impact. Zorn stiffened and groaned once; Daxon staggered and nearly fell, then ran on, but was conscious of sticky warmth flooding down his side.

The other smugglers had already vanished over the crest of the hill, and the *Starfire* was now hidden in boiling clouds. O'Grady was going to leave without them!

Cursing under his breath, Daxon ran faster; only at the last moment did he spot the chasm opening in the rock, almost under his boots.

"Hold on for your life, Zorn!" he cried, and vaulted into space. Wide as the chasm was, he could have easily leaped it under ordinary circumstances: for Marshawke Daxon was no ordinary man. Zorn's dead weight worked against him, however, and his fingers clawed desperately at the edge of the abyss a moment before losing their hold. Down, down he fell, as laser fire whistled through the space he'd occupied scant milliseconds before.

Daxon spotted a projecting edge of rock and grabbed for it. He caught it, and the rock held; but to his horror, he felt Zorn slipping, falling free. As he looked over his shoulder he beheld Zorn plummeting down, limp as a broken doll, staring up with wide unseeing eyes. Daxon had been carrying a dead man.

Thief though he was, Daxon felt an involuntary prayer for the man's soul rise to his lips. He looked up at the narrow strip of sky and beheld the *Starfire* rising gracefully against the sun. Had the crew made it aboard? Even as he wondered, laser fire came from some source too near to allow him time for reflection. Using the force of will that had made him a legend in the renegade underworld, Daxon pulled himself up on the edge, groping for a better handhold.

To his astonishment, his hand seemed to disappear in midair. Understanding instinctively what he had found, he threw himself forward at what appeared to be sheer rock wall but was in fact an illusion, a trick of light to conceal the tunnel mouth that was really there. Daxon rolled and came up on his feet, staring around, all his senses sharpened by danger. Slowly, silently he drew his laser pistol. Beyond the tunnel mouth, outside, the whine of laser fire was louder; the troops had come up to the edge of the abyss and were firing down, now, at what must have been Zorn's just barely visible corpse. Daxon held his breath and waited for them to stop and move on.

He was in a smooth-walled passage that led into the depths of the island, but not into darkness; far down its length

was an eerie blue glow. On the wall immediately opposite
where he stood a steel plate was set into the wall, with the
words SITE 317 inscribed upon it.

Daxon began to edge his way along the tunnel, moving
with the silence of a great cat. Something about the blue light
drew him, for a reason he was never afterward to explain
satisfactorily. Down he went and down, into the subterranean
lair of... what?

After a hundred paces the tunnel opened out into a room,
lit by the blue glow that had become stronger and brighter as
he had descended. Daxon stepped into that room and caught
his breath at what he saw there.

The blue glow was emanating from a great vault made of
what appeared to be transparent glass. Floating within was a
girl, naked, dreaming, and her long hair was the color of fire
and moved like flame in the slow currents of the heavy fluid
that imprisoned her.

Daxon walked like a man in the grip of enchantment. He
knew her: surely he knew her, had always known that graceful
body, that face at once childlike yet possessed of a somber
dignity. He knew that her eyes, when they opened, would be
black as smoldering coals in her pale face; he knew that her
hair was fragrant with myrrh and attar of roses, that he'd
buried his face in its burning waves. When had he done that?
How did he know these things?

Impossible memories rose to assail him, of places he'd
never been, in an era long past. Suddenly he remembered the
sea, and the man he'd been once, a man with nobler
aspirations perhaps than mere smuggling, and the girl's name,
which had been... Mendoza.

He could not say with any certainty just who he had been,
or why he remembered these things; it was enough that he
remembered the girl, and knew that she was his true love. This
he knew beyond all doubt, as tears streamed down his
unshaven face.

Acting on impulse, Daxon aimed his pistol at the imprisoning glass and fired. The whole side of the vat gave way and flooded its contents outward: but he was there to catch her as she was spilled free, and he held her above the glittering blue tide and splashed to a couch at one side of the room which he had not previously noticed.

There he lay her down. She was shivering, trembling with returning life, only barely conscious. He knelt beside her, unable to keep his mouth from hers any longer; and her lips were warm as he kissed her, and opened in surprise as she woke to him.

Yes, that was the mouth that had haunted him in dreams, all the years of his life. He had wanted to kiss that coral mouth, stroke that body of ivory, wind his hands in the copper hair unbound at last for him, for him, she was his now. None of the others had mattered. This was the one he'd searched for, never knowing.

"Mendoza," he gasped. She opened her dark eyes and saw his dear familiar face: her incoherent cry of joy echoed in that cavern.

Lewis got up and stumbled into the bathroom, where he pulled a handful of tissues from the dispenser and dried his streaming tears. Blowing his nose, he sat down again and reached for the keyboard.

They melted into another kiss. Daxon knew that whatever had sundered them in the past, he would never let her slip through his fingers again; somehow he knew that at last, after centuries of heartbreak and false starts, their story was truly beginning.

And though they were going to escape from that dark prison and soar free of the Company, though they were about to go on to a life of wonderful adventures together, this perhaps would be the moment to wreathe around in flowers as their happy ending: the ending of their separation and lost years. Love had triumphed at last.

Lewis read it over, wiping away the tears that still welled in his eyes. It wasn't good enough, it never was; he couldn't write worth a damn.

He sagged at the table, looking out from the circle of light into the shadows of his room. It was late. Almost no sound in the grand old hotel, where the mortals on night shift leaned half asleep at their posts. A wind moving through the dark garden. The quiet surge of the sea. Less quiet surging from Joseph's room, where a certain rhythm of sounds and voices suggested that Joseph wasn't alone.

Lewis got up and opened the compartment in his suitcase that concealed the flask. He found a chilled bottle of mineral water in the minibar and a glass, poured himself a drink, and added gin. He went back and sat in the circle of lamplight, sipping his drink, reading over what he'd written.

The bed still waited on the other side of the room, as narrow and cold as before. He wasn't ready to face it yet.

"You know, guy, you're not getting enough sleep," Joseph remarked at breakfast. "You look like hell."

Lewis shrugged and warmed his hands on a cup of herbal tea. Bootlegged coffee was harder to come by than gin.

"Maybe we should concentrate on relaxing today. There's a nice golf course here. You play golf?" Joseph asked.

"From time to time," Lewis said.

"A lot of nice greens." Joseph indicated the brochure he'd picked up at the front desk. "Oldest miniature golf course in the world. Famous pitch-and-putt course. World-Class Restored Course of the Stars. That's in Avalon Canyon, here." He opened out the brochure and held it up so Lewis wouldn't miss the point he was making: Avalon Canyon pointed straight behind the town, toward the palisades.

"That looks challenging," Lewis said. "Perhaps we can stroll up there and see."

"We can check it out, anyway. And look, just a little way farther up the road is that memorial thing, with the library. You wanted to see that. And it looks like there's some hiking trails behind the library. Sounds like a great way to spend the day, getting lots of fresh air and exercise. I bet you sleep tonight." *I've got it all figured out. We walk up there today, see what the best route is for getting into the interior, and then come back. Dinner, early bedtime, and as soon as it's dark and you're in bed with your eyes shut, you turn on a little device I'm going to slip you. It'll zap the datalink, but if anybody's monitoring you, they won't be able to tell, because you'll have gone to bed so they'll think it's normal to be getting a black screen. Is that subtle or what?*

Bravo, Joseph.

Thanks. I have a zapper too. We get dressed again and sneak out, head straight up Avalon Canyon, and you can look for your secret whatever it is all night if you want. As long as we're back in our beds by morning when transmission resumes, nobody will ever know we were up there.

"Yes," Lewis said aloud. "Let's do that. Fresh air and exercise, that's what I need. What a Facilitator you are!"

"Just fulfilling my program," Joseph said, grinning. He looked at Lewis's untouched tofu waffle. "You going to finish that?"

"Be my guest," said Lewis, pushing it across the table to him. "Let's go as soon as you've finished, shall we?"

"Mm," Joseph agreed, mouth full.

It was a bright and hopeful morning, if a rather silent one. In all the terraced restaurants, trays of breakfast were being sent back by disgruntled merrymakers, to be replaced by trays bearing tomato drinks festooned with celery or chaste bottles of mineral water. Even Laurel and Hardy looked a little green around the gills as Joseph and Lewis passed them, though they tipped their derbies gallantly.

At Sumner Avenue the two real immortals turned right and walked in the direction of the interior, through the residential district with its high narrow Victorian houses, and beyond, where they entered Avalon Canyon Road. Once they had passed through the maze of screening pepper trees, they got their first clear view of the long valley that ran back into the interior.

It was surprisingly wild-looking. Great sleek mountains faced one another, ignoring the emerald-green golf course that climbed their lower slopes. The road ran up the right-hand side of the valley, between stone walls that blazed with flowering vines, and a double row of palm trees spread vast fanned crowns over most of its length. Looking up at them, Lewis caught his breath. He remembered Edward and Mendoza walking together here, under these enormous palms. These were the trees in his dream.

"Nice golf course," said Joseph pleasantly. *What's wrong?*

Look at this green valley. Joseph, I think the agricultural station was here. This had to have been Mendoza's prison.

You have some psychic hunch about this, huh?

Call it what you like. She was here.

A hundred and fifty thousand years ago, maybe.

Lewis exhaled sharply. "Yes, this *is* a nice golf course. Let's see more of it, shall we?"

They walked on, and the valley was quiet in the sunlight, and the mountains watched them.

Tell me something, Lewis. We didn't really come here because you had some kind of vision or dream. You turned up some hard evidence about whatever it is we're looking for, didn't you?

Yes. What do you think I am, a complete fool?

Lewis, I wish to God I knew what you are.

Lewis set his chin and marched stubbornly on, so that Joseph had to hurry after him, passing in and out of the shadows cast by the great palms.

In less than an hour they came to the head of the valley, which narrowed gradually beyond the golf course until the road was running up its center, through a green twilight cast by great old mahogany trees that grew down the flanks of the mountains on either side. Here a pair of ornate gateposts rose, supporting between them

a wrought-iron arch bearing the words THE WILLIAM K. WRIGLEY ME-
MORIAL GARDEN AND LIBRARY.

They looked through the arch. There was an open area like an
amphitheater, full of sunlight and air, and the paved road gave way to
a raked gravel one branching off into neat beds of endemic plants.
Looming above the garden, backed into the mountain beyond, was a
stone tower seven stories tall, reached by sweeping staircases to the
right and left that converged on a terrace at its base.

Joseph and Lewis walked up through the botanical garden, half
expecting a familiar figure to rise from her work and look in their direction. Nothing moved but a raven, which swooped down to land
on the path and cocked a bright inquisitive eye at them. It did not
speak. At the monument they took the left staircase, ascending
through figured bronze doors, climbing to the central courtyard with
its patterned tile walls, its friezes of pink-and-green stone carved with
birds and sea creatures.

It was a tomb fit for a Moorish emperor, not for a chewing gum
magnate. His family had thought so too, because they'd had his
body removed shortly after his death and reinterred in some sensible
little American cemetery on the eastern seaboard. And so the tomb
here stood empty, in all its lonely and absurd grandeur, until a certain Kronos Diversified Stock Company offered to excavate the heart
of the mountain behind it and put in a library worthy of ancient
Alexandria.

This Joseph and Lewis learned from a brass plate set beside the
door of the elevator that would have taken them down into the library, had it not been locked. The plate further informed them that
actual physical visits to the library were by appointment only, on
certain days of the week, to persons with the proper academic credentials.

"Well, that's a sign of the times, I must say," remarked Lewis in
disappointment. *The Company again. Good lord, there are probably
books I acquired for them in there.*

Joseph shrugged. "Who reads anymore?" *It's very Company, though, isn't it? Collect a huge mass of something really valuable, put it in an unbelievably safe place where the monkeys can't get at it, and sit on it. Nice piece of design. Bet it's safe from electromagnetic pulses and anything else that could happen.*

"What a pity." Lewis put his hands in his pockets and strolled out into the courtyard, looking down the right-hand staircase. "There appears to be a trailhead over there. Do you suppose we could follow it to the other side of the island?"

They could and did, up a steep switchback grade. It brought them, after an hour's steady labor, to the top of the coastal ridge. The view was well worth the climb: sea in all directions dotted with white sails, the long valley opening out to their right with the little white town at its end. To their left, wild canyons descended to the windward shore, beyond a fence posted with the sign NO ADMITTANCE. ENDEMIC SPECIES PRESERVE.

Somewhere down there, transmitted Lewis, staring.

You think so? Joseph pretended to shade his eyes with his hand, scanning intently. He turned this way and that, recording, interpreting, analyzing. *I don't find anything, Lewis. And that's good. I'm picking up definite Company signals off at the other end of the island, and some from the library below; but nothing in this quarter. It's called Silver Canyon on the maps.*

I don't read any trails going in or out, either.

You're sure this is the place?

Joseph, I know it. Standing here, I can almost hear her voice.

Not as bad as I thought. Just a few square miles of wilderness nobody cares about. No alarms, no security techs. I hope you brought working clothes?

Naturally.

And you're not going to die of disappointment if we don't find anything?

We'll find something, Joseph.

Tonight, then. Joseph yawned and stretched. "Some view, huh? I could use a sandwich right about now. Want to head back down?"

Back in town, the very picture of relaxed vacationers, they spent an enjoyable afternoon idling. They ate lunch at one of the terraced restaurants, and played several games of miniature golf on a course set up as an English-style formal garden complete with maze and marjoram knots. They took several tours, including the noted glass-bottomed boat ride. They dressed formally for an early dinner and went to the Avalon Ballroom to hear swing music played by a Benny Goodman reenactor with his reenactor band. Charlie Chaplin wandered over to their table and attempted a conversation in mime. They tipped him, and he went away.

As they walked back to the Hotel Saint Catherine, Joseph lurched a little on the stair and bumped into Lewis. Lewis felt something slipped into the pocket of his dinner jacket.

That's the signal killer?

That's yours. I've been playing around with a model Latif designed. It looks like a class ring. Slip it on. When you're back in your room, go through the whole business of getting undressed, getting into bed, turning off the light, closing your eyes; then activate the ring by turning the bezel mount to the left. It's good for ten hours. Then get up and put your work clothes on. I'll meet you in the hall.

I feel like James Bond.

Cool, huh?

There was nothing remarkable about two gentlemen in formal dinner dress going to their rooms at ten o'clock in the evening. There was nothing remarkable about their reemergence twenty minutes later, dressed in simple exercise suits of dark-gray cotton fleece and dark running shoes. A certain amount of daily exercise was mandated by law in the twenty-third century, and many people preferred to jog in the cool of the evening.

So nobody noticed the two gentlemen as they pounded dutifully along Casino Way and then Crescent Avenue, or as they turned up Sumner. When they neared Avalon Canyon Road, an observer might have found it curious that they were increasing their speed, inasmuch as they were now going uphill. But all the golfers of the day were long since sprawled in front of entertainment centers with drinks in their hands, so there was no observer. Which was a good thing, because just past the pitch-and-putt greens the two gentlemen, shifting into hyperfunction, accelerated into blurs and vanished up the canyon, on the dark road under the white stars.

Where do we start?

Good question. Joseph looked down from the spine of the island, regarding the impenetrable dark mass of trees. He switched to infrared, and it lit up for him. Ordering a topographical analysis, he saw the whole landscape behind his eyes, neatly lined and graded. Beside him, Lewis was doing the same thing.

Let's start with the nearest ridge and work our way along it, scanning downhill as we go, said Joseph.

Good thinking. We're looking for caves and electromagnetic anomalies that would suggest old excavation.

That's what I thought.

They jumped the fence and moved out together, silent in the gigantic silence of that night. Not a bird called, the crickets had fallen still, no wind moved in the trees. Even the surf washing the rocks far below made no perceptible sound.

Here's something. Lewis transmitted.

Joseph whirled to scan. He found the anomaly and analyzed; moved in a little closer for greater detail. *Old mine adit, probably.*

How old is it, do you think?

We'll see.

They worked their way down the hill slowly and found the adit, half collapsed and masked by bushes, invisible to mortal eyes even by daylight. Joseph extended his scan, detected the remains of wooden supports, analyzed the extent of their decay. *I'd have to say 1890s, plus or minus a decade. That doesn't fit, though, does it?*

No. What we're looking for should be much older. Something prior to 1492.

You think your mystery is from a pre-Columbian civilization? It might be.

Wow. Okay, let's move on.

They went back up the hill and continued along its crest. They found evidence of three more adits, all dating from the same era, then traces of grading that might have been a road for pack horses, also from the late nineteenth century. There were a number of spot anomalies where holes had been. The holes might have been dug for buried treasure or camp latrines, or might have been the work of extraordinarily busy ground squirrels. When they came to the end of one ridge, they made their way down and up the side of the next and began again. Two hours went by in this way, yielding no caves and nothing else of interest.

In the third hour they entered a region west of their starting point, where even the ground squirrels had never chosen to burrow. Lewis was silent and withdrawn, and Joseph ran a diagnostic on himself for malfunction. It didn't seem possible they'd found a place where *nothing* had ever disturbed the soil.

Then, abruptly, it showed up on both their internal screens at once: an anomaly bigger than any they had seen yet, undoubtedly a cave. There was something else, too.

What the hell is that? Joseph stopped in his tracks.

Is that old aircraft wreckage? And there's . . . some kind of masking wave. It's cloaking most of an acre. To hide the wreckage from discovery, or is this one of your bunkers, Joseph?

No. Joseph was staring hard at the anomaly. *I know where all the bunkers are, and there are none on this island.*

There aren't?

I can tell you one thing for certain: the masking isn't being generated by any Company technology. That's one weird frequency.

There's a cave there, all right. I don't know what the wreck is, though. And I'm not picking up any life signs, are you?

No.

But I think there's a dead mortal.

Edward. It must be Edward. Lewis started for the anomaly at a run.

Joseph stood gaping a moment before he ran after him. *Come back here. Are you nuts? Was this what you dragged us up here after? A goddam dead Englishman?*

I thought— Nennius implied—

They skidded to a stop just short of the anomaly. Lewis stared down, white-faced, at the old wreckage: a small Beecraft of the kind that had been popular just before antigravity was patented. Its stubby wings and fuselage had smashed on impact, but the cockpit was intact. A skull grinned through the windshield at Lewis, an ordinary mortal skull, nothing remarkable about its shape.

When did you talk to Nennius? said Joseph, seizing Lewis by the arm.

Last year. He told me about Edward, he said his disappearance might have been connected with a cave up here. Lewis had begun to shake.

Joseph let go of his arm and doubled over, as though he was going to be physically ill. *You fool. How could you have been so stupid as to tell Nennius—of all people—about what we've been doing all these years?*

I didn't! It happened by chance. We ran into each other on a cruise, and he told me the story to pass the time.

Then he knew about you, Lewis. The Company finally noticed your prying into old secrets, and they sent him after you. He set a trap, and we've walked right into it. Mendoza's not here, and neither is Edward. We've got to get the hell out before the security techs come for us. Joseph straightened up and looked around, preparing to run for his life; but it was too late.

"We have weapons," a drippy little voice informed them.

Both turned. There, instead of the phalanx of security techs they expected, stood three small pale men, dressed in what appeared to be golfing ensembles. They did indeed have weapons, and the weapons were trained on Lewis.

"You don't do anything smart, this time," said the foremost of the men. "We wait here until the others come for us. Then we take you home."

Joseph, they're only after me, transmitted Lewis, deadly calm. *You can get away.*

"For Christ's sake!" snarled Joseph, and winked out, to reappear between Lewis and the pale men. "Go, Lewis! Look, you stupid little—ow!"

Lewis, who had obediently winked out and reappeared thirty yards away, heard Joseph's howl of pain. He saw the pale men firing again, and watched in horror as Joseph fell.

Then he was beside Joseph, caught hold of him, and they were away, this time getting as far as the next canyon before Lewis lost momentum. When they stopped, Joseph tottered a moment and fell again. He struggled to pull himself up but seemed unable to use his left arm and leg.

Lewis crouched over him. *My God, I've killed us both.*

Joseph struggled, making croaking noises. His face was terrifying: the left side slack, the left eye turned up sightless and white. The right eye rolled wildly as he strained to see over Lewis's shoulder. Lewis followed his stare to behold three little globes of light floating over the ridge, coming after them.

Betrayed, said Joseph. *Company told them, deal. Find you. Company let them take—* He went into a seizure.

Lewis, supporting his head, looked across the canyon in quiet despair. The lights came closer. *Can you see, Joseph? Can you hear me? Uh.*

I'll lead them away from you. I'll go as far as I can. They might

forget there were two of us. Try to crawl to cover. If you can make
it to morning, most of your systems ought to reset, and you can get
away. I am so very sorry about this, Joseph.

    Lewis.

But Lewis had winked out, and at the head of the canyon Joseph
heard a shout and saw a waving figure, dark against the skyline.

"Here I am! Up here, you wretched imbeciles!" yelled Lewis, and
dashed over the top out of sight. The three lights froze and then
moved after him with uncanny speed, drifting above the brush like
balloons. Joseph was left in darkness. He tried to keep from passing
out from the pain, which was unlike anything he'd experienced in his
twenty-odd thousand years.

After a moment he was able to coordinate his right arm and leg
sufficiently to drag himself backward, half upright in the deeper
gloom of an ironwood thicket. Panting, he tried to run a self-
diagnostic. As he did so, he heard a distant crashing, a faint shout
from Lewis, something Joseph couldn't make out.

There was another light on the ridge across from him.

Right eye widening, Joseph crouched back into the shadows.
Someone whined in the darkness beside him. But there was no one
beside him. On the opposite ridge a lot of lights now moved fast, all
in a line, like ants following ants, following Lewis, up and over the
ridge. A torchlight procession. The Hollywood Bowl performance of
Midsummer Night's Dream. When was that, 1938? Max Reinhardt's
stupendous, colossal extravaganza. Fairies in the trees with lights.
Shine, little glowworm. Joseph went with Lewis, had drinks afterward in the bar at Musso and Frank's, Lewis in his tuxedo elegant
and so funny critiquing the show over his martini, acting out the
worst moments, Joseph laughing and laughing—

A flare of light in his face, a tremendous vibration. He was flat on
his back looking up at the biggest damn full moon he'd ever seen. But
the moon didn't notice him, it rose majestically and drifted up over
the ridge, following all the little horrible lights. It dipped out of sight
on the other side, but he could still see the glow through the trees.

As he was levering himself upright again, with unbelievable effort, he heard far off a long, wavering cry of agony.

Lewis!

He toppled and fell, going into another seizure. When it subsided, he grappled frantically at roots, stones, anything to pull himself along, anything to go in the opposite direction from the monstrous light, scuttling like a crab, blindly going faster and faster, and gravity was helping him now, because he was rolling, tumbling, oh *shit* he'd forgot about the cliffs—

Roaring air for a moment, and then a deafening crash as he hit the water. Darkness and deathly cold. Smashed like a bug. But he wouldn't drown, would he? He was immortal.

He was floating face up when the full moon reappeared, drifting over the top of the cliff. He gasped and flailed, but once again it took no notice of him. It rotated, and he saw it was a beautiful craft really, a glowing drop. It hesitated a moment before moving out to sea, picking up speed as it went but still zigging and wobbling unsteadily, as though piloted by idiots.

He watched it leave. It had no need to come back: it had caught what it had been hunting for so long.

San Pedro

Man? boat? Dead? Not dead?

Joseph was instantly awake, his eye narrowed. He waited until he felt the prodding beak again, nudging his painful ribs.

Not-man? Dead?

Alive! He grappled with his right arm and clung, sinking his teeth into its dorsal fin for good measure as the dolphin screamed and darted under, trying frantically to throw him off. He hung on, through a long icy bubbly ride.

Ow ow! Not-man, off! Not-man, off!

Hear me.

Okay!

Seek boat. You swim me to boat. In boat, I stop bite, you go.

Okay, the dolphin agreed sullenly, and they rose slowly to the surface. The dolphin cast about for a ship, located one, and swam for it awkwardly, still giving a stealthy flip now and then in hopes of dislodging Joseph, who gripped it like grim death.

Not soon enough for either of them, the animal closed with its object, a small craft cutting through the darkness under power. It was towing a dinghy.

Baby boat, Joseph indicated. The dolphin swam to the dinghy. Joseph lunged and got his leg over the side, then his arm. He rolled gasping into the bottom of the dinghy, as the dolphin called him dirty names and swam away.

He looked up at the stars. Late, look how far they'd wheeled across the sky. He closed his eyes for a moment, and when he opened them, the sky was pale, the stars had disappeared. Gray air, stale smells, and suddenly a very large tanker was taking up most of the view. He lurched up on his right elbow. The left side of his body was still dead.

Important things to do right now:

1. Reactivate signal killer.
2. Get out of dinghy before you are noticed.

Joseph groped for his left hand, pulled it into his lap, twisted the bezel on the ring, and felt a comforting little jolt. He writhed around and took his bearings.

He was traveling into San Pedro Harbor courtesy the good ship *Bobbi Jo,* which seemed to be making for a berth near the old Ports o' Call sector. He made a tentative attempt to access a map; he got one! Los Angeles County. In the last moments before the *Bobbi Jo* docked, he scanned the map, made a plan, and rolled over the side into murky water.

Ten minutes later, he was crouched shivering under a boat dock, snarling at the crabs who advanced, intrigued by his condition. Finally he killed a few of them and cracked them open, and sucked the meat out of the pieces of shell.

He stayed there all day, unnoticed by anyone. By nightfall his left leg responded to commands somewhat, though he was still blind and deaf on the left side and unable to use his left arm at all. In the afternoon he reactivated the signal killer.

When the evening grew late and quiet, he crawled out and up to the marina. Filthy, unshaven, staggering, he looked like any of the other zombies who roamed the night. He quickly found the paths they used, the alleyways and ugly places where they passed freely, invisible to others. Before morning he found his way to the city wall. He waited near an access port and watched. At dawn a convoy of transports lined up to exit. He shambled to the last one, swung himself up on its loading step, and hung on for dear life. He didn't worry about being seen. Nobody cared about people going *out* to Los Angeles; it was only the incoming transports that were searched for refugees.

He clung like a limpet as the transport picked up speed, following the route of what used to be the old Harbor Freeway. As it drew near a certain overpass in Compton, he launched himself and fell, rolling and tumbling down the embankment, to come to rest against an ancient chain-link fence in a nest of blown paper and trash. The rest of the world collected its garbage to run fusion plants: not Los Angeles.

He lay there bleeding, running a self-diagnostic. Contusions, minor cuts, no more.

Growling at no one in particular, he dragged himself upright and stumbled along the verge, until he was able to find an offramp. He seemed to have sustained a scalp wound, and now the blood was running down into his good eye. Blinking, he made his way into Watts and shambled down Avalon Boulevard, looking through the ruins for an address.

Nobody bothered him.

The mission was easy to spot. It was the only intact building for blocks, had once been a big rambling private house, and there was a line of people stretching out the door onto the front porch. They looked at him, appalled, except the young man in some kind of monastic habit who was addressing them, handing each one a form to fill out. Joseph wiped the blood from his eye and read the sign mounted above the porch: THE COMPASSIONATES OF ALLAH. He lurched forward and began to crawl up the stairs.

Somebody finally thought to nudge the brother and tell him there was a white guy getting into line. The young man snapped, "No whites treated here—" Then he saw Joseph and stopped, gulping. Joseph fixed him with his good eye, which the blood was obscuring again, and tried to form words. He couldn't, quite.

An elderly lady groped in her pocket for a handful of gray paper napkins and held them out to Joseph timidly. He accepted them and wiped his bleeding face. She told the young brother she thought Joseph might be Mexican. He leaned forward and told Joseph, in Spanish, that this was a blacks-only immunization center. Joseph just stared at him, breathing harshly.

"Maybe Filipino?" somebody else suggested.

Joseph raised his hand and made a writing gesture in midair.

The people in the line conferred briefly among themselves and decided that maybe the brother had better take the stranger inside before he died on the porch. Thoroughly unnerved, the young man went to the door and opened it, pointing inside. Why was Joseph moving so slowly? Blood loss. Internal hemorrhaging. Estimate fugue state in four minutes fourteen seconds, if self-repair not initiated prior to that time.

Inside was a waiting room. The young man held open a door marked EMERGENCY CARE for Joseph, waving at him to go in, but Joseph spotted the one marked ADMINISTRATOR and pushed that instead, and went through.

A thin-featured black man in old-fashioned reading glasses was going over forms at a desk. He glanced up in irritation at being interrupted, and his eyes widened at the sight of Joseph. Limping just ahead of the young man, who had run after him, Joseph grabbed a grease pencil from a jar on the desk and got its cap off. On the back of a form he wrote, with infinite care, the word *Suleyman*.

The Administrator looked at him sharply.

That was the last clear impression Joseph had for a while.

He was on a cot in a locked room. Mortals had carried him there. There were compresses on his wounds. It was day. He moved convulsively, twisted the bezel of the ring. Still safe.

It was night. He had a blanket now. Bandages too. The ring, again. Still safe.

Still night, but there were mortals moving around him, cutting away his torn and filthy clothing, washing him, bandaging him again, exclaiming over his bruises. Black men, all in the same monastic robes. They were talking to him, trying to get him upright, into white cotton pajamas. They put shoes on his feet. They pushed his arms through the sleeves of a long coat. Then, thank God, they let him lie down again.

Somebody was feeding him broth. Did he think he could manage with a straw? He tried. He managed, mostly, and somebody wiped away what had run from the slack corner of his mouth. He thought they would let him sleep then, but here were more of them, back with a stretcher. They moved him onto the stretcher and took him out into the night air. It was foul and cold. Old petroleum sump nearby. He was riding in an ambulance—when did that happen? An ambulance but no siren. He remembered the ring again.

They told him to be quiet, that they had to wait for the gate patrolman who knew them.

A shipyard? He had the sudden awful feeling that he was still crouched under the dock, eating crabs, and had only dreamed he made it this far. No, they were explaining that he had no papers, but Suleyman had arranged passage anyway. It was just getting light as he was carried on board the ship, big square freight barge, unlovely thing. Down to a tiny dark closet of a room. The fusion drive boomed steadily somewhere close. They all went away and left him, except the man in the reading glasses. Darkness. The ship was moving out. He could sleep now.

He slept for a long time in the darkness. Brother Ibrahim never left him. Joseph explained about the ring, how it had to be twisted every ten hours. Brother Ibrahim knew. Suleyman had made the ring? Sort of. It was all right.

Day was nearly as dark as night, except for long slanting fingers of sunlight that somehow found their way down into the hold and through his ventilation grate.

He woke weeping, weeping for Lewis, and Brother Ibrahim comforted him. You have no souls, he explained in Arabic, and so need fear no fires of hell. But if your friend was serving Allah's purpose, he died in glory and light, and feels no pain, which is the best that can possibly be hoped for such creatures. Moreover, he is remembered eternally, for God forgets nothing, and surely that is a kind of eternal life.

Joseph agreed hazily. But how had they come to be speaking in seventh-century Arabic?

You spoke first, Brother Ibrahim told him in mild surprise.

Oh, you're a scholar?

Yes, Brother Ibrahim was a scholar.

Sunlight stripes followed by darkness, followed by sunlight. He could see a little out of his left eye now, he could manage the straw better. He could work the thumb on his left hand. Brother Ibrahim told him the wounds were healing.

The smells changed. He could smell land. Then, a flood of air and light, and mortals came in through the doorway. More brothers. Moonlight? Brief muttered conversations in French. Brother Ibrahim was coming with him, must deliver Joseph into Suleyman's hands himself, he had promised to. They reached an agreement, and the stretcher was taken up again. Joseph was carried out into the night, tilting this way, tilting that way, and into the back of a van with Brother Ibrahim crowded in beside him. A long, long drive.

Fez

J OSEPH."

Suleyman was looking into his eyes.

"Joseph, you're not self-repairing fast enough. We're going to help you."

"Will it hurt?"

"We'll have to shut you down to do it."

"That figures," Joseph grumbled, and lost consciousness again.

Silence, incredible silence. He was alone, and damaged.

Well, of course he was damaged. Shot twice by a death ray, fell off a cliff, was half drowned, and jumped from the back of a convoy speeding through Watts.

No, he was *really* damaged.

His eyes were swollen nearly shut, his sinus cavities plugged solid and throbbing. Someone had done maxillofacial surgery on him, broken his nose . . .

His datalink was gone. Not offline, not even temporarily disconnected. Gone. Surgically removed.

Joseph peered around cautiously, and found he had no difficulty turning his head. He lay in a bed, in a pleasant room with windows shaded against the sun.

"Joseph?"

He met Suleyman's somber gaze.

"Tell me what happened to you, Joseph. I need you to tell me as quickly as you can."

Joseph gave him the briefest version of the story, about the stupid little men who'd been after Lewis for years and finally caught up with him. About the weapons they had, that could ruin the biomechanicals on an operative.

Suleyman looked grim. "There's more to the story than that, though, isn't there?"

"Yeah," Joseph replied. "What have you done to me, Suleyman?"

"Modified you. We had no choice. You won't need the signal disrupter anymore, at least. You're officially dead now, Joseph, as far as the Company's concerned. You don't exist. But they may have a problem solver hunting for you anyway, and we can't risk their finding you here."

Joseph lay there blinking, unable to take it in.

Suleyman went to the window, looking down into the street below. "We'll get you back on your feet again, of course, and I can give you a list of contacts. You'd heal faster if we had a regeneration tank, but the closest ones are in that bunker you showed me, and I don't think you want to go there. Once you've recovered, though, you'll need to run. You're a hazard to my people."

Joseph nodded.

"I am truly sorry about this, Joseph, sorrier than you can know. A lot has happened in the last few weeks. When you're well enough, you're going to have to tell me the whole story, from the beginning, no lies, nothing left out. Do you understand? And the others are going to want to talk to you."

"Okay," said Joseph, but was distracted by the echoes that were beginning in his head.

Suleyman scowled at him and crossed swiftly to his bedside. He leaned down and looked hard at Joseph, then straightened up. "Latif!" he shouted.

Joseph didn't know what happened after that.

He wasn't well for a long time, even after they repaired him. The Company wasn't with him anymore. Nobody was watching him, but nobody was watching *over* him either. For some reason his body seemed to believe it was mortal again. Systems faltered or gave out for no apparent reason, and Latif would be suddenly there beside him with a stabilizer cabinet, cursing, pounding on his chest, telling him it was all in his head.

His head wasn't at its best, certainly. He had long periods of clarity, but there were still intervals when the echoes would come, when he had to wait, to listen, trying to unravel them, and he couldn't focus on anything else then. When Joseph was able to think once more, Suleyman would come sit beside him and resume the debriefing. It went on for days. They pried out every detail from his story, going back over the events. Sometimes Suleyman brought in other people, operatives Joseph didn't know, and had them listen.

The more Joseph told the story, the more terrible it seemed to him, until he could scarcely believe what he'd done. There were times when he lay there weeping helplessly, desperate to redeem himself with Dr. Zeus, ready to go crawling to confess everything, excuse anything, if the Company would only take him back. He wanted his old life again. He'd never wanted trouble. He didn't want to be alone, cut off, adrift.

One afternoon he opened his eyes, and Nan was sitting beside him, holding his hand. He smiled.

"Joseph, dear," she said. "We've found out something."

"What?"

"The details of your story are confirmed. You did take a room at the Hotel Saint Catherine on 5 August, and so did Lewis. On 6 August you were both seen in town. On 7 August the maid went to your rooms and found the beds unmade and all your luggage still there, but no sign of either one of you. Three days later, just as the manager was about to call the police, two men representing themselves as your attorneys came to the hotel and removed your personal effects. They paid what you owed and left. The manager was disinclined to pursue the matter further."

"Ah," said Joseph.

"I broke into your personnel file. I examined Lewis's, too. The last entry shows that you were transferred from long-term active duty in Madrid to a location known only as Site 489. Lewis's last entry shows a short-term mission to Arkham, Vermont, following which he, too, was transferred to Site 489."

"Same place."

"Joseph," she said, squeezing his hand. "Both entries are dated 5 August 2276. The day before the accident happened."

He stared at her as that sank in. "Then the Company did plan it," he whispered.

"Someone planned it," Nan said. "Someone let those creatures know where Lewis was. And you were meant to be taken with him."

"I was right," he said dully. It didn't make him happy.

"Now we know," Nan said, her voice precise and quiet, "that a site number is a designation not of place but of fate. It signifies permanent disposal of some kind, or at least what the Company imagines to be permanent. Lewis has been disposed of. So has Mendoza. So has Kalugin. So have you, as far as they are aware. Why, Joseph?"

"We were poking around. Getting into secrets."

"And my dear Kalugin, who never did anything but follow kind impulses at the wrong moment? Or poor unhappy Mendoza, who loved a mortal man?" Nan's voice hardened. "What happened to them, Joseph? Are they really lost, has the Company found some way to reverse immortality? Or are they hidden away in bunkers, like your friends the old Enforcers?"

"I know what they did to Lewis," said Joseph. "I know what they did to me. If the Company doesn't know how to kill us, the little stupid men do. Maybe. Though I'm not dead. Maybe Lewis isn't dead, either." But it was a mistake to say that, for it brought terrible images to his mind: Lewis alive and unable to die no matter how desperately he wanted to, helpless somewhere. Joseph began to tremble.

Nan held him, but her voice was like steel now. "We really must find out. Don't you agree? Before more of us join the ranks of the disappeared? Because the rate of disappearance has accelerated. In the last week, fifty operatives were transferred to sites designated by numbers. The week before that, it was twenty-seven. How many of them were people we knew, Joseph? Will we be obliged to rebel?"

He closed his eyes. "This is it, isn't it? The pieces are beginning to fall into place for 2355. Infighting and treachery. Is this where the Silence starts?"

"I wish I knew," she replied.

The following day he woke to see Victor standing beside his bed, white-faced with anger but composed. "So it's true?" he said. "They gave Lewis to—those things?"

"Yes," Joseph said. "The little stupid people."

"Worse perversions of humanity than our own damned father Budu, I can tell you. Homo Umbratilis, the Company called them."

Man of the shadows? thought Joseph foggily. He said, "You know something about them?"

"Oh, yes," Victor said, pulling up a chair and sitting down. His fists were clenched on the arms of the chair; Joseph noticed this because Victor was wearing white gloves indoors, which was strange. "Filthy little dwellers under rocks. Idiot craftsmen. Responsible, I daresay, for all the legends of dwarves and kobolds and malevolent fairies. Marginally human, but debased and retarded for all their genius. I don't know what the Company did to earn their hatred; but it seems they set themselves the task of disabling our operatives."

"They got Lewis once before," Joseph said. "But the Company saved him that time."

"I know," said Victor, tight-lipped. "I was there when we revived him. I was his, how would you describe it—? His handler. It was my job to see how fully he recovered, how much he remembered about the incident. And when he did remember, it was my job to see that he forgot again."

Joseph regarded him a long moment. "You've done some dirty work in your day, haven't you?" he said at last.

"Vile things," Victor said. "I marvel I don't leave stains where I walk. Listen to me, Joseph. There was a black project. It was by sheerest accident that Lewis blundered into one of their warrens the first time. When the Company rescued Lewis and saw what the little monsters could do—no operative had ever been so badly disabled—they captured and bred some of the damned things, to see if such genius could be turned to Dr. Zeus's advantage. But they could never get enough of them, the creatures didn't breed well, the males tended to die young. So Dr. Zeus crossbred its subjects with Homo sapiens, and had slightly better success.

"And then the Company discovered that the free ones were still after Lewis. They can focus on only one idea at a time, but they focus with dreadful intensity, and they never give up. They got it into their heads that they could perfect their weapon against us if they could recapture Lewis and study him.

"Dr. Zeus shipped him off to New World One, out of their reach. I was sent there a while to observe him. His memories hadn't returned, so I reported that he might go back to active duty when the Company had further use for him.

"I thought it was all over. I thought the creatures had all been captured." Victor tugged absently at his gloves. "There were no more reports of fairies in the world. All the old stories were being dismissed as superstition. I didn't know they'd simply got better at hiding themselves. But the Company knew. The Company watched Lewis, waiting to see if the creatures had forgot about him."

"And they hadn't," said Joseph.

"No. They were lurking after one of the Company's half-breeds when he led them to Lewis, quite by chance. And then the hunt was up again. You know what happened after that. Lewis fled to you, after all."

"The Company creamed them again."

"No, as it happened. It would appear that some sort of contact was attempted at that time. The Company wanted to reach an agreement with them."

"Just to get Lewis out of the way?" Joseph was aghast. "What had he done? All we ever did was talk about trying to find Mendoza."

"Oh, you did other things." Victor gave him a shrewd look. "You know that perfectly well. You might have been able to get away with it—you're a Facilitator—but not Lewis. He'd developed a fondness for certain Company secrets, for one thing. And it began to be obvious that his lost memories were returning. But I'm afraid that wasn't the whole reason he was marked for disappearance."

"What?"

"The creatures wanted Lewis for experiments," said Victor, spreading his gloved hands. "Well, the Company decided to let them have him. And if you can't imagine why our masters might want someone, anyone, to devise a weapon against us—but you're not that naive."

Joseph just stared at him.

"Things are rather sticky, just now. Rumors are flying, distrust and paranoia abound, rebellion is in the air. Personally, I can't imagine how the Silence is going to wait until 2355 to fall," he said.

"Me either," Joseph said.

"But it will," Victor mused. "Giving us seventy-four years to prepare ourselves. I can't say I find the prospect of my own death that alarming. I certainly merit capital punishment, several times over, and if you knew the details of my very unpleasant career, you'd agree with me. But Lewis was a gentleman, and he didn't deserve what they did to him." He looked at Joseph with his pale catlike eyes. "Neither did poor old Kalugin. I begin to suspect that even our father wasn't as bad as he seemed, set beside the monsters who created him."

Joseph lay his head back on the pillow, exhausted. "But what do we do?"

"I must go on playing the game for another few decades. I haven't much choice," Victor told him. "You, however, now have a certain freedom denied the rest of us. If you're a clever fellow—and your history persuades me you're very clever indeed—you'll put it to good use. You can go wherever you wish. Set traps for guilty parties. Pursue the truth. I strongly recommend that you begin in San Francisco."

"San Francisco, huh?" Joseph narrowed his eyes.

Victor got up and went to the door. He paused there a moment. "And you might want to take a shovel with you."

Latif disconnected the diagnostic apparatus. "See? Not a damned thing wrong anymore," he told Joseph. "I told you."

"My nose hurts," Joseph complained.

"Psychosomatic. So you weigh an ounce less than you used to. Big Brother won't be in your head, either. No more worrying about making the Company suspicious over those embarrassing little power surges that happen too often."

"Nobody seems to suspect the bunch of you," Joseph grumbled, rising from the chair.

"There's a power station across the street." Latif bared his teeth in a smile. "Neat, huh? All kinds of interference, and there's nothing anybody can do, so it's ignored. Not that anybody would question Suleyman, anyway."

"People have questioned me," Suleyman told him, watching from the sidelines. "Nobody's untouchable, son. Never forget that."

"I'd like to see Dr. Zeus try to double-cross you!" Latif said.

"No, you wouldn't," said Suleyman and Joseph at the same time.

Latif shrugged and went to the weapons cabinet, where he drew out a high-speed ballistic handgun and checked it. "Ready when you are," he told Joseph. "Bunny-slope setting, okay?"

Joseph poised on one of a number of blue circles painted on the floor. Latif took careful aim and fired at him point-blank from a distance of three meters.

Joseph was gone, of course, before the bullet reached him, having winked out to one of the other circles. Latif whirled, though still moving at mere mortal speed, and fired again; Joseph was gone to another circle. His choice of circles was random. Another shot, and another circle, and so on, until the clip was empty.

"Normal response time, normal readout," Suleyman said. "Next level."

Latif reloaded. Joseph took his position on the first circle again, and the game resumed, but with the difference that Latif was now moving at Joseph's speed. The game was over in a few seconds, and Joseph was still unharmed.

"Normal response time, normal readout," repeated Suleyman. "This seems as good a time as any to tell you about the coup attempt. Next level."

"Excuse me?" Joseph looked up from watching Latif's trigger finger. Latif fired anyway, and the game began again, at the same speed, with the variation that Latif was now attempting to anticipate Joseph's next position rather than the one he happened to be occupying at that particular millisecond.

"Normal response time, normal readout. Yes, you remember I mentioned things were getting a little edgy up there? It seems the Plague Club made a premature bid for power. Either that or someone in the ruling cabal finally took notice of my warnings and mounted an operation against them," Suleyman said. "Next level."

Latif reloaded, grinning. The next level was like the previous one, only faster, and utilizing the circles that had been painted on the walls and ceiling also.

"Really?" Joseph said, panting slightly.

"Normal, normal. Yes. Most of the Company personnel will never hear about it, but all the executive operatives had to be informed. Perhaps I should say *explained to*; we couldn't help but notice something was going on. Normal, normal. Next level." Any mortal in the room at this moment would have thought Suleyman was talking to himself, as the other two immortals were moving far too quickly to be seen. Of course, no mortal could have heard what Suleyman was saying over the roar of continuous gunfire.

Suleyman continued: "Quite a few executive assignments of long standing have been unexpectedly reshuffled. One hundred and six operatives of differing grades have been transferred to numbered sites over a period of six weeks. There have been some promotions. There have been three outright arrests, which as you know is extremely rare."

The noise stopped suddenly, and two figures became visible through the clearing gun smoke.

"Damn, this gun's melted," said Latif. Suleyman looked at him in mild reproach.

"So who got arrested?" gasped Joseph, leaning forward and bracing his hands on his knees.

"Nobody you know. They were, however, very high in the Plague Club cabal, subordinates only to Labienus. He didn't get arrested, which I find interesting." Suleyman took the ruined gun from Latif and examined it thoughtfully. "An intercabal purge to free himself of anyone still loyal to Budu, perhaps. Of the operatives who were sent to numbered sites, about half were known members of the Plague Club. Of course, many weren't. Lewis, for example. I'm certain he was never a member. You—" Suleyman sighted along the barrel. "You, I'm giving the benefit of the doubt." He tossed the warped thing away in disgust.

"Thanks so much," Joseph said, mopping his face with a towel.

"You're welcome. And I received a commendation from our masters, in appreciation of my dogged attempts to warn them of this possibility, and their assurances that it has been dealt with. They continue to depend on my unshakable integrity and loyalty. Isn't that nice?"

Joseph rolled his eyes. "If they're throwing around words like *loyalty*, things must have got pretty shaky up there."

"So I guess it will quiet down, now," said Latif.

Suleyman and Joseph looked at each other.

"Maybe," said Suleyman. They walked together out of the diagnostic room. He drew a deep breath. "So, Joseph. You tested out fit and fine. You're completely recovered and ready to be cut loose. You understand."

"I guess." Joseph sighed and flexed his shoulders.

"You are the security risk from hell, man," Latif said.

"He knows that, son. My people have too much at stake. There are mortals who would lose their lives. There are immortals who would lose more. We haven't seen Joseph, haven't heard from him, have no idea what became of him. He is lost and will stay lost. It shouldn't be too hard for a man of his experience."

"I owe you, Suleyman—" Joseph began, but Suleyman held up his hand.

"In return, he will forget anything he saw concerning my immunization program." He looked at Joseph sternly. "To each his own rebellion."

"And if you tell anybody about the program," added Latif, "it won't matter how lost you are—I will come after you and I will find you, man."

That evening a solitary traveler slipped out of a side gate and made his way to a public transport stand. A ticket was purchased, in cash, for the coast. At Casablanca the traveler got out and moved through the darkness to the waterfront, where great cargo ships waited for morning. He found the one he wanted. No mortal security guard saw him run aboard, quicker than a rat and quieter.

The traveler found his way among the shipping containers, seeking one with a broken seal, inching between the stacks in the darkness. When he found the container he needed, he prized it open and slithered in, clambering up through boxes of electronic equipment to the top, where there was a comfortable clearance between the roof of the container and his face. The traveler stretched out and sighed, feeling secure.

No mortal would have been able to bear a stateroom like that, but it had its advantages. Cargo ships were not subjected to the same rigorous security measures air transports were. They were too useful for smuggling, for one thing. The official argument was that terrorists always took planes. In any case the cargo ships traveled so slowly that no mortal who had places to go and things to do would choose one as a method of transport.

Joseph, of course, wasn't mortal, even if he felt not quite as immortal as he had been.

He closed his eyes and set his internal clocks, factoring in emergency protocols. He began to breathe very slowly, and more slowly still. Gradually he slipped into a voluntary fugue state. He was only dimly aware, hours later, when the ship backed ponderously from her berth and made her way out into the Atlantic. By the time she was well out to sea, he had shut down entirely. He rested, waiting, dreaming.

He didn't dream particularly well. The great voice was booming in the darkness, impressively echoing and quite unmistakable. "And when he opened the fifth seal, I saw under the tabernacle, the souls of them that were killed for the word of God, and for the testimony they had, and they cried with a loud voice saying: how long tarriest thou Lord holy and true, to judge and to avenge our blood on them that dwell on the earth? And long white garments were given unto every one of them!"

"Don't you tell *me* about John of Patmos," Joseph heard himself growling. "I knew the guy, okay?"

But the speaker rose from his table and stood, lit only by the single candle that had enabled him to read, and the light fell on the long folds of the scholar's black robe and on the face. The eyes above the wide cheekbones were shadowed, but a spark glinted there, and light glinted on the teeth.

"And it was said unto them that they should rest for a little season until the number of their fellows, and brethren, and of them that should be killed as they were, were fulfilled!" shouted Nicholas Harpole, holding out his hands as though he were about to present Joseph with something. So eloquent was his gesture, so well acted, that Joseph stepped forward half against his will to see what it was, though he knew there was nothing there.

But there was something in his hands, after all: a sheet of mirrored glass. Joseph looked at himself and saw a snarling dog face, foam dripping from the jaws. And more: stretching into the darkness behind him, a vaulted bunker with row upon row of open coffins, each containing a figure robed in white. There were too many to count, but Joseph could see the two in the foreground with perfect clarity. Mendoza and Lewis, too pale, too still.

"You bastard," Joseph wept. At least he was weeping inside; the dog's face showed no emotion. "They're your victims, you know that? You got them both. Couldn't stay dead, could you? Reached out of your grave and made them love you, and it destroyed them. Age after age, you come back." Joseph reeled, trying to think what else had happened, what else he had said and done, in that prison cell so long ago.

Chortling, he drew back his fist, ready to deliver a sound right hook to Nicholas's jaw. Up he soared, into midair, laughing to himself, but he connected with nothing. After a moment's breathless pause he looked down to find himself hurtling into a red canyon with a tiny ribbon of blue water winding through it, far below.

Down he tumbled, thinking in resignation that this too was déjà vu. Then, crash, he'd made a hole in the ground just his own size and shape, and he knew that the big Englishman would be looking down from his great height at the puff of rising dust and sneering.

And in fact that was what he was doing, as Joseph saw when he dragged himself out of the hole. Sneering down from horseback, no less, as though he wasn't tall enough already, and resplendent in a fine tailored Victorian traveling ensemble.

He made a covert gesture, and Joseph tensed, thinking he was going to draw a hidden weapon. Instead he produced a shovel out of nowhere, and threw it at Joseph's feet. Joseph jumped backward.

"Seek for thy noble father in the dust, Hamlet," said Edward Alton Bell-Fairfax contemptuously, and, turning his horse's head, he galloped away.

"You think you're so smart," Joseph shouted after him. "You quoted it wrong, big shot!"

He turned and looked over his shoulder to avoid falling into the hole again, but to his amazement he saw that the hole had changed: it was no longer the size and shape of his own body but much bigger, as though it had been made by his father.

San Francisco

THE CARGO VESSEL *Hanjin* maneuvered slowly into Island Creek Channel and moored there, dropping anchor. Her captain went ashore to register her arrival with the proper authorities. Her crew were showering, sprucing up for a night on the town.

Joseph, deep in the hold, woke in darkness and listened a long while. He heard the crew leave, all but the night watch. He heard the great city grow quiet as the hours went by. When he judged the time to be right, he crawled from his hiding place and crept up on deck, avoiding the surveillance cameras that swept back and forth relentlessly.

Watching for the proper moment, he dropped over the side and swam ashore. He made his way to Third Street and trudged along it, passing the big ballpark, squelching all the way up to Market. Here he paused a moment before turning left and walking up Market as far as Grant. At Grant he turned right and went into Chinatown.

He walked more slowly now, scanning as he went. He disabled the security system of a small grocery store, broke in, and loaded the pockets of his long coat with fruit, protein bars, bottles of water, and herbal tea. He hurried on from there and sought out an apartment building, an older and less desirable one. Half its units were presently vacant, its security systems offline. It still took five minutes' work to persuade the elevator to take him up to the eighth floor, which was completely without tenants.

He broke into one unit and settled himself on the floor, where he gorged on what he'd stolen from the market. His body received it gratefully. He was overwhelmed with the need for real sleep, now, and sprawled in a strategically chosen corner near a window and let himself rest.

It was late afternoon when he awoke. It was later by the time he finally got the elevator down to the street and exited from the building by a service door.

He did not go to Sacramento yet. He walked back to Market Street instead, through the going-home crowds, pacing up its length until he found a major department store. He went in, found a holomap of the store, noted where the hardware and sporting goods departments were, noted moreover what kind of security system protected the store. Then he left and went down to stroll along the Embarcadero, a grubby little man in a long coat.

When it grew dark, he went quietly to the back door of a restaurant and disabled its security system. The cook, bending over the oven to take out a pan of rolls, felt a faint chill. He looked around to see where the draft came from and saw, to his astonishment, that an entire casserole of lasagna had vanished. So had two loaves of fresh-baked bread.

A mile away, Joseph leaned back against a pier piling and ate, watching the lights of Oakland glitter across the water. When he finished, he buried the evidence of his meal and waited until the crowds all went home, the floaters, the cyclists, the performance artists. He waited until the lights in the towers began to wink out. Then he walked back up Market Street and stole a truck.

A City Parks and Recreation Department agvan, to be precise, from a transit yard south of Market. The yard wasn't locked. No point, when vehicles were capable of floating over fences. Car theft was virtually unknown in the twenty-third century anyway, thanks to alarms that could not be disabled by the most determined mortal. Five minutes after Joseph strolled into the transit yard, he was piloting the agvan around the corner of Market and Second to the main entrance of the department store.

No subtle cyborg tricks on the lock this time. He just broke and entered, and went into hyperfunction as soon as he heard the faint high scream of the alarm. The security cameras saw no more than a blur racing up and down the fire stairs and through the departments he needed. Rapidly, things began to appear in the back of the van as though teleported there: three cases of high-energy bars, a crate of bottled water, two tarpaulins, an electronics tool kit, picks and shovels, a sleeping bag, clothing, and, last but not least, a sixty-gallon fusion trash receptacle.

Long before the security officer staggered out to see what was going on, the agvan was roaring away down Grant Avenue.

Joseph slowed as he turned left onto Sacramento, up one of the desperately steep hills that made motoring so memorable in the days of manual transmissions. He climbed slowly, scanning as he went, and passed Waverly Place. On the right-hand side of the street he found what he had been seeking. He had to get out and stare, though, peering through the fence. Why couldn't he be wrong about his worst fears once in a while?

There was no house at that location, above Waverly Place. There was a tiny fenced park, walled around by towering buildings. What Joseph had been seeking registered as ten feet down, under the neat flowerbeds and pristine lawn.

He got the simple lock open and went right to work, draping the fence with tarpaulins to mask his activities. He brought out the tools and the trash receptacle. He walked the length of the little park, scanning again, moving his head this way and that as though listening for something. When he had it pinpointed, he began to dig, quickly.

The first shovel broke after half an hour, when he'd gone down six feet. Then there was a hard impacted layer, clay and ash, tumbled bricks; he used a pick to get through that. It was the stratum from the 1906 earthquake, the truth buried so far under the pretty flowers, the past that the present was built on. When Joseph brought up a piece of human skull, one eye socket hooked on the business end of the pick, he stopped and went in with another shovel, more carefully.

Charred mortal bones, fragments of wood, bits of brass. An opium pipe. A bronze hatchet head. Joseph peered at it and made out the characters that told him it was the property of the Black Dragon Retribution Tong. More bones, more hatchet heads, and something that didn't grate or clank under his shovel. Soft and dull, like leather.

Joseph dropped the shovel at once. He knelt and began to dig with his hands, crying silently, tears running down his face and silvering in his beard.

He found an arm first, fragments of its rotted coat dropping away as he lifted it out: withered sinew, tarry flesh, the leather of the skin strangely supple even so. Bright glint of metal, ferroceramic at the bone end. He lifted it, and it flexed like a snake. Clawlike fingers curled into a fist as he watched. It was a very big arm, wasted and shrunken though it was.

He set it on the edge of the hole and kept searching. Here was a gigantic thigh, still wearing riveted rags: Levi Strauss jeans, for God's sake. The rest of the leg followed, but the foot had been hacked off. Eventually he found a boot, with a bit of ankle and gimbal joint protruding from its top.

The rest of the body was battered and hewn but in one piece, except for the head. He found it, after a long moment of panicked scrabbling in the hole. You really don't want to know what it looked like.

Joseph crawled out and attempted to fit the body into the trash receptacle. With some effort he got it to flex, and pushed it down. He placed the head in too, more or less in its own lap, and the arm and leg and foot, and closed the lid. He rolled the receptacle awkwardly to the back of the agvan. Having secured it, he got in and drove to

Van Ness, took Van Ness to Lombard, and took Lombard to the Golden Gate Bridge, just as mortals had done for the last four centuries.

The bridge had changed. Its scarlet towers were supported now by antigravity banks, and it had twisted and broken and been repaired more times than could be counted. It was still something to make you catch your breath, whether you were mortal or immortal.

The agvan roared across it under the unsleeping lights and disappeared into the wall of fog that was tumbling down the Marin headlands.

Mount Tamalpais

Joseph PULLED TO the side of a particular mountain road and got out, sniffing the air. Morning on the wind, even if there was no appreciable light in the sky yet. He scanned and spotted the entrance to the bunker, which, predictably enough, was where he had found it a century earlier. He unloaded the agvan, lugging things up a steep hill, following a deer trail through madrone and manzanita. Last was the trash receptacle, and he blessed its little wheels that allowed him to drag it along the trail.

When he'd secured everything at the bunker's door, he staggered back down and leaned into the cab of the agvan to program its autopilot. He backed away and watched as it rose smoothly and rotated. It sped off, back to the distant transport yard in the city. He climbed back up the hill.

Having worked the seal on the door, he went down the long echoing passage, dragging behind him the trash bin full of discarded god.

Abdiel was very old, but he didn't know he was very old. His memory wasn't all that good. Looking in a mirror wouldn't have reminded him: he appeared perpetually twenty, and a young twenty at that, wide dark eyes with a sort of startled Bambi expression, lots of soft curling black hair and a soft dark beard.

He didn't know he'd looked like that for the last thirty thousand years. He wasn't very bright.

But bright enough to do his job, and follow the few simple commandments with which he had been programmed. There are seven holy shrines, he had been told. Thou shalt go from the first to the second, and from the second to the third, and so to the seventh, when thou shalt go back to the first again. At each shrine shalt thou labor, as thou hast been instructed; and when thy labor is done there, thou must bear witness and travel to the next place appointed. Thou shalt not fail in this, neither shalt thou speak of thy task to any mortal thou mayest meet without the shrines.

Nowadays it generally took him about twenty years to make a full circle. When he came back to the first shrine, he was always surprised to see his own handwriting on the chalkboard, because he never realized until that moment that he wasn't arriving there for the first time. The moment he erased the board, it was always as though he'd erased the realization too, for with proof of the past gone, the past ceased to exist for him.

Abdiel was a failed immortal, but if his brain was like a sieve, his body at least was perfectly untiring, ageless, beautiful. Accordingly, the Company had found a use for him, making the most of his plight.

He walked up the side of Mount Tamalpais, keeping to the recreational paths because they were easy, and he liked to follow the line of least resistance. He smiled and stepped aside for every jogger he encountered, keeping his eyes modestly downcast. His clothes were nondescript and a little shabby, though not too shabby, because he didn't like being arrested as a vagrant. It kept him from his duties, and nothing mattered except his duties.

The fog was rolling up the mountain now, drifting like a reverse avalanche from the sea, a torrent of boiling silver in the afternoon light. It floated over the laurel groves and the yellow meadows of autumn, soothing all that dustiness with cool moist air. Abdiel drew it into his lungs gratefully, thanking it for obscuring his way from the mortals. He was invisible in the fog when he sprinted off the path and down through the moss-hung trees to the dark fold in the rock that he'd seen in his dreams.

Yes, there was the doorway to the seventh shrine. He'd completed his pilgrimage at last. He addressed the seal, and it opened for him. He crept in reverently, hurrying down the long tunnel toward the celestial light.

He didn't remember having been here before, so he wasn't as surprised as he might have been to see that there was another person in the shrine, moving about in one of the side chapels. This shrine looked very much like the sixth shrine, which he vaguely remembered, because he'd been there most recently: the soft light, the sweet fragrance, and the blessed ones floating in their dreams.

He set down his pack. The motion drew the attention of the other person, who stepped out of the side chapel and looked at him. "I'll bet you're Abdiel," the person said, scanning.

Abdiel nodded. "Are you one of the Masters?" he asked, for the other man wasn't a mortal. The man narrowed his little black eyes and smiled.

"Why, yes," he said. "I am."

As soon as he told Abdiel this, Abdiel knew that it must be so; and though the man looked nothing like the Masters that Abdiel had seen, being grubby and rather small, instantly Abdiel's mental picture of *Master* had reconfigured to resemble the one who stood before him.

"Pleased to meet you," Abdiel said, smiling back.

The Master considered him. "I notice you have no datalink, Abdiel. That must be because your appointed tasks are so top secret and important, right?"

"Yes." Abdiel looked earnest. He wasn't sure why his duties should be top secret, but he certainly knew they were important. "I've found the seventh shrine at last."

"No kidding? Well, good for you. What are you going to do now?"

The Master was testing him! "See that all is clean and in order," Abdiel said fervently. "Check pumps number A3 and C5 in each unit

[292]

for corrosion. Monitor alkaline balance of regenerative fluids. Check thermocontrols. Check lighting regulators. Check integrity of all seals. Monitor vault integrity and report any cracks, leaks, or evidence of stresses. Bear witness to my labors. Sir!" He saluted snappily.

"Excellent," the Master said, and his smile twisted up into his beard at one side. "Now, you know, of course, that you can't tell anybody you've seen me here? That it's top secret?"

"Oh, yes, sir." Abdiel saluted again.

"Okay, then." The Master rolled up his ragged sleeves. "You run along and do your job, and let me do mine."

"Are you preparing one of the blessed ones for eternal rest?" Abdiel said, looking past him into the side chapel. Something was stretched out on the steel table in there.

"That's right."

"Gee, do you need me to help?" Abdiel looked eager. "I've never done that. I just look after the ones who are resting already."

"You do, eh?" the Master said thoughtfully. "Maybe you can help me. Are you strong?"

"Really strong!" Abdiel held up both arms and made fists to show his muscles.

When the Master led him into the side chamber, Abdiel drew back in horror at what he saw lying on the table there. "Oh. That's one of the evil ones!" he said, averting his eyes.

"Why do you think so?" the Master asked, watching him.

"Well, he's all dirty and horrible and dead-looking, and the blessed ones are never like that," Abdiel said, trying not to see. "The blessed ones are clean and whole and sleep in the heavenly light. The evil ones sleep where it's dark and dirty, and they get all withered and ugly."

The Master took up the bucket of regenerative solution with which he'd been washing the thing on the table. "Do you know why that is, Abdiel?"

"Because—" Abdiel faltered, then remembered that the Master had tested him before. "Because the blessed ones have worked hard for the Masters, and deserve a nice rest in a shrine. But the evil ones disobeyed, so they have to sleep in the other place."

"And where's the other place, Abdiel?" The Master was bathing the blind eye sockets, the great brown snarling teeth.

Abdiel shuddered and looked away again. "Where you got him from."

"Smart boy, Abdiel," the Master said. "Now, I'll let you in on a little secret. We Masters are all-wise and all-merciful. Sometimes we forgive the evil ones their sins and take them out of the other place and put them here instead. That's what I'm doing now. This guy wasn't all bad, you know. Only he's got to be repaired before he can heal in the heavenly light. See?"

"I guess so." Abdiel made himself raise his head and look at the ruined giant on the table. Oh, he needed repairs terribly. Dermal integrity breached in thirty-eight places on ventral surface. Left pedal support structure disarticulated, left foot avulsed. Left leg avulsed at pelvic articulation, femur analogue frame dented at supports 5, 8, and 13. Right arm— Abdiel ran to the sink and threw up.

"That's okay," the Master said cheerfully. "Good thing you got rid of your lunch before we really got to work. Now, blow your nose and come help me. I'm going to need you to hold him still so I can reattach his leg."

It wasn't a very nice experience. Once the leg was reattached, the great body jerked and twisted, and the bright gimbal of the pedal support structure moved unnervingly until they got its horrible black foot on and sutured in place. The arm was even more frightening, but the head was the worst of all. As soon as the Sinclair chain gimbal was reconnected, even before the muscles could be tugged back and sutured into place, the head began to turn, the fearsome jaws to clash. What remained of the structure of its eyes clicked and fluttered as though trying to see. Abdiel had to run for the sink again.

It didn't bother the Master, though. He just kept working away.

"Now, you see why it's so important to obey us Masters and do your job?" he lectured Abdiel. "Wouldn't it be awful to suffer the way this old guy has? You don't ever want this to happen to you."

"Gosh, never ever!" gasped Abdiel, pulling himself upright and wiping his mouth.

"So you will keep the commandment about silence, right? Because it would be just too awful to break it and turn out like *him*." The Master gritted his teeth and reached up into the neck to pull down one end of a severed tendon. He reconnected it and went on. "Now, I've pretty much got the hard parts over with, so you can go on and do your regular work. Run along."

Abdiel was only too glad to go, out into the heavenly light where the blessed ones slept, fresh and clean every one of them. He busied himself with his assigned tasks and soon forgot all about the nastiness in the side chapel, in fact he was quite startled a week later when the Master came walking down an aisle between the vaults, lugging the ugly old man who was all put together now.

"Hi there," the Master said. "Where's an empty vault, Abdiel?"

Abdiel showed him. The Master climbed up nimbly and dropped the body into the regenerant, where it bobbed for a moment before being drawn in. Then it sank, settled, and, seen through the pure blue glow, seemed no longer quite so dead. Was it moving? Were the shriveled limbs stretching out?

"That's a nice sight," said the Master. "Wasn't as hard as I thought, either. I feel like celebrating! You want a granola bar, Abdiel? My treat." He held out a nubbly confection, and Abdiel accepted it thankfully. He hadn't remembered to eat in days, and his own stash of Power Crunchies was back at the entrance in his pack. The Master drew out another bar and unwrapped it, and they stood there chewing companionably, looking up at the floating figure.

"Will he get better now?" Abdiel asked.

"Oh, yeah," the Master said with his mouth full. "Now that he's all put together, his self-repair will take over and the nanobots will bring him up to specs, rebuild anything he's missing, get the organs functioning again. His brain's offline, but that's the protective fugue.

It might take years, but one of these days he'll look just like the rest of the people in here. Like the big guys, anyway."

"What about his heavenly crown?" Abdiel asked, indicating the circlet all the other floating figures wore.

"Oh. Well, he was pretty bad, even if he got forgiven, so I don't know if he'll get one of those," the Master said. "We'll see."

Abdiel nodded, feeling compassionate and hoping the old man would merit a crown. The crowns were terribly important, and must never, ever be taken off a sleeper, because they gave the blessed ones good dreams. Evil ones, of course, had nightmares.

The rest of that time the Master walked with Abdiel, observing him at his duties. He was interested in everything Abdiel did, and asked him a lot of questions. He particularly tested Abdiel on the access codes to the terminals that connected the bunker with the Masters in their distant abode of delight. Abdiel passed every test. The Master congratulated him and told him he was a good operative. When at last Abdiel chalked his witness on the board, shouldered his pack, and walked away down the tunnel to the mortal world, he turned and waved at his new friend, buoyed by a pleasant sense of self-worth.

By the time he was walking along Highway 1, however, he'd forgotten the Master ever existed. All his attention was fixed on finding the mysterious first shrine, which he'd heard was off somewhere in a land far away...

Joseph in the Darkness

So THERE IT IS. So here we are.

You're getting better, father, I can tell. You still look like a murder victim six times over, but at least you don't seem to have been dead quite so long. Some day soon you'll start growing back the soft tissues of your eyes, your liver, your heart, all those things the rats...

What if she...

I wonder how you got on the wrong side of the Black Dragon Retribution Tong, father, in an opium cellar on Sacramento Street, just minutes before the 1906 earthquake? Must be quite a story. You'll tell me someday. Or maybe Victor will. I have a feeling he knows. He could never have inflicted those hatchet wounds, he's half your size. And yet something happened when he spit on you. I wonder if it has any connection with those gloves he never takes off.

Were the hatchetmen sent later? Were you unconscious then? Did Labienus set you up? Was he power hungry? Were you a little inconvenient to have around with your rigid moral code? If it wasn't your own people, was it the Company? It's just like something the Company would do. I can testify to that.

This is what the Company does to all its operatives, sooner or later, isn't it? None of us actually dead, but we'd be luckier if we were. Those of us who behaved ourselves get to dream away time in a nice warm bath. Those of us who haven't behaved? They find an excuse to lower the boom on us, one day when we least expect it. Then we're abandoned to rot in a grave like you were, or handed over to the enemy like Lewis was, or used and thrown away like Mendoza so nobody would ever discover the truth about her...

The Company must have watched us all, weighed every incident, heard every word we said, and waited, keeping score. They could afford to wait years, hundreds of years, thousands of years, and while we worked so faithfully for them, the list of marks against us grew longer.

Maybe I deserved what happened to me, and maybe you did, too, father, but Lewis? What harm did he ever do anybody? And yet I can't imagine what he's suffering now, if he's not so damaged he's past suffering. Poor romantic idiot.

Was he in love with Mendoza? Was he in love with the Englishman? With both of them? Did he even know? He never gave up trying to find them. He wasn't a coward, like me.

She's still lost, my little girl, and maybe in some dungeon blacker than the one in Santiago, with hotter coals. What would they do to a Crome generator? Try to disconnect her extra talents? Experiment on her? She's not in here now, I know. I've looked. If there's the least chance she alone can go forward in time, she alone can discover the truth about 2355, the Company will have locked her away some place a lot more secure than this; and they'll never let her out.

I should have gone after her sooner. I should have gone after you sooner, too.

He was right, the goddam Englishman. I screwed up just like Hamlet. You handed me the truth about your betrayal right at the beginning of the play, and I delayed, procrastinated, because I was scared, wasn't sure, didn't want trouble. Now look. I've lost everything I had, and the curtain's coming down on a stage littered with bodies.

But we'll write a new last act, won't we, father? When I get you out of there, we'll make a plan. You were always a lot better at battle strategies than I was. It'll be easy. I still have the Company access codes Lewis downloaded to me, we know where all the bodies are buried, and we have seventy-four years to get ready.

Maybe we'll set all the Old Guard free, and see how they feel about what's been going on. And then! Wouldn't that be great, father? All of us together again, one last time? I couldn't save Lewis, but we can avenge him. Lewis and all the other innocents. Will we go after treacherous bastards like Nennius? Will we hunt down the masters who have lied to us so shamelessly, for so many thousands of mortal lifetimes? Is 2355 payback time? Is it time to sing the Dies Irae?

Yeah! *For behold, the Lord cometh out of his place to punish the inhabitants of the earth for their iniquity: the earth also shall disclose her blood, and shall no more cover her slain. In that day the Lord with his sore and great and strong sword shall punish leviathan the piercing serpent, even leviathan that crooked serpent; and he shall slay the dragon that is in the sea!*

I can quote Scripture too, you know.